but call on a true Scout and there you will find bravery espoused in their oath, and loyalty that will vanquish any foe. Marie's assiduous zeal for history discovers ordinary Scouts who indeed became extraordinary heroes.

~Paul Thrower
Scoutmaster Troop 514, Southlake, Texas

What a blessing to have been invited to read *Underground Scouts*. The story, history, and writing checked all the boxes that make a book memorable for me. I recommend this book to anyone wishing to learn more about the Scouts in Poland who participated in the Warsaw Uprising at tremendous peril to themselves and the people and country they loved deeply.

~Elaine Mazurek Stephens
Polish American Council of Texas
Third Vice President

This book [*California Trail Discovered*] contains history, literature, geography, and STEAM all in one! As a homeschool teacher, I appreciated how all of these subjects were woven together in one place, and as an avid reader, I loved that the lessons did not make the storyline feel awkward or forced. Pacing in this story was excellent, and character development was not sacrificed on behalf of action, as there was an abundance of both. I loved reading Daniel's story; I highly recommend it!

~Rachel Summey
Homeschooling Mom
Richardson, Texas

Marie Sontag once again displays her brilliant talent for storytelling in this book. The hardships, the endurance, the conflicts, plus the emotional depth of the characters all come to life in this wonderful tale of resilience and tenacity! [*California Trail Discovered*] is historical fiction that is filled with rich detail and perfectly tuned for the middle grade reader. It left me craving for more!

~Roberta Hendricks,
Reading Intervention Specialist
Pampa, Texas

While reading *Yosemite Trail Discovered*, I felt like I was really in California being a part of the gold rush with these characters. In the story, there was a moment when Virginia's character surprised me. It's worth reading to find out. The story made me want to read another one written by Dr. Sontag.

~Joy T.
Age 13

UNDERGROUND
SCOUTS

Also by Marie Sontag

The Bronze Dagger
The Alabaster Jar
The Silver Coin

The Whitcomb Discoveries
California Trail Discovered
Yosemite Trail Discovered

UNDERGROUND SCOUTS

Book 1 of the WWII Rising Hope Series

MARIE SONTAG

WordCrafts

Underground Scouts
Copyright © 2022
Marie Sontag, PhD

Paperback ISBN: 978-1-957344-39-3

Cover and map design by Harits Farhan

Published by WordCrafts Press
Cody, Wyoming 82414
www.wordcrafts.net

Warsaw, Poland

Warsaw's Districts

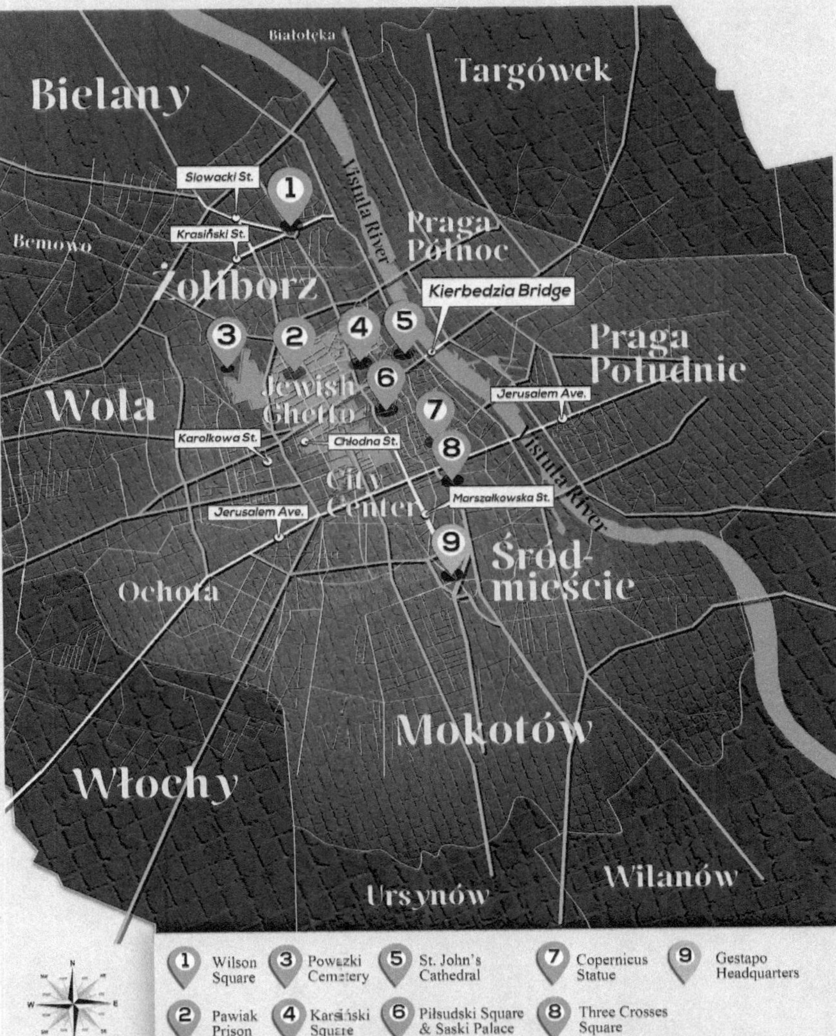

WARSAW BATTLE LOCATION

1. **St. Anthony's Church:** *Krzysh dies*
2. **Saski Gardens:** *German stronghold*
3. **Zamoyski Palace:** *Hide out in the cellar*
4. **City Center:** *Home Army Headquarters*
5. **Królewska Street:** *Storm through holes in apartment dwellings to meet up with Colonel Monter's men to stage a counter-attack against German advances*
6. **Marszalkowska Street near Królewska:** *Hunker down to hold the German line at Królewska to keep the enemy from advancing south to City Center*
7. **Wilanowska Street:** *Ordered to retreat south after Dirlewanger bombs the area*
8. **Napoleon Square:** *Dirlewanger ordered Stukas to bomb this area, and had the Nebelwerfer in Saski Gardens fire incendiary rockets into City Center*
9. **Holy Cross Church and St. Alexander's Church:** *Dirlewanger bombed and incinerated these churches, knowing citizens had gathered there for sanctuary*
10. ***Bajka* Ship**
11. **Paint Factory**
12. **Bank of Poland**

To those who gave their all for Warsaw's Rising,
especially the Boy Scouts and Girl Guides.
Thank you for instilling within me a love for
Poland and its people.

To our "adopted" family in Warsaw,
Stanisław, Basia, Henry, George, and Mary Piechowicz
We wish we lived closer.

To my father, Ed Reik,
whose father's last name was Reikowski.
I wish I had known both of you better.

NORTH SEA
LATVIA
POLAND
BELARUS
Katyn Forest
U.S.S.R
Warsaw
Kock
Pinsk Marshes
Vistula Riv.
Lubartów
Kovel
Kiev
Lviv
UKRAINE
Dniester Riv.
Dnieper Riv.
Donets Riv.
Slovakia
Hungary
MOLDOVA
Romania
Serbia
Danube Riv.
Yalta
Bulgaria
Kosovo
BLACK SEA

To see a sequential and alphabetical list of characters in the book, go to page 287. There you'll also find pronunciations for Polish names and discover which characters were historical and which ones were fictional. A link to a downloadable list of these characters, including pictures, can be found at:
www.mariesontag.com/books/underground-scouts/

CHAPTER 1

Be Prepared–Czuwaj!

Midmorning, September 8, 1939
Palmiry, Poland, Kampinos Forest

Tadzio stood with his family in the entry way of their summerhouse. He clenched his teeth to calm his coiling stomach.

Poppa, his battered suitcase in hand, stepped to the door and turned the brass handle. One more second and he'd be gone. Again.

I should stop him. Tadzio lowered his gaze and shook his head. *No. Today is no different.*

But today *was* different. Today, Germany declared war on Poland.

He twisted a loose thread hanging from the cuff of his Boy Scout shirt and inhaled a quick breath. "Why do you have to leave now, Poppa? We need you. The war—"

With a sigh, Father released the door's handle and turned. Deep circles beneath his eyes showed darker than usual. "I'm sorry, Tadzio. I know I haven't been home much this past year." He ruffled Tadzio's dark blond hair. "I know I have missed out on many events. And after meeting with your scoutmaster today, I realize how important your scouting activities are. However, I must go on a special business trip. We will talk more when I return."

Poppa glanced at Magdalena who stood with stooped shoulders next to Mother. The vanilla and lavender scent of his aftershave hung in the air as he shifted his gaze back to Tadzio. "You're thirteen now, son. Even though Magdalena is older, I expect you to take over as man of the house."

Magdalena sniffled into her lace handkerchief.

Squeezing five-year-old Henio's hand, Mother studied Poppa with tear-rimmed eyes. She kissed his cheek and offered what looked like a forced smile. "Come back to us soon, Henryk."

Once again, Tadzio fingered his wayward thread. "Poppa?" His voice came soft. "Can you at least tell us when you'll be back?"

"I can't give you any details." He lifted Tadzio's chin. "When I return, I'll explain everything. For now, obey Mother and listen to your scoutmaster. Take care of the family until I return."

As Father walked out the door, Tadzio tamped down the sharp taste of garlic and onions that rose to his throat—compliments of last night's dinner. Although anger boiled in his belly, he wanted to run after him, wrap his arms around his waist, and scream, *No, Poppa. Don't leave us now!*

Earlier that morning, Andrzej, Tadzio's sixteen-year-old patrol leader, had driven to their summerhouse with their scoutmaster and two other scouts in tow. Father and the scoutmaster had then retreated to Poppa's study. They remained there and spoke in hushed tones for almost thirty minutes.

Tadzio hated mysteries. He wanted an explanation. He stood outside the doorway until Poppa and his scoutmaster finished. When they exited, his scoutmaster's pressed lips advised him not to ask questions.

Now, two hours later, his scoutmaster joined him and his family on the white-columned porch to bid Father goodbye.

As Tadzio shielded his eyes from the late-morning sun, his breath caught in his throat. *When will I see Poppa again?*

With solid steps, his father deposited his suitcase in the trunk of Andrzej's black Fiat 518, then strode across the yard and into the barn. He emerged minutes later, dragging two bulging suitcases. Hoisting them into the back seat of Andrzej's car, he slid in next to them.

"Thank you for coming today, Professor Handelsman," Mother said to the scoutmaster. "I know your talk encouraged my husband."

"And his words inspired me," the scoutmaster said. "Your husband is a brave man."

Arching a brow, Tadzio turned to his scoutmaster. "Professor, what did you and my father discuss?"

Professor Handelsman raised his chin and gazed out across the yard. "Later, son. Not now."

The stench of petrol flooded Tadzio's nostrils as Andrzej revved the Fiat's engine. Seconds later, chauffeuring Father, the patrol leader pulled out of the graveled driveway and onto the Kampinos's forest-lined road.

The scoutmaster stroked his walrus mustache and turned to Tadzio and Magdalena. "Andrzej will be back in an hour. I'd like you and the other Scouts to join me in the study when he returns. I will tell you then what you need to know."

Tadzio opened his mouth to say, *Tell us now*, but the professor's scowl stopped him.

Frustrated, Tadzio re-entered the house and shuffled into the parlor. Their Böesendorfer piano beckoned him from the far corner. Its black and white ivories invited him to hammer out his swirl of emotions beneath the weight of his fingers. In the past, music had always served as his constant companion. He hoped it would do so again as he sought refuge from the world's harsh realities in a Schubert sonata.

The other Scouts went their separate ways until Andrzej returned from his mysterious errand.

At three o'clock, Andrzej's Fiat crunched across the pebbled driveway. The professor motioned the Scouts to follow him into the study.

Once everyone settled into a leather-backed chair, Professor Handelsman eased the study's heavy oak doors shut.

Tadzio's chair seemed to swallow him whole as he slouched into its ample seat.

The professor sat behind Poppa's cherry wood desk, adjusted his rimless spectacles, and gazed at the group. "Sources tell me it's only a matter of days before German soldiers march through here on their way to Warsaw. Boy Scouts and Girl Guides from several cities have banded together with Warsaw's Scouts to take a stand against the Nazis who will pour into the capital. It won't be easy. If you have any qualms about joining the effort, say so now."

Confused and frustrated, Tadzio supported his jaw with a fisted hand. He wanted to shout, but only managed a whisper. "Joining what effort?"

Stefan shot Tadzio one of his cocky half-smiles. "The Polish Underground, you moron."

Their scoutmaster's chair squeaked as he shifted his weight and stroked his mustache. "The Scouts are not really *joining* the Underground." His voice came thick and heavy. "We are merely choosing to help the cause, as it were."

Bullies. Tadzio avoided them. For as long as he could remember, Stefan, a Scout his own age, had bullied him. Now, for the sake of Poland, their scoutmaster challenged him to confront the Germans.

Tadzio gazed around the room—first at Andrzej, then Lech and Stefan, his best friend Krzysh, and finally his sixteen-year-old sister, Magdalena. She stared back, her dark, brown eyes wide with uncertainty. What would Magdalena say? Would she follow Andrzej and Lech's lead?

Biting her lip, his sister brushed a lock of her shoulder-length, dark brown hair behind one ear and squeezed her eyes shut.

Tadzio pulled in a ragged breath. What would happen to Mother and little Henio if he and Magdalena joined the resistance?

Their scoutmaster continued. "What I am about to ask from all of you is a personal sacrifice on behalf of Poland. Your final decision is, of course, up to you. As for your family, Tadzio and Magdalena, the caretakers of your manor house have pledged their lives to protect them while your father is away on business. If you decide to join us in the cause, they will look after your mother and little brother. You must each make your own decision."

A hush filled the room. The Scouts' pale faces betrayed the struggle that plagued them all.

Tadzio broke the spell. "I mean no disrespect, Professor." He squirmed in his seat. "I don't know why my father had to leave, but since he's gone, my family is my priority."

Squaring her shoulders, Magdalena inched forward on her chair. "And earlier this week my father's brother and his wife were killed when a bomb hit their apartment building in Warsaw." Her voice quivered, and she dug her nails into the sides of her chair. "That's why we're here at our summerhouse. Now, we're also caring for our orphaned eleven-year-old cousin, Józefina."

Tadzio nodded. "Since I am the eldest son, my first responsibility is to my family."

"Well spoken, son." Professor Handelsman studied Tadzio over the top of his glasses. "As I said, the caretakers of your manor house have pledged to watch over your family while your father is away, but I understand why you must make your mother and little Henio your priority."

The professor glanced at the other Scouts. "What about the rest of you?"

Tadzio's patrol leader, Andrzej, spoke first. His pensive gaze narrowed, and he pinned Tadzio with a stare. Apparently, Andrzej didn't accept his excuse. "As we know, this is what we've prepared for all summer. It comes as no surprise." Andrzej jiggled his left leg. "The Scout training we received in the Kampinos Forest these past few months—first aid, food storage, water purification, map reading skills, Morse Code, riflery—it all prepared us for this moment. I will give my all for Poland."

Lech smoothed back his thick, black hair. "Andrzej's right. Unless you were living in a vacuum, we all knew the Germans would come for us. I say it's time to take a stand."

First Lech, then Andrzej, and finally Lech's younger brother, Stefan, rose to their feet. Standing with raised chins, they punched their fists into the air and shouted in unison. "*Czuwaj! Czuwaj!*"

Glued to his seat, Tadzio shook his head. *Czuwaj?* Their Scout motto mocked him. As a Scout, he had pledged to be vigilant. Awake. Prepared. But this? No. He couldn't shout *Czuwaj*. Not now. Nothing had prepared him for this.

Tadzio glanced at Krzysh. His heart squeezed as his best friend pulled his knees to his chin and clasped his hands over his ears. No. Krzysh wasn't up to the task, either.

Krzysh tried to hide it, but Tadzio knew better. His best friend was crazy with fear over his parents' fate.

On September 1, when Germans first bombed Warsaw, Father drove the family to their summer home in the Kampinos Forest. Krzysh and his nine-year-old sister Lucyna had accompanied them. Krzysh's parents promised to join them as soon as they took care of business in the city. Later, Krzysh's parents sent a message saying a bomb leveled the Bank of Poland just as they were leaving—the same bank where Tadzio's father worked. Now, Krzysh's parents were recovering in a hospital somewhere in Warsaw. That made it Krzysh's responsibility to care for his sister.

Tadzio shifted his gaze to Magdalena. Like him, she remained in her seat.

Beads of perspiration trickled down Tadzio's back. His stomach twisted into a knot. He ran out of the room, barely making it to the bathroom before spewing his afternoon meal into the toilet.

Ashamed, he glanced at his reflection in the mirror and shook his head. *Guess I was right. I don't have what it takes to fight the Germans.*

Before turning in for the night, Mother coaxed Tadzio and Magdalena into performing their violin and piano arrangement of Chopin's Etude in E.

With wide eyes, Professor Handelsman turned to Tadzio's mother. "I didn't know Chopin wrote an etude for piano and violin."

Mother pursed her lips, making her sleek Greek nose appear even more slender. "Actually, Professor, Tadzio has written a piano arrangement of Chopin's Piano Etude in E Major to accompany Magdalena as she plays the melody on the violin. They had hoped to perform this new arrangement for the Chopin Young People's Concert this fall. They worked on the piece all summer."

"Well, well." The professor clapped his hands and motioned everyone into the parlor. "Tadzio, my boy, I knew you had talent on the rifle range, as well as archery and map skills, but I had no idea you possessed such musical ability. By all means, we must have a command performance."

Stefan shoved his way past Tadzio as he entered the room. "Right. He's just a regular *Mr. Perfect.*" With a sigh, Stefan flopped down on the dark green sofa.

Angered by Stefan's cutting comment and embarrassed by the attention, Tadzio's face burned. He lowered his head and plodded to the piano.

The professor sat in the winged Queen Anne chair next to Stefan and leaned toward the Scout. "Not perfect, Pan Lutowski, skilled." His voice grew low. "You have skills as well. After all, you chose to leave with me tomorrow morning. Tadzio chose to stay behind."

Balling his hands into fists, Tadzio ticked a jaw muscle. Perhaps the professor hadn't meant for him to overhear his remark to Stefan, but he had.

Mother settled Henio and the other children next to her on a couch across from the professor. Andrzej and Lech sat on parlor chairs near the piano.

Smoothing his mustache, the portly professor addressed the group. "Did any of you know that, according to Chopin's biographer, the composer once told his copyist he believed he'd never written a more beautiful melody than that found in his E Major Etude?"

Tadzio raised a brow. He'd never heard that story.

Others shrugged and shook their heads.

The professor nodded. "Once, when Chopin was listening to a recording of this etude, he raised his arms like this." The elderly man stood and clasped his hands above his head. "When the piece ended, legend says Chopin exclaimed, 'O, Poland, my fatherland!'" As if in prayer, Professor Handelsman lowered his hands and sat.

The scoutmaster continued, "As you all know, after the Polish cadets rebelled against Russia in 1830, Chopin never returned to Poland. How he loved his homeland! You can hear the longing for his country in every strain of the piece." Professor Handelsman's tired eyes revealed a wistful look. "He wrote the Etude in E Major two years after he left Poland and, as I said, never returned." The professor pulled in a long breath. "Ahh. What a fitting melody for us this evening."

Tadzio peered closer at his scoutmaster. Were those tears in his eyes?

He knew Chopin left Poland in 1830 when Russia's czar sent troops into their country. His grandfather told him stories about how the cadets at Warsaw Military College had rebelled against the czar. One of those cadets had been Grandfather's Great-Uncle Tadeusz, for whom Tadzio was named.

How proud his grandfather had been of his great-uncle. Grandfather explained how the Russian czar before Nicholas I had allowed the Poles their own parliament and constitution. But when Nicholas I came to power, he abolished the Poles' self-government and restored strict Russian rule. Having obtained a taste of freedom, the Poles staged a rebellion. Within a year, Nicholas I defeated the cadets and their supporters. The czar sent 25,000 patriots and their families to Siberia—including Grandfather's Great-Uncle Tadeusz.

Last year, when his family vacationed with Grandfather at their summerhouse, the elderly man had shared, "Although my Great-Uncle Tadeusz was sent to Siberia, his family evaded capture because they hid in this summerhouse. This is a very special place for our family." That was the first time Grandfather had mentioned this tidbit of family history. A month later, Grandfather died.

Tadzio saw history repeating itself. This time, it was the Germans threatening Poland's freedom. Now, he and his family sought refuge at the summerhouse.

Tadzio glanced at Magdalena. She stood next to the piano with her chin resting on her violin, her bow drawn across her strings, and her elbow raised as she waited for his downbeat.

After nodding his head twice, the magic began.

Magdalena's lilting melody and Tadzio's restful two-four rhythm transformed the room into a unity of emotion for the fatherland of Poland.

Of a yearning for freedom.

Of love.

Of family.

Of everything good in life.

And, for one brief moment, it eased the painful knowledge that the enemy, like inky mists of darkness, crept across the forest floor, seeking to snatch it all away. Even Stefan, who appeared to hum along with parts of the melody, seemed grateful for the little concert. Before Tadzio and Magdalena reached the song's climax, the younger children fell asleep.

As the last notes faded and Magdalena lifted her bow from its strings, Lech sighed. "That was amazing."

Magdalena blushed. Avoiding Lech's gaze, she placed her Roth violin in its coffin-shaped case. "Thank you."

Lech stood and placed a hand on hers as she fastened the latch. "I've never heard anything so beautiful."

Professor Handelsman stood and gave a slight cough. "Andrzej, Lech, Stefan. Set your alarms for 5:30 a.m. We will leave right after breakfast."

Magdalena shot Lech a puzzled look.

Lech stared back at her. A pained expression flooded his eyes. His mouth opened as if to say something, but the professor coughed again.

The elderly scoutmaster nodded toward Tadzio's mother. "Thank you for your hospitality, Pani Dombrowska. No need to see us off tomorrow. We will care for ourselves and be gone before you rise."

Tadzio squeezed his eyebrows together. He wanted to know where they were going, but, having chosen to stay behind, he knew he had no right to ask. Angry with the Germans, himself, Father, and everyone else in general, he kissed Mother on the cheek and ambled off to bed. Krzysh followed ten minutes later.

When Tadzio arose the next morning, Professor Handelsman, Andrzej, Lech, and Stefan had already left. While he and Magdalena set the table, Mother prepared a breakfast of tomatoes, avocados, and eggs.

"Do you know where Professor Handelsman has gone?" Tadzio asked Mother.

"Off to do important Scout work, I suppose." She wiped her hands on a towel. "But I appreciate you staying here to help with the children. I know you'd much rather be off with them."

Tadzio wasn't so sure he'd rather be off with the Scouts. He could only imagine what kind of danger they might encounter.

CHAPTER 2

The Secret Chamber

September 23, 1939
Palmiry, Poland

On the afternoon of September 23, after endless games of hide and seek with the younger children, Tadzio demanded a break. "It's time for the live Radio Warsaw concert."

Magdalena took up her favorite spot on their green-velveted sofa. "What's on today's schedule?"

"Władysław Szpilman." Tadzio grinned. Szpilman was one of his favorite pianists. Electronic whirs belched from the Philco cathedral radio as Tadzio dialed the knob and tuned in the station.

Soon, blazing strains of Chopin's emotional Fantazja-Impromptu filled the room. Like moths to a flame, everyone gathered in the parlor.

During Chopin's romantically haunting Nocturne in E flat, Magdalena held her fingers aloft, as if conducting. "See? Things are not so bad in the city."

Tadzio wagged his head. Didn't anyone else hear bombs exploding behind the live broadcast?

Szpilman's next selection, Chopin's third movement of Piano Sonata No. 2, quickened his pulse. Chopin's Funeral March. *Pray for the dead.* His insides churned. *Is this a prelude of things to come?*

After the program, everyone trailed out of the room.

Tadzio leaned back in the winged Queen Anne's chair and absorbed the station's recording of Rachmaninov's Piano Concerto #2. The somber tones darkened his mood even more. Although no longer a live broadcast, he imagined bombs bursting behind every strain. As the single notes of the second movement faded, the station went dead.

Tadzio glanced at the grandfather clock next to the parlor window. It chimed 3:15. The program shouldn't be over. He fiddled with the dial. Nothing. Bombs must have hit the station.

Tadzio shook the mute radio, then thumped it.

"What did the wireless ever do to you?" Krzysh chuckled as he entered the room. "Seriously," he added, "did the broadcast get interrupted?" Krzysh pulled a book from a nearby table and sat on the green couch.

Tadzio couldn't muster strength to respond. He simply nodded. Hoping to keep morbid questions from forming, he pressed his fingers against his temples. Questions arose anyway. *Are my friends in Warsaw still alive? What about Krzysh and Lucyna's parents? Is Father—* Frustrated and powerless, Tadzio moved to the piano and pounded out a scherzo.

Thirty minutes later, Henio tugged his sleeve.

A dissonant clash of notes erupted.

"Henio!"

His little brother pulled again. "I want to play outside."

Tadzio scowled and yanked his sleeve from Henio's grasp. "Leave me alone. Find Cousin Józefina and color pictures."

Krzysh snapped shut his Horatio Nelson book. "That was harsh, don't you think?"

Running toward the kitchen, Henio wailed, "Momma, Tadzio yelled at me."

Tadzio narrowed his eyes at Krzysh. "Mind your own business."

"Tadeusz Dombrowski!" His mother shouted.

Clenching his jaw, Tadzio returned to the fast-paced scherzo he struggled to master.

Mother called again. "Tadzio, you promised to help with the children." Her thin, high-pitched voice sounded close to tears.

Tadzio dropped his hands to his lap. Wallowing in his own frustration and worry, he hadn't thought how Warsaw's bombing and his father's absence might affect his mother.

The sound of ripping paper and a girl's shriek rose from the next room.

"Lucyna, is that you?" Krzysh ran out.

Tadzio followed.

Lucyna, Józefina, and Henio lay on the kitchen floor, wildly scribbling over each other's pictures.

"Mine's better."

"No, mine."

"Yours is ugly."

"You can't draw anything."

"Can too. Momma says I draw pretty."

"My Mommy is hurt."

"My Momma is—"

The children broke down and bawled.

Tadzio's mother squeezed her eyes shut and moaned. Tugging at hair pinned to the back of her head, she ran out the side door.

Magdalena joined Tadzio in the kitchen just as Krzysh scooped up Lucyna.

"Everything will be okay." Krzysh brushed back moist strands of hair from his sister's face.

Lifting Henio, Tadzio kissed his little brother's warm, soft cheek as he hugged him to his chest. "I'm sorry, Henio."

Magdalena bent down and enveloped her young cousin in a hug.

Józefina melted into Magdalena's embrace. "My momma," she whimpered. "My momma."

Smiling, Henio lifted his chubby hands and pinched Tadzio's cheeks. "Let's play hide and seek."

Magdalena rolled her dark brown eyes. "Not again."

"There must be something else we can all do together." Tadzio shook his head, but let a smile tug at a corner of his mouth.

Krzysh and Magdalena stared at Tadzio with blank faces, then laughed.

No. Hide and seek it was.

Krzysh sighed. "But can we start from someplace other than the kitchen? Let's begin in your father's study."

The children agreed and headed down the hallway.

Reaching the study, Tadzio gasped. His father's silver chess pieces were strewn across the polished oak floor. Tadzio's face burned. "Who opened Father's set?"

Krzysh released his sister's hand and bent down to pick up the chessmen. "Lucyna and I played War with these earlier today while you practiced. I'm sorry. We forgot to clean up."

Tadzio put Henio down and helped Krzysh return the figures to their black-velveted case. "Father doesn't even let *me* play with these." He frowned.

"I said I was sorry." Krzysh slammed the box shut.

Kneeling back-to-back, the boys stood.

Krzysh bumped into Tadzio.

Knocked off-balance, Tadzio sprawled and crashed into the bookcase. His forehead smashed into a brass bookend.

A wall panel slid open, revealing a hidden room.

Silenced ruled as the children gaped into the darkness.

Tadzio swallowed hard, then took a tentative step forward.

The others followed.

Trembling, Tadzio ventured deeper into the room. A musty smell filled his nostrils. Glancing around, he guessed the enclosure was about the size of his bedroom in Warsaw. In the dim light, an old kerosene lantern sitting on a ledge caught his attention.

Magdalena joined him.

Dancing his fingers along the dusty shelf, Tadzio found a box of wooden matches. He struck a match and lit the lantern, illuminating a small knob near the opening. He pulled it.

The chamber's door slammed shut.

Magdalena screamed. "Tadzio! We're trapped!"

CHAPTER 3

The Germans

Late September 1939
Palmiry, Poland

Tadzio pulled the knob a second time. The door opened.

"Never do that again!" Magdalena punched his arm. "You scared me to death."

Even though his forehead throbbed, Tadzio laughed. They'd discovered Grandfather's secret chamber where Great-Great-Great-Uncle Tadeusz's family once hid from Czar Nicholas I.

The children jumped up and down. "Again, again," they shouted, clapping their hands. "Can we come in?"

"Sure."

Tadzio waved them into the hidden room.

Faded green army cots filled the small space. The youngsters flopped down and rubbed their noses as wisps of dust rose.

With drooped shoulders, Krzysh shuffled in. "I'm sorry about the chess set. Are you okay?"

Tadzio touched his forehead. A lump had already formed. "Don't worry about it. It was an accident. Besides. Bumping into each other helped us discover this secret room." Tadzio surveyed the chamber. "This should keep the little ones busy. We can tell them it's their secret playhouse."

Krzysh nodded. "At least it'll give us a break from playing hide and seek."

Pressing a finger to her lips, Józefina shook her head. "Let's keep this room *very* secret."

At dinner that evening, Henio announced to the adults, "We have a secret playhouse."

Józefina scowled.

"Ouch!" Henio yelled around a mouthful of potatoes. "Józefina kicked me."

Tomasz, the eldest caretaker, raised an eyebrow. "We wondered when you'd stumble across that secret place. Did you know it once saved the family of your grandfather's Great-Uncle Tadeusz when he was a cadet at Warsaw Military College?"

Magdalena shot Tomasz a puzzled look. "You know about the room?"

Tomasz nodded as his wife, Halina, passed him a bowl of cooked turnips.

Halina picked up the story. "Your grandfather told us about it when he first hired us as caretakers." She tapped her chin. "Let's see, if Tadeusz was your grandfather's great-uncle, that would make him your—"

Halina's eighteen-year-old son, Feliks, jumped in. "That would make Cadet Tadeusz Magdalena's great-great-great-uncle."

The corners of Magdalena's eyes crinkled as she returned his blue-eyed gaze.

Feliks' father poked the air with his fork, as if underscoring facts. "Yes, well, when the cadets at Warsaw Military College rebelled against Czar Nicholas I, the czar exiled them all to Siberia. He then sent Russian soldiers to round up all their relatives. Cadet Tadeusz got word to your grandfather's family, and they hid in that secret chamber. You wouldn't be here today if it hadn't been for that room."

Tadzio's mother passed Tomasz the plate of tomatoes. "And, who knows? That room may one day prove our salvation."

As Krzysh predicted, the secret room kept the youngsters busy for weeks. Krzysh helped Tadzio line the walls with additional shelves so the children could store bandages and make-believe medicines to play hospital. Tadzio and Magdalena added a few dishes and costumes so the children could play house and dress-up.

On another shelf, they stored toy weapons for playing pirates, as well as a battery-operated lantern. On the highest ledge, out of the children's reach, Tadzio and Magdalena placed a bag of caramels they'd brought from Warsaw. While the children played, Tadzio practiced the piano. Magdalena and Krzysh spent most of their time reading.

During the last week of September, Tadzio overheard Tomasz and Halina in the kitchen speaking in hushed tones. "Don't tell the children yet," Tomasz said. "It will break their hearts. While gathering supplies in Palmiry, I heard Warsaw surrendered to the Germans yesterday."

"Tomasz!" Halina wailed. "We said we would never surrender."

"Things change when staring into the face of a starving child. The city people have no food, no water, and no medicine. What are they to do?"

Halina let out a *tsk*. "Any news yet of poor Krzysh and Lucyna's parents?"

"The last I heard, they were fighting serious infections. Then, the place where they were staying was shelled, and they had to move to another makeshift hospital. There's been no word since."

The kitchen's screen door creaked open and slammed shut. Mother's voice interrupted the caretakers. "Tomasz and Halina, would you please join me in the barn? I think there's a leak in the roof. I'd like you to take a look."

Tadzio wanted to ask Tomasz more about Warsaw's surrender, but a distant wail from Henio stopped him. He headed down the hall toward Henio's voice. Magdalena and Krzysh trailed behind him.

Henio's voice led Tadzio to Poppa's study where he lay sprawled on the oak-wood floor. Tears streaked Henio's face, and he groaned as he clutched his ankle.

Tadzio shifted his gaze from Henio to Lucyna.

Squeezing her brows together, Lucyna pointed to the desk. "Henio was playing paratrooper. He jumped off your father's desk. We put a pile of blankets inside the playroom for him to land on. He missed. I think he hurt his ankle."

Pointing a finger at Lucyna, Józefina scowled. "It was all *her* idea."

"Józefina encouraged him to do it." Lucyna stuck out her tongue.

After waving a dismissive hand, Magdalena motioned to Krzysh. "Grab the first aid kit from the playhouse. "Tadzio, get Mother. Tell her Henio's hurt."

As Tadzio took a step, machine-gun fire pierced the air. He inhaled a gasp and held it. Was it possible for your heart to beat right out of your chest?

His father's parting words flashed in his mind. *I expect you to take over as man of the house.*

Gasping for breath, Tadzio thrust Magdalena and the children into the secret room. He yelled for Krzysh to join them, but his friend didn't move.

"Krzysh!" he shouted again. "Get in here!"

Krzysh stayed frozen in place.

Seizing his friend's shirtsleeve, Tadzio yanked him inside. He then turned to Magdalena. "I'm going to the kitchen to grab a few things. If I'm not back in a minute, pull the knob and shut the door."

Magdalena clutched Tadzio's hands. "Wait! What's happening?"

"Do as I say. Don't leave this room."

Running to the study's window, Tadzio peeked out from behind the tall curtains. Two German personnel carriers and a staff car had parked next to the barn. A soldier atop a carrier aimed his machine gun at the old building and let off another round.

Oh, God! Mother's in the barn! Trembling, he ran to the kitchen and filled a large glass bottle with water. He then grabbed a metal pail and tossed in a chunk of cheese, a knife, and a loaf of bread.

Rat-a-tat-tat!

He glanced out the kitchen window. Tomasz and Feliks crouched near an opening on the barn's second floor. They trained their rifles on the soldiers manning the machine guns.

Blam! Blam!

One gunner tumbled off his carrier.

A blaze of shots exploded from the second carrier.

Tomasz and Feliks tumbled to the ground.

Covering his mouth to stifle a shriek, Tadzio willed himself to move.

He couldn't.

Motionless, he stared at the caretakers lying face down in the mud.

A distant cry from Magdalena thawed him. Tucking his supplies under his arm, he sprinted back to the secret chamber.

"Pull the knob!"

CHAPTER 4

The Well

Late September 1939
Palmiry, Poland

Tadzio dashed inside. The panel door swished shut. Dropping his supplies to the floor, he reached for the battery-operated lantern and clicked it on.

Magdalena leaned closer and whispered. "What's happening? I heard gunfire."

Eyes wide, Tadzio pinched his lips closed and shook his head. He silently willed her not to ask questions. His stomach spasmed. Hoping to corral his runaway emotions, he pulled in a deep breath and offered Magdalena a raised eyebrow. "Henio's ankle?"

Appearing to understand, Magdalena sat on the cot next to their little brother and gently flexed his foot.

Henio winced, but didn't cry.

Standing, she removed a few rolled-up bandages from a box overhead.

Tadzio lifted the lantern. "We can only leave the light on for a minute." His mind whirred. Would Germans soon storm the house? "We don't want to run out the battery." Like a column of marching ants, beads of sweat trickled down his spine.

Józefina whined. "I hate the dark."

He tried to soothe her with a half-smile. "So do I." He clenched his jaw, hoping to keep his voice steady. "When I turn off the light, we'll play a little game."

Józefina stuck out her lower lip. "What kind of game?"

Magdalena nodded at Tadzio as she finished bandaging Henio's ankle. She stood, grabbed the bag of caramels they'd stored on the top shelf, and gave everyone a piece. "Here are the rules." She put her hands on her hips and grimaced her best schoolmarm face. "Eat your candy now, and then we'll shut off the lantern. No one is to talk or make a noise until Tadzio turns it back on. If you remain completely quiet until we have light, I'll reward you with another caramel."

Józefina opened her mouth as if to object, but Magdalena put a finger to her lips.

Frowning, Józefina took the candy and stretched out next to Lucyna.

Magdalena curled up on the other cot with Henio.

Huddled in a corner, Krzysh wrapped his arms around his knees. Spotting a stool near the opposite wall, Tadzio sat and clicked off the light.

After a while, the children's breathing came in calm, even intervals. He guessed they'd fallen asleep. He, however, worked to remain alert. When his feet tingled, he stood and wiggled his toes to bring them back to life.

A faint light bled in between the panel and the wall. He crept to the corner where Krzysh hunkered down. "Are you okay?" he whispered.

Krzysh didn't respond.

He laid a hand on his friend's shoulder. Vibrations from Krzysh's trembling body worked their way up through Tadzio's hand to his arm. Worried the quivering would prove contagious, Tadzio groped back to his stool.

After several minutes, Tadzio moved to the chamber's door. He strained to pick up any noise. Far off, he heard gruff German voices shout orders. A minute later, the kitchen's side door creaked open and slammed shut. The thud of boots tromped across the wooden floors.

Closer.

Closer.

More gruff German voices. More bellowing.

A German shouted something outside the secret chamber's door. A female answered. *"Nein."*

Mother! His skin prickled, and he clamped a hand over his mouth.

He didn't know what the German had asked, but he recognized his mother's voice and her response. *Nein*—no.

The soldiers tossed books off Poppa's shelves, slid drawers out of his desk, and rustled papers. Tadzio prayed they wouldn't accidentally pull on the bookend that opened their chamber's door.

In the semi-darkness, Tadzio sensed a faint movement from Krzysh's corner. His friend came to stand beside him.

"My mother's out there," Tadzio whispered.

"I know," Krzysh whispered back. "They asked her if anyone else is in the house."

Tadzio pulled in a sigh of relief. Unlike him, Krzysh had studied German in school. He could translate whatever the Germans said.

A sudden chill enveloped him. His mother had just protected them by telling the Germans no one was in the house. Tadzio bit his lip. *But who will protect her?*

Another German voice shouted, "*Aus! Alle raus!*"

"He's ordering everyone to leave," Krzysh whispered.

Boots trudged across the study's floor and down the hallway.

About fifteen minutes later, engines revved. Vehicles crunched pebbled stones beneath their wheels as the transport carriers pulled away.

Believing it safe to turn on the lantern, Tadzio flooded the room with light. The children woke and Magdalena handed out their promised treats.

Tadzio passed around the water jar, along with pieces of cheese and bread. Pretending it was still part of the game, he told them they'd stay in the chamber overnight. The bucket in the corner would serve as their toilet. Although their charges protested, Magdalena had enough candies to reward their compliance. Tadzio didn't want to take any chances. What if the Germans returned, or more took their place?

The next morning, Tadzio opened the chamber's door. "I'll exit first and make sure it's safe. Everyone stay here until I get back." Once more, he pressed his lips into a flat line and gave Magdalena his *don't-ask-any-questions* face.

Józefina stamped her foot. "I want to go too. It smells in here."

Reaching for the bag of candies, Magdalena shook it. "Our game is almost over, Józefina, but I think we have enough sweets for one more round. Those who can stay here without complaining until Tadzio returns will get the last pieces."

Tadzio shot Magdalena a faint smile and stepped into the study.

Krzysh grabbed his arm. "Since you and I are orphans," Krzysh said, "we need to stick together. We can't do that if I'm sitting on the floor hugging my knees."

Tadzio clapped Krzysh on the back as they walked down the hallway toward the kitchen. He wondered if Krzysh would feel the same when they found Tomasz and Feliks' bodies lying in the mud near the barn.

Reaching the kitchen, Tadzio gazed out the window where the German carriers had stood the day before. No bodies lay on the ground.

"Let's check outside." Tadzio yanked in a quick breath, hoping to strengthen his resolve to face whatever he found.

Krzysh nodded.

Relying on hand signals they'd learned at Scout camp two months ago, Tadzio led Krzysh through a search of the grounds. Signals like *halt, move forward, freeze,* and *take a knee* had come in handy when they'd played capture the flag at camp. But this was no game. He surveyed the front, side, and back of the house, but found no Germans. He relaxed his shoulders.

Krzysh stood tall and placed his hands on his hips. "Looks like it's all clear."

Nodding, Tadzio jerked up his head. "Wait. My mother. We haven't seen any sign of her. Or Halina, our groundskeeper's wife."

"You're right." Krzysh pinched his lower lip between his teeth. "And what about your groundskeeper and his son? Do you think the Germans took everyone with them when they left? What were they looking for in your father's study?"

Tadzio's stomach dropped. He had no idea what the Germans hoped to find at the manor house. But he did know what happened to Tomasz and Feliks.

Krzysh tilted his head. "Maybe we should check inside the barn and over by the pond."

Tadzio shivered. *Maybe we shouldn't.* What if Germans had dragged Tomasz and Feliks' dead bodies into the barn, or dumped them in the pond? As if a cold January wind had blown off their frozen pond, he tugged his arms to his chest. But it was September. The pond wasn't frozen.

Tadzio searched the outbuilding but found it empty. Even their two horses and cow were gone. He could only hope the Germans had taken his mother and Halina as prisoners and buried Halina's husband and son somewhere nearby.

As he and Krzysh passed a stand of birch trees in their trek toward the pond, the old dry well came into view. Just like a flash flood muddies still waters, the sight of the well stirred up memories and feelings he thought he'd forgotten.

Tadzio stopped in his tracks.

The well's wooden bucket still dangled over the top of the well. The frayed rope still attached the bucket to the crossbeams. Gazing at the weathered container, Tadzio covered his ears, but it didn't drown out the silent echoes of his panicked, unanswered screams for help. Cries he'd shouted eight years ago while playing hide and seek with his father.

He saw himself as that five-year-old who climbed atop the bucket and lowered himself into the well. Holding onto the rope, he'd told himself he would only go down far enough to avoid being seen. Then he'd pull himself up.

He gasped as he relived the same air-pushed-out-of-your-lungs feeling he'd experienced when he lost control of the rope and fell. A pain shot through his leg as he saw himself lying at the bottom of the dry well, his leg bent beneath him. It had taken his father over an hour to retrieve him from that dark hole.

Shame washed over his frame. The same scared five-year-old boy still lived inside of him.

Krzysh signaled to move forward.

Shaking his head, Tadzio stood frozen in place. He felt as though his clothes had transformed into bricks, making it impossible to move.

Krzysh moved behind a pine. Peering out, he once again signaled Tadzio forward.

Once more, Tadzio silently said no.

Krzysh poked his head out and glanced one way, then the other. Satisfied, he crept to another tree and scanned the area again.

Tadzio remained in place.

Krzysh strode over to Tadzio. "What's the matter? Do you see something?"

Tadzio continued to stare at the well.

Following his friend's gaze, Krzysh gripped Tadzio's shoulder. "You don't think your mother is—" He squeezed harder. "Stay here."

Krzysh sprinted over and gazed inside. Spinning around, he shouted, "It's empty."

A coldness filled Tadzio's chest. He hung his head and shuffled back to the house.

When the boys reached the secret room, Tadzio pulled the book-end and opened the door. "Game's over. Come out now."

The children squealed and ran into the study.

"Somebody made a mess." Henio gazed wide-eyed at the books strewn across the room.

The kitchen door creaked open and banged shut.

Magdalena's face went white.

Had the Germans returned? Every muscle in Tadzio's body quivered. He wished they could sink into the floorboards. If he moved to reopen the secret chamber, the new intruders might hear it. Afraid Henio or one of the other children might call out, he pressed a finger to his lips.

CHAPTER 5

The Return

End of September 1939
Palmiry, Poland

"Tadzio? Magdalena?" a familiar voice rang out from the kitchen.

Tadzio blew out a breath he didn't realize he'd been holding. "We're in the study."

Magdalena called out. "Oh, Andrzej I'm so glad you're back!" She ran down the hallway. Tadzio followed her, with Krzysh and the children close behind.

Andrzej, Lech, and even Stefan greeted them with smiles, handshakes, and thumps on the back.

The professor rested a hand on Tadzio's shoulder. "Looks like you made the right decision to remain here and protect the children, son. We were conducting drills in the Kampinos Forest when we heard the Germans ransacked your summerhouse." His voice lowered. "We feared the worst. I'm glad you are all okay."

Tadzio cast his gaze to the floor and spoke almost in a whisper. "Not everyone, sir. Tomasz and Feliks are dead. My mother and Halina …" His lips quivered, and his nose burned.

The professor twitched his silver moustache. His eyes misted over. "What happened to the women?"

Lifting his head, he pushed out his next words. "I don't know, sir. We couldn't find them anywhere. Maybe the Germans took them as prisoners."

The professor gazed deeply into Tadzio's eyes, as if evaluating his strength. "Most likely, my boy, most likely. And it will be our job to get them back."

The elderly Scout leader patted Tadzio's shoulder as he watched the children try to outdo each other in telling the Scouts about their secret hiding place. He then turned back to Tadzio. "Son, do you think you're ready to join us now?"

Tadzio hadn't told Magdalena about the caretakers' deaths or the disappearance of their mother and Halina. If he joined the Scouts to help overthrow the Germans, who would take care of Magdalena and the children?

Before he could answer, Henio tugged his sleeve. "Tadzio? Where's Momma? I want to show her my ankle."

Tadzio crouched and ruffled Henio's soft brown hair. "She had to go away with Halina on a brief trip. She'll be back before you know it."

Wide-eyed and open-mouthed, Magdalena shot Tadzio one of her *what-are-you-not-telling-me?* looks.

Before she followed up her gaze with an interrogation, Tadzio stood and held up a hand. "Magdalena, why don't you take the children to the study and get them started on a game? Professor Handelsman has some important news to share with all of us when you come back."

Once Magdalena settled her charges in the study, the professor invited her to join them around the enamel-topped kitchen farm table.

Tadzio's hands trembled. He interlaced his fingers, hoping to steady them. Fighting to control his voice, he related the story of Tomasz and Feliks' deaths and the disappearance of his mother and Halina.

He squeezed his toes inside his shoes, bracing for an outburst from Magdalena. Instead, she thrust her head forward, tucked in her almond-shaped chin, and pressed her palms to the table.

She glanced at Andrzej, then at Lech. "What can we do to get them back?"

"First things first." The professor studied the Scouts' faces. "Is everyone here fully committed to the cause of Poland?"

"Yes, sir." Tadzio nodded. So did Magdalena, Krzysh, and the others.

"Then I will pass on to you the news I received from the council last night. As a Scouting organization, we've decided to work closely with the Underground Army to fight against the German occupation. Besides our prewar oath, we are asking Scouts to add one more line to their pledge. The additional vow is: 'I pledge to you that I shall serve with the Gray Ranks, safeguard the secrets of the organization, obey orders, and not hesitate to sacrifice my life.'"

Krzysh raked his hand through his light brown hair. "What are the Gray Ranks, Professor?"

"It's the code name for Polish Scouts. We will have our own head-quarters, but work closely with the Home Army, contributing to their resistance operations." The professor let his tired gray eyes search out each Scout before he continued. "So, are you all willing to make this additional Scout pledge?"

Tadzio jumped to his feet and held up the three-fingered Scout sign.

Chairs scraped across the wooden floor as everyone stood.

Their Scout leader shook his head and blinked several times, as if stunned by the unanimous response. He rose and repeated each phrase of the new Scout Oath, followed by a chorus of voices from the Scouts.

Once finished, the Scouts continued to stand, their right hands holding aloft the Scout sign.

Lech finally broke the silence. He shot his fist into the air and shouted, "*Czuwaj!* Be prepared!"

Everyone joined with upraised fists. *"Czuwaj!"*

A knock at the door interrupted their shouts.

Everyone except the professor froze.

Moving toward the door, the Scout leader called over his shoulder, "Not to worry. I am expecting visitors."

Tadzio followed the professor. Outside stood a party of six people—an elderly couple, a middle-aged couple, and two young men. Professor Handelsman shook the eldest man's hand. "Ah, the Reikowski family, correct? You received your papers, I trust?"

The other Scouts joined them in the marbled entryway.

"Please, come in," the professor said.

The other men shook Professor Handelsman's hand as they entered, and the women removed their headscarves.

The professor pointed to Tadzio and Magdalena. "These are the children I told you about. They will leave shortly after our midday meal." He flourished his arm across his chest, as if taking in the entire manor house. "This is the residence you will care for while they are gone. I know you will be good stewards of the home while the family is away."

Swallowing hard, Tadzio gazed at Magdalena.

Her eyes widened, but she didn't ask any questions.

Neither did he.

As they finished their midday meal, their scoutmaster supplied them with marching orders. "I must return to our camp in the woods. Andrzej will escort all of you, including the little ones, to Warsaw. Once there, report to the makeshift hospital on Karolkowa Street where you'll receive further instructions."

"What about those people, Professor?" Tadzio kept his voice low and inclined his head toward the back bedrooms where the newcomers were settling in. "Who are they?"

"The less you know, the better." The scoutmaster rubbed his mustache between his thumb and forefinger. "You can trust them to take care of your manor house. As to your travels, there is still a functioning railway from Palmiry to Warsaw. If stopped, tell the Germans you were visiting relatives in Palmiry during the bombing, but are returning to your families in the capital. Here are your new names." The professor handed each person important looking papers. "Memorize this information."

Tadzio saw his own picture staring up at him from a new identity card. Now, however, his name read Jerzy Kowalski.

Krzysh's cheeks flushed. "A makeshift hospital? Is that where my mother and father are recuperating?"

The professor pressed his lips together. "I don't know, son. You'll have to ask when you arrive."

After their meal, Professor Handelsman joined them outside for a brief prayer, then bid them goodbye. "I am not sure if or when we shall see each other again." The elderly man's gray eyes moistened. "May God go with you."

Their leader headed west, back into the Kampinos Forest.

Tadzio raised a hand. "Goodbye, Professor." He stole one more glimpse at the manor house before heading east.

Will I ever see Mother or Father again?

CHAPTER 6

Two Jewish Orphans

August to September 1939
Thalau, Germany, to Warsaw, Poland

Thirteen-year-old Benyameen stared out the train window as Yacov fidgeted with the carved wooden horse on his lap.

Yacov nudged his older brother. "Tell me again the story of when Poppa made this horse. And how he and Momma were heroes when they saved those people from drowning."

A space between his ribs ached as Benyameen lifted the wooden piece from Yacov's hand. The small toy was the only thing left from their parents. Yacov was only five when the Nazi took them away. His little brother had no idea why his parents disappeared, so Benyameen made up a story to honor their memory.

Turning the toy over in his hand, Benyameen sighed. "Yacov, I think you've heard me tell the tale so many times, you should be the one telling it by now." He handed the carving back to Yacov just as the train's engine released a *whoosh* of steam.

"Look." Benyameen tapped his window, glad to change the subject. "We've arrived at the Warsaw-Gdańsk Station. This is where we get off."

As they stood to leave, Yacov gazed up at Benyameen with wide eyes and tugged his shirt. "Things will be better for us here in Poland than they were in Germany, right Benyameen?"

Benyameen's mind whirred with scenes from the past month. How he and Yacov hid in an abandoned cellar for two weeks while his brother, now seven years old, recovered from a fever. How he'd finally gone to Herr Feinberg's shop to beg the Jewish proprietor for medicine to quiet Yacov's cough. How, worst of all, he'd witnessed the Feinberg family's arrest, their attempted escape, and their bloody deaths at the hands of the Gestapo. And, finally, he knew Mrs. Feinberg had sewn train tickets and false passports inside the pocket-linings of her children's clothing. He searched the Feinberg boys' bullet-ridden bodies and found them, then used them to take him and Yacov to what he'd hope would be the safety of Poland.

As they stepped off the railway car, Yacov tugged his shirt again. "Things will be better for us here, right, Benyameen?"

"I can't make any promises." Benyameen tossed the flour sack containing their few belongings over his shoulder and enveloped Yacov's hand in his.

As they left the train station, Benyameen fixed his gaze on the more well-dressed people and, out of habit, trailed them. If he had to steal food or money, he'd pocket it from the richer folk. More likely they'd be able to afford it.

The sights and sounds of Warsaw jangled his nerves, as if balancing across a canyon on a fallen log. The fast-moving, slurred speech flooding his ears sounded nothing like his native tongue's clean, crisp syllables.

With Yacov in tow, Benyameen scurried into an intersection, keeping his eye trained on a couple in front of him.

The clatter of a horse-drawn cab bounding down the brick-paved thoroughfare startled him. Benyameen sucked in a breath and stopped in the middle of the street.

The horse whinnied and pawed the air with his front legs.

Red-faced, the driver spit out a string of unintelligible words as he brought his carriage to a halt.

Guessing the man had shouted Polish curses, Benyameen shook with embarrassment. Attempting an apology, he gazed up at the mustached man. "*Es tut mir Leid.*"

Once again, the driver uttered a string of words. Waving the boys aside, he continued on his way.

His heart pounding, Benyameen led Yacov to the other side of the street. He stopped and took in gulps of air.

"I hope all the Polish people aren't mean like him," Yacov said as he panted. He leaned against Benyameen's leg. "He sounded really mad."

Benyameen ruffled Yacov's hair. "I'm sure we'll meet some nice people."

Pulling in a few more calming breaths, Benyameen focused on his mission. *We'll find a place to hide near the more well-to-do area of town. From there, I'll look for an odd job or scavenge for food.* Before he took his next step, he heard familiar German words behind him.

"Kann ich Ihnen helfen?"

Someone just asked him if he could help. Without thinking, Benyameen whipped around. *"Ja!* We could use some help."

He stared into the kind, smiling face of an elderly gentleman robed in a button-downed black kaftan that reached his ankles. The man's gray beard hung at least a foot below his chin. On his head, like a small crown, sat a black yarmulke.

Benyameen raised his brows. *A Jew—like me!*

Before the man spoke again, a middle-aged passerby dressed in a double-breasted suit tipped his black fedora. *"Dzień dobry, panie Lebowski."*

"Dzień dobry, panie Woźniak." Herr Lebowsi nodded his head.

The man in the fedora continued on his way.

Benyameen squinted and studied the Jewish gentleman standing in front of him. "So, you're not German? Are you really Polish?"

Before the elderly man could reply, Yacov tugged Benyameen's shirt. "I'm hungry. When can we eat?"

"Just a minute, Yacov." Benyameen squeezed his brother's hand. "Let me talk with this gentleman."

Herr Lebowski patted Yacov's head. *"Ja, und nein.* Yes, and no, to answer your question. I have been on the train with you since Poznan where I visited my sister and her family there." The man patted Yacov's head again. "I am a German Jew. Like my sister, I now live in Poland. My sister and her family moved here five years ago. I came twenty years before that. I overheard you and your brother speaking German on the train and realized you were probably fleeing Germany because of the Jewish persecutions there." Herr Lebowski raised his head and glanced around the busy street. "I am afraid, however," he lowered his voice to almost a whisper, "the same fate awaits us here as well. That is why I went to Poznan. I urged my sister and her family to leave Poland and move as far east as possible. Even to Russia, if need be. I don't think we Jews are safe from the Germans, even in Poland. I believe the Nazis will come here soon enough."

Yacov tugged Benyameen's shirt again. "Benyameen, what should we do? Should we go to Russia?"

Benyameen shook his head at Yacov, then turned his attention back to the Jewish man. "What about you, Herr Lebowski? Will you travel to Russia with your sister?"

The old man chuckled. "I have moved enough for two lifetimes. During Germany's Great War, I immigrated to Poland. My life is here now." He extended his hand and pointed to the two-story building across the street. "That is my shop."

Although Benyameen couldn't decipher the gold-lettered Polish words emblazoned on the building's front windowpane, he recognized the owner's name—Lebowski. Spotting the display of rings, earrings, and necklaces, he identified it as a jewelry store.

Herr Lebowski straightened and rubbed his back. "And I am getting older by the minute. Let us stop jabbering out here. Do an old man a favor. Follow me inside for a bowl of soup."

Benyameen and Yacov joined Herr Lebowski for dinner, slept in his cellar that evening, did chores for him the next day and then for the next several weeks.

One morning while watching Herr Lebowski repair a ring, Benyameen held aloft a tool. He studied its black-knobbed end and long, narrow, metal shaft. Just below the knob, another shaft protruded like an upside-down L. It had a rosewood handle.

"What's this tool for?" he asked the elderly jeweler.

Releasing the magnifying glass that hung around his neck, Herr Lebowski lifted the tool from Benyameen's hand. "This is called an Archimedes drill," he explained. "I will use it to increase the setting size on this ring for a ruby the German colonel asked me to add. The ring used to contain a diamond, but his new girlfriend prefers rubies."

Benyameen continued to examine the tools. He loved watching Herr Lebowski work. Perhaps, if they stayed long enough, he'd even teach him the trade. His heart pinched at the thought. He could only hope. The jeweler already told him that since his only living relative was his sister he didn't mind having two visitors stay with him for a while.

Near the end of August, Benyameen sat with Yacov and Herr Lebowski in the kitchen above the jewelry shop as they ate their midday meal.

After Benyameen finished his potato pierogi, he turned to Herr Lebowski. "Do your sister and her family ever come to visit you here in Warsaw?"

The elderly man wiped his gray beard with his cloth napkin and wagged his head no. "My sister's husband has held a grudge against me ever since they first married."

Yacov slurped the last of his soup and put down his spoon. It clanked against his ceramic bowl. "Does your sister have any children?"

"Ja." Herr Lebowski sighed. "I miss them terribly. You see, our father was a cantor in the synagogue, a very religious man, and—"

"What's a cantor?" Yacov said.

Herr Lebowski's grayish-blue eyes twinkled when he smiled. "He's the one who leads the Jewish people in prayer and song. My father had a powerful baritone voice. He loved leading the congregation in song." The gentle old man brought a hand to his chest. "It broke my father's heart when my sister married someone outside the faith."

"Outside the faith?" Yacov scrunched his nose.

The jeweler drew in a deep breath, exhaled, then continued. "My sister married a man who wasn't Jewish. Since my father was a leader in the synagogue, he had to follow tradition and treat my sister as though she had died. Even though I never regarded her that way, her husband decided he wanted nothing to do with our family. That was over twenty years ago. My father is now ten years in the grave.

Even so, whenever I visit my sister's family, her husband refuses to speak with me."

Yacov frowned. "That's awful."

"But enough about me." Herr Lebowski's voice took on a gravelly, aged tone. "We must finish our soup before it gets cold, ja?"

Herr Lebowski told Benyameen that, as long as he found him and Yacov hard working and trustworthy, he would provide them with food and shelter. Daily, the kind gentleman reminded Benyameen that trust must be earned. Desperately wanting to earn the old man's trust, he vowed to never violate it.

As Benyameen had hoped, Herr Lebowski continued to teach him more about the jewelry business. In the evenings, once chores were finished, he also taught him and Yacov how to read and write in Polish.

On the morning of September 1, everything changed. After showing Benyameen how to repair the clasp of a locket, Herr Lebowski sent him to buy bread.

Strolling down the block to Babinski's bakery, the whine of an engine buzzed in his ears. Gazing up, the sight of a low-flying plane froze his blood. His heart raced. Black crosses on the wings' undersides and a Nazi symbol on the plane's tail meant only one thing. Germany's *Luftwaffe* had followed him even here.

Before Benyameen could urge his feet forward, a canister-shaped object whistled down. He crouched and covered his head.

Boom!

The ground rolled beneath him. He stumbled and fell. Windows across the way shattered, propelling missiles of glass into the street.

Skirting around chunks of broken concrete, collapsed buildings, and a few dead bodies, Benyameen tripped and ducked his way back to the jewelry store. Discovering that it still stood, he leaned over and breathed a sigh of relief.

Later that night as he lay on his cot, Benyameen couldn't sleep. The explosion of bombs and the crash of broken glass reverberated in his head. He tossed and turned until a whimper arose from Yacov's corner of the cellar.

He's just murmuring in his sleep. Benyameen held his breath and waited. Soon, all was quiet.

Tugging his blanket closer to his face, Benyameen shifted his weight on the cot.

Yacov thrashed. "Yamee, help me! No! Stop! Help!"

Kicking off his blanket, Benyameen scurried to his brother's side. Gently shaking Yacov's shoulder, he attempted to rouse him from whatever nightmare held him captive.

He couldn't.

A few minutes later, Herr Lebowski's gravelly voice called out from the top of the cellar stairs. "What is it, boys?"

The steps creaked as the jeweler descended. Dressed in his nightshirt and holding aloft a kerosene lamp, his presence brightened the room.

"I can't wake him up." Benyameen pinched his lips into a flat line as he bent over Yacov. He worked to put on his responsible, older-brother face, but his insides shook. "I think he's having a nightmare."

Herr Lebowski set the lantern on the floor, knelt next to Benyameen, and cupped a hand over Yacov's forehead. "There now, son." His voice came soft and soothing. "You are safe. Nothing here will hurt you." The gentle man hummed a tender melody as he stroked Yacov's head.

The humming transformed into words, but in a language Benyameen didn't recognize.

By the time Herr Lebowski finished, Yacov had stopped thrashing, letting out only an occasional whimper.

Tears stung Benyameen's eyes. He tried to blink them away. "That was beautiful. What were you singing about?"

As Herr Lebowski dragged over a nearby chair, its wooden legs scraped across the cement floor. He picked it up and carried it to Yacov's cot. Sitting with a heavy sigh, he explained, "It is a song my father wrote. He composed it to teach us words from the *Tanakh*, our holy writings."

Benyameen tilted his head. "But I didn't understand any of the words."

"I was singing in Hebrew." The aged man's eyes moistened. "My father fashioned it from a text in the Book of Psalms and combined it with words from the prophet Zephaniah."

Hebrew. Benyameen shook his head. He'd never heard the language spoken before. His parents weren't religious Jews. The song's lilting words and the cantor's somber melody awed him. He widened his eyes. "Please. Tell me what the song means."

Herr Lebowski's solemn expression melted into a grin. "Roughly translated, it means, 'I am the Lord your God. I am always with you, and I am mighty to save. I take great delight in you. I will quiet you with my love, and I will rejoice over you with singing. I am a father to the fatherless, and, like a father carries his son, so I will carry you in the day of trouble.'" Herr Lebowski closed his eyes. "I always felt safe when Father sang that to me."

Benyameen replayed the tune several times in his mind. The soothing melody warmed his soul. "I wish I had grown up with a father." He pulled in a deep breath. "I can't imagine what it would be like to have a father sing to me."

CHAPTER 7

The Siege

September 1939
Warsaw, Poland

For the next few weeks, German planes and artillery pounded Warsaw. Benyameen trusted reports that France and Great Britain would soon come to Poland's aid. Hadn't he heard on Herr Lebowski's wireless radio that, after Germany's unprovoked attack on Warsaw, the two European countries had declared war on Germany?

By the third week of September, Benyameen lost hope of Poland receiving help from either Britain or France. Like his fate as an orphan, Warsaw's citizens had to survive on their own.

On the afternoon of September 24, the shop bell jangled and Benyameen glanced up.

Herr Lebowski shuffled in, returning from his trip to the market.

Yacov, standing next to Benyameen, grasped his brother's hand. "Will we have something to eat now?"

Benyameen eyed Herr Lebowski's hands. Empty. As empty as his stomach. His heart cracked, and his stomach spasmed. He studied the old man's face and kaftan. Gray. Residue from the bombed-out city had turned his elderly friend into an ashen ghost.

"I'm sorry, boys." Tears stained the man's wrinkled face. "I have failed you. I thought I could keep you safe here in Warsaw. But now the city is in flames, and there is nowhere to buy food. Not even with my diamonds."

Herr Lebowski slumped on a stool behind his empty jewelry

counter. He withdrew a tiny, black-velveted pouch from his coat pocket. He emptied its contents. Two small gems clinked onto the glass countertop. He sighed. "With the bombing, I expected no one would want to buy jewelry. That's why we locked up my merchandise in the cellar safe. But I thought that, surely, someone would trade bread for diamonds. I was wrong."

The whistle of shells and the sudden boom of explosions pierced the air. Benyameen scooped up the diamonds. The floor shook. The crackling of splintered wood, like lightning striking a tree, rang from somewhere nearby.

People wailed.

A horse screamed.

Herr Lebowski shoved the boys toward the back. "Quick! The cellar!"

Another shell whistled. Benyameen grabbed Yacov's hand and pulled him to the basement. The sound of shattering glass followed him down the steps, echoed by Herr Lebowski's footfalls.

When Benyameen lit the kerosene lamp, he grimaced. Blood oozed from the elderly man's head. Hoping Yacov wouldn't see it, Benyameen tried to divert his attention. "Yacov, please look in Herr Lebowski's trunk over in the corner. I think I saw a deck of cards in it. We might be down here for a while. Since there are three of us, perhaps I can teach you how to play Skat."

While Yacov rummaged through the chest for the cards, Benyameen inspected the jeweler's head. A shard of glass pierced his right temple.

Benyameen bit his lower lip. "While we were running to the basement, a shell must have blasted the storefront. It looks like a piece of shattered glass hit your head before you reached the stairs."

Fingering his temple, Herr Lebowski winced.

Benyameen reached to pull out the glass.

"No. Don't remove it yet, son." Herr Lebowski touched his head again. "We should have some clean cloths nearby to wrap my wound as soon as you pull it out. But first, I need to tell you something important. Just in case I—"

Yacov ran back with the cards. "Here they are." He held out the deck and glanced from Benyameen to Herr Lebowski. His small brown eyes grew into large-sized marbles. "Why is Herr Lebowski bleeding?"

"Yacov, I'll teach you how to play Skat after we fix Herr Lebowski's cut." Benyameen laid a hand on Yacov's shoulder. "He got hit with a little piece of glass before he made it downstairs. I promise, after we stop the bleeding, we'll play cards."

Yacov nodded. "What can I do to help?"

"I saw some clean clothes in the trunk. Bring me something from the chest to wrap his wound after I pull out the glass."

Yacov obeyed.

After guiding Herr Lebowski to a chair, Benyameen tore the shirt Yacov brought over and ripped it into strips. He pulled out the shard and quickly bound the old man's head.

Touching the bandage, Herr Lebowski nodded. "Well done, son. Where did you learn how to do that?"

Benyameen glanced away. His nose burned as vague memories of his father surfaced. He swallowed hard. "When Yacov was five, my father led a troop of Boy Scouts in Germany. I watched him give first aid lessons to the boys in his unit. By then the Scouts were forbidden to meet. My father held gatherings anyway. The next night, my mother and father …" Although the night the Brown Shirts took his parents away happened two years ago, he still found it difficult to put the memories into words. Besides. The tale he'd given Yacov of his parents' deaths had nothing to do with the truth he'd almost shared with Herr Lebowski. For Yacov, it was only a story of a carved horse and two heroic parents.

The old jeweler grimaced and nodded. "I understand. No need to explain."

Herr Lebowski turned to Yacov. "Let's see those cards, boy."

Yacov handed him the deck.

"Very well, then, Benyameen," Herr Lebowski said. "Teach us how to play your German game of Skat."

Benyameen pulled over one of the cots to use as a table and sat next Yacov on the other cot.

"Wait." Herr Lebowski held up his hands. "Before we begin, I need to show you something." Moving to his safe in the far corner, he waved the boys over. "You must learn how to open this in case I ever need you to retrieve something for me."

Benyameen's heart thumped. "It's not necessary, sir. We don't need to know how to open your safe." *Is he testing me?* Either his old friend wondered if he'd ever steal from him, or he was worried he might not survive his head wound.

Herr Lebowski waved them over again. "No, I insist. Benyameen, bring the lantern."

Reluctantly, Benyameen obeyed.

"See this knob here, and the surrounding numbers?"

Benyameen nodded.

"First, you turn this dial right, to nineteen." Herr Lebowski turned the dial. He stopped, then twisted left. "Next, dial left past zero and keep going until you reach two, then stop. Finally, turn right to six." When he finished the sequence, he pulled on the door's handle. The safe emitted a click, and he swung the door open.

Benyameen raised the lantern and peered inside. Two shelves were stacked four layers high with black boxes.

Herr Lebowski pulled out a box and opened it. Jewels of various colors sparkled in the lantern's glow.

"If anything should happen to me, I want you to take my gems and get as far away from Poland as possible." Herr Lebowski held Benyameen with a stare. "Don't let the Germans capture you. Live on for me, as if you were my grandsons. Can you do that for an old man?"

Yacov grinned. "Does that mean we can call you Grandpapa?"

Herr Lebowski ruffled Yacov's hair and smiled. "Sure, you can call me Grandpapa."

Benyameen repeated. "Nineteen, two, six. That's easy to remember. It's the year I was born. 1926." Benyameen's eyes stung. "But we don't need to take your jewels, because nothing's going to happen to you. France and Great Britain will rescue Poland any day now." Blinking tears from his lashes, Benyameen added, "But we would be honored to call you Grandpapa."

Herr Lebowski returned the box and shut the safe. "France and Britain had better come soon." He chuckled. "If they don't, this old man will die of starvation."

Noticing a fresh patch of blood soaking through Herr Lebowski's bandage, Benyameen led the jeweler back to the cots. "I need to wrap your head with more cloths. Then I think you should rest for a bit."

"But, Benyameen," Yacov whined as he held up the cards. "You promised."

"We'll have to save our game for later." Benyameen grabbed a blanket from the other cot and covered Herr Lebowski.

The elderly man didn't argue.

Taking the lantern with him, Benyameen pulled Yacov over to the trunk where he'd placed their bag of belongings from Germany. Opening the sack, he glanced at Yacov. "I have an idea, but I need your help."

Yacov rolled his eyes. "Unless you've hidden a loaf of bread in there, I don't think there's anything in that old sack that can help us right now."

Instructing Yacov to hold the lantern higher, Benyameen knelt and peered inside the bag. "It's not bread." Benyameen searched the bag and grinned as he withdrew his prize. "A knife."

Yacov stuck out his lower lip. "How is a knife better than a loaf of bread?"

Brushing the cellar's dust from his trousers, Benyameen stood. "When that last bomb exploded, I heard a horse screech. If it's dead, it might still be lying out there."

Yacov's eyes went wide. "You don't mean we're going to eat dead horse meat!"

Benyameen let a corner of his mouth pull up. "I'm hungry enough to eat a horse, aren't you?"

"I suppose so." Yacov frowned. "But I don't think I'll like it."

"Trust me, Yacov. We have to do this. We have to do whatever it takes to survive. For us, and for Herr—I mean, for us and for Grandpapa."

Yacov grinned. "I like calling him Grandpapa."

Benyameen draped an arm over Yacov's shoulder. "Me too. Now, let's go get some dinner."

CHAPTER 8

Return to Warsaw

End of September 1939
Palmiry to Warsaw, Poland

Magdalena twisted her shoulder-length hair into a bun and pinned it atop her head before heading to the train station with the children and the Scouts.

"Does everyone have their new identities memorized?" Andrzej asked as their little group plodded toward the Palmiry depot.

Magdalena clutched Henio's hand and hurried to keep pace. "You want us to read and walk at the same time? You must slow down if you expect us to do that. The little ones are having a hard time keeping up."

Glancing back at Magdalena, Andrzej raised a brow. "I'm sorry. I wasn't thinking." He slowed his stride.

Magdalena pressed her lips into a flat line and nodded, satisfied Andrzej admitted he wasn't infallible. *Just because he thinks he should lead, doesn't mean he always knows what everyone needs.*

"But we have to memorize our new identities before we board the train in case we're questioned by the Germans."

Magdalena furrowed her forehead. "What if we make it a game?" She playfully swung Henio's arm. "I know. Henio and I can pair up. Tadzio, you work with Józefina. Krzysh can pair up with Lucyna, and Lech and Stefan will quiz each other."

Tugging her hand, Henio flashed her an impish grin. "You and I will make a great team."

She grinned. "That's right. And, Andrzej will be our gamemaster. I'm sure he'll like that."

Andrzej gave her one of his *what's-that-supposed-to-mean?* looks.

She ignored him. "Once we review our new identities with our partners, Andrzej will quiz us." She read Henio the information on his new identity card as they tromped forward.

The others did the same. By the time they reached the station, everyone had their identity details memorized. Andrzej declared Lech and Stefan winners, since they sounded the most convincing when quizzed.

"That's not fair." Józefina whined. "They're older than we are. I think we should play a new game."

Magdalena forced herself not to roll her eyes. "Yes, Józefina. We will play a different game once we board the train."

After taking their seats, she turned to the children. "Let's play Guess What I See. Józefina can go first."

Józefina clapped her hands as the train chugged forward.

About halfway to Warsaw, a German soldier moved down the aisle, stopping to speak to a few travelers.

When he reached Magdalena, he tapped her shoulder. "*Papiere, bitte.*"

Magdalena let her jaw drop. She assumed he wanted to check her identity, but wasn't sure. She didn't understand German.

Sitting across the aisle from her, Krzysh leaned over. "He wants to see your papers—your identity card."

Her hand trembled as she retrieved it from her purse. *What if he asks me details?* She held her breath as she handed her card to the soldier.

The young man grinned as his fingers touched hers.

Her mouth went dry, but she let a corner of it curve up into what she hoped he'd take as a pleasant, flirtatious smile.

The soldier returned her information without asking questions.

When the train reached Warsaw, Andrzej suggested they walk the rest of the way to the Karolkowa Street hospital.

Magdalena shook her head. "That's at least twelve blocks. I don't think the children can walk that far."

Reaching inside his trouser pocket, Andrzej pulled out a few *złotys*. "We don't have a lot of money, but we can probably afford to hire a carriage to take you and the children there." He pointed at Tadzio, Lech, and Stefan. "The four of us can walk."

The others nodded, and Andrzej flagged down the next horse-drawn buggy.

The old, open-air carriage creaked as Magdalena and the children stepped aboard.

The thin horses raised their graying heads and snorted.

Andrzej gave the driver directions to the makeshift hospital, paid the cab fare, and flashed Magdalena a spirited grin. "We'll be waiting for you at the hospital."

Magdalena arched an eyebrow. "Not if we get there first."

The lift of their lighthearted banter quickly faded as the buggy bounced down the war-torn streets of Warsaw. Magdalena's chest burned as she eyed avenues littered with mounds of broken glass and brick, sidewalks twisted and battered by weeks of bombings, blackened window frames of burned-out shops blankly staring back at her like rows of blind people. The scenes combined to form an unblinking witness of the city's devastation. And, as if shrouding Warsaw's former glory, a dense veil of ash draped dead horses, broken carriages, and even corpses.

Worse than the scenes of destruction, the putrid stench of death and an acrid smell of ash assaulted her senses. Like an overpowering mix of rotten fruit, garlic, and three-week-old cabbage, the foul odors made her gag. She leaned to the side of the carriage, fighting the urge to vomit.

As the carriage turned left, Henio tapped her arm and pointed straight ahead. "Who are those people?"

She swallowed her bile and eyed the scene in front of them, quickly forcing Henio's arm down.

A group of German soldiers in gray-green uniforms crossed the street. More roamed the sidewalks. Some barked orders. Others examined people's papers. A few pushed citizens with upraised hands against the side of a building.

Magdalena's pulse raced. "Those are German soldiers. For now, we have to be nice and do what they say. And it's not polite to point at them."

When the carriage arrived at the hospital, she thanked the driver and gathered the children inside. As far as she could tell, the other

Scouts hadn't arrived yet. That thought brightened her doleful mood.

"Magdalena!" A young blonde dressed in a doctor's white overcoat left the side of a patient and, running over, enveloped her in a hug. "I'm so glad you got here safely."

"Anna?" Magdalena returned the hug and stepped back to study the girl at arm's length. Could it be? Yes. Her Girl Guides leader, Anna Zawadzka. Thin and frail, Anna looked as though she'd aged at least five years since she'd seen her last. Magdalena tugged the stethoscope hanging from the girl's neck. "So, are you a doctor now?"

"I wish." Anna shook her head. "I would be more useful to these poor people if I had the skills of a physician. I'm just doing what I can—putting our Girl Guides' first aid training to good use."

Magdalena shifted her gaze to the bedridden patients, and a cold, helpless fear clutched her heart. The moaning sea of men, women, and children stared back at her with hopeless, painfilled eyes. Some lay wrapped in bloodied bandages. Others were bound in casts, or had missing limbs.

Józefina tugged Magdalena's coat sleeve. "I'm hungry."

Studying the children's confused faces, Magdalena blinked back a wave of hopelessness. She offered Józefina a slight grin. "Of course you are, sweetie. Perhaps my friend here can show us where to get a drink of water?"

Anna nodded. "Of course, of course. Our kitchen is over here."

While Anna settled the children at a table with tin cups of water and a handful of crackers, Magdalena asked about Andrzej and the other Scouts.

"They haven't arrived yet." Anna pointed at two metal chairs around another table near the children, and the two sat. "But, Professor Handelsman told us you were coming, and made provisions for everyone." Anna glanced at the children. "Especially for the little ones."

Magdalena's stomach knotted. The children were her responsibility. Why were others making plans for them without consulting her? She tilted her head to the side and parted her lips.

Anna held up a hand. "I'll explain more when the boys get here."

Before Magdalena could press for more information, a nurse entered and spoke with her former Girl Guides leader in hushed tones.

Anna stood. "I'm sorry, Magdalena. I'm needed on the floor. Wait here with the children until Andrzej and the others arrive."

About ten minutes later, when the boys walked through the hospital doors, Andrzej shot Magdalena a playful grin. "Guess you beat us."

Right now she didn't care who reached the hospital first. She did care, however, that plans had been made for her and the children without her knowledge.

"What's going on, Andrzej?" She forced her voice to remain low, but, like balls of fire, an intensity of heat enflamed every word that escaped her lips.

Not seeming to notice the tension between Andrzej and Magdalena, Anna came over and hugged the boys. She ushered them all to a circle of metal chairs near the back corner of the makeshift hospital.

"What about the children?" Magdalena asked as Anna invited them to sit.

"Oh, don't worry about them." Anna waved a hand. "One of our volunteers is keeping them busy rolling bandages while we talk."

"That's just it, Anna." Magdalena sat taller in her chair, its cold metal back pressing against her bony spine. "I do worry about the children. They are my responsibility. If plans are being made for them, I need to be consulted."

"Of course, of course. And you will be." Anna glanced down at her hands, then eyed Andrzej. "But first, I must tell you, Andrzej, that my brother needs to meet with you as soon as possible. The usual place."

Andrzej nodded.

Crunching her brows, Magdalena shot Andrzej a quizzical look. *Now what's she talking about?*

Andrzej gave Magdalena a slight shake of the head, then turned to Anna. "Before I meet with him, we need to get the children settled. Have we found a place for them to stay?"

Heat rose from Magdalena's chest to her throat. *A place to stay?* Alarm bells sounded in her head. She gripped the seat of her chair as the room began to sway. "Anna, as I said before, if there's any planning to be done about the children, I need to be a part of it."

Anna nodded. "Yes, of course, Magdalena. But, you must understand, some things had to be decided in advance." Anna leaned toward Andrzej. "The landlady of the building next door has a room available. She will rent it to Magdalena and the children for a small fee, but the funds have already been provided."

Things were moving too fast. Magdalena clenched her jaw and stood. "Anna, I don't—"

Anna held up a hand to Magdalena, keeping her eyes trained on Andrzej. "And, while Magdalena helps us here at the hospital, the apartment manager will care for the children during the day."

The room spun. Magdalena grabbed the end of a nearby iron bedframe to steady herself. The smell of urine, blood, and antiseptic filled her nostrils. Her knees buckled. Falling, she hit her head on something cold and hard.

Everything went dark.

When Magdalena opened her eyes, she was no longer in the hospital. "Where—where am I?" She struggled to sit, but a middle-aged woman at her bedside placed a cold compress on the back of her head and gently urged her down.

"You're safely tucked away in your new home. Don't you worry." The plump middle-aged woman clucked her tongue. "I daresay, you and those children have been through a lot these past two days. You need a bit of rest. Lie still, and let Auntie M take care of you."

Was this was a dream? She recalled losing her balance and hitting her head. How did she get here? She glanced at the foot of the bed where Lech and Andrzej sat.

"Auntie M?" Andrzej addressed the kind woman. "Why don't you let me explain some things to her."

Józefina's shrill voice suddenly cut through the paper-thin walls. "I'm telling on you! You're not sharing."

Henio gave a muffled, whimpering cry.

"It's okay, Henio." Lucyna's little voice soothed. "Józefina can't help it if she's mean."

Auntie M made a clucking noise with her tongue and smiled. "Yes, well. You boys explain things here. I'll sort out matters out with the children."

Pulling his chair to the side of Magdalena's bed, Andrzej smoothed the sides of his woolen trousers. "Auntie M is part of the Underground. She's also—"

"What kind of a name is Auntie M? And what do you mean, *part of the Underground?*" Magdalena's head throbbed, but she maneuvered to prop herself up. "What have you gotten us into?"

Andrzej patted Magdalena's arm. "You just had a bad fall, Magdalena. Try to stay calm."

She yanked her arm away and wriggled to sit taller. "Don't you tell me to stay calm, Andrzej Romocki. Ever since you've assumed control of our little mission, everything's spun out of control."

Andrzej pinned her with a stare. "Things *are* out of control, Magdalena." He narrowed his eyes. "In case you haven't noticed, there's a war on. Our country is out of control. The world is out of control. Now, you're going to listen to me, and you're not going to interrupt."

Blinking, Magdalena struggled to absorb the force of his words. He'd never spoken so harshly with her. Unable to contain her ragged emotions, a tear slid down her cheek.

Lech jumped up and poured her a cup of water from the pitcher on the nightstand. "Lighten up, Andrzej. We've all been through a lot." He handed her the drink.

"Thank you, Lech." She cradled the cup and sipped. "At least one of you can still act like a gentleman."

Andrzej blew out a breath. "Things are moving fast, Magdalena, and we don't have time for hysterics. As I was explaining—"

Magdalena let her jaw drop. "So now I'm hysterical?"

A muscle in Andrzej's jaw twitched.

She immediately regretted her accusation.

"No, you're just being a girl."

She narrowed her eyes and inhaled a quick breath, but held her tongue.

Andrzej smoothed his trousers again. "Right now, I need you to be a Girl Guide. A Girl Guide who, like us, recently took a pledge as a member of the Gray Ranks." His words picked up speed as his gaze met hers. "A pledge to safeguard the secrets of the organization, obey the orders of the Gray Ranks, and not hesitate to sacrifice your life. Are you still willing to do that?"

She glanced away. He was right. A lack of control always made her afraid. And, today, she'd stared fear in the face as never before. She studied the tin cup in her hands. "What do you need me to do?"

Andrzej pulled in a breath. "Professor Handelsman noticed you excelled in first-aid training this summer at camp. That's why he got you a job working at the hospital with Anna while Auntie M cares for the children."

"Auntie M is the one you said is part of the Underground?"

Andrzej nodded. "Yes. Her sons and husband were killed when the Germans first attacked Warsaw. Their apartment building is right next to the makeshift hospital." He lowered his voice. "You see, the hospital's part of our cover."

The bump on the back of Magdalena's head pulsed. "Cover?"

Lech leaned in. "It's our base of operations. As Professor Handelsman explained, it's less conspicuous to pass messages going in and out of a hospital than it is going in and out of an apartment or a restaurant."

Fighting the urge to assert control, Magdalena kept her voice even. "And when was all of this decided?"

Andrzej jiggled his leg. "When we went back to the Kampinos Forest. Remember, back at your summerhouse? Professor Handelsman invited you, Tadzio, and Krzysh to join us, but you decided to stay behind."

She nodded. Things were beginning to make sense. "So what else is planned? What about Tadzio?"

Before Andrzej could continue, Lech broke in. "Anna's brother, Zoshka, that's his code name, has rented an apartment one block east of the hospital where he stays sometimes. Tadzio, Krzysh, Stefan, and I will live there too. That way we'll all be close to one another."

"I thought Anna's brother's name was Tadeusz." Magdalena furrowed her forehead, but it made her head hurt more. "Why would he want to be called Zoshka? That's a girl's name."

Lech arched a bushy brow. "That's what makes Zoshka such a great code name. Who would guess that a great Gray Ranks leader was using a girl's name?"

Magdalena glanced from Lech to Andrzej. "So, do you two have code names?"

Lech grinned. "Not yet. But I suppose we will once we get started with our activities."

She glanced sideways at Andrzej. "What kind of activities?"

"Don't worry about that right now." He leaned forward and placed his hands on his knees. "Just get your strength back. Anna will tell you more later. She'll look in on you this evening."

As Andrzej stood to leave, Magdalena grabbed his arm. "I haven't thanked you for all you've done." She grasped his rough hand and squeezed it tightly. "Thank you for taking such good care of Tadzio, the children—and me. I don't know where we'd be without you."

He looked down and squeezed her hand back. "Of course. Just rest now. And don't worry about the children. Auntie M will take good care of them. Lech and I have a meeting with Zoshka. We'll check on you tomorrow."

As Andrzej reached the door, Lech stood and lightly kissed Magdalena on the top of her head. "I still can't stop thinking about that violin piece back at the manor house," he whispered in her ear. "I hope I can get another concert soon." He lightly touched her fingertips before following Andrzej out the bedroom door.

CHAPTER 9

The Catholic German

Mid–September 1939
Wegrow to Warsaw, Poland

The crisp September wind cut through the open collar of Lieutenant Hosenfeld's gray woolen overcoat. He fisted it closer to his neck as he rounded the corner of a Polish barn. Earlier this morning, his commander ordered him to investigate news of a skirmish near a barn just outside the town of Wegrow, the town where he'd been stationed since the beginning of September.

So far, this war was nothing like the Great War. The war where he'd been honored with the Iron Cross. What glory for the Fatherland would be found in solving a barn dispute? He was tired of waiting. When would they take part in the siege of Warsaw?

Peering inside the hay-filled barn, he spied a German soldier arguing with a school-aged boy. The youth kicked and screamed as the soldier attempted to drag the lad out. Hosenfeld took note of the insignia on the man's collar. A lieutenant, just like him. He also noticed the *SS* lightning patches on the man's gray-collared uniform. The *Schutzstaffel*. From the few encounters he'd had with members of Hitler's elite Protection Squad, the *SS*, he knew to keep his distance. Disciplined and brutal, these men reported directly to Heinrich Himmler, not, as he did, to the Armed Forces High Command.

As Hosenfeld entered the barn, he weighed his words carefully. "*Bitte*. Please, what seems to be the problem here?"

"Not that it is any of your business," the *SS* soldier snapped, "but I caught this boy stealing hay requisitioned for use by the *Waffen-SS*. He will be shot as an example to others."

The boy looked the same age as his own son, perhaps only ten or eleven.

Flailing his arms in a useless effort to escape the soldier's grasp, the boy cried out. "It's not your hay! This is my poppa's barn. It's his hay!"

Hosenfeld stepped closer. "You can't kill that boy. He's only a child!"

The *SS* soldier, still grasping his hay thief, whipped out his pistol and pointed it at Hosenfeld. "This is not your business! If you wish to make it your business, I shall shoot you also!"

Hosenfeld swallowed hard and stopped in his tracks.

Without releasing the child or lowering his Luger, the *SS* lieutenant waved his pistol toward the barn doors, ordering Hosenfeld out.

Hosenfeld's mouth went dry. His tongue seemed too large for his mouth. He saw the image of his own, son, Detlev, as the boy thrashed beneath the soldier's grasp. A tingling numbness crept from his toes to his legs. He stiffly turned and trudged out.

Drang nach Osten. Our yearning for the East. Hosenfeld once again muttered the propaganda phrase he'd heard Herr Hitler repeat so often. Yes. Germany needed to reclaim the eastern territory stolen from them after the Great War. *Drang nach Osten.*

For the first time, however, the phrase failed to inspire.

The boy's defiant cries continued for a few more seconds as Hosenfeld increased the distance between himself and the barn.

A young boy's scream.

Blam!

Then, silence.

Every muscle in his body twitched as echoes of the deadly shot bounced off the surrounding buildings. Hosenfeld slipped to a knee.

What else could I have done? If he had tried to save the boy, they'd both be dead.

His stomach spasmed, as if his intestines had turned inside out. Making the sign of the cross, he offered a prayer for the boy's soul.

Then, as if switching off a light, he rose and returned to make his report.

For the next three weeks, nightmares haunted Hosenfeld as he fever-ishly tossed between sweated sheets. Night after night, the Polish boy's face appeared in his dreams, pleading for help. During Hos-enfeld's struggle to wake from his nightmares, the boy's face slowly morphed into that of his son. He went to Mass every Sunday and lit candles for the boy's soul. Hopefully, the nightmares would go away once he received a more permanent assignment.

At the end of September, his captain called him into his office, a building formerly occupied by the town's mayor.

With a cigarette pinched between his lips, his captain shuffled papers and waved him to sit in a wooden chair in front of his desk.

Hosenfeld obeyed, forcing himself to sit still and upright. He had no idea what the captain wanted. He'd never been able to read the man.

The captain's square jaw and high cheek bones, coupled with his swimmer's build, offered an intimidating persona that kept most men at a distance. Removing his cigarette and blowing out a wisp of smoke, the captain raised his pack. "Cigarette?"

Hosenfeld nodded, pulled one out, and lit it with a lighter from his coat pocket.

Leaning back to study his subordinate, the captain tapped a few ashes into an empty tin can on the corner of his desk. "Now that the Poles' capitulation is final, I have your new assignment."

Inhaling the acrid smell of the surrounding smoke, Hosenfeld stiffened his backbone and nodded. "Wherever I am needed, sir."

"You will leave immediately for Pabianice where you will finalize the construction of a prisoner-of-war camp." The captain crushed the stub of his cigarette. "Soon, many of the captured fighters from Warsaw will be transferred there."

"Thank you, sir." Hosenfeld prepared to stand, but the captain motioned him back into his seat.

"That is not all. If you do well with the camp's administration, you will be promoted to captain. Once Warsaw is firmly in our control, you will be given a unit command and oversee the College of Physical Education there."

Captain of my own unit. Maintaining a stoic face in front of his commander, Hosenfeld exhaled a final puff. "Thank you, sir. Whatever is needed for the good of the *Reich.*"

Assuming their business was now concluded, Hosenfeld put out his cigarette, stood, and offered a *Sieg Heil.* He'd hoped to see more battle, but what else could a previously wounded, forty-four-year-old veteran of the Great War expect?

Annemarie would be pleased. That evening, he sat down and wrote his wife a letter.

Dear Annemarie,

Good news! The stubborn Poles have finally surrendered, and I will soon be promoted to the rank of captain. Not that their surrender was without great effort on our part, of course.

The Luftwaffe dropped over 500 tons of bombs, and we had to shell the people heavily before they were brought to their knees. In the end, they sacrificed over 40,000 civilians. Fifty percent of their capitol city was damaged. What a tragic waste of people and resources.

After a short stint overseeing a prisoner-of-war camp in a town called Pabianice, I will transfer to Warsaw were I will administrate the College of Physical Education. Our weary soldiers will spend their R&R time there in order to stay in peak physical condition. I am sure you will appreciate this news, since this position will keep me off the battlefield. It will also allow me to send home a larger paycheck, substantially more than the petty teacher's salary I had before I left.

Give my love to Detlev, Anemone, Helmut, and Uta.

One brisk morning, about a week after his transfer to Pabianice, Hosenfeld pedaled a bicycle from his barracks to the newly completed prisoner-of-war-camp. A young Polish woman along the road waved him down. Dressed in an over-sized gray suit coat and a dusty, dark-green woolen dress, he couldn't help but notice her bulging abdomen. Beneath one arm she toted a rolled up blanket, and beneath the other she clutched a heavy-looking rucksack.

"*Bitte.*" She flagged him down.

Hosenfeld pulled up beside her.

"My husband was seriously injured while fighting to save Warsaw," she said in faulty German. "They say he was captured and taken to a prisoner-of-war camp near Pabianice. I have walked four days from Warsaw to bring him medicines, food, and a blanket."

"I am sorry," Hosenfeld said. "But, I do not think I can—"

Before he could finish, the woman dropped the blanket to the ground and opened the rucksack. "I must get these to him." She fisted away a tear from her dirt-smudged cheek. Opening the pack, she pointed to the various medicines and bandages, along with a loaf of bread, a large chunk of cheese, and a bottle of Polish vodka.

Noting the woman appeared ready give birth any day, Annemarie suddenly came to mind. His wife had been thirty-six weeks pregnant when he left for war. He received the good news of Uta's birth a week before he arrived in Wegrow.

He dismounted his bicycle. "What is your husband's name?"

"Stanisław Cieciora." The woman never let her eyes meet his. Instead, she looked off to the side, blinking often and hard.

Hosenfeld pulled out a pencil and paper from his shirt pocket and jotted down the name.

"Please, sir." The woman glanced at Hosenfeld and quickly looked away. "He is very ill, and I am afraid they will just kill him. I am going to have our child soon, as you can see." She touched her protruding stomach.

Hosenfeld straightened his officer's cap. "Your husband will be home again in four days' time." Shouldering the rucksack, he strapped the rolled-up blanket to his bicycle. "I will see he gets these. Go home now, and take care of yourself."

Four days later, Hosenfeld arranged for a transport truck taking goods to Warsaw to also shuttle Stanisław Cieciora home to his wife.

A month later Wilm Hosenfeld knelt in a Catholic church in Warsaw where he worshipped at Mass next to his grateful friends, the Cieciora family. Although his friendship with them made him feel less guilty about his inability to save the Polish boy in the barn, he still had a job to do. But, at least he could still maintain a semblance of morality as he did it.

CHAPTER 10

A Tearful Goodbye

November 1939
Warsaw, Poland

Yacov felt older than his seven years as he carefully carried Grandpapa's midday meal down the creaky wooden staircase to the shop below. Maybe he'd already turned eight. It was hard to keep track of the days when you lived in another country. When you spoke another language. When you were in the middle of a war.

He was glad that, since Poland had surrendered to the Germans, the bombing had stopped. He and Benyameen had moved from the basement to a bedroom above Grandpapa's shop. The top floor also housed Grandpapa's bedroom, the kitchen, and a bathroom. For the first time since Yacov could remember, he and Benyameen were living in a real house and sleeping in real beds.

After his brother prepared the midday meal of soup and cabbage rolls, he instructed Yacov to take a portion down to Grandpapa.

Carrying down the meal, Yacov saw Grandpapa had a customer. He was a tall man dressed in a German uniform.

When he recognized the man, Yacov almost dropped his plate.

"Herr Hosenfeld!" Yacov rushed the plate to Grandpapa, then wrapped his arms around the tall German's legs.

Patting the boy on the head, the soldier crouched down and studied the lad at eye level. A grin spread across his face. "Yacov, my boy. I thought I'd never see you again. How did you get here to… Never mind. Don't tell me. I'm just glad to see you safe and well."

Yacov glanced at Grandpapa. Noticing the older man's frown,

Yacov rushed to explain. "Grandpapa, this is Herr Hosenfeld, the schoolteacher I told you about. Remember? Benyameen and I told you how we met him in Germany shortly before we came here."

Grandpapa raked his spindly fingers through his long beard and wagged his head. "I'm sorry son, I don't recall that story."

"Surely, you must remember." Yacov planted his tiny palms on the glass case that separated him from Grandpapa. "Last month, when we could finally buy some apples, I told you about the last one I'd eaten back in Germany. How I'd stolen one from a fruit seller in Thalau. That was a little before I got sick. Herr Hosenfeld saw the seller snatch me, so he told the man I was his nephew and paid him for the fruit."

The tall captain grinned. "That's right. We'd never met before, but after I rescued Yacov from the fruit seller, I saw he had no shoes, so my wife and I bought him a pair. We then invited Yacov and his brother Benyameen to our home for a meal. Annemarie says that, on my teacher's salary, I can't afford to adopt every orphan I see, but at least I can buy him shoes and offer him a meal."

Yacov raised his foot. "And, see? I'm still wearing them."

Grandpapa cleared his throat. "And now, Herr Hosenfeld, the schoolteacher, is a captain in the German army."

The old man glanced at Yacov with tired eyes. "I think you should go back upstairs now, Yacov. Thank you for bringing my meal. Return to your Polish language studies with Benyameen."

Captain Hosenfeld stood, removed his cap, and laid it on the glass counter. "There is no need to fear, Pan Lebowski." He addressed the jeweler in his faltering Polish. "I am only here to buy a bracelet for my wife. I haven't seen her since my promotion to the rank of captain, and I want to bring her a special gift when I go home next month on leave."

Yacov only understood about half of what the soldier said, but he got the general idea. Speaking to the captain in German, he asked, "How is *Frau* Hosenfeld? And Detlev? Is he still catching tree frogs?"

Grandpapa cleared his throat again and rounded the counter. "Please, Yacov. Go back upstairs and finish your studies. Let me complete my business with the captain."

Yacov let his head droop. "Yes, Grandpapa." He shuffled to the stairs and mounted the first step, but stopped and turned. "It was good to see you, Herr, I mean *Captain* Hosenfeld. I hope to see you again soon."

The soldier gave the boy a grin that didn't quite reach his eyes. "It was good to see you too, Yacov."

Taking a few more steps until he could no longer see Grandpapa, Yacov crouched behind the railing.

"*Sprechen Sie Deutch?*" The captain asked Grandpapa.

"*Ja,* I speak German," Grandpapa said.

The captain continued in German. "I didn't want to say anything in front of Yacov, Herr Lebowski, but it's no longer safe for you, Yacov, or Benyameen to remain here in Warsaw. Is there somewhere you can go?"

"I am tired of running." Grandpapa scratched the few gray hairs that remained on his head. "Yacov and his brother are safe here. They have special identities now. Officially, they are Catholic, if you know what I mean. Only you and I know their real names and religion. For me, however, it is too late."

Captain Hosenfeld lowered his voice. "I have heard that Hitler will eventually move all Warsaw Jews to a special area within the city. I'm not sure when this will happen, but you'll be forced to wear a yellow armband showing the Star of David. Any Jew refusing to wear an armband will be shot. Or worse. Is there someone living east of here who would take you in?"

Before Grandpapa answered, the bell above the shop's door jangled.

"Good afternoon, Pan Woźniak," Grandpapa greeted the new visitor.

"Good afternoon, Pan Lebowski," the gentleman said.

"I will be with you as soon as I finish with the captain."

"No hurry," said Pan Woźniak. "I enjoy viewing your merchandise." The man chuckled. "Even though there is little I can afford to buy."

Yacov shifted his position to catch a better glimpse of Captain Hosenfeld. The German leaned over the counter and spoke closer to Grandpapa's ear. Yacov couldn't make out what he said. A minute later, the shop's bell clanged as Captain Hosenfeld left.

"What was that all about?" Pan Woźniak asked the jeweler.

Grandpapa spoke softly. "Remember that offer you made last

month to buy my shop? If you promise to keep Yacov and Benyameen on as apprentices, I am ready to make a deal. I think it is time to retire."

Yacov gasped. *Grandpapa is going to abandon us? How could he?* Chills ran through him, as if someone had pushed him from the warmth of a wood-burning stove into a knee-high snowdrift. He had to tell Benyameen. Turning to bolt up the stairs, he stopped when the shop's bell rang out again. Yacov squeezed his head through two of the banister's posts. What other bad news had walked through the door?

Two young men rushed in whom he'd never seen before. The boys leaned over to catch their breath.

"Quick." The taller youth ran to Grandpapa's counter. "Can you hide us, please?"

The second boy, spotting Grandpapa's customer, glanced at Pan Woźniak, and then at Grandpapa. "The Blue Police are after us. We need your help."

The Blue Police? Benyameen had told him about them—Polish policemen who were overseen by the Germans, and forced to ensure the people's compliance with German laws. Yacov tried to guess the taller boy's age. Noticing his face had the shadow of a mustache, he guessed perhaps five or more years older than Benyameen. Maybe the boys were part of the Polish Underground. Benyameen talked about them too. Or maybe the young men were just hoodlums.

Grandpapa nodded at the boys. "*Tak.* Yes." He grabbed the taller boy's wrist and tugged him toward the staircase. "Hurry. Up the stairs and out the bedroom window. From there, you can jump to the building next door and escape over the rooftops."

The young men darted past Yacov and pounded the steps two at a time.

A few seconds later, a Blue Policeman ran into the shop and waved his pistol in the air. "Did two thugs just come in here?"

Pan Woźniak stepped forward. "Yes. But we told them to leave. If you hurry, you can still catch them. I think they ran around the corner."

"If you're lying"—the police officer pointed his gun at Pan Woźniak—"I will come back and shoot you myself." He turned and rushed out the door.

Grandpapa placed a hand over his heart.

Scurrying down the steps, Benyameen almost ran into Yacov when he neared the bottom. "What's going on?" he asked Yacov. "Two young men just ran into Grandpapa's bedroom."

Before Yacov could answer, Pan Woźniak addressed Grandpapa.

"Pan Lebowski, I am still very interested in purchasing your shop. Can you give me a tour of the second floor? Now?"

Benyameen let his mouth drop open.

Yacov wanted to tell Benyameen about Herr Hosenfeld and about Grandpapa's plan to abandon them, but he couldn't push out the words.

"Benyameen," Grandpapa called out. "Please come down and watch the shop for a few minutes."

Benyameen continued down the steps as Grandpapa escorted Pan Woźniak upstairs.

Yacov trailed the men.

The older youths stood at the window in Grandpapa's bedroom, studying the street below.

"He's gone now boys," Pan Woźniak said.

Grandpapa stared at Pan Woźniak, his graying caterpillar brows crunching together until they almost met in the middle. "You know these two?"

Pan Woźniak nodded.

The blond-haired boy blew out a breath and flopped on Grandpapa's bed. The old coils creaked with the burden. "That was close, Zoshka."

Zoshka remained at the window. "Too close, Alek." He let out a sigh and sat next to his friend. "We can't afford to take any more chances like that."

Alek thumped his friend on the back. "But Zoshka, after we removed those German street signs and replaced them with the Polish ones, the German delivery trucks had no idea where to go!"

Alek turned to Pan Woźniak. "Uncle Ludwik, you should have seen it. The stupid Germans drivers can't read Polish, and, since we took down their German street signs, they didn't know which way to go. When they stopped to ask directions, I sent them completely out of the way. It was beautiful!"

Grandpapa shot Pan Woźniak a quizzical look. "Uncle Ludwik?"

Pan Woźniak nodded. "Alek, Zoshka, this is Pan Lebowski. I might buy his shop. It could make a good safehouse for us in the near future."

Yacov could only wonder what that meant.

A few days later, everything changed. As soon as the sun set, Grandpapa locked the door and drew the shades. When he gathered with the others near the back of the store, he scooped Yacov up into his arms for a hug.

Yacov wrapped his arms around the old man's neck and returned the embrace. "Grandpapa, I don't understand why you have to go. Don't you love us anymore? Did I do something bad?"

"No, no, my boy." Grandpapa returned Yacov's hug. "You have done nothing wrong. I love you and Benyameen very much. But I must go away for a little while."

Yacov glanced at Benyameen, and then at Grandpapa's traveling bag on the floor.

Pan Woźniak patted Grandpapa's shoulder. "You must go now so you can reach the next safehouse before curfew. Zoshka has the wagon out back."

Yacov wiped his damp cheeks across Grandpapa's bearded face, perhaps for the last time. Nothing had made any sense since Captain Hosenfeld visited their shop. Grandpapa explained bad Germans would soon come and take Grandpapa away if he didn't go somewhere safe. But why couldn't he and Benyameen go with him? And couldn't they ask Captain Hosenfeld for help? The captain was a good German. At least, he thought so.

Prying Yacov from Grandpapa's arms, Pan Woźniak lifted him into his own.

Yacov rested his head on his new friend's shoulder. It wasn't the same. Uncle Ludwik had no hair on his face and hardly any on his head. Yacov's tears fell freely onto the man's tan woolen sweater.

Uncle Ludwik adjusted Yacov's weight on his hip. "I'll take good care of the boys," he told Grandpapa. "With the Allies' help, this could all be over soon."

Uncle Ludwik's words didn't sound convincing.

"Goodbye, my grandsons." Grandpapa kissed Yacov's cheek. Bending down, he wrapped Benyameen in a hug. "Take good care of your brother, Benyameen." Grandpapa's voice came thick. "And, both of you, make your beds every day." He wagged a finger at Benyameen. "Don't forget to make your beds."

Benyameen pinched his lower lip between his teeth. "We will, Grandpapa. Every day."

A youth rushed in through the back door. Yacov recognized him as Zoshka, the young man who fled from the Blue Police earlier that week.

"We have to go—now," Zoshka said in a low voice.

Grandpapa picked up his travelling bag and walked toward the back entrance. With his hand on the door knob, he turned and gazed at the boys once more. "Shalom."

The Suitcase

Independence Day, November 11, 1939
Warsaw, Poland

Tadzio tugged the gray woolen blanket more snugly around his shoulders as he shifted on his iron-frame bed. He didn't want to get up. Today, he and Krzysh would conduct their first Gray Ranks mission for the Underground. A glance at Krzysh's bed told him his friend had already gotten up. Krzysh's earlier reluctance to help the Underground had all but disappeared. He now enthusiastically referred to today's assignment as a "spy mission." But the way Tadzio saw it, they just had to pick up a suitcase from someone at St. Alexander's Church and bring it back home.

Home. How could he call living with three other messy boys a home? Besides himself, Krzysh, Lech, and Stefan, they also occasionally shared their living space with two older boys, Rudy and Alek. Leaders of the Beeches Patrol, Rudy and Alek sometimes stayed overnight, especially when Zoshka, Anna's brother, came to visit. When that happened, Andrzej also came over. Then Andrzej, Rudy, Alek, and Zoshka would stay up all night, conspiring in hushed tones.

Whenever Rudy and Alek visited, they trained the boys in what they called "the art of stealth travel." At first, they simply taught them how to monitor their surroundings. After weeks of noticing minute details whenever he went out, it began to it come naturally. Eventually, Tadzio could recognize an unknown person in the street if he ran into him twice in one day. And if someone followed him for any length of time, he sensed it, as if he had some sort of human radar concealed on his body.

Yesterday, on his way to his underground science class, he got the impression someone was trailing him. It seemed silly that he had to go to class in secret, but, since the beginning of November, the Germans had closed all schools for Poles over the age of twelve. When only three blocks from the apartment, where his illegal science class was held, he stopped in front of a shop window. Using its reflection to observe people behind him, he noticed the same tall man he thought he'd seen a block earlier. Tadzio quickly crossed the busy intersection and disappeared down a side street.

This morning, all he wanted to do was sleep. Before long, he slipped in and out of a dream. His muscles tensed, and his heart pounded as he raced down Karolkowa Street. A Gestapo agent chased after him, firing shots above his head. Then the dream shifted. He gagged as he took a sip of bitter tea. He looked everywhere for sugar but couldn't find any.

"Tadzio, wake up."

As if from a distance, Krzysh's voice cut through his fog. Only half awake, Tadzio remembered sugar was in short supply because of the German occupation. He'd have to drink his tea unsweetened or buy some saccharine on the black market.

Krzysh shook his shoulder.

Opening his eyes, Tadzio awoke. Good thing. He hated bitter tea.

Twenty minutes later, Tadzio paid their fare as he and Krzysh hopped onto an electric streetcar that drove past Powąki Cemetery. Tadzio shuddered as he glanced out the window. Snow blanketed the cemetery's barren ground and lightly dusted its outcroppings of tombstones.

Poor Krzysh. The remains of his parents now laid buried beneath that snow. Last month, his friend learned his parents had died at the end of September from injuries they sustained during Warsaw's bombing. However, instead of retreating into himself, Krzysh found ways to fight back against the Germans. That's probably why Krzysh was so excited about today's first mission.

As the tram turned south toward Chlodna Street, Tadzio

considered the fate of his own parents. Five weeks ago, he and Magdalena found out his mother and their caretaker's wife Halina were housed in Pawiak Prison. That was about six kilometers from where they lived. How could they be so close and yet so far away?

Polish prison guards recently smuggled out information that Halina and his mother were being questioned concerning the whereabouts of his father. If his mother or Halina knew anything about his father, why didn't they tell the Germans? And where was his father? Did he have any idea what they were going through? Did he even care?

When the tram neared Saski Gardens, Tadzio nudged Krzysh. "What time is it?"

Krzysh pulled out his pocket watch. "It's 9:50. We've got more than an hour before our eleven o'clock handoff."

"Let's get off at Saski Gardens," Tadzio said. "We can walk through Piłsudski Square on our way to the church."

Returning his watch to his pocket, Krzysh glanced at Tadzio. "Why bother visiting the square? There won't be any Independence Day celebrations today." A muscle flexed in Krzysh's jaw. "Only God knows when we'll see a free Poland again."

Tadzio shrugged his shoulders and sighed. "For the past two years, our family visited Saski Gardens and Piłsudski Square on November 11 to celebrate Independence Day. I guess I want to do it for them."

At the next stop, Tadzio and Krzysh stepped off the tram and trudged through the foot-deep snow until they reached Piłsudski Square. Tadzio stopped in front of the Tomb of the Unknown Soldier. Standing beneath the colonnade-topped arch that housed the tomb, he lifted his right hand to give the three-fingered Scout salute.

Krzysh grabbed his arm and pushed it down. "Do you want the Germans to know you're a Boy Scout?" Krzysh hissed.

"What's wrong with that?" Tadzio frowned.

"Haven't you noticed?" Krzysh pointed at the tomb. "No soldiers are standing guard there. Our Polish Army no longer exists. Poland no longer exists." Krzysh glanced around the square. "Even an innocent Scout salute can get you arrested." Krzysh lowered his voice. "Our patriotism has to be more inconspicuous now."

Tadzio knew Krzysh was right, but he didn't like it. His head hurt. He thought about all he'd recently lost. His mother was in prison, and his father had abandoned them. He, Magdalena, and Henio no longer lived together. Tadzio had no real place to call home. Even his homeland wasn't really his anymore. A sour taste filled his mouth.

Tadzio surveyed the square. Small groups of Polish citizens milled about. He squinted as the morning sun reflected off the snowbanks. Near the eastern end of the square, a few children tossed snowballs at each other. The cold November wind whipped across his face and stung his eyes. He tugged his woolen scarf more tightly around his neck.

Studying the Saski Palace, Tadzio shifted his gaze from its northern wing to the southern end before allowing his attention to rest once again on the colonnade-topped arcade connecting the two wings.

He nudged Krzysh. "Did you know that Chopin's father taught French here at the Saski Palace?"

Krzysh shook his head. "No. Was that when the Saski Palace was a secondary school?"

Bending down to form a snowball, Tadzio didn't answer right away. The cold made his limbs and mind sluggish. "Right," he finally said. "After my father started working at the bank, I used to visit Saski Palace every week after my piano lessons. I thought it would make me feel closer to Chopin and to my music. And, somehow, closer to my father."

Krzysh raised a brow. "Did it?"

Tadzio threw his ball into a snowbank. "A little. Before my father got so involved in his work, he also played piano. Chopin was his favorite composer." Tadzio gestured toward the right wing of the palace. "The Chopin family used to live there. They could remain in the palace as long as Chopin's father taught here. Chopin also went to school here during those years."

Gazing at the palace, Krzysh pulled his knitted cap more firmly around his ears. "Back then, Poland was part of the Prussian Kingdom, wasn't it?"

"Right." Tadzio pinched his eyes together. "It seems like we've always belonged to someone else."

"Not always," Krzysh said in a low voice.

Standing in silence for a moment, Tadzio pulled in a deep breath. "That's true. We governed ourselves for over a thousand years before Russia, Prussia, and the Hapsburgs carved us out of existence. But, after that, it was over a hundred years before we regained our freedom. That's a long time not to have the world recognize you as your own country."

Following Tadzio's example, Krzysh bent down, formed a snowball, and tossed it across the square. "True, but after the Great War, we got our country back again."

Tadzio shrugged. "Yes, but look how long that lasted. Only twenty years. Now, once again, others have stolen our freedom."

Krzysh threw another snowball, this time at Tadzio's feet. "They've stolen our freedom, but they'll never extinguish our patriotism."

Tadzio wasn't so sure.

The boys strode down New World Street in silence. They waited for several German motorcycles with sidecars to roar by before crossing. A little farther on, they neared Poland's Academy of Sciences.

Krzysh checked his watch again. "It's only 10:15. I don't think we should arrive too early. It might look suspicious if we're standing around, doing nothing for forty-five minutes."

"Then let's stop at the Academy of Science. Next to Saski Palace, it's my second favorite place to visit on a Saturday."

Krzysh extended his arm. "Lead the way."

Ascending the Academy's steps, Tadzio stopped to admire the building's arched entrances and white columns. He then let his gaze rest on the bronze monument of Copernicus in front of the building.

Glancing from the statue to Tadzio, Krzysh finally broke the silence. "I get it, Tadzio. Music and science. Two things that make you feel all is right with the world."

Tadzio shook his head. "No, Krzysh. Things will never be right in Poland as long as other countries rule us. But Chopin and Copernicus—they belong to Poland. No one can take them from us."

Krzysh pointed to the statue. "Remind me again what Copernicus is holding."

Stepping forward, Tadzio gestured to the figure. "In his right hand, Copernicus is holding a drafting compass. In his left hand, he's holding a celestial sphere. The sphere shows how the sky looks as seen from Earth."

Krzysh pushed out his lips as if he'd just sucked a lemon. "Knowing you, I have a feeling those items mean more to you than just scientific tools."

"You're right." Tadzio nodded. "To me, they've always represented precision and perspective. Looking at the compass reminds me we have tools to measure things. It helps me feel grounded. And the sphere reminds me to see things from more than just my own limited perspective. Seeing them again today, I realize that no matter how dark things are, somewhere in the future things will work out."

Krzysh checked his watch. "Well, I think nature sometimes needs a little help to get things worked out—like the suitcase we're supposed to pick up. I don't know what's in it, but Alek and Rudy made it sound pretty—"

Tadzio broke in. "Krzysh! Come look at this. I can't believe it." Tadzio leaned in and studied the pedestal's inscription. "Someone's hammered away the lettering on this plaque. It used to say, 'To Nicolaus Copernicus from a Grateful Nation.' Now you can't read it at all. Who would do that?"

After glancing at the defaced letters, Krzysh strode to the other side of the statue. "And look over here. Someone posted a German sign on this side."

Meeting up with Krzysh, Tadzio studied the new plaque screwed into the statue's base. He threw up his hands. "What does it say?"

Krzysh read the inscription aloud. "*Dem Grossen Astronomen Nicolaus Copernicus.*' It means, 'To the grand astronomer, Nicolaus Copernicus, from your grateful German Nation.'"

Tadzio balled his fists. "First the Germans invade our country and pretend to own everything we've built. And now they pretend Copernicus was German, not Polish!"

"What can we do?" Krzysh shrugged.

"I guess that's why we're on this mission."

Krzysh checked his watch again. "It's 10:30. We'd better get over to the church."

Fifteen minutes later they reached Three Crosses Square. As instructed, they waited beneath the columned portico. To pass the time, Tadzio studied the faces of people milling about the square.

A short man in a black, knitted cap approached. In one hand, he gripped a beat-up dark brown suitcase. A brisk wind whipped through the square and flapped open his unbuttoned woolen coat. The stranger paused, plunked down the suitcase, and swiftly secured his coat's belt around his waist. Retrieving the suitcase, he moved toward the boys. When he reached Tadzio, he asked, "Do you know when St. Alexander's Church was built?"

Tadzio's mouth twitched. He recognized the contact question, but couldn't recall the agreed-upon response.

Stepping forward, Krzysh said, "It was first built in 1820."

With a sigh, Tadzio let his muscles relax. Although St. Alexander's Church was really built in 1818, the correct contact response was 1820.

"Thank you." The stranger handed Krzysh the suitcase. Casually glancing around, the man whispered, "You must protect this suitcase with your life. Do not open it. If stopped, do not let anyone take you into custody. Do you have a weapon?"

Tadzio raised his eyebrows. "You mean like a gun?"

The man nodded.

Tadzio shook his head.

"If the Gestapo find out what's in there," the man said, "they'll arrest you and torture you until they learn everything you know about your contacts. Believe me, you don't want that to happen."

Tadzio swallowed hard.

With his back to the square, the man tugged open his woolen coat. Reaching inside, he pulled out a revolver and offered it to Krzysh.

Krzysh nudged Tadzio. "You take it. You're a better shot than me."

Not sure whether his hands were shaking out of fear, the cold, or maybe both, Tadzio grasped the gun. He quickly shoved it into his waistband and buttoned up his coat.

"Godspeed," the man said. Turning around, he trudged across the square.

Taking turns carrying the suitcase, the boys took a different route home.

After twenty minutes, they reached the intersection of Wolska and Karolkowa. Tadzio grabbed Krzysh's arm. "I just remembered. There's a police station further down Karolkowa."

"Then I think it's your turn to carry the suitcase." Krzysh handed off the package.

"Oh, great. Thanks a lot."

Krzysh flashed him a weak smile. "What are friends for?"

After walking several more blocks, Tadzio stopped. "Let's go east down Żytnia as far as Gibalskiego, then head north. From there we can cut through an alleyway that leads back to Karolkowa. That will almost bring us to our flat's door."

Krzysh nodded. "Good idea."

"And, Krzysh," Tadzio added, "it's your turn to carry the suitcase."

Shops and cafés lined Żytnia's short block to Gibalskiego. Above them rose apartment complexes three stories high. From one café, the smell of fresh bread and cooked onions made Tadzio's stomach rumble. He hadn't eaten anything since they'd left that morning.

At the corner where they were supposed to turn down Gibalskiego, Tadzio spotted a Blue Policeman exiting a watch repair shop. Glancing at Krzysh and noticing he gripped the suitcase even more tightly, Tadzio figured he'd seen him too.

"Maybe we should turn around and go back the way they we came," Krzysh whispered.

Knowing the Blue Police collaborated with the Germans, Tadzio shook his head. "That might look suspicious. We should just keep going."

Krzysh nodded. "As long as you have the pistol handy."

The boys reached the corner and then turned left at Gilbaskiego. Tadzio saw an alleyway up ahead. If confronted, they could turn in there.

A minute later, they heard the Polish police officer's steps behind them. "Halt please. I'd like to see what's in your suitcase."

CHAPTER 12

The Transmitter

November 11, 1939
Warsaw, Poland

Tadzio didn't stop for the policeman. Instead, he hurried into the alleyway.

Krzysh followed.

"Stop!" the police officer shouted again.

Tadzio unbuttoned his coat in case he needed to pull out his gun.

When the policeman huffed around the corner, he grabbed Krzysh by the collar and shook him. "When the police tell you to stop, boy, you'd better obey! Now, what's in the suitcase?"

Krzysh glanced at Tadzio with wide eyes and studied his unbuttoned overcoat.

"What do you think we have in our luggage?" Tadzio grasped the sides of his open coat without revealing the revolver.

Still clutching Krzysh's collar, the policeman raised his chin. "You boys don't look so tough. I bet you've only got black-market items in there. Perhaps saccharine?"

Tadzio raised a brow and stared at the officer. "Well, I'd advise you not to sweeten your tea with our sugar substitute. I think we have something you'd find even sweeter."

Tadzio glanced where Krzysh kept his watch and hoped the policeman would take his bluff. With the absence of sugar since the beginning of the occupation, and with artificial sweeteners in short supply, it seemed reasonable two young boys might traffic in black-market saccharine. Such a minor offense, however, probably wouldn't warrant a visit to Gestapo headquarters. Tadzio wanted the officer to think they might offer him a bribe if he ignored the contents of the suitcase.

A corner of the man's mouth curved up. He released Krzysh. "So, do you mean to offer me a different kind of sweetener if I let you go?"

Krzysh glanced at Tadzio who still stared at his hidden watch. He then grinned and nodded at the officer. "Yes. How about this?" Setting down the suitcase, he withdrew his pocket watch and handed it to the man. "That's a fine timepiece," Krzysh said. "Perhaps even better than the one you took to the repair shop."

The policeman inclined his head. "How did you know—" Not finishing his sentence, he rotated the timepiece in his hand as he examined it.

Angry voices rose behind them. Tadzio glanced up to see what caused the commotion.

A group of people had gathered at the alleyway entrance and were pointing at the Blue Policeman.

The officer took in the scene, then refocused on the boys. "Well, thank you for giving me the *time of day* lads." He snickered and tucked the watch into his trouser pocket. "You can be on your way now. But make sure you stay out of trouble."

As soon as the man left, Tadzio leaned over and rested his hands on his knees. He pulled in several deep breaths.

"That was close," Krzysh said. "For a minute, I thought you were going to have to shoot him."

Tadzio smirked. "With the police station so close, I didn't think that would be a good idea." He waved Krzysh forward. "Come on. Let's get this suitcase home."

Later that evening, Tadzio slipped through the back door of the Karolkowa hospital with the suitcase in hand. Five minutes later, Krzysh came in through the front. At four and five-minute intervals, Andrzej, Lech, Stefan, Alek, and Rudy also joined the group. Anna and Magdalena were already working in the hospital with patients.

Once everyone arrived, all the Scouts sat in a circle near the back of the room as Krzysh related news of their escape from the police.

Alek crossed his arms and leaned back. "That was some quick thinking, boys."

Magdalena nodded and shot Tadzio a half-smile.

Shifting his position on his metal chair, Tadzio raised a brow. "So Alek, can you tell us now what's in the suitcase?"

Alek turned to Rudy. "I'd better let the brains of our organization explain that."

Although a year younger than Alek, nineteen-year-old Rudy was the more serious of the two. And, since Professor Handelsman and his wife had recently gone into hiding because of their Jewish roots, Rudy now served as the group's scoutmaster.

Rudy glanced in Tadzio's direction, but seemed to ignore his question. Instead, their new scoutmaster squeezed his thick, reddish-brown eyebrows together and shifted his gaze to Magdalena. "Anna tells me you did very well during your Morse code training at the Girl Guide's Camporee this summer, Magdalena. I hear you earned your first level certification."

Blushing, Magdalena nodded. "Yes, and considering I fainted on my first day here at the hospital, I think I'd do much better as a radio operator than as a nurse."

Rudy ran a hand through his disheveled mop of reddish-brown hair. "Then, how would you like to work as a telegraphist instead?"

Krzysh leaned forward. "Is that's what's in the suitcase? A transmitter?"

Rudy grinned. "You mean, you really haven't opened it yet?"

"You told us not to." Tadzio frowned.

"Good answer." Rudy nodded. "Yes. Our contact gave you a radio transmitter. We also have a receiver and a recorder, but those were damaged during the siege."

Tadzio leaned forward. "I could help you repair them."

"He's sort of a science genius," Krzysh volunteered.

Andrzej jiggled his leg and turned to Tadzio. "If you could repair the receiver and the recorder, we'd be the first Scout group in the area to set up a transmitting operation."

"That's right." Rudy tugged his right ear. "The Wawer Scout troop, just southeast of here, has one. They're eager to set up a communication link with us to coordinate activities. But we can't do that until we have a working receiver and recorder."

Rudy rubbed his chin. "Lech and Stefan, retrieve the recorder and receiver from the safehouse and help Tadzio get the parts he needs to repair them."

"Will do," Lech said.

Rudy stood. "Anna, I'll arrange for Magdalena to receive training as our radio operator. Do you think you can survive here without her at the hospital?"

Anna and Magdalena exchanged glances.

Tadzio knew how much Magdalena hated working as a nurse.

Anna smiled at Magdalena. "I think we can manage without her."

CHAPTER 13

Murder in Wawer

December 1939
Warsaw, Poland

By the third week of December, with the help of Lech and Stefan, Tadzio got the receiver and recorder running. When not at the hospital or working on the radio, Tadzio spent time with Magdalena and the children at Auntie M's flat.

At the end of the month, Auntie M invited the Scouts over for Christmas Eve dinner. She had used her black-market connections to purchase fruit, nuts, and flour for the feast. The sweet woman baked long, white Christmas loaves covered with poppy seeds. She also made two of Tadzio's favorite Christmas treats: gingerbread and spice cakes. For the Christmas Eve meal, she made pierogi with sauerkraut and mushrooms. They also had fish, potatoes, and sauerkraut salad.

After dinner, as Tadzio, Lech, Stefan, and Krzysh donned their coats to return to their own flat, Andrzej turned to Magdalena. "Don't forget. Be ready to leave tomorrow by 6:30 AM. We want to arrive at the safehouse early so we have time to test the equipment."

Andrzej's tone sounded as tight as the muscles in his face. There was a lot at stake. Rudy had put him in charge of this operation. Tomorrow would be their first test of the transmitter. They would receive a call from the Scouts in Wawer at ten o'clock on Christmas morning.

Magdalena smoothed down the turned-up collar on Andrzej's black woolen coat. "I'll be ready. Everything will go as planned."

Once Andrzej left, Lech turned to Magdalena. "Please be careful tomorrow." He laid his hands on her shoulders. "This isn't a game. If anything happened to you—"

Magdalena put a finger to his lips. "Oh, Lech, don't worry." She pulled his gray woolen cap down more firmly around his ears.

Grabbing Magdalena's wrists, Lech stepped closer and kissed her on the lips.

Tadzio let his jaw drop.

Blinking, Magdalena stepped back and opened her mouth to speak, but no words came out.

Lech turned and trailed Stefan out the door.

Unable to resist, Tadzio moved to Magdalena and grasped her wrists. "Oh, Magdalena, please be careful tomorrow. If anything happened to you—" He leaned in and pretended to give her a kiss.

Magdalena pushed him away. "Oh, get out of here." She grinned.

Krzysh batted his eyelashes at her. "Goodnight, Magdalena."

Tadzio thumped Krzysh on the back as they strode down the street to their own apartment.

At seven o'clock the next morning, Andrzej, Magdalena, and Tadzio arrived at the safehouse carrying what looked like shopping bags full of vegetables. To Tadzio's surprise, the safehouse turned out to be a jewelry store. The owner of the store, a short, balding man, let them in through the back entrance.

The diminutive man led Tadzio and the others up a creaking wooden staircase to the floor above. "We can set up here in the kitchen." He pointed to a table where two boys sat finishing their breakfast. Tadzio placed his bag next to them.

"This is Yacov and Benyameen," the man introduced the boys.

The younger boy looked up. "Uncle Ludwik, do you want us to go outside now and keep a lookout?"

Andrzej pinched his brows together as he removed the vegetables from the top of his bag, and then the transmitter hiding beneath them. "Uncle Ludwik?"

The owner ruffled the younger boy's blond hair and glanced at

Andrzej. "The boys call me Uncle Ludwik. That's what I'd like all of you to call me now. Benyameen and Yacov were living here with the jeweler, Pan Lebowski, until I advised him to find a safer place to live. I bought the jewelry store from him, mostly because I realized this would be an excellent cover for our activities. Now, I also serve as these boys' uncle."

Uncle Ludwik put a hand on Yacov's shoulder and crouched down to speak with him at eye level. "Yacov, you and Benyameen won't need to go out and watch yet. First, we have to get all the equipment set up. Why don't you and Benyameen go to your room and make your beds?"

Yacov nodded and scampered off.

"Uncle Ludwik?" the older boy asked. "If it's okay with you, I'd like to stay and observe. I've always been interested in electronics, but I've never seen the equipment up close."

Uncle Ludwik glanced at Andrzej.

Andrzej nodded. "It's okay with me, Benyameen. If it turns out you have a knack for this sort of thing, we could give you some training. We always need more skilled operators."

Benyameen rubbed his hands together. "I'd like that very much."

After unpacking all the vegetables, Tadzio connected the transmitter to the power outlet. The tubes began to glow. He mounted the quartz and turned a knob. The small control bulb burned brightly.

Benyameen's eyes grew large.

Tadzio pointed to the wall behind the kitchen table and handed the transmitter's transducer to Benyameen. "Can you hang the antenna there on the wall?"

"Of course." Benyameen removed a calendar from the wall and hooked the antenna on its nail.

Tadzio placed a tiny bulb surrounded by a wire ring on the table, close to the antenna. The bulb lit instantly. "Okay, the transmitter's working."

"How did you do that?" Benyameen asked.

Andrzej stepped up to the table. "Sorry, Benyameen, no time to explain now. Maybe you and Tadzio can talk later." He shifted his attention to Tadzio. "Are the recorder and receiver ready to go?"

Tadzio adjusted a few knobs. "I'm having trouble with the receiver. I need to make some adjustments."

By now, Yacov had returned. While Tadzio worked with the equipment, Andrzej reviewed everyone's assignments. "Tadzio, Magdalena, and I will stay inside to transmit and receive messages. Uncle Ludwik, Benyameen, and Yacov will serve as outdoor lookouts. As you know, the enemy has listening posts operating twenty-four hours a day. If the Germans find any stations broadcasting they haven't heard before, they'll report on the spot." Andrzej ran a hand across his face.

"Once they pick up on our signal, and they will, they'll use directional antennas between listening posts to find out where our reception is the strongest. After that, they'll send out either a plane or a mobile unit to locate our position. So, lookouts, if you see a plane or any mobile unit, report it immediately. Also, watch for any cars that pull up and remain parked without the driver leaving. If that happens, we'll need to promptly evacuate. Finally, watch for anyone milling around the area, either alone or in a group. Report anything that seems suspicious."

By ten o'clock, Tadzio had everything ready.

Magdalena pressed the transmitting key and tapped out their call sign. Then, in international code, she signaled she was going over to reception. After adjusting her earphones, she stared at the transmitter.

Tadzio searched her face. Had she heard anything yet? Her expression remained the same. Could something be faulty with the equipment? The agreed-upon wavelength with Wawer remained silent.

By 11:30 AM, Andrzej shook his head. "We told Wawer if we didn't make a connection by now, we'd try again tomorrow night. That's what we'll have to do."

Tadzio shut down the transmitter and turned to Andrzej. "But curfew is at 8 PM. If we're out on the street after that, we could get arrested."

Andrzej nodded. "Then I guess we sleep here tomorrow night."

Before eight o'clock the next evening, Tadzio once again helped carry bags of vegetables to Uncle Ludwik's jewelry shop.

Benyameen taught them how to play Skat. At 10 PM Tadzio set up the equipment.

Yacov said he'd stay awake to help, but by 10:45 PM he had fallen asleep with his head resting on the kitchen table. Uncle Ludwik carried him off to bed while Tadzio tuned in the frequency. Benyameen and Uncle Ludwik took up positions at the windows. Magdalena clicked out their call sign, then switched over to reception. A few minutes later, she bounced in her chair, pointing to her headphones.

Tadzio plugged in the tape recorder and observed the dots and dashes that appeared.

Magdalena decoded each letter until she had the entire message. Suddenly, her jaw slackened. She dropped her pencil.

Andrzej, peering over Magdalena's shoulder, snatched up the decoded dispatch and read it aloud. "Germans arrest 120 innocent Poles in Wawer tonight after Polish hoodlums kill two German officers. Germans say the arrests are punishment for the murders. More information to follow."

A week later, they received a follow-up report. Out of the 120 people arrested in Wawer, they sentenced 114 to death, even though they weren't responsible for the officers' murders. According to the Germans, the Poles were "collectively responsible" for the German officers' deaths.

CHAPTER 14

Vomit Bombs

February 1940
Warsaw, Poland

Signs of German oppression increased daily. When Tadzio and Krzysh went to the library, they found it closed—indefinitely. At one of the tram stops on the way home, the Germans rounded up several Jews and took them away. They weren't wearing their required Star of David.

Krzysh grumbled. "I'm tired of the little errands Andrzej gives us. I want to do something that really gets back at the Germans."

"Keep your voice down." Tadzio lowered his head. Even though they sat in the back of the tram, and the Germans sat in the front, there was always the possibility of German sympathizers within earshot.

"What else can we do?"

Krzysh leaned closer. "Stefan told me he and Lech sabotaged several street signs last week. They switched some of the German street names the Germans put up, and their supply trucks ended up going in the wrong direction."

Tadzio raised a brow. "Did Andrzej okay that?"

Krzysh snickered and shook his head. "No. Lech overheard Rudy and Alek talking about it, so he and Stefan did it too. Stefan also said he and Lech made vomit bombs and threw them into restaurants where only Germans are allowed. Isn't that a great idea?"

"No, it's not." Tadzio shook his head. "That's just stupid. What if they get caught?"

Krzysh sighed and leaned back in his seat. "At least they'd die doing something."

The tram jerked to a stop. People near the front mumbled something about a roadblock ahead.

Tadzio caught his breath as soldiers boarded the tram.

"*Papieren,*" the uniformed men shouted. "*Papieren. Schnell.*"

Tadzio's hands shook as he reached for his wallet. He glanced at a young man across the aisle.

Grasping the seat in front of him, the young man gazed around with wild eyes.

A gray-haired woman next to the man patted his hand. "It'll be okay, Piotr. Just stay calm."

As the soldiers drew closer, Piotr darted off the tram.

Tadzio stood to follow the action.

A soldier on the sidewalk whipped out his gun.

Blam!

Piotr, grasping his abdomen, fell to the ground, writhing in pain.

Hanging his head out of the tram's window, Tadzio vomited onto the street.

Blam! Another shot.

With his stomach still churning, Tadzio pulled his head back inside the tram.

"*Papieren,*" shouted a voice next to him.

Numb with fear, Tadzio didn't respond.

Krzysh poked him. "Show the soldier your identity card."

Trembling, Tadzio took out his card.

The German glanced at it, then back at Tadzio. "Jerzy Kowalski. Only thirteen, eh? And you work as a hospital orderly?"

Krzysh translated for Tadzio.

Tadzio nodded yes.

"That's good." The soldier's mouth twisted into a wicked smile as he showed Tadzio's papers to the German behind him. "See here, Schmidt? This one's too young. We only want boys fourteen and older. But at least he does a job suited to Poles. It says here he cleans bed pans." The soldier laughed and threw the ID card in Tadzio's face.

"*Aus!*" yelled another soldier a few rows behind Tadzio. He guessed the German had found a boy older than thirteen. The soldier dragged a young man off the tram and shoved him into the street. Others pushed him into a group of about thirty other boys and men they'd already gathered.

Angry and helpless, Tadzio's heart raced as the soldiers shoved their captives against the side of a building. They beat anyone found with a gun or knife. They then pushed their prisoners into an enclosed army truck.

To no one in particular, Tadzio asked, "Where are they taking them?"

A woman in front of Tadzio clutched her grocery bag more tightly to her chest. Fear pinched her face. "I've heard they ship them off to Germany as slave labor for the Reich."

As the tram lurched forward again, Tadzio turned to Krzysh and whispered. "Tell me again about those vomit bombs."

CHAPTER 15

Forbidden Music

End of April 1940
Warsaw, Poland

Throughout the winter and spring of 1940, the Nazis tightened their noose on life in Warsaw. More and more teens disappeared, giving the street an empty, haunted feeling.

When the Germans cut the Poles' monthly ration of coupons, Tadzio supplemented his hospital orderly pay by working as a waiter in a local café. He used the extra money to buy food on the black market for Auntie M and the children.

While Tadzio and Krzysh mopped the hospital floors one afternoon near the end of April, Magdalena rushed in. "Auntie M's planning a party next week to celebrate Constitution Day," she said. "She hopes it will lift everyone's spirits. Can you two make it?"

His muscles taut, Tadzio set his mop in the corner and blew out a breath. "The way you ran in here, I worried something bad had happened." He wiped sweat from his forehead with his shirtsleeve. "I can't come. I'm working at the café all that week."

Magdalena pouted. "Oh, please. Our upstairs neighbor has a piano, and she said we could use it. I suggested you and I give a little concert for the party. Can't you trade shifts with someone?"

He hadn't played piano since they left their summerhouse last September. As he recalled the event, his fingers automatically wriggled out the first phrase of Chopin's Etude in E Major. His heart soared at the thought of playing again. "Will we be able to practice together before then?"

Magdalena brightened. "Yes. Our neighbor said we can come by and practice whenever we want."

Tadzio's stomach growled. "Invite me to dinner tonight, and I'll work out my schedule."

"Hey, how about me?" Krzysh broke in.

Magdalena grinned. "Sure. I'll cook for both of you tonight. See you at six."

Between Tadzio's two jobs, his underground school studies, and occasional errands for Andrzej, he found time to practice several pieces for the party, including the Etude in E Major he and Magdalena had played at the manor house. By May 3, they'd prepared an evening of entertainment for the celebration.

On the day of the event, Tadzio helped Magdalena set out snacks on Auntie M's dining table while the children played in the bedroom.

"I only wish Professor Handelsman could be here," Magdalena said. "At least he and his wife are safely hidden away."

With a rumble from his stomach, Tadzio reached across her and helped himself to one of the miniature ham sandwiches.

Magdalena slapped his hand. "Those sandwiches are for the guests."

Tadzio shrugged. "I don't live here. I'm a guest."

Lech sat next to Stefan on the living room couch and stretched his legs. "Magdalena, are you performing the violin piece tonight that you played last September?"

She avoided Lech's stare. Tadzio raised a brow. According to what Magdalena had shared with him, she hadn't talked much to Lech since he gave her a kiss on Christmas Eve.

Lech moved to the other side of Stefan, closer to Magdalena. "I certainly hope you are playing that piece, even though it's by Chopin. Can you believe the Germans have forbidden us from listening to any music by the great composer, just because he was Polish? How absurd."

"Yes, we plan to perform the etude again." Without looking up, Magdalena continued to rearrange the sandwiches on the plate. "If you'll excuse me, Lech, I need to help Auntie M in the kitchen."

As she left, Lech blew out a heavy breath.

Tadzio waited to be sure she was gone, then grabbed another

sandwich. A self-satisfied grin spread across his face. He enjoyed the tasty food and the fact that Magdalena no longer seemed interested in Lech. After biting into his finger food, he sat in a metal chair across from Stefan and Lech.

A moment later, Krzysh emerged from the bedroom where he'd been taking care of the children. When he noticed the sandwich in Tadzio's hand, he helped himself to one and squatted on the floor next to Tadzio.

Stefan nudged Lech. "Tell Tadzio and Krzysh what you did last Saturday."

A smile flickered across Lech's face. "I went to the Bristol Hotel near Piłsudski Square and sat at a corner dining table. I hid behind a German newspaper and sat there reading it as if I was one of them!"

"Fantastic." Krzysh slapped his knee.

Tadzio wagged his head. "Yeah. Fantastically stupid. The Bristol Hotel is off-limits to Poles. What if you got caught?"

Lech drew back his shoulders. "Of course it's off-limits, Dombrowski. That's what makes it so exciting! I wore the right clothes, acted arrogant like the Germans, and managed to get by with the little German I know. Those stuck-up Krauts in their fancy uniforms—downing huge tankards of beer and eating plates full of sauerkraut. And guess who I saw walk in, hanging on the arm of a German officer? That tall, blonde Polish woman, Danusia. Can you beat that?"

"Danusia Ristau?" Tadzio leaned forward. "She manages the café where I work." A chill ran through him. Had she suspected he worked for the Underground?

"Right." Lech nodded. "Any idea why she'd be having dinner with a German?"

Tadzio narrowed his eyes. "Does Andrzej know about this?"

"It's Morro, not Andrzej," Krzysh said as he poked Tadzio's side.

Tadzio sighed. He wasn't used to calling Andrzej by his code name.

Lech leaned back on the couch and picked at a few loose threads on the armrest. "You mean, did I tell Morro about going to the Bristol Hotel? No. And I'm not *going* to tell him, either."

The apartment door opened. Andrzej entered with two neighbors from the upstairs flat. Auntie M's small sitting room soon filled to capacity. With all the tasty food, laughter, and fun, Tadzio put Lech's news on hold. Before long, Auntie M announced it was time to move up to the neighbor's apartment for their concert.

Tadzio had almost forgotten how much he enjoyed playing for others. His excitement rose as his fingers found their familiar positions across the keys. After performing a few solo pieces by Beethoven and two by Mozart, Magdalena joined him for their finale, Chopin's Etude in E Major. The harmonies of his pulsing beat and Magdalena's melody transported him to another world—a world where everyone spoke the same language, where emotions rose and fell with the music, and where they cheered as one for having experienced it together.

As he readied to strike the keys more forcefully for an upcoming crescendo, whispers went up among the listeners.

Andrzej's voice cut through the piece. "Tadzio, stop," he ordered.

Tadzio's hands froze in midair. He resisted the urge to hit the next chord.

Andrzej stood and addressed the crowd. "Auntie M reminded me that this piece is by Chopin. Since the Germans recently declared it illegal to play anything written by him, I think it's wise to end the concert here."

Tadzio's heart fell as he glanced at those around him. Lech, red-faced, scowled, but Andrej's stone stare seemed to silence him. Others' pinched faces and downcast eyes betrayed their fearful thoughts.

"Morro's right," Auntie M said. "I can vouch for those gathered here. We're all true patriots, but there might be listening ears in other apartments—people who would gladly report us for disobeying the current law. Best we not rock the boat."

Although the party seemed officially over, many neighbors stayed. One went to the piano and pecked out the melody of a Bach tune. Two talked of the weather, and a few spoke in hushed tones about the black market.

Not wanting to speak with anyone, Tadzio stepped out onto the balcony. He settled himself in a wicker chair overlooking the back-yard garden and studied the star-filled sky. He located the North Star—something he and Father used to do. Like a soft blanket, a warm sensation enveloped him. In his ever-changing world of uncertainty, at least the stars remained predictable.

A few minutes afterward, Andrzej and Magdalena strolled out. Tadzio sat in a corner behind a large plant. He almost called out, but then changed his mind. If he stayed hidden, he might hear something he could use later as brotherly *ammunition*.

Andrzej placed a hand on the railing and turned toward Magdalena. "I have something I need to tell you." His tone sounded dark and serious.

"And I have something I need to tell you." Magdalena's voice sounded playful as she placed her hand next to his.

Andrzej stuffed his hands in his pockets, gazed up at the moon, then back at Magdalena. "All right. You go first."

"I know you heard Lech kissed me on Christmas Eve." Magdalena glanced out over the balcony. Her voice sounded small. "But perhaps you hadn't heard that I didn't kiss him back."

"So, are you saying you don't have feelings for Lech?" Andrzej dug his hands deeper into his pockets.

"I'm saying, I don't have feelings for Lech the way that—" She turned toward Andrzej. "I don't have feelings for Lech the way I have feelings for you."

Tadzio edged forward in his wicker chair.

Andrzej grasped her hands. "Magdalena, we both have important work to do. We can't afford to get sidetracked by our emotions right now."

She pulled her hands away and turned toward the railing. "Yes, we *do* have important work." Her pitch rose. "Our freedom is important. Poland is important. But if we have to deny our feelings, what good is freedom? Or a country?"

Andrzej rested his hand on her shoulder. "Please don't say that, Magdalena. I wanted to speak with you out here tonight because I have some news about your mother."

Almost losing his balance, Tadzio grabbed the sides of his chair to steady himself. Hopefully, they hadn't heard the noise. He continued to peer at them from behind the plant.

With a gasp, Magdalena seized Andrzej's arms. "What have you heard about my mother? Is she all right? Have they released her?" Magdalena's words came fierce and fast. "What about Halina?"

Like a metronome set on allegretto, Tadzio's heart thumped faster. He leaned out from behind the plant to get a better look.

"We found out from some of the Polish guards that your mother is still in Pawiak Prison." Andrzej held her gaze. "The Gestapo have repeatedly questioned her about your father, but she insists she doesn't know where he is. We've also heard that Halina is very ill."

Magdalena sniffled. "Is my mother well? Have they hurt her? Tell me the truth, Andrzej."

"The guards told us they have transferred both Halina and your mother to the prison hospital." He brushed back a strand of Magdalena's long, dark hair. "Your mother has pneumonia. They're not sure yet about Halina's diagnosis."

Magdalena's sniffles turned to sobs. "Oh Andrzej, is there any way to free them?"

With a shake of his head, Andrzej grasped her hands. "No, but your mother smuggled out a message. She's asked that you, Tadzio, and Henio walk past the prison hospital next Monday at noon. The guard said she'll appear at one of the windows facing the street. Although she wants to see all of you again, she doesn't want Henio to know. She's afraid it might upset him if he sees her but can't go to her. Only you and Tadzio should glance up."

Magdalena tottered for a moment. "Oh, Andrzej."

When he reached out to steady her, she wrapped her arms around his neck.

Just then, Lech stepped out onto the balcony. "Hey, Morro, you're needed in the—" Lech stopped when he saw Andrzej embracing Magdalena.

The two swiveled their heads in Lech's direction.

"You're needed inside," Lech finished.

Since he had the next day off, Tadzio planned to stay in his apartment and read a book until Magdalena came over. Before he left the party last night, Magdalena said she'd stop by the next afternoon.

He figured she wanted to tell him the news Andrzej had shared.

Before she arrived, Krzysh approached him in the living room. Krzysh nudged his foot. "Can I borrow your bicycle today?"

Tadzio lowered his book and cocked his head. "Sure, but what's wrong with yours?"

"Stefan's going to use it. He and I are taking a bike ride."

Tadzio raised his book to eye level and spoke from behind it. "So, you and Stefan are chums now, eh?" He didn't care that he had an edge to his voice. Krzysh was his friend, not Stefan's. What had changed?

Krzysh leaned closer. "Lech taught us a trick." He withdrew a liquid-filled bottle from his pocket and held it up.

Tadzio peered over his book and sniffed. "What's in there?"

"Something that will heat things up for the Germans." Krzysh grinned.

"Whatever you're planning, it's not worth it. You'll get caught for sure."

Krzysh frowned and slapped the back of Tadzio's book. "Well, it beats sitting around here, doing nothing. Maybe you don't care that the Krauts have your mother in prison, but my mother and father are lying dead in a grave. I plan to do something about it." Krzysh tromped to the door and slammed it shut behind him.

Tadzio had picked up the toxic aroma of the liquid in Krzysh's bottle. Petrol. Most likely, Krzysh and Stefan planned to smash the bottles against a building or sign, and then set the gasoline on fire. He wanted to tell Andrzej about their scheme, but didn't know where to find him. He searched the house for Lech, but he wasn't around either.

An hour later when Magdalena arrived, he relayed Krzysh and Stefan's plans.

She shook her head. "It's crazy, but I almost can't blame them. It's frustrating to feel like we can't fight back." She told him about their mother's message.

Tadzio pretended to hear about it for the first time. "I'm scheduled to work the noon shift at the café on Monday, but Staś will take my place. He's always asking for more hours."

Magdalena squeaked out a sob and turned her head.

Grasping her hands, he squeezed them. "Are you sure you can handle seeing Mother behind prison bars?"

Magdalena's larynx bobbed as she swallowed and blinked away a tear. "I have to. For Mother's sake. Who knows what horrors she's endured in prison? She needs to know we're okay. It might give her the strength to go on." Magdalena brushed her face hard with the back of her hand.

Tadzio bit the inside of his cheek. How would he hold up when they saw Mother again?

CHAPTER 16

A Prison Visit

May 1940
Warsaw, Poland

On Monday morning, Tadzio led Magdalena and Henio to the tram stop on Pawia Street. Tadzio told Henio they needed a little family time and were going to a café for a late breakfast.

"This is so much fun," Henio said as the trio ambled down the sidewalk toward the café.

Tadzio and Magdalena each held one of Henio's hands. Every few minutes, Henio jumped so his brother and sister could swing him between them. Each time, Tadzio's heart leapt with him. He'd forgotten how much he enjoyed time with his siblings.

After a breakfast of hard-boiled eggs, lettuce, tomato, and onions, they continued down Pawia Street until they reached the prison. The muscles in Tadzio's face twitched as he studied the prison windows near the hospital wing. Several bells from nearby churches tolled noon.

Henio glanced up at his brother. "Why are we stopping here?"

Tadzio furrowed his forehead. He hoped Magdalena would come up with an explanation.

"I thought we'd play a game." Although Magdalena's voice came strained and thin, she continued. "We're going to stand here for three minutes and see how many trams go by. We're going to count to ourselves, and not say anything out loud. After three minutes, if you count the same number of trams as we do, I have a special treat for you."

"Oh, that's an easy game, Magda." Henio grinned. "You know I'm a good counter."

"We'll see." Magdalena flashed Henio a smile that didn't quite reach her eyes. "Okay. Three minutes starting—now."

Henio stood as straight as a soldier and faced the street.

Tadzio swiveled his gaze to study the prison windows, searching for a glimpse of his mother. When she first appeared, he didn't recognize her—not with her disheveled hair and gaunt face. When she smiled, however, there was no mistake. His stomach twisted.

Magdalena gasped. She'd seen her too.

"Shh," said Henio. He tugged on Tadzio and Magdalena's hands without shifting his attention from the street.

A burning love surged through Tadzio, intertwined with a sense of dark hatred. How could he experience both emotions at the same time? His heart broke for his mother, but his love was almost drowned out by his hatred of the Germans who had taken her away.

After a few minutes, his mother blew them a kiss and waved goodbye.

Tadzio held up a hand, willing her to wait. He boosted Henio onto his shoulders. "Time's up," Tadzio told him.

"Two trams." Henio beamed.

Grasping Henio's legs, Tadzio nodded. "Right. Magdalena, I guess you owe this boy a treat." Tadzio turned so his mother could glimpse Henio's face.

Mother pressed a hand to her mouth, then brushed tears from her eyes as a brave smile flickered across her face.

"I know I've got that treat here somewhere." Magdalena rummaged through her purse. She paused, as if struggling to hold back a sob. "Well, if I can't find it, I guess I'll have to give it to you when we get home."

Tadzio released his grasp on one of Henio's legs and waved good-bye to his mother.

"It's okay," Henio said to Magdalena. "It was a treat just to eat breakfast together today. I like it when we're a family."

"So do I." Tadzio swallowed hard. "So do I."

Andrzej visited the boys' flat later that evening. Tadzio told him about Lech's stunt at the Bristol Hotel. He also told him how Lech had seen Danusia, his café manager, on the arm of a German officer. "Do you think it's still safe for me to work there?" Tadzio asked as Andrzej sat on their sagging couch. "Do you think I should quit?"

"Don't make any changes right now." Andrzej leaned his head back and stretched his neck muscles. "Who knows? This information could be very helpful. Just be careful when you're around her."

Tadzio decided not to tell Andrzej about Stefan and Krzysh's bottle-throwing adventure. Seeing his sick mother behind prison bars had tapped his own reserve of German hatred—and his desire to do something about it.

Later that week, while emptying hospital bedpans, Tadzio asked Krzysh about his bike ride with Stefan. "So, what did you and Stefan do with those bottles the other day?"

"Are you sure you want to know?" Krzysh shrugged.

"Yes, I do. Where did you go?" Tadzio held his breath as he emptied the last bedpan.

Motioning for Tadzio to follow, Krzysh didn't speak until they were out back. "Lech gave us several bottles filled with petrol and we rode over to Wilson Square. You know that big wooden billboard near Meinl's store?"

Tadzio smirked. "You mean the one covered with German posters? The ones with absurd regulations, like German Governor Krüger's law that he will shoot any Jew not wearing the Star of David? Or arrest anyone who plays Chopin music?"

Turning on the spigot, Krzysh filled a pail with water. "Yes," he nodded.

"So, did you do something to it?"

A smile spread across Krzysh's face. "At five o'clock—that's when the square's the busiest and it's easier to blend in with the crowd—we smashed the bottles against the billboard. When they broke, the petrol soaked into the posters, and we set them on fire. You should have seen it. The entire square lit up!"

Tadzio's chest burned as he seized a second pail and filled it with water.

"I know you think it's stupid." Krzysh shook his head. "But I can't tell you how good it felt."

"Actually, I don't think it was stupid." Tadzio picked up a mop leaning against the building and handed it to Krzysh, then grabbed another mop propped up next to the door. As they carried their mop buckets into the hospital, Tadzio paused. "And, Krzysh? I think you're braver than me."

CHAPTER 17

The Raid

October 1940
Warsaw, Poland

Magdalena exited the tram on New World Avenue and scurried to her box-office job. As she walked the next two blocks, she contemplated all that had taken place since Germany's invasion last September.

She winced as she recalled Mother's thin form gazing at them through the bars of the prison hospital in May. It had hardened her resolve to do whatever she could to thwart the German occupation. She wished Andrzej had more jobs for her as a telegraphist. Even with the few times she sent and received illegal messages for the Gray Ranks, Warsaw's frequent power outages made the transmission work unpredictable and exasperating.

Her illicit high school classes in teachers' homes and her occasional Scout activities consumed most of her day. Despite that, she recently applied as a part-time ticket operator when a job opened at the theater. Like Tadzio, she wanted to earn extra money. If only her brother offered more support.

She understood why the underground government had warned Poles not to patronize public playhouses. On some nights she'd even helped Scouts paint slogans around the city that read, "Only pigs attend cinemas." Most movie theaters only showed Nazi German films, preceded by propaganda newsreels. The Germans edited the few Polish reels shown in Warsaw to eliminate any reference to their national symbols, and to cut out the names of Jewish actors and producers.

"But I'm not attending the shows," Magdalena argued with Tadzio. "I'm only selling tickets." Besides, now that she'd turned seventeen, the job gave her an excuse to wear her new make-up, her over-the-knee gray skirt, and her most recent purchase, a smart woolen jacket. She felt especially pleased with how the jacket's petal peplum accentuated her thin waistline.

In October, Uncle Ludwik offered Magdalena the opportunity to use her theater-ticketing job as a contact point for passing coded messages. She eagerly agreed. The box office had a great deal of traffic in the afternoon, and no one paid attention to the people who called there. It was easy to sit in her cubicle and smile at the emissaries Uncle Ludwik sent. Under the pretense of buying tickets, agents delivered or collected messages for other Underground personnel.

She didn't tell Andrzej about passing the notes because the job had nothing to do with the Gray Ranks' activities. Besides, she and Andrzej hadn't talked much in the past five months—not since May's Constitution Day.

She also hadn't spoken very often with Lech. Not since he kissed her last year on Christmas Eve. She smiled at the thought. That had changed last month when he caught up with her after her secret physics class at a teacher's home.

"I am so embarrassed about kissing you on Christmas Eve," Lech had said. "I'm sorry I was so forward. Can you forgive me?"

She not only forgave him, but also let him walk her to her flat every day after that. She shared her aspirations to become a concert violinist once the war was over. He spoke of someday earning his own business. Yesterday, he revealed that his calculus teacher allowed them to listen to a BBC Polish Service broadcast on his illegal wireless when they finished their lesson early.

As she neared her ticket booth, Lech's whistle broke her reverie.

Her muscles tensed. "What are you doing here?" She lowered her voice to a whisper. "I don't think you should meet me at work."

Ignoring her reprimand, he glanced at her from head to toe, and whistled once more. "Wow, is that a new jacket?"

"Why yes." Her cheeks warmed at Lech's gaze.

"Well, I approve." He grabbed her hand and spun her in a circle.

When she faced him again, she grasped his other hand and grinned. "Thanks for the compliment, but, seriously, what are you doing here?"

"Can't a guy take his girl out to a show?"

"Oh?" Magdalena offered a teasing smile. "So now I'm *your girl?*"

Lech pulled her a closer. "Of course you are. We've walked home after our secret classes for over a month, haven't we?"

"Yes, we have." She locked her gaze onto his and pressed her palm to his heart. "But I'm not sure that makes me *your girl.*"

"Oh, I think it does." He grinned and brushed her lips with his. "And it's time I take my girl out to the theater. I've worked hard at the tannery and picked up other side jobs. We deserve a treat. Please give me two tickets for tomorrow's show, *Forgotten Melody.*"

Magdalena pinched her lips together. "Lech, you know the underground government doesn't want us to attend any movies."

Lech dropped her hands and stepped back. "The Germans tell us what we can and can't do, and now our own underground government wants to boss us around. Well, I'm sick of it." He pushed back a wayward strand of his thick, black hair. "The movie's a fun comedy produced by Polish people. We deserve something light-hearted to help us deal with the pain and suffering we see every day."

Magdalena put a finger to her chin and considered his arguments. When the movie first came out, a year before Germany's invasion, Father promised to take the family to view it. He never did. Now, Father was gone. She changed her tack.

"So, you want to buy two tickets for tomorrow's presentation." She arched a brow and raised her chin. "And what makes you assume I'm available tomorrow night?"

Lech bowed low. "Magdalena, my dear, would you do me the honor of joining me for a movie tomorrow evening?" He gestured toward the theater. "I thought we'd see *Forgotten Melody.* If I can get the ticket girl of this establishment to sell me two admissions."

"Why, yes." She giggled. "I think I am available then. I would be delighted to join you for a picture."

After checking in with her manager, Magdalena slipped into the ticket booth.

Lech pushed his money through the glass cut-away and retrieved the tickets she handed him. His fingers rested on hers for a few seconds. "I'll stop by your flat at seven o'clock." He winked. "And I'd love for you to wear that brown jacket again."

Magdalena quirked a brow. "Good—since it's the only nice thing I have."

After Lech left, business picked up. Her box office sold tickets for both cinemas and live theater, so she had customers all afternoon, mostly German. Just before closing, Uncle Ludwik stepped up to the booth.

"I'd like two tickets for tomorrow's presentation." Uncle Ludwik slid a white envelope through Magdalena's ticket window.

Magdalena opened the envelope and read the enclosed note. *Tomorrow night, usual place, 8 PM. Important job. Tell no one.* She furrowed a brow.

"You *do* still have tickets available for tomorrow's show, don't you?" Uncle Ludwik asked.

As if an old crust of bread had lodged in her throat, she swallowed hard. Uncle Ludwik needed her for a telegraphist job. Saying yes to him meant breaking her date with Lech. And she couldn't tell him why.

"Of course, sir." As they had agreed, Magdalena pretended not to know Uncle Ludwik. "I have tickets for tomorrow's show, *Forgotten Melody*. That's no problem."

Pretending to draw up two admissions, she placed the note inside the envelope and slid it back through the window. Her answer told Uncle Ludwik she consented to the job and would arrive at the jewelry shop by eight o'clock tomorrow night.

As the Underground agent left, Magdalena shook her head. *Choosing patriotism over love. Sounds like something Andrzej would do.*

After her physics class the next day, Lech, as usual, caught up with her on Żytnia Street to walk her home.

"Lech, about tonight—" she began.

"Yes, at seven o'clock sharp." He held out his hand, offering to carry her notebook.

She handed it to him. "I won't be able to make it. Something important has come up."

Lech grasped her shoulder and shot her an icy stare. "More important than going out with me?"

His hazel eyes darkened as he tightened his grip.

She reached up and touched his cheek. "Lech, you know I want to go out with you, but I should have checked with Auntie M before I said yes. She needs me this evening. I'm so sorry. I'll make it up to you."

Lech gave her a crooked smile. "Really?" He released her shoulder. "Well, as long as you make it up to me. I'll hold you to that promise."

They continued on their way toward their flats. When they reached Karolkowa Street, they went their separate ways.

At eight o'clock that evening, Magdalena knocked on the jewelry store's back door. Three raps, a pause, then two more raps. Her stomach did flip-flops. It had been several weeks since Uncle Ludwik asked her to send a message.

Benyameen let her in then shut the door. "Everyone's upstairs. Uncle Ludwik says to go right up."

Magdalena entered the kitchen area of the second floor. Her nerves skittered when she noticed two strangers with Uncle Ludwik. She raised a brow.

"Not to worry," Uncle Ludwik said. "These are friends of mine."

Her taut muscles relaxed a little, but her stomach felt queasy.

"Thank you for coming," he said. "Our usual telegraphist couldn't make it, and we have an important message to send."

A young man of about twenty sat by the radio. Benyameen helped him test the equipment.

An older gentleman of about forty with short-cropped blond hair stared out the window. "Zofia's giving us the all-clear signal," he said. He turned, blew out a puff of smoke, then crushed his stub of a cigarette in a nearby ashtray.

Why did her hands tremble? She worked to steady them as Uncle Ludwik handed her a message. Someone had written it in a code she'd never seen. The only word that made sense was the name "Wojtek" sprinkled throughout the note. Working to calm her stomach, she sat at the table and tapped out the transmission.

Before she finished, the man at the window cried out. "Ludwik, shut it down! Zofia's giving us the warning signal. Two black cars just pulled up across the street."

Magdalena froze.

Uncle Ludwik yanked out the radio's plug. "Quick," he shouted at the young man at the transmitter. "Out the window. I'll hide the short-wave. Jump to the next balcony like we planned. Hurry over the roofs to the end of the block. Nowak and Magdalena will follow."

Everyone rushed around in a whirl of activity, but Magdalena couldn't budge. Her limbs went numb like when she fell through the ice at the manor house pond.

"Move girl, move!" Uncle Ludwik shouted. "No time to panic. Out the window now. Take Benyameen and Yacov with you."

Yacov dashed out of the bedroom. "Uncle Ludwik, what about you? You have to come too."

"I'll be along soon." Uncle Ludwik bent down and hugged Yacov. "Now go." He placed Yacov's little hand in Benyameen's.

Magdalena felt Yacov tug on her skirt. In a fog, she rose from her chair and followed everyone out the window.

CHAPTER 18

The Move

October 1940
Warsaw, Poland

Everyone vaulted to the adjacent building's rooftop.
"Hurry." The blond man waved for them to follow as he scurried to the next building.

Magdalena stole a glance back. Even though the sun had set, she still made out two black cars parked across from the jewelry shop. She shuddered as Gestapo agents pushed Uncle Ludwik toward one of them.

After following the others down a fire escape, she alternately ran and walked three kilometers with Benyameen and Yacov in tow.

No one spoke, but her mind whirred. *What will happen to Uncle Ludwik? What about the radio transmission I never finished sending?* As with the other traumas she'd experienced since Father left, she stuffed her unanswered questions deep inside.

She shook with fear and exhaustion when she finally reached the Scouts' flat and pounded on their door.

No one answered.

"They've got to be here." She rapped again. Still no answer. She rattled the handle. Locked. "Where could they be?"

Yacov tugged her hand. "Will Uncle Ludwik be okay?" His tiny voice sounded as scared as she felt.

Magdalena pressed the trembling fingers of her free hand to her lips. "I don't know. Let's go over to the hospital and see if they're over there."

When she entered the back door, she let out a sigh of relief. The Scouts were assembled in a circle around Anna's desk. She rushed over and, spotting two empty chairs next to Anna, settled Benyameen in one of them. Taking up the spot next to Anna, she lifted Yacov to her lap and reported the Gestapo's raid on the jewelry store.

Lech's nostrils flared. "You told me you had to do something for Auntie M." He leaned forward and scowled. "You lied to me."

"I'm sorry." Magdalena shifted her gaze to the cement floor. "Uncle Ludwik warned me to tell no one." Saying the brave man's name out loud brought tears to her eyes. She balled her fists to hold them back.

Lech stood, raised his metal chair, then slammed the legs to the ground. "How can we work together if we can't trust each other?"

"Sit down," Zoshka said as he glared at Lech.

He thumped it again, then sat.

With arched eyebrows, Zoshka faced Magdalena. "You're sure you saw the Gestapo arrest Uncle Ludwik?"

Her words caught in her throat. She could only pull in a breath and nod.

He turned to his sister. "Anna, take Yacov to Auntie M's and introduce him to Henio. Ask if he can spend the night. And Lech, Benyameen will stay with you and Stefan."

"Sure." Lech nodded, but continued to scowl at Magdalena.

His searing gaze twisted her insides. She glanced away.

"Alright then." Anna stood, attempted a smile, and extended a hand to Yacov.

The little boy shook his head and wrapped his arms around Magdalena's neck. "I don't want to go anywhere without you or Benyameen."

Magdalena smoothed Yacov's blond hair and met Zoshka's gaze. "I will introduce Yacov myself. It won't take long." Not waiting for Zoshka's approval, she carried her small charge to Auntie M's.

When she returned, Zoshka summarized what he'd already told the others. "As I've explained, this hospital is shutting down next week." He leaned forward. "Magdalena, Anna, Tadzio, and Krzysh, here are your updated ID cards authorizing you to work at the Żoliborz Hospital."

After handing them out, Zoshka leaned back in his chair. "Auntie

M's sister has offered to rent us rooms in her two-story home on Felinski Street. Her code name is Auntie L. Her place is only six blocks from that hospital, and—"

"Zoshka!" Heat flamed Magdalena's face. She held up a hand and swallowed back a wave of anger. "How can you be so matter-of-fact when I just told you the Gestapo arrested Uncle Ludwik?"

Zoshka drew his thick brows together. "Magdalena, we can't allow ourselves to wallow in our emotions. We'll have time to mourn our losses once the war is over. Until then, we must maintain our focus."

Wallow in our emotions? Magdalena's intestines twisted. She shifted in her chair.

"He's right," Anna whispered in her ear and squeezed her hand.

Despite Anna's efforts to comfort her, bile rose from her stomach to her throat. Maybe she wasn't cut out to be part of the Gray Ranks. She glanced at Zoshka. The Scout leader's razor-like stare bore through her.

"As I was saying," he continued, "we must maintain our focus. With the capture of Uncle Ludwik, Benyameen and Yacov will now join our little group. They'll share one of the second-floor bedrooms in Auntie L's house."

Magdalena studied Zoshka's pinched face. He appeared more worried than ever. "Wait, wait." She again held up a hand. "Why is this hospital closing? And why are all of us moving in together?"

Rudy ran his fingers through his unruly mop of reddish-brown hair. "Remember when the German governor, Fischer, announced he would soon divide Warsaw into three separate living areas? One for Poles, one for Germans, and one for Jews?"

Magdalena nodded.

"Well, the Jewish area's western boundary is only six blocks from our Karolkowa Hospital. The Gestapo won't allow them to leave their section of town, so we no longer need a clinic here. Zoshka wants us to relocate farther north."

"And yesterday," Anna added, "there was a manhunt in Wilson Square. The Germans took Auntie L's husband and her three sons. Her other two boys are Polish Air Force pilots and live in London. Since she's all alone in her house now, we will rent rooms from her."

Magdalena smirked. She glanced first at Andrzej, then Lech. "So, we'll all be one big happy family. I can hardly wait. When do we leave?"

"We head out at dawn tomorrow." Andrzej smoothed his trousers. "Walk over in small groups, about an hour apart from each other. I've written out a schedule." He passed everyone an agenda and a map. "Memorize it, then destroy it. See you all at Auntie L's."

CHAPTER 19

Avenge Wawer

December 22–24, 1940
Żoliborz District, Warsaw, Poland

Two months had passed since they moved in with Auntie L. Tadzio woke up in a foul mood. Yesterday, he spent the morning working at Żoliborz Hospital. Then he worked late at the café because his replacement never showed up. Now that it was Sunday morning, he wanted to sleep in. Why had he promised Magdalena he'd go with her and Henio to the ten o'clock Mass? Magdalena had reminded him yesterday that it was the last Sunday before Christmas. He knew she was trying to guilt him into going. It had worked.

As Tadzio stumbled out of bed, he brooded. *I wish Mother and Father were here.* He tried not to wake Krzysh or Benyameen as he rubbed his eyes and shuffled to the washroom. He envisioned his own family of five bundled up in their winter coats as they trudged together to St. John's Cathedral. Today, only three of them would pass through the church doors.

"We take the trolley all the way to Old Town Market, then on to the church," Magdalena reminded him as they tromped through the foot-deep snow to the tram stop.

"I know." Tadzio scowled. "Just because I haven't gone with you to church every Sunday doesn't mean I forgot how to get there. You're so bossy."

"I am not." Magdalena threw back her head. "I just want to get there on time. To do that, we need to be sure we get on the right trolley."

Once they boarded the tram, Tadzio shut his eyes and let his mind wander. Anger brewed behind his eyelids. He'd lost so much this past year. Would things ever return to normal?

After a few blocks, the trolley stopped. Tadzio opened his eyes and took in their surroundings.

"This doesn't look like Old Town," Henio said as he glanced out the fogged-over window.

"It's not." Tadzio leaned across Magdalena and Henio and wiped the window with his mittened hand. "I know we got on the right tram. I wonder why we're stopping here at Piwna Street."

An old man sitting across from Tadzio rubbed his gloved hands together. "Looks like another roundup."

The woman sitting next to the man groaned. "Jesus, Mary, and Joseph." She made the sign of the cross, bowed her scarf-covered head, then pressed her hands to her lips.

Tadzio's stomach twisted, and not from hunger. Images from the last roundup he witnessed flashed across his mind. Unlike the last time, he was now fourteen. The Germans could *legally* take him from the tram and send him to work in Germany.

The elderly gentleman spoke again. "I heard the Germans took away over 20,000 people this past September. The ones who weren't sent to work in German factories were shipped off to the city of Oświęcim in southern Poland."

A young man sitting two rows in front of them turned in his seat. "The stupid Germans can't even pronounce Oświęcim, so they just call it *Auschwitz*. I've heard that the Nazis eventually plan to ship all the Jews who now live in the Jewish Ghetto to concentration camps they're building there in Auschwitz."

A woman's voice rang out from the rear. "All the Jews from the Ghetto? That's impossible. You're talking about almost 400,000 people! Surely the Germans wouldn't send 400,000 people to concentration camps!"

"You're right," the elderly man spoke again. "The Germans wouldn't do that. I hear they're building a new concentration camp in Treblinka. That's much closer to Warsaw than Oświęcim. They'll probably send most of Warsaw's Jews there."

Magdalena, squeezed between Tadzio and Henio, spoke up. "Well, some Poles won't let that happen. They'll stand up for what's right."

Shocked by Magdalena's brashness, Tadzio pinched her.

She turned and scowled at him.

The older gentleman leaned across the aisle to catch Magdalena's attention. "You're right, young lady. Some brave Poles *will* stand up for what is right, only to be shot down by German machine guns."

A chill ran through Tadzio. He shuddered. Gazing above the assorted hats and caps of the people sitting in front of him, he scanned for soldiers. Not seeing any, he tugged Magdalena's coat sleeve. "Let's get off here and walk to St. John's. It's only about two blocks south."

Magdalena nodded.

Tadzio trudged through the snow with Magdalena and Henio until they reached the corner of Grodzka. He then turned right.

Henio walked between his siblings, gripping their gloved hands. "I'm cold," he whined.

Magdalena pointed ahead, down the narrow, brick-lined street. "It's not much farther. See those steps near the end of this street? That's the Jesuit church. Right next to it is St. John's."

"Oh, I can walk *that* far." Henio's tone brightened.

Tadzio grinned as he squeezed his brother's hand. Henio's sweet spirit always cheered him up.

Father Wacław's sermon offered Tadzio a flicker of hope.

"Our Epistle reading for the Fourth Sunday of Advent is from St. Paul's letter to the Corinthians," the priest began. "These words still provide hope for us today. St. Paul told the early Christians not to judge events before the appointed time. The apostle wrote, 'The Lord will bring to light what is hidden in darkness and will expose the motives of men's hearts.'"

Father Wacław turned his attention to a man in the fourth pew—a German officer.

Tadzio followed the priest's gaze. Why was the soldier there? Was he at Mass to spy on the priest? Was he a church member? No, that couldn't be. He glanced at the anxious faces surrounding him and guessed some of the other parishioners wondered the same thing.

Still studying the German officer, Father Wacław continued. "In God's timing, He will bring to light what is hidden in darkness. He will expose the motives of men's hearts. Our job, as our reading in Luke reminds us today, is to prepare the way of the Lord. We are called to help make crooked roads straight and rough ways smooth so that all of mankind can see God's salvation."

The priest pulled in a breath and continued. "In a few days, we will celebrate our Lord's birth. We must remember that Jesus was a person of history whose words, miracles, and sinless life showed Him to be God in the flesh. He lived, died, and rose from the dead in order to forgive our sins and enable us to love those who persecute us, as well as to stand up for what is right. May God give us wisdom to do both—to love those who persecute us, and to stand up for what is right and good."

Muffled coughs rose from the congregation as Father Wacław vacated the pulpit and returned to the altar.

Tadzio's mind wrestled with the message. How could God possibly expect him to love German soldiers, like the one sitting a few rows in front of him? How was he supposed to love people who jailed, kidnapped, and killed innocent people? How could he love people who imprisoned and probably tortured his mother and Halina? And how could God expect him, a fourteen-year-old, to stand up against an entire army? Someone who hadn't even been able to stand up for, or even protect himself from bullies at school?

After Mass, Father Wacław waited at the church door to shake parishioners' hands. The German officer exited before Tadzio.

Father Wacław grasped the soldier's hands between his. "I'm glad you joined us for Mass today. I hope you come again."

"I hope so too, Father," the German nodded. "I hope so too."

When Tadzio shook hands with the priest, Father Wacław leaned in. "I want you three to stay for a moment after everyone leaves. I have some information for you."

Tadzio's mouth went dry. He shifted his gaze to Magdalena. She nodded. They went back inside and waited in the foyer's warmth.

As Tadzio twisted his woolen cap between his hands, his mind raced. Why had the priest asked them to wait? Was there another message from Mother? Did Father Wacław know something about Poppa?

After the last parishioner left, the priest motioned for Tadzio, Magdalena, and Henio to join him in a pew near the back of the church. Once seated, Father Wacław glanced around the empty church, then rested his gaze on Tadzio. "Last week in Pawiak Prison, I gave the Last Rites to a dying prisoner."

Magdalena gasped and held her hand over her mouth. "No! Was it Mother?"

The priest held up a hand. "No, no. Your mother is alive. However, while I was there, an informant told me the Germans plan to move your mother, Halina, and about 500 other prisoners within the next few weeks. The SS plans to take them to the Warsaw West Station. From there, they will load them onto cattle trains and take them to northern Germany."

Tadzio let his jaw drop. "Isn't that where the Germans built Ravensbrück, the women's concentration camp?"

Magdalena pinched Tadzio's arm. She scowled and inclined her head toward Henio.

Bile rose to Tadzio's mouth. Poor Henio didn't know what a concentration camp was. But they did. Rudy had told them about it. He said Ravensbrück was a women's prison work camp about eighty kilometers north of Berlin. It primarily jailed women and children. *How do you explain that to a five-year-old?* Tadzio wondered.

Tadzio turned to the priest. "Father, about your sermon today." Tadzio shifted his gaze to the floor. "I don't think I even *want* the Lord to give me the power to love the Germans." He glanced back at the priest. "But I do want His power to make the crooked ways straight."

The man rested a hand on Tadzio's shoulder. "Son, I'll pray the Lord empowers you to do both."

When Tadzio returned to Auntie L's house, he found the Scouts seated in the parlor. While Magdalena settled Henio and Yacov upstairs, he stood in front of the fireplace and relayed Father Wacław's message to the others.

As he spoke, his pulse picked up speed. "We've got to do something," he concluded, fixing Andrzej with a stare. "Let's rescue the prisoners when they're transferred to the train station."

Magdalena entered the parlor and sat next to Andrzej on the magenta brocade couch. "That might work," she said.

Andrzej shook his head. "Even if we knew the exact day and time the prisoners were being moved, the Underground can't risk it. We don't have enough men or guns for that."

"But Andrzej." Tadzio held out his hands as if offering a plea. "We could—"

"No." Andrzej stared him down.

Magdalena stood, put her hands on her hips, and leaned close to Andrzej. "We're talking about my mother. What if it was your mother?"

"Magdalena, I—"

Before Andrzej could finish, Magdalena burst into tears and ran from the room.

Heat coursed through Tadzio's veins. Like a tree limb snapped off by rapids, pent-up rage broke through Tadzio's resolve of self-control. He kicked one of Henio's wooden toys across the room, crashing it into the far wall. "I can't just stand around and do nothing. There's got to be a way to fight back."

Benyameen nodded. "I agree. There's got to be something we can do."

Krzysh, sitting near the brick fireplace, blew out a breath. "I hate to say it, but Andrzej's right. If we try to rescue them, it'll be a massacre."

Both Lech and Stefan grunted their agreement.

"Tadzio, you know Krzysh is right," Lech said. "We'd get slaughtered."

"That's easy for you to say." Tadzio glared at Lech. "Both of your parents are dead." He glanced back at Krzysh. "So are yours."

Tadzio's angry words sucked the air from the room.

After a beat, Lech balled his fists. He stood and marched toward Tadzio. "Dombrowski, I've a good mind to rearrange your face. Why don't you and I—"

Stefan ran to his brother's side and tugged his arm. "He didn't mean it, Lech. Let's just all calm down."

"Let me go." Lech shook him off.

"That's enough." Andrzej stood and fisted his hands to his waist. "Fighting each other won't help. I know you're all angry and frustrated. So am I."

Lech and Stefan returned to their seats seats just as Magdalena re-entered the room.

"There is one thing we can do." Andrzej clenched his jaw. "It won't rescue your mother, but at least we'll be doing *something*."

Tadzio raised his head. "What's that?"

With a determined gaze, Andrzej eyed each Scout. "Earlier this week, Zoshka told me about a Christmas Eve event planned by the Wawer Gray Ranks. He wants us to join them."

Magdalena's eyebrows rose to her hairline. "And, of course, by *us*, you mean both the Boy Scouts *and* the Girl Guides."

"Of course." Andrzej nodded. "On Christmas Eve, the Gray Ranks plan to paint graffiti all around Warsaw to commemorate the Wawer Massacre. Remember last year, just after Christmas, when the Germans in Wawer sentenced about 100 innocent Poles to death?"

"That was the first coded message I ever received." Magdalena crossed her arms. "The Scouts in Wawer told us German officers were killed by two Polish criminals. Even though they caught the murderers, the Germans said the Poles were *collectively responsible*."

Tadzio rubbed his chin. "I remember. Because two German officers died, they slaughtered 114 innocent Poles. All for the actions of two stupid criminals."

"That's right." Andrzej eyes widened. "And this Christmas Eve, the Gray Ranks will paint, *We Will Avenge Wawer* throughout Warsaw. When the Germans wake up Christmas morning, we want them shaking in their boots, wondering how we'll exact our revenge."

Tadzio threw up his hands and plopped down next to Krzysh. "A lot of good that will do. They'll just force us to paint over it."

Magdalena scooted to the edge of the couch. "But at least the Germans will know not all of us will cower in the face of their brutality. And it will encourage the people in our city. I think half the battle is giving people hope. No matter how small our actions might seem."

A muscle ticked in Andrzej jaw. "You're wrong, Magdalena. Giving people hope is *more* than half the battle."

On Christmas Eve, Tadzio, Krzysh, Benyameen, Stefan, and Magdalena crept from the house to join Lech and Andrzej at the appointed rendezvous spot. A few minutes after they arrived at the abandoned theater on Krasiński Street, Lech and Andrzej joined them with paint buckets and brushes in hand.

Tadzio pulled his woolen scarf over his nose to ward off the bitter wind that whistled through the theater's boarded up windows.

"The Gray Ranks from Wawer will blanket the Old City area," Andrzej said, handing one of the paint buckets to Tadzio. "We'll paint any vacant walls near Wilson Square. Stay within a whistle's ear-shot of each other."

Lech and Andrzej handed out the rest of the supplies.

"How do you want us to team up?" Tadzio said.

Andrzej pointed to Krzysh, Tadzio, and Benyameen. "You three work together. Stefan and Lech, you two team up. Magdalena and I will form a third group."

At this news, a corner of Magdalena's mouth turned up. She seemed pleased with the arrangement since she and Lech hadn't patched things up yet.

"Morro," Lech addressed Andrzej by his code name, "what if we get caught?"

"Same as always." Andrzej tugged his woolen cap over his ears. "Give the distress whistle to alert the others. Try to escape if you can. If you're captured, only give your code name. And by all means, don't squeal on another Gray Ranks member."

With a raised brow, Lech asked, "Do you have the Luger?"

Andrzej tapped a slight bulge at his side. "I'll only use it in an emergency. We're expected to accomplish this mission without a hitch. It's Christmas Eve. The Germans won't expect anything tonight."

Tadzio led Krzysh and Benyameen to their assigned spot.

After ten minutes of painting *Avenge Wawer* on the sides of buildings, Benyameen stopped. "You know, we could cover a lot more territory if we found a shorter way to write Avenge Wawer."

Tadzio blew on his gloved hands. A cloud of condensation rose with it. "You're right, Benyameen. We've graffitied the words on several buildings down this street. Maybe now we can use only the first two letters. PW—*Pomścimy Wawer*. Avenge Wawer."

"Good idea." Krzysh thumped Tadzio on the back and painted "P".

"I have an idea," Benyameen said, stepping closer. He added a longer downward stroke to Krzysh's "P". He then swiped two upward strokes at the bottom to form a "W"—⚓.

Tadzio trudged over and examined the symbol. "Hmm." He stepped back. "That makes it look like an anchor with a loop on top."

Benyameen and Krzysh studied it for a moment.

"You're right," Krzysh said. "It forms a *kotwica*. An anchor. Let's paint a *kotwica* with a loop on top from now on. It'll go faster, and people will still get the message."

Tadzio worked with renewed energy. "PW," he said, as he painted the new sign. "You know, it could also stand for *Polska Walcząca*—Poland Fighting." He repeated the phrases to himself. *Pomścimy Wawer*—We will avenge Wawer. *Polska Walcząca*—Poland Fighting. He continued to draw the anchor sign and loops on the next section of the wall. *If only we could fight with more than words and a paintbrush.*

Despite the cold, heat rose from his chest to his throat. He envisioned Wawer's scene last Christmas when Germans lined up 114 innocent boys and men against a wall, then shot them in cold blood. He conjured up the image of his mother behind prison bars. He then visualized himself pressing the barrel of a gun against a German's head. And yet, in this scene, no matter how hard he willed, he couldn't picture himself pulling the trigger.

A flicker of movement near the corner made Tadzio drop his paintbrush. A chill ran through him as the form of a German officer appeared.

CHAPTER 20

Captured

December 24, 1940
Żoliborz District, Warsaw, Poland

The officer drew his pistol. "*Hände hoch.* Hands up high!" Dropping his bucket and brush, Tadzio raised his hands. He was about to give the distress whistle when Benyameen stopped him.

"Wait. I know this man. This is Captain Hosenfeld." Benyameen peered closer at the German. "Captain Hosenfeld, it's me, Benyameen. Yacov's brother."

The officer inclined his head. "Benyameen?"

With his hands still raised, Benyameen nodded. "Yes, sir. You visited Herr Lutowski's jewelry shop a year ago to buy a gift for your wife. And last month, Yacov and I saw you in Wilson Square. You handed out shoes to bare-footed Polish boys on the street. I couldn't believe a German was doing such a kind thing. Then Yacov reminded me you once bought him a pair of shoes when you found him barefoot in Germany."

The captain furrowed his forehead and lowered his gun. "Yes. Benyameen. I'm sorry to meet you again under such circumstances. But don't you know I can have you arrested? What is this graffiti?" In his faltering Polish, the officer read the words splayed across the wall. "*Pomścimy Wawer.* We will avenge Wawer."

Benyameen had told Tadzio about this German officer, but Tadzio hadn't dared to believe it.

"Put your hands down, boys." Captain Hosenfeld holstered his gun.

"If you promise not to attack me with your paint brushes, I promise not to shoot you. I am on my way home from a dinner, which is why I am alone. However, if other Wehrmacht officers were with me, or heaven forbid, the Gestapo, I'd be forced to arrest you. Go home now. Go back to your warm beds."

Bending down to secure the lid on his paint can, Tadzio peered more closely at the German. He recognized him as the officer he'd seen at church.

Captain Hosenfeld adjusted his cap. "If you know of other groups out tonight, tell them to go home as well. There are at least two Gestapo teams patrolling this area. I hope I won't see you out here again." The German turned and disappeared around the corner.

Widening his eyes, Tadzio glanced at Krzysh and Benyameen. "We should warn the others."

Removing his gloves, Krzysh put two fingers to his lips and let out a loud whistle.

Tadzio picked up his brush and paint can. "Let's make sure they're okay before we head home." He led Benyameen and Krzysh down the street to where he'd last seen Magdalena and Andrzej.

Tadzio spotted them about halfway down the block. His stomach dropped.

Pressed up against a wall, Andrej and Magdalena stood spread eagle with a Gestapo policeman at their backs, his semi-automatic trained on them.

In a panic, Tadzio ran up behind the German and slammed the paint can into the back of the man's head.

The German's knees buckled. He dropped his pistol in the snow and collapsed to the ground.

Blood pounded in Tadzio's ears. "Run!" he yelled.

As Magdalena and Andrzej turned around, the fallen policeman reached out and grabbed Andrzej's leg.

Andrzej fell face first into the snow.

"Grab the gun!" Magdalena screamed.

Tadzio couldn't move. As if in slow motion, the scene played out in front of him. Andrzej and the German wrestled in the snow. Andrzej, without success, kicked to free himself from the man's grasp.

"The gun!" Magdalena screamed again.

Krzysh rushed past Tadzio. He scooped up the Luger and squeezed off a burst of fire. A second later, the man lay dead.

The white snow near Tadzio's feet slowly changed to red. It then morphed to brown as Tadzio retched. The putrid smell of vomit shocked him back to reality.

Andrzej scrambled to his feet. "Let's get out of here. Now!"

Magdalena tugged Andrzej's arm. "What about Lech and Stefan?"

"I'm sure they heard the shot." Andrzej seized the pistol from Krzysh's shaking hand. He clapped Krzysh on the shoulder and headed down the block.

Tadzio and the rest followed.

After Andrzej led the others to Feliński Street, he stopped and peered around the corner. "Go back," he hissed to Tadzio and the others. "Go back."

Tadzio peered past Andrzej and glimpsed Lech and Stefan at the other end of the block. The brothers had their hands raised as they approached. Two Gestapo policeman pointed pistols at their backs.

Tadzio and the others retreated back the way they had come. Back toward the dead policeman in the snow.

From somewhere behind them, a car door opened.

The sound of fists meeting flesh snapped through the air, followed by a shout from Lech. "Run!"

Tadzio and the others froze in their tracks.

A shot rang out.

A scream.

Seconds later, Stefan barreled around the corner, right into Tadzio.

A doorway in the building next to them opened.

"Quick," a voice called out in the dark. "In here."

Someone pulled Tadzio and the other Scouts through the doorway and up a stairwell.

A car squealed around the corner, slowed to an idle, then sped away.

CHAPTER 21

Political Prisoners

December 1940–January 1941
Żoliborz District, Warsaw, Poland

Two days later, Lech returned to Auntie L's house.

Tadzio's pulse raced as he ran upstairs to Lech and Stefan's bedroom. The Scouts gathered to hear how Lech had escaped the Gestapo.

Tadzio tried not to stare at Lech. The cuts above his swollen eyelids, his bruised, puffy cheeks, and his bloodied split lip told their own tale. Lech also wore a bloodstained bandage around his right upper arm where, Tadzio guessed, the Gestapo had shot him the night he was caught.

"They shot me after I told Stefan to run," Lech said. "But the bullet only grazed my arm. They took me to Gestapo Headquarters and beat me, hoping I'd give up the names of those responsible for the Avenge Wawer event." The Scout winced as he attempted a grin. "I only gave them fake names. I convinced the Gestapo I'd bring them more information if they let me go, so they did."

Andrzej raised his chin. "So they don't know your real name, or where you live?"

Lech shook his head no. "I had my fake ID and told them I was a friend of Danusia Ristau. As soon as I said that, the beatings stopped."

Andrzej's eyebrows pinched together. "Who is Danusia Ristau?"

"Remember?" Tadzio said. "We told you about her after Auntie M's Constitution Day party last May. She manages the Heartbeat

Café where I used to work. Lech saw her once at the Bristol Hotel in the company of a German officer. We think she's probably a *Volksdeutscher.* You know. A Pole with a German heritage."

"Right," Lech nodded. "She was born here, but her parents came from Germany. She pretends to be on the side of the Poles, but receives special treatment from the Germans because her loyalties lie with the Germans, not with us. I think she secretly passes on information to the Gestapo when she overhears conversations in her café with customers who have Underground connections."

"Give me a pistol." Stefan balled his fists. "I'll see she gets what she deserves."

Andrzej held up a hand. "That's the job of the Underground Government's Judicial Committee, not us. Trust me. She'll get what she deserves."

Lech glanced around the room. "Where's Magdalena? Did the Gestapo grab her too?"

Stefan grinned and clapped Krzysh on the back. "No, thanks to Krzysh. A German had his Luger pointed at Andrzej and Magdalena, but Krzysh grabbed the Kraut's pistol and shot him dead."

Gazing at Krzysh, Lech's eyes widened. "Wow. You're braver than you look, Piechowicz. Good job!"

Tadzio grimaced. Stefan didn't mention that he was the one who made the German drop his gun when he hit him over the head with a paint can. At least Stefan didn't tell Lech that Krzysh grabbed the gun because he froze. And Stefan also didn't say anything about him throwing up after Krzysh shot the man.

Andrzej glanced at Tadzio, then back at Lech. "To answer your question, Lech, you were the only one who got caught. Right now, Magdalena's taking the children out for a walk."

Just then, Magdalena burst into the room, ran over to Lech, and knelt in front of him. "Auntie M told me you were all in here." She gently fingered Lech's arm below his bandage. "Has a doctor looked at this? And your face. You should put some ice on it. I'll see what I can do." She quickly left.

Tadzio turned to Krzysh. "Well," he whispered. "I guess that relationship is back on."

The first Sunday in January, Tadzio joined Magdalena and Henio again for the tram ride to St. John's Cathedral. And once again, there in the fourth pew, sat Captain Hosenfeld.

After Mass, while trudging to the tram stop, Tadzio overheard the conversation of a couple walking in front of them.

"They say the Wehrmacht officer is a friend of the Cieciora family," the husband said to his wife. "Didn't you notice Pan Ciecioras sitting next to him?"

The wife, bundled up in her blue woolen coat, shook her head no. "But Pan Cieciora fought against the Germans when they first invaded Warsaw. Why would he be friends with one of them?"

Tadzio slowed his stride to keep pace behind the two.

The husband pressed his brown fur hat more firmly onto his head. "I heard the German officer got Pan Cieciora released from a prison camp just before the Ciecioras had their first baby. They have been friends with him ever since."

Tadzio glanced at Magdalena. "Hosenfeld." He spoke in hushed tones. "The officer who caught us painting *Avenge Wawer* in Wilson Square."

Magdalena raised her snow-flaked brows and nodded.

The following week, Tadzio was busier than ever at Żoliborz Hospital. Since their teachers had cancelled their secret classes for the holidays, he volunteered for extra shifts.

On Friday afternoon, Zoshka rushed into the hospital and called for Anna. Tadzio glanced up from across the room. He stopped stocking medicines into a cabinet and strained to hear their conversation. It sounded like a discussion about Scout business.

Tadzio picked his way between rows of patients to get closer.

Anna shook her head. "No. Magdalena is at the box office right now. Lech went to pick her up. But Tadzio's here. What happened?"

Zoshka arched a brow. "I have news about their mother, but I think we should wait and tell them at the same time."

A patient with a bandaged head reached out and grabbed Tadzio's arm. "Water. Please." The man's voice sounded weak and scratchy. "I've been calling out for over an hour."

Finding the man's tin drinking cup, Tadzio filled it from a nearby pitcher. He lifted the patient's head and pressed the cup to his dry, cracked lips.

The injured man slurped down the liquid.

Still cradling the patient's head, Tadzio's heart lurched when he gazed at his torso. The doctors had amputated one of his arms at the elbow.

The man followed Tadzio's gaze. "The Germans grabbed me in a round-up a few days ago," he said. "They took about two hundred of us away on trucks. I heard they were going to put us on a train headed for Germany, so when I saw a chance to jump, I did. Unfortunately, the truck behind us rolled over my arm. I escaped intact, except for my arm."

"You should try to rest." Tadzio laid the man's head on his pillow.

When Tadzio glanced again at Zoshka and Anna, they were moving toward the front door to greet Rudy and Alek, who had just entered. They all then moved to Anna's desk and sat.

A moment later, Lech and Magdalena rushed in.

"Lech told me you have news about my mother," Magdalena said. "What is it?"

Anna glanced up and met Tadzio's gaze. She waved him over.

Sitting on a metal chair across from Magdalena, he noticed his sister grasped Lech's hand in a death-like grip. *Yes. Those two are definitely back together.*

Zoshka rubbed a hand across his face and let his gaze meet Tadzio's, then glanced at Magdalena. "The Gestapo loaded 500 Pawiak prisoners onto trains early this morning and sent them to Ravensbrück. Your mother and Halina were among them. They've been labeled political prisoners, accused of working with the government-in-exile."

"No!" Magdalena clamped a hand over her mouth and sobbed as she buried her head in Lech's chest.

Gathering her in close, Lech nuzzled her glossy black locks. His eyes flooded with grief, but as he raised his head, Tadzio cringed at the anger that suddenly darkened his countenance.

Zoshka cleared his throat. "I'm sorry. There was nothing we could do."

A strange burning crept up Tadzio's legs. His mind flashed back to the afternoon they all sat around the kitchen table in their summerhouse with Professor Handelsman. The afternoon he swore the new Scout oath to safeguard the secrets of the organization, obey orders, and not hesitate to sacrifice his life.

Yes. When the time came, he'd willingly sacrifice his life.

CHAPTER 22

New Recruits

January–August 1941
Żoliborz District, Warsaw, Poland

A few weeks after receiving Zoshka's news about the Pawiak prisoner transfer, Andrzej moved the boys to a two-bedroom flat on Krasiński Street, a few blocks from Auntie L's house.

"We're stepping up our involvement with the Underground," Andrzej explained. "It's safer for Magdalena and the children if we're not all under the same roof."

While moving his things into the bedroom he would share with Krzysh and Benyameen, Tadzio confided to Krzysh, "I wonder if this is really about our increased Underground activities, or if Andrzej just doesn't want Lech and Magdalena living together in the same house? Personally, I think it's a good idea."

"At least Andrzej's keeping Lech busy," Krzysh said as he piled his few belongings on top of his bed. "Since Lech lost his job at the tannery because of his arm, I thought he'd be moping around the apartment all day. But his new job working for the Underground newspaper seems to keep him occupied."

Tadzio stopped placing his clothes in the armoire and turned to Krzysh. "I wonder if Andrzej could get me a job delivering the *Information Bulletin?*"

"You already have a job at the hospital and the new café. Now you want a third job?" Krzysh threw a pair of pants at Tadzio's head.

"Hey!" he said. "What was that for?"

"Those are your pants, not mine." His friend continued to sort through the small pile of clothes on his bed. "And besides, are you sure you're not just interested in a job with the Underground paper because Stefan's working there now? It's not a competition, you know. We also need to keep up with our studies."

Squeezing between Krzysh's bed and his, Tadzio folded the rest of his clothes and transferred each uneven stack into one of the wardrobe's drawers. He had enjoyed living with Henio and Magdalena at Auntie L's, but if moving out meant he'd be more involved in Underground activities, he was all for it. He had to admit, however, he would miss the women's cooking. Since the five boys all had different work schedules, they would now purchase and make their own meals. He might be losing weight in the next few months.

One night after working at the café, Tadzio brought home a copy of the *New Warsaw Courier*, the German propaganda newspaper. Someone had left it on a café table. Relieved to be off his feet, he sipped a cup of tea as he sat on their second-hand couch to scan the pages.

"Why are you looking at that garbage?" Lech said as he strode in from work. "I thought you didn't understand German. Even if you did, don't you know you can't trust anything it prints?"

Tadzio lowered the paper and scowled. "I've picked up a little of the language. And, yes, I know it's all propaganda, but it was free, so I took it."

"Well, here's the latest copy of the *Bulletin*." Lech tossed a copy onto Tadzio's lap. "You can believe what you read in there." He flopped down on the other old couch they'd squeezed into the small living area. "The *Bulletin* is in such demand that we've expanded distribution to include our end of town. If you still want a piece of the action, we could use more help delivering bundles to secret distribution locations."

Tadzio quirked a brow. "Really? Sign me up. When do I start?"

Eager for a newspaper that printed the truth, Warsaw's citizens snatched up copies of the Underground's *Information Bulletin* like fresh perogies. Tadzio appreciated Lech finding him a job transporting large quantities of the paper to secret transit spots. Twice, he eluded arrest by the Gestapo while making his bundled deliveries. As the weeks wore on, however, more reports came in of Scouts getting arrested for delivering the Underground's newspaper. Although concerned, it didn't stop him from making his rounds.

Near the end of January, Magdalena invited Tadzio and Krzysh over for dinner. They gratefully accepted.

After a tasty meal of mushroom perogies and cabbage rolls, Magdalena began to clear the table, but Auntie M held up a hand.

"Auntie L and I will take care of this," Auntie M said. "We know you have important business to discuss with Tadzio and Krzysh."

Tadzio's pulse quickened. "Important business? What's going on, Magda?"

Sitting across from Tadzio and Krzysh, Magdalena pressed her palms flat on the table. "You both know a few months ago Anna assigned me to lead a young group of Girl Guides, right?"

The boys nodded.

"This week, Lucyna and Józefina asked to join my troop since they're now eleven and thirteen."

Tadzio rubbed his jaw. "Why do I sense you have more news than just Józefina and Lucyna becoming Girl Guides?"

Pulling in a breath, his sister continued. "For the past week, the older girls in my troop have delivered copies of the *Information Bulletin* to residents on our block. The Underground asked us to expand our route to include the next two streets. Lucyna and Józefina want to deliver them too."

Krzysh shook his head. "Lucyna's too young."

"And so is Józefina." Tadzio balled his fists. "It's too dangerous. I won't allow it. Haven't you heard about the recent arrests?"

Magdalena arched a brow. "You won't allow it? Who put you in charge of everyone?"

Heat rose to Tadzio's chest. "Father did when he left. He said I had to be the man of the house. With Uncle Julek and Aunt Ewa gone, we're the only family Józefina has left. I forbid it."

Magdalena placed her hand on Tadzio's. "I understand. But you two can't protect the girls forever. They see what's going on. They want to join the fight. I think we should let them."

With a sigh, Krzysh leaned back and glanced at Tadzio. "Seems to me it's already decided."

Tadzio gave a reluctant nod.

On February 3, Tadzio took an early morning shift at the café. Having arrived at 6 AM, he breathed a sigh of relief when the wall clock's hands moved to 1 PM. As he grabbed his woolen coat from the rack near the entrance, Krzysh rushed in.

"Tadzio, I need to—"

Tadzio held up a hand. Krzysh looked as white as the snow blanketing the sidewalk. "Not here," he whispered. Shouldering his coat, he led his friend outside.

After the café's door jangled shut behind them, Krzysh blurted out his news. "Lucyna, Józefina, and two other girls from Magdalena's troop were just picked up near Wilson Square. They had just started their deliveries of the *Information Bulletin* when the Blue Police arrested them. Magdalena says Józefina had a satchel-full, but the other girls hadn't picked up their bundles yet. The police suspected the other girls also planned to deliver the *Bulletin,* so they took all of them to Gestapo Headquarters for interrogation."

Tadzio knees buckled.

Grabbing his elbow, Krzysh steadied his friend and glanced around. "Do you think Józefina will admit that Lucyna and the others were also *Bulletin* messengers?"

"Let's hope not." Tadzio's voice came out in a hoarse whisper. He imagined his face had now turned as white as Krzysh's.

Ten days after the girls' arrest, Auntie M received a message from one of her Underground contacts. All the Scouts assembled in Auntie L's parlor to hear the news.

"One of the Pawiak guards works for the Underground," Auntie M said. "He told me Józefina broke under Gestapo interrogation. She told the Gestapo that all the girls were *Bulletin* messengers. They're now being held at Pawiak prison in a large cell for minors."

A shudder ran through Tadzio.

Magdalena wailed. "How can the Germans torture little girls? It's evil. Pure evil!" She buried her head in Lech's shoulder and sobbed as they sat together on the magenta couch.

Lech wrapped his arm around her shoulder.

"My girls! my girls!" Magdalena moaned. "It should have been me, not them."

Tadzio glanced sideways at Krzysh who sat next to him on the floor. His friend had buried his face in his hands.

"Oh, Lucyna," Krzysh's muffled voice cried out.

Tadzio's stomach rose to his throat.

Auntie M pulled out a handkerchief, dabbed her eyes, and continued. "Later, my contact said he overheard the girls talking while they peeled potatoes in the kitchen with other female prisoners." She paused to blow her nose. "Józefina told the girls she broke under the Gestapo's interrogation, but that she would change her confession. She promised she would tell the Gestapo she only implicated them to make the torture stop. She promised the girls she'd say she was the only one delivering the illegal publication."

Even though his throat constricted with emotion, Tadzio pushed out his questions. "Magda, did you say Józefina was the only one actually carrying copies of the *Bulletin* when they were arrested? Lucyna and the others hadn't picked up their bundles yet, right?"

Magdalena glanced at him with red eyes and nodded.

He drew his brows together. "If Józefina takes back her confession and says the other girls weren't distributing the *Bulletin*, maybe the Gestapo will let the others go."

Auntie M nodded. "We'll just have to pray and not give up hope."

Krzysh continually asked Auntie M if she'd heard any more news about Lucyna and the other girls in prison, but a month passed without any word.

On March 20, as soon as Tadzio got home from his secret history class, he snatched up the latest issue of the *Information Bulletin*. He read that the Germans had closed all the gates to the Jewish Ghetto. Streetcars that had previously traveled through the middle of the Ghetto were now rerouted outside its perimeter. Over dinner, he discussed with the others what this new isolation of the Jews meant. No one had any ideas.

German brutality escalated throughout the spring of 1941. Street arrests, public executions of civilians for trivial reasons, and even public hangings occurred daily. On Saturday, May 3, Andrzej arrived at the boys' apartment just before curfew.

"Where've you been, Andrzej?" Lech asked. "We haven't seen you for weeks. Got any missions for us?"

Andrzej plopped down on one of the threadbare couches and raked a hand through his usually well-combed hair. "I just met with the Underground leaders. We listened to a speech given by England's Prime Minister, Winston Churchill." Andrzej withdrew a crumpled paper from his shirt's pocket. "From the tone of Churchill's message, it sounds like the Allies might soon come to our aid." He unfolded the note and read it aloud.

Every day, Hitler's firing squads are busy in a dozen lands. Monday, he shoots Dutchmen; Tuesday, Norwegians. On Wednesday, the French and Belgians stand against the wall. Thursday is the day the Czechs must suffer. And now there are the Serbs and the Croats to fill his repulsive bill of executions. But, always, on all the days, there are the Poles.

"So, the Germans brutalize us even more than they do the other Europeans." Lech shook his head.

"Not that it's much comfort." Tadzio shook his head. "But at least we know the Allies are aware of our situation. Maybe now they'll offer us more than just words of pity and actually do something."

Throughout the month of June, Tadzio noticed that Lech and Magdalena spent almost every spare moment together. Lech had turned twenty in May, and Magdalena had turned eighteen in June. Tadzio had wondered if Lech would propose to her on her birthday, but the day came and went with no proposal. He was actually relieved. Although Lech threw himself into any underground work that came his way, Tadzio had reservations about him. He believed Andrzej and Rudy felt the same way.

Tadzio frequently heard Andrzej and Rudy advise Lech not to get romantically involved with Magdalena. Lech simply accused Andrzej of jealousy.

On a warm night in July, after Tadzio came home from working at the café, Lech and Andrzej argued outside the apartment.

"You're just mad because she chose the better man," Lech said.

A few weeks later when Rudy visited, Lech and Rudy argued in the boys' kitchen.

"You can't tell me what to do." Lech shoved Rudy against the wall.

Rudy narrowed his gaze and raised his chin. "I'm just saying that soldiers can't divide their affections between a love-life and their training. Both will suffer."

Lech stepped back. "Just because you and Andrzej hold ranks in the Underground Army doesn't mean you can tell me what to do in my personal life." Lech turned and stomped out the door.

In late July, Auntie M and Auntie L invited the boys over for dinner. After everyone sat, Auntie M said, "I have some bittersweet news."

All eyes turned to the elderly woman.

"Since the Germans have now declared war on the Soviet Union, we've been told the Gestapo will release less important prisoners. Our contact inside Pawiak Prison reported that when the Gestapo brought Józefina in for further questioning, she told them she only claimed the other girls were delivering papers so the torture would stop. Her interrogator asked if she realized that by admitting she lied, she would have a more severe punishment. Józefina reportedly said, 'I know, but I couldn't live knowing I accused innocent people.' As a result, they sentenced her to Ravensbrück. The Gestapo will free the rest of the girls by the end of the week."

Tadzio's breath caught in his throat. Ever since leaving the manor house in the fall of 1939, a heavy weight had pressed down on him. He wasn't sure he could take much more.

He recalled a moment before the war, during the spring of 1938, when he had helped Father change a tire on the family's green Opel. The memory vividly replayed in his mind of when the car jack wasn't working properly. He and Uncle Julek grasped the car's front bumper and lifted it whileFather slipped the wheel into place. The car didn't seem heavy when both he and his uncle lifted it, but, when Uncle Julek lost his grip, Tadzio was left holding it by himself. Searing pain shot through his shoulders and forced him to let go.

He felt the same way now. First, his aunt and uncle died. Then they received news of Krzysh's parents' deaths. Józefina would soon join his mother and Halina in Ravensbrück. Would they all end up in a German concentration camp? Or worse?

Later that evening, Tadzio told Andrzej, "I'm going to snap if I can't do more to fight the Germans."

"You've got to be patient," Andrzej said in a low tone. "I *can* tell you the Home Army and Underground Government have plans for an uprising against the Germans in the near future, but we have to wait for the right time. If we stage the uprising too soon, it might fail."

Andrzej's news did little to cheer him. He wasn't sure how much longer he could hold on before he took matters into his own hands.

CHAPTER 23

Training Exercises

September 1941–January 1942
Żoliborz District, Warsaw, Poland

Throughout the fall of 1941, Tadzio maintained a busy schedule. He delivered bundles of the Underground's newspapers before dawn. After that, he attended secret high school classes. Most afternoons and evenings he worked at the café or Żoliborz Hospital. He made time, however, for any radio transmission assignments Andrzej gave him and Magdalena. His Scout work always came first.

In mid-October, Magdalena invited him over for dinner to help Krzysh's sister, Lucyna, with her history homework. As usual, Lech and Andrzej were at his flat, fighting about Lech's relationship with Magdalena. Glad he'd already finished his homework, Tadzio readily agreed.

"Tadzio's always been good in history," Magdalena told Lucyna as they ate together in Auntie L's kitchen. "I could never keep all those dates straight."

Tadzio swallowed his spoonful of soup, then winked at Auntie L and Auntie M. "The only dates Magdalena could ever keep straight were those she had on Friday and Saturday nights, and what boy was coming which day."

Henio grinned. "Now she doesn't even have to worry about that because she only dates Lech. Are you going to marry him soon, Magda?"

Tadzio chuckled. At seven, Henio still had his childhood charm.

"Yacov punched Henio's arm. You're not supposed to ask questions like that."

A twinge of guilt gripped Tadzio's heart. He'd spent little time with his brother since moving in with the Scouts on Krasiński Street. Yacov, now nine, acted more like Henio's older brother than he did.

Magdalena cleared the table and washed dishes, while Tadzio and Lucyna reviewed her schoolwork.

"What's the assignment you're having trouble with?" Tadzio asked.

Krzysh's twelve-year-old sister spoke in a soft voice. "At school, we're not allowed to learn Polish history. We can only study German and math." She leaned toward Tadzio and almost whispered. "After school, instead of going home, we take different routes to my teacher's house. After we arrive, she teaches us Polish history. I'm supposed to write a paper about the war heroes Kościuszko and Kiliński." Lucyna pressed her lips together. "I know nothing about either one." She sat back in her chair. "Krzysh said you're much better at history than he is. Can you help me?"

Tadzio smiled. "I'd love to. Did you know there's a statue of Jan Kiliński only about three kilometers from here? Maybe Krzysh and I can take you there next Saturday."

"I'd like that." A faint smile flitted across her face, then faded.

Tadzio's insides pricked. With their busy schedules, neither he nor Krzysh had spent much time with their siblings.

Auntie L strode into the kitchen with an armload of books. "My husband had a few history volumes on a parlor shelf. I hid them when the Germans closed all the libraries last year. Maybe you'll find something helpful in them."

The lines in Auntie L's face had deepened since the Germans rounded up her husband and sons three months ago. "Thanks Auntie L." Tadzio offered her a weak smile as she set the books on the table. "These will be a great help."

As Tadzio opened a thick, leatherbound book, a hint of vanilla tickled his nose. *Ahh. The scent of learning.* He inhaled the fragrance, then flipped through the pages until he found Kościuszko's portrait. "Let's start with him." He positioned the hardback so Lucyna could see the war hero's picture. "Kościuszko was a Polish nobleman who believed in equality for all Poles. In 1791, he was friends with many who created Poland's first constitution. It was the first of its kind in Europe."

"Wow." Lucyna flipped a blonde braid behind her shoulder. "I didn't know we had the first constitution in Europe." She withdrew a pencil and paper from her book bag and jotted down notes.

A stack of soup bowls clattered as Magdalena placed them in the oak hutch behind the kitchen table. "Yes." Magdalena turned to Lucyna. "The first constitution in Europe. After America, we were the second country in the world to govern our sovereign lands with such a document. However, unlike America, our constitution didn't last long."

Tadzio scowled at his sister.

"Is that true, Tadzio?" Lucyna pulled her brows together.

"It's sad, but true. It only lasted nineteen months." Tadzio clenched his jaw. "It didn't last because our new system of laws limited the Polish nobility's power. Rather than live under a government that gave peasants a measure of equality, the greedy nobles paved the way for Russia to invade Poland. We weren't an independent nation again until 1918."

Lucyna's eyes widened. "Why would the nobles do that?"

"They wanted power over the peasants, even if it meant Russia was in charge," Tadzio said.

"That's awful." Lucyna scrunched her nose

Tadzio nodded. "Kościuszko thought so too. In 1794, he led an uprising to overthrow Russia. The enemy outnumbered him three to one, but that didn't deter him."

Magdalena, drying a cup, approached their table. "At least that's better odds than we have against the Germans."

Tadzio glared at her. Why was she trying to discourage Lucyna?

He read a few more paragraphs, then summarized the information. "Before the 1794 uprising against Russia, Kościuszko went to America. In 1776, he fought alongside American colonists during their War of Independence." He glanced back at Magdalena and smirked. "And the British outnumbered the Americans by *more* than three to one."

Lucyna smiled. "The Americans won that war, didn't they?"

Tadzio nodded.

"I think it takes more than soldiers to win a war." Lucyna brightened.

Tadzio grinned. "You're pretty smart. Are you sure you're Krzysh's sister?"

"I won't tell him you said that." Lucyna chuckled. She then leaned back and sighed. As if deep in thought, she tapped her pencil against her lips. "The Germans may outnumber us, but I think it takes more than soldiers to win a war. Things like hope, bravery, and believing in something that's worth dying for."

"I agree." Tadzio's eyes burned. He considered the courage Lucyna had already displayed—volunteering to deliver the Underground newspapers; her arrest, her imprisonment. And she was only twelve.

He opened another book and paged through it. Once again, he inhaled its sweet, pungent odor. His mood lifted. "Here's a picture of Jan Kiliński. He was a shoemaker, not a soldier, but during the Kościuszko Uprising he led a group of peasants to overtake the Russian ambassador's home in Warsaw. Although wounded twice, Kiliński survived the uprising. That's why we have a statue of him in Krasiński Square. He embodies our Polish virtues of bravery and patriotism."

The sound of running water meant Magdalena was back at the sink. "Tadzio," she called out above splashes, "don't forget to mention that the Kościuszko Uprising failed. Russia took over most of Poland for the next 126 years. Poland, as a nation, no longer existed between those years."

Tadzio harumphed. "Magdalena, I thought *I* was the one giving the history lessons."

Lucyna jotted down a few more notes, then gazed up at Tadzio. "So, Kościuszko's uprising failed?"

"Yes."

"And the cadets' 1830 rebellion against Russia failed?"

He winced against a razor of pain. His history lesson wasn't going as well as he'd hoped. "Yes."

Lucyna glanced down at her paper. "But, in 1791, we *did* create the world's second constitution. And even though we weren't an independent nation again until 1919, we eventually *did* win back our freedom."

Tadzio's flagging spirits stirred as Lucyna's blue eyes brightened.

Magdalena came over and sat. "Yes, but that freedom only lasted twenty years. Like Kościuszko and the cadets, we've lost it once again. This time, to the Germans."

He refused to let Magdalena's despondency dash his hopes. He snapped the enormous book shut and pulled in a lungful of air. "You're right, Magdalena. But now the Germans must deal with us."

By the time Tadzio returned to his apartment, Andrzej had left. He didn't see him again until late October.

"I have an announcement," Andrzej said as he unexpectantly arrived.

The five boys squeezed around the apartment's kitchen table. Tadzio's nerves jangled as he tried to read their Scout leader's face. He wasn't sure he could handle any more bad news.

Andrzej's forehead furrowed as he glanced at those around him. "I know you've all felt frustrated the past few months. You've heard rumors of Gray Ranks operations. It's true. Some Scouts have bombed German supply trains and raided arms depots."

Murmurs went up around the table.

Andrzej held up a hand. "I've participated in some of these activities but haven't invited any of you to join the operations. So, despite my warnings, some of you have taken it upon yourselves to burn German posters, steal German signs, and throw vomit bombs into German theaters and restaurants." Andrzej shot Lech and Stefan a wry smile. "However, you'll be glad to know, the Underground Army has now increased their training efforts to prepare for an uprising—to get ready for open fighting."

As if a taut band had loosened across his chest, Tadzio inhaled a full breath of air. *Finally. Plans to strike back against the Germans.*

Andrzej continued. "You've seen little of me this month because I've been training with the Underground Army. I'm proud to announce that I now hold the rank of Lance-Corporal."

Tadzio let his jaw drop.

Rising to his feet, Benyameen saluted.

"Did they give you a group of soldiers to command?" Lech asked.

Andrzej pressed his lips into a flat line and nodded. "They told me to find five good recruits. I said I knew just the men." A smile creased his face. "I'm looking at them right now."

Tadzio's skin prickled with pride. He wished Father could see him now—at fifteen, a member of Poland's Underground Army.

On the morning of November 27, Tadzio and the boys filled their backpacks with equipment and walked three-quarters of a kilometer to the Warsaw-Gdańsk Railway Station. They hid beneath the arched train bridge near the stationhouse and waited for Andrzej's signal.

Tadzio breathed warm air into his mittened hands. "At least last night's snow flurries have stopped," he whispered to Krzysh.

A long train pulled into the station and stopped. Steam hissed out from beneath its engine as a red-capped stationmaster and a few white-clad German nurses milled about the station's platform.

Andrzej whispered to Tadzio, "That train's loaded with wounded German soldiers returning from the Russian Front. They're being taken to hospitals in Germany."

Eventually a red flag went up, a whistle blew, and the train moved on.

Fifteen minutes later, Andrzej motioned and they boarded the train headed for Choszczówka.

After traveling nineteen kilometers to a wooded area, the group disembarked. Andrzej led them in marching drills. He taught them how to scout the terrain to determine movement and maneuver conditions. They practiced attack and storm techniques. Through the trees, they occasionally glimpsed other groups conducting similar exercises.

By dusk, Andrzej led them back to the train station.

Tadzio barely noticed the train's stops on the return trip. He couldn't remember the last time he felt so bone-weary.

January 1942

January of the New Year brought a fresh flurry of German demands.

After working all afternoon at the café, Tadzio sneered as he read their newest order posted in Wilson Square.

All skis and ski boots must be handed over for
German soldiers fighting in Russia.

When he reached their flat, he flopped down on the threadbare couch and read the latest issue of the *New Warsaw Courier* he'd brought home from work. He scoffed at the German's justification for their latest law.

> At this moment, our German soldiers need skis for their bloody battles with the Red Army, the tool of world Communist Jewry. Your cooperation in supplying the needed skis and ski boots will enable the soldiers to put an end to this threat once and for all.

The next day, Tadzio attended his underground high school literature class at Professor Lewandowski's house. The professor sat in his living room, wrapped in a brown woolen coat, a gray scarf, and woolen mittens that revealed his fingertips.

"I'm sorry, Tadzio," the professor said as Tadzio entered. "I depleted my coal ration this month, so I have no heat."

Tadzio shuddered, envisioning an afternoon in the professor's cold house. Like the professor and the five students sitting around him, he too left his coat on.

"I will conduct today's lesson while you do some physical work to help you keep warm." A corner of Professor Lewandowski's mouth turned up. "Please follow me into the kitchen."

Five pairs of varnished skis, three saws, and a pile of bricks lay on the floor. "Form three teams of two please," the professor said, pointing to the supplies.

Tadzio arched a brow.

The professor chuckled. "No sense in giving skis to the Germans that we can use to warm our homes. While you cut, I will teach."

Tadzio glanced at Jolanta Dylewska, a girl he'd known from music class before the war. "If you hold a ski, I'll cut."

Jolanta inclined her head. "But what are the bricks for?"

Tadzio piled three blocks upon one another, then laid a ski on the mound. "You grasp the ski while I cut."

"I see." Jolanta grinned and grasped the long flat runner.

The other students followed suit.

"Today," the professor raised his voice above the din of saws, "we will discuss a Polish poem by Count Zygmunt Krasiński. Krasiński wrote this poem after the cadets' failed rebellion against the Russian Czar in 1830. As I read the poem, see if you recognize the origins of the various metaphors Krasiński employs. Also, look for parallels between the poem's original historical context and our present political situation."

Tadzio cared little for poetry. However, listening to the professor recite Krasiński's poem while he cut up skis—ones now useless to German soldiers, but very useful for warming the professor's home—definitely piqued his interest.

"Oh, and by the way." The professor glanced at Tadzio. "Are any of you familiar with Chopin's Opus 74, Number 9, also known as *The Melodia?*"

Surprised by the professor's Chopin reference, Tadzio stopped sawing. "*The Melodia?* Yes, sir. I'm familiar with it, but I've never played it."

The professor raised his index finger. "Perhaps that's because *The Melodia* is not a solo piano piece. It's a piano accompaniment to a melody Chopin wrote for a vocalist. The words Chopin intended the vocalist to sing are from this Krasiński poem."

Tadzio now gave the professor his full attention.

Clearing his throat, Professor Lewandowski held up his book to read the poem, but Jolanta raised her hand.

"Excuse me professor, but last year I sang *The Melodia* for one of my music exams. Would you mind if I sing it in the background while you read?"

"Not at all, my dear." The professor smiled. "We would be honored."

Tadzio glanced around the room. He knew many of the students from previous grades. Most had shown little interest in music or poetry. Now, however, they all leaned forward to hear the professor read as Jolanta softly sang.

Under their crosses' cruel weight they stand
  To see from the mountain top, the Promised Land.
Their eyes shine with transcendent light
  To see their people descending.
They see the regions they will never enter,
  The horn of plenty they will never taste!
And here their bones will lie unremembered,
  Perhaps forever.

Tadzio considered the poem and the melody. Would he soon share the fate of the 1794 war heroes? Like his grandfather's great-uncle and those who fought in the cadet's rebellion of 1830, would foreign powers also crush him under their tyrannical heel?

He shivered, but not from the cold. Like Krasiński, would he never see a free Poland again? Would his bones—perhaps soon— lie somewhere, unremembered?

CHAPTER 24

The Kotwica, an Anchor of Hope

February–April 1942
Żoliborz District, Warsaw, Poland

Auntie M's Napoleon-styled mantel clock chimed three times. Energy surged through Magdalena, proud she'd been able to stay up three hours past midnight. As she and Lech had previously arranged, she unlocked the front door. A minute later, Lech, shivering from the February cold, entered.

She motioned him in, then sat cross-legged in front of the parlor's fireplace.

Lech removed his coat and gloves, then sat beside her on the blue- and rose-colored Aubusson rug. He rested his palms on his knees and flashed her a Cheshire grin.

"What are you smiling about, mister?" She grasped his icy fingers. "Brrr," she shuddered and rubbed his hands between hers. "Can you tell me now why you're here so late?"

He grabbed her hands and kissed them. "First, have I told you lately how much I love you?"

Her face grew hot, and not from the meager fire in front of them. "A few times, but I always like to hear it again."

He leaned forward and kissed her.

Despite the cold, warmth flooded her body.

He returned his hands to his knees. "Alek asked me to help him with something today—well, technically, last night." He raked a hand through his thick, black hair. "Remember how the Germans defaced the Copernicus plaque when they first occupied Warsaw?"

"Yes." She nodded as she studied his face. The fire's smoldering embers reflected in the gold flecks of his hazel eyes. She forced herself to focus on his words. "Tadzio told me the Germans hammered out the statue's Polish sign, 'To Nicolaus Copernicus from a Grateful Nation,' and installed a new plaque that read, 'To Nicolaus Copernicus from the German Nation.'"

Lech rocked back and forth. It reminded her of when Henio couldn't wait to pour out a story. She crossed her arms as if his pause annoyed her. In reality, a new chill ran through her. What had Lech and Alek done?

"Tonight, Alek and I stole the German plaque." Lech slapped a hand on his knee.

"Shh." Magdalena put a finger to her lips. "Not so loud. You'll wake the entire household." She shivered as she bumped his knee with her fist. "If the Germans find out you had something to do with taking down their sign, they'll hang you in public for sure. What were you thinking?"

A corner of his mouth turned up. "I was thinking I'd make you proud. When Warsaw wakes up today and sees the German plaque missing, it'll raise their hopes. Show them someone's willing to push back."

Uncomfortable with the risks he took, Magdalena shook her head and shifted her gaze to the cooling fireplace. "I suppose that's true. We need a lot of encouragement right now." She paused, then turned back toward him. "Lech Lutowski, I'm not sure if I should be proud or mad at you."

He grasped her shoulders. "I don't care if you're proud or mad, as long as you give me another kiss." He pressed his lips to hers.

Warm, deep, inviting. Her body tingled. She kissed him back—longer and harder than she'd ever done before. Moving as if in a trance, she wrapped her arms around him. Finally, unable to breathe, she pushed him back and pulled in a full breath. "I—I'm working a long shift at the theater today and tomorrow. After that, however, I'd love to see your handiwork on the Copernicus statue."

He grinned his full-toothed grin. "How about Saturday?"

"I'll pack a picnic lunch." She squeezed his knee.

He inclined his head. "A picnic in February?"

"Sure." She widened her eyes. "Bring a blanket to keep us warm. Of course, because of food rationing, it'll be a small lunch. And we'll have to eat quickly so we don't freeze. But it will still be fun. I know just the place. It's a short walk from the statue."

The following Saturday, despite food shortages and the February chill, Magdalena packed a lunch for their stroll to Staszic Square to see the Copernicus statue. When they arrived, they found the square full of people. Most of the visitors stood in a semi-circle around Copernicus, commenting on the missing plaque.

"Would you look at that?" said a stooped woman standing next to Magdalena. "Who'd be brave enough to steal the German placard?" The woman placed a hand over her chest. "It encourages this old heart of mine."

An elderly man standing behind the woman spoke up. "This looks like the work of the Underground." He gathered his gray scarf more tightly around his neck and lowered his head. "And I hear many young people have volunteered to stage an uprising soon."

Magdalena grasped Lech's arm. He'd told her about his training exercises in the woods to prepare for Warsaw's Rising.

Lech flashed her a knowing grin then kissed her cheek.

A middle-aged man wearing wire-rimmed glasses and a black knitted cap joined the discussion. "We Poles have always been proud of our heroes. Our history. Our heritage. When I first saw that evil German sign on Copernicus' monument, I felt as though someone had punched me in the stomach."

The older gentleman shook his head. "So did I. The audacity of the Germans to pretend that Copernicus was a German and not a Pole. It restores my hope in Poland's future to see that someone had the fortitude to remove that accursed sign."

The twinge of anger Magdalena had felt over Lech's risky behavior now melted into pride. She stood on her toes and pecked his cheek. "Before lunch," she asked, "could you take me to see the Kiliński statue?"

Lech's thick dark brows pulled together. "Okay. But are you sure you want to walk that far? It's about twelve blocks from here. Why do you want to see that statue?"

A chilly wind blew through the square. Magdalena secured her woolen scarf more firmly around her ears. "A few months ago, Tadzio helped Lucyna write a report on Jan Kiliński, and Tadeusz Kościuszko. I knew little about them, but his information piqued my interest."

Lech wrapped an arm around her shoulder and kissed the top of her head. "I don't care much for history, but sure. Anything for my girl."

When they neared the Kiliński site, a crowd blocked her view of the statue. As she drew closer, Magdalena's heart lurched. The crowd no longer blocked her view. The statue was gone.

A young boy gazed up at his father. "Poppa? How can a big bronze statue like that disappear?"

"I don't know, son."

"Here comes Mayor Kulski," someone in the crowd shouted.

As heads turned, several people spoke at once.

"Maybe the mayor knows what happened."

"Let's ask him."

"He's a good man."

"I wouldn't want to be him right now."

The crowd parted as the Polish mayor of Warsaw stepped forward to speak. "Citizens of Warsaw." The mayor held up his hands to quiet the crowd. "Early this morning, German Governor Fischer ordered the removal of our Kiliński statue. He said it was in retaliation for what he called a *hooligan's prank*. A few days ago, someone stole the German plaque from the Copernicus monument." The mayor wagged his head. "I was powerless to stop its confiscation."

Magdalena studied the people surrounding the mayor. Some in the crowd raised their arms and cheered, grateful someone stood up to the Germans. Others, perhaps mourning the loss of the statue, remained quiet and lowered their heads. Many, like deflated balloons, stood with slumped shoulders.

If the people only knew what was going on behind the scenes. How Lech, Alek, and other Scouts were risking their lives to buoy their spirits. She wished she could cheer them on with the zeal that now swelled her heart—the expectation of a strong Poland in the near future.

The mayor continued. "Governor Fischer has not yet informed me of the statue's whereabouts, or whether he plans to return it. For now, we'll have to keep the memory of Warsaw's heroes alive in our hearts. As soon as I learn more, I will let you know."

With that, the mayor left.

"So, where will we eat lunch?" Lech asked as the crowd dispersed. "Here?"

Magdalena furrowed her forehead. "Aren't you upset about the missing Kiliński statue?"

Lech shrugged his shoulders. "At least I know the Germans took us seriously when we stole their plaque. Many of the people here were proud someone finally stood up to them."

Lech was right. She shouldn't let the missing statue dampen her spirits. She swung their clasped hands between them and led Lech toward their picnic's destination. "I'll tell you where we're going for lunch if you'll let me share what I learned from Tadzio about Kiliński."

Rolling his eyes, Lech readjusted the picnic basket's shoulder strap. "I thought you didn't like history. But if it gets me lunch faster, I'll listen."

Magdalena led Lech toward Krasiński Square. "I didn't care much for history until a few months ago," she began. "Tadzio came over last October to help Lucyna with a report about Warsaw's 1794 war heroes."

"Tadzio sure loves books," Lech said.

Magdalena nodded. "I never appreciated his enthusiasm for learning, but his talk with Lucyna affected me. For example, I never understood why Kiliński meant so much to the people of Warsaw. I'd heard he was a shoemaker and city councilman, but I didn't know he was a strong supporter of our 1791 Constitution and a leader in Kościuszko's 1794 Uprising."

A cloud passed overhead as they crossed another street. "Kind of like me," Lech said when they reached the other side. "Rudy thinks I'll never amount to anything. He only sees me as a common worker. But, like Kiliński, I can aspire to greatness. I'd make a great leader if Rudy, Morro, or Zoshka would give me half a chance."

"Yes, you could." Magdalena stopped in the middle of the sidewalk and gazed up at him. "I think you can accomplish anything you put your mind to." She stood on tiptoe and pecked his cheek. "And I'd be proud to be by your side as you do it."

Sliding the picnic basket's strap off his shoulder, Lech set it on the ground. He pulled her close and kissed her as if he'd never let go.

"Excuse me." A scratchy, low voice came up behind them. "You two are blocking the sidewalk."

Lech released Magdalena and chuckled. "I'm sorry, sir. Young love."

Embarrassment flamed Magdalena's cheeks.

The elderly man smiled and saluted them with his cane. "I was like that once. Ahh, to be young and in love again. God bless you both."

"Thank you, sir," Lech said. "Same to you." He raised the basket's strap to his shoulder and turned to Magdalena. "Now, where were we?"

Magdalena flashed him a wry smile. "You mean the kiss, or our talk about Poland's heroes?"

"The kiss, of course."

She playfully swatted his arm. "We need to keep walking."

A mock pout lined his face. "If you insist."

"Seriously, Lech," Magdalena said as they continued down the sidewalk. "Did you know that, after we created our Constitution, the nobles opposed it? They believed it gave the peasants too much power. They encouraged Russia to invade us, thinking it would return some of the power they'd lost under our new laws."

Lech nodded. "I did know that. But we won back our freedom in 1919."

They reached a corner and waited for traffic to pass.

"Yes, we did," Magdalena said. "But with Germany's invasion, that freedom only lasted twenty years."

Lech waggled his brows. "Like yours, if you stray too far from me." He grasped her gloved hand and grinned.

She tugged on his arm. "Ha, ha. Hilarious."

After crossing the intersection, Magdalena stopped to readjust her scarf. "I think I'm beginning to understand why everyone's so willing to give up everything in our fight against the Germans."

"I'd be willing to give up everything," Lech said. "Except you."

Magdalena frowned. Her heart picked up speed. "Do you really mean that?" She held him with a stare. "If you had to choose between me or a free Poland, would you really choose me? Even if it meant living under German or Russian rule?"

Lech's jaw stiffened. "Every time. Given the choice, I'd always choose you."

A chill ran through her. She shivered, unsure if that was the answer she wanted to hear.

A few weeks later, Lech visited Magdalena at the theater booth. "Alek discovered where the Germans hid Kiliński's statute. They stashed it in the National Museum's basement."

Magdalena slipped a hand through her booth's narrow opening. Lech grasped it.

A fearful dread slid down her throat. "Please tell me you won't do anything crazy."

Lech glanced around, then kept his voice low. "There's no way we can get the statue out of the museum, but Alek and I plan to graffiti the building. We'll write, 'People of Warsaw—I am here. Jan Kiliński.' What do you think?" Lech grinned.

After making sure no customers were near, Magdalena grabbed Lech's wrist. "I think it's dangerous, but I know it will inspire people. You and Alek make quite a team."

Lech scrunched his eyebrows. "Yeah, but we have to be careful that Zoshka, Rudy, and Morro don't find out until after we pull it off. They don't want us taking unnecessary risks. They only want us drilling for an eventual uprising. But what if that day never comes? I can't just sit around doing nothing."

She rubbed Lech's hand, hoping to soothe away the anger that brewed behind his eyes. It frightened her. One minute he'd laugh hysterically. The next moment, he'd smash his fist into a wall.

Lech's forehead furrowed. "To make matters worse, Rudy and Morro keep saying I shouldn't be involved with you." He smacked his palm against the booth's counter.

Magdalena jumped.

"They say it's a distraction. I just think they're jealous."

Magdalena traced a gentle pattern across the top of his hand.

The fire in his eyes simmered. He pulled in a breath. "You'll never guess what Alek and I are going to do after we paint the graffiti."

Bracing herself, Magdalena widened her eyes. "What?"

"After we announce the statue's location, we'll put a new plaque on the Copernicus monument. It's going to read, 'For removal of the Kiliński statue, I am extending winter by two months. Signed, Copernicus.'" Lech leaned back and laughed.

Magdalena shook her head. She couldn't help but chuckle along with him, but she also couldn't push away the trepidation that tickled her spine.

After Lech and Alek's museum graffiti and plaque replacement, the Germans cut back Warsaw's food rations even more. Some people complained, but many said those minor acts of rebellion were worth the price.

During the months of March and April, Magdalena accompanied Auntie M and Auntie L on bi-weekly train trips to the countryside to purchase black-market potatoes, cabbage, and sugar. Today, as they returned to Warsaw, she stared out the window in search of any policemen patrolling the station platform. She rehearsed the scene in her mind. If she saw any, she'd toss the food hidden beneath her clothes out the window.

As the train whooshed to a stop, Auntie M patted Magdalena's arm. "Relax, dear. God will see us through."

Magdalena's lower lip trembled. She let out a whimper. "How can you be so sure, Auntie M?"

The gray-haired woman paused for a moment. "We know God is love. He's also merciful and just. His character never changes. Of that we can be sure, even in the worst of times."

Magdalena's throat thickened. She inhaled a deep breath to push out her next words. "Then why has God allowed the Germans to starve us? And to slaughter innocent people right in front of our eyes?"

"Evil men make evil choices." Auntie M *tsked*. "But that doesn't change who God is. You know that Auntie L and I read a portion of Scripture together every morning, right?"

Magdalena nodded. She'd seen this on the occasional mornings when she got up early. As a Catholic, she wasn't encouraged to read the Bible for herself. However, these women honored opportunities to read Scripture as if it was a form of Communion.

Auntie M leaned her head closer. "This morning we read a passage from the book of Hebrews. It reminded me that God's character is unchangeable. In the end, evil men's actions will never thwart God."

"That's right." Auntie L added. "Ultimately, our hope lies in the fact that God's nature of love, mercy, and justice never changes, regardless of what's going on around us. The passage Auntie M and I read said, 'We have this hope as an anchor for the soul, firm and secure.'"

Magdalena considered the women's words. A hope as firm and secure as an anchor. Like the symbol now graffitied throughout Poland—the *kotwica*. Yes, that's what she needed right now. An anchor for her soul. An anchor of hope. Hope that, despite the evil times, Poland and her faith in God's unchanging character, would emerge triumphant.

CHAPTER 25

A Letter and a Betrayal

Warsaw Sporting Complex
September 13, 1942

Captain Hosenfeld checked his pocket watch. Only one more hour before his shift ended at the Warsaw Sports Complex. With all the events staffed and scheduled for the rest of the month, he used the extra hour to write a letter home to his wife.

My Dearest Annemarie,

How I miss you. On some days, I wish you were here with me. Last evening, I attended a performance of the Strauss operetta, Die Fledermaus. I longed to have you on my arm as I spied other German officers and citizens with their wives. We were all dressed in our finest as we attempted to escape the reality of this offensive war, if just for a few hours.

Then again, I am so glad you are not here to witness the tragedies I see on a daily basis. The SS often take people away and shoot them for no reason.

Last month, a Polish shopkeeper who sells me fruits and vegetables told me about his wife who visited a friend in the maternity ward of the Jewish Ghetto. This woman saw the Gestapo come and take away all the babies, throw them in a sack, and toss them into a hearse. She said the wails of the infants and mothers tore at her heart. Especially as those Gestapo animals laughed while carrying out the despicable deed.

Several weeks ago, I had dinner with Gerhard Stabenow, head of Warsaw's Security Services. In order to distance himself from the

SS's mass murder of human beings, he dehumanized the poor Jewish victims by labelling them as "ants" and "vermin." When he talked about the deportation and gassing of Jews in places like Auschwitz and Treblinka, he simply labelled the acts as "resettlement."

Until last week, I found it difficult to believe some of the atrocities rumoured to take place at those concentration camps. A Special Commando Unit officer who attended a fencing tournament I organized recently confirmed the stories. This officer was so upset, he completely forgot we were in a large company of people, including a top Gestapo man. The Commando officer told me that, while in the town of Sielce this past July, his unit was ordered to drive thousands of Jews out of their ghetto and march them to the nearby railway station.

He said the train didn't come for three days, so the Jews had to wait out in the summer heat without food or water. When the train finally came to transport the Jews to the concentration camp, he and his men had to cram two hundred of them into cattle cars that were only large enough for forty-two people.

I confess, I am quite anxious about what the future holds for us. I cannot understand how we have been able to commit such crimes against defenseless people.

Longing for you,

Wilm

Hosenfeld folded up the letter and tucked it inside his uniform's jacket. Compartmentalizing the tragedies he'd just revealed, he turned his thoughts once again to the routines of daily life. "Maybe I'll pick up a few fruits and vegetables on my way home."

January 3, 1943

Before leaving for his 6 AM deliveries of the *Information Bulletin* bundles, Lech rubbed his hands together to ward off the chill of the frosty morning. After buttoning his coat, he slung his satchel of papers over his shoulder.

Suddenly, Zoshka burst through the door. An icy blast whooshed in with him. The Scout leader looked and smelled like he hadn't bathed in several days. As Zoshka unbuttoned his coat, he asked, "Aren't Alek and Rudy here yet?"

Lech's eyes went wide. "I haven't seen them for over a week. Why? Has something happened?"

His friend tromped to the front room sofa and flopped down, not even bothering to remove his coat. "We finished a job two days ago. Said we'd regroup here by six this morning."

Dropping the satchel of newspapers slung over his shoulder, Lech sat on a threadbare chair across from Zoshka. "What was the job?"

Before the leader answered, Rudy and Alek rushed in.

"Zoshka!" Rudy shouted. "You made it out safely. Thank God!"

The three Scout leaders embraced and thumped each other on the back.

"Sorry we're late." Alek took off his belted trench coat. "We had a hard time getting out of Kraśnik."

Running a hand through his short, reddish-brown hair, Rudy joined Zoshka on the couch. "*SS* men with guard dogs stood watch at the Kraśnik train station, so we had to find another way home. Fortunately, an old farmer smuggled us out in his pickup. We hid under a pile of vegetables. He drove us to the next town where we caught the next train home."

Alek dragged a chair out of the kitchen and sat next to Lech. "You should have seen it, Lech." Alek gestured with his hands. "Zoshka commanded the Scout's Assault Group in Kraśnik. It was our job to blow up German trains that were on their way to—"

Scowling, Zoshka held up a hand. "Lech, weren't you just on your way out? Looks like you have papers to deliver."

Lech bristled in his chair. Obviously, the Scout leaders had just taken part in a covert operation, and as commander of the Scout's Assault Group, Lech realized Zoshka wanted to make sure the mission remained a secret.

Narrowing his eyes, Lech glared at Zoshka. "I think I've earned the right to be part of these secret missions. I've stolen German street signs, thrown vomit bombs into German theaters, and helped Alek take the German plaque off the Copernicus statue. I graffitied the whereabouts of the Krasiński statue, and even got arrested during the Avenge Wawer action."

A corner of Alek's mouth turned up. "He's got a point."

Running a hand over his stubbled face, Zoshka sighed. "It's not up to me. The Scout's Assault Groups operate under the direct command of the Home Army. I'll have to check with my superiors."

"Lech hasn't earned the privilege of joining an assault group." Fire rose in Rudy's eyes as he turned to Lech. "Both Morro and I have ordered you to cut things off with Magdalena, but you refuse to do it. When you're out there blowing up trains or carrying out assassinations, you can't think about how your girlfriend will feel if you get killed. Assault Group members must remain focused at all times. This isn't a game. We depend on each other. Personal distractions get people killed."

The springs of the sagging couch groaned as Zoshka shifted his weight on it. "Like I said, it's not up to me. I'll talk with my commander in the Home Army and get back to you."

"You do that." Lech fisted his hands. "I'm ready to blow up some Germans." He grabbed his satchel and stomped out the door.

Two weeks later, Zoshka visited Lech. "You've got your wish. The Polish Underground government recently passed a death sentence on the Gestapo agent, Louis Herbert. The Underground Judicial Committee declared him guilty of murdering one of our Assault Group's explosive experts. I need one more recruit for our death squad mission."

Blood pulsed in Lech's ears. He'd waited for the day he could join the Assault Group and prove his worth. "So when will it happen? What do you want me to do?"

"First, you have to know," Zoshka said, rubbing the back of his neck as if working out a knot, "we don't do this on the whim of the Underground. Their authority comes from our elected leaders in London where they fled after Germany's invasion. We don't take the law into our own hands."

"I understand." An electric current surged through Lech's body.

"You must understand that our government-in-exile still runs Poland's affairs. However, they do so through a group of Underground proxy leaders here in Warsaw."

"Yeah, yeah. I don't need a lecture in politics," Lech sighed.

Zoshka ticked a muscle in his jaw. "As an Assault Group leader, It's my job to carry out the Judicial Committee's death sentence on Herbert. My team needs one more lookout."

Lech nodded. "I'm in."

On the evening of the scheduled assassination, Lech stood under the streetlamp on the northwest corner of Valor Street as he watched Zoshka and Alek enter the Gestapo agent's apartment building. As instructed, he lit a cigarette and reviewed his orders. If he saw any suspicious activity outside the apartment building, he was to crush the cigarette under his heel. If the cigarette burned down before Zoshka and Alek left Herbert's apartment, he'd drop the cigarette and light another.

Rudy and other members of Zoshka's Assault Group stood on the adjacent corners and did the same.

Thirty minutes later, the Gestapo agent entered his apartment building. Before long, Zoshka and Alek sauntered out.

How can they appear so cool? Lech wondered. *They just murdered a man.* The thought sent a chill through him. *Could I do the same? Yes. I'll prove myself—if our leaders ever give me the chance.*

Lech crushed his cigarette under the heel of his boot and headed in the opposite direction.

The following week, Lech helped Zoshka, Rudy, and Alek remove important papers and a cache of weapons from the apartment of Jan Blonski. Blonski had worked with the Underground since the beginning of the war, but recently died in an operation conducted by another Assault Group. Lech started to read one of the papers he was collecting when Rudy slugged him in the arm.

"Move it, Lech," Rudy said. "You don't read it. You just pack it."

"If I'm sacrificing my life, I think I should know what for."

"Then you don't belong in our Assault Group."

The Scout at the window suddenly called out. "Zoshka, our man on the street just stomped out his cigarette. Something's wrong. We need to leave. Now."

Lech's heart jumped to his throat. He swallowed hard and stuffed as many papers as possible into his satchel before following everyone out the door. As planned, they all wandered off in separate directions. Lech was halfway down the street before soldiers shouted out behind him.

"Halt!" Lech turned and saw two uniformed Germans with their backs to him. They were pointing P38s at Rudy as he ran down the street in the opposite direction.

Shots rang out. Rudy clutched his shoulder before he turned the corner. The soldiers followed.

Lech's heartbeat didn't slow until he arrived back at his apartment.

No one heard from Zoshka, Alek, or Rudy for the next two weeks. Every knock on the apartment door froze Lech's blood. Had the three leaders been captured? Was the Gestapo coming for him next?

Then, without warning, Rudy showed up at the apartment one evening with his arm in a sling.

Lech sat with Benyameen, Stefan, Krzysh, and Tadzio at the kitchen table eating dinner.

"What happened to you?" Benyameen asked, staring wide-eyed at Rudy's sling.

"I didn't feel like stopping when a German told me to, so they shot me in the shoulder." Rudy eyed the boys' half-emptied plates. "Got any more of that stew?"

"You can have the rest of mine," Lech said. "I'm supposed to meet Magdalena at Auntie L's right now anyway."

Rudy scowled. "What? You promised to cut it off with her. When Zoshka finds out, you're finished."

"Where is Zoshka?" Tadzio put down his fork. "We haven't seen him in weeks."

Rudy rolled his lips inward and shook his head. "We received a tip that the Germans ordered his arrest, so he's hiding out in the country until things cool down."

Lech clenched his jaw. "So who's in charge of the Assault Group now?"

"I am." Rudy's face twisted. "And as far as I'm concerned, you're off the team."

The boys gaped at Lech, but said nothing.

Lech's chair scraped across the wooden floor as he shoved it back. "Why? Because I won't cut things off with Magdalena?" Lech stood, stepped forward, and clutched the neckline of Rudy's sweater. "Well, I've had enough of your crap. Get out of my way." Lech shook Rudy off, then bumped his injured shoulder as he stomped past.

Rudy let out a cry, but lunged for Lech with his good arm. "Not so fast." He grabbed Lech by the back of his shirt. "Outside with me. Now."

The chilly night air did nothing to cool Lech's temper. Shaking off Rudy's hold, he turned on his heel to confront him. "Who do you think you are? You can't boss me around. I've got a good mind to pound you into the ground right now."

"Unbelievable." Rudy spat. "Who am I? Really? I'm a scoutmaster, and you're a Gray Ranks Scout. And, didn't you also sign up to be part of the Home Army under Andrzej's command?"

Lech narrowed his eyes. Anger flamed his body as he curled his fists.

Rudy continued his tirade. "In addition to being your Scout leader and the Assault Group leader, I'm also a corporal in the Home Army." Rudy poked a finger at Lech's chest. "And you're a what? A private." His voice rose. "Do you even know what an oath is, much less how to keep one?"

Rudy pushed himself under Lech's nose. "As part of our Assault Group, and as part of the Home Army, you promised to obey orders. If that means you give up your girl, then you give up your girl. Or maybe you can't handle being part of something that's bigger than you."

Lech opened his mouth to respond.

Rudy cut him off. "I told Zoshka that I didn't think you belonged in our Assault Group, much less in the Home Army. I don't think you've got what it takes."

With his hands still curled, Lech grit his teeth. He pictured one of his fists landing in Rudy's face. Until an image of Magdalena floated across his mind. Her dark, soft, lavender-smelling hair. Her almond-shaped face. Her soft, sweet lips. She'd never forgive him if he struck Rudy, especially with his injured shoulder.

Lech let out a low growl and sneered at Rudy. "I've got what it takes. You'll see." He turned and walked away.

He planned to walk the four blocks south to Auntie L's house, but, instead, he headed northeast. As he plodded on, Magdalena filled every thought. He wondered why he hadn't proposed to her yet. *Money.* He didn't want to be like his father.

Thinking about his father made him taste blood. He knew the man felt embarrassed that he couldn't provide for his family, so he walked out on them when Lech was six. He never returned.

Lech desired to have enough money set aside when he proposed to Magdalena. Yes. That's why he hadn't proposed yet. He didn't want to lose her. And who was Rudy to tell him he couldn't have her in his life and be a soldier too? He'd show him.

Twelve blocks later, Lech found himself standing in front of an apartment on Potocki Street. "Hello Danusia," he greeted the tall blonde who answered the door. "I have some information for you."

CHAPTER 26

Operation Arsenal

February–March 1943
Żoliborz District, Warsaw, Poland

Tadzio received a frantic call from Magdalena at eight o'clock that evening. "Have you seen Lech? He was supposed to come to Auntie L's tonight."

"He was here," Tadzio said. "But he and Rudy had an argument, and they both stormed off."

"I'm worried." Magdalena's tight voice trembled over the phone line. "He never misses our planned time together—unless he's up to something. Have him call me back. No matter how late."

Tadzio's gut knotted. Maybe Lech took Rudy's warning seriously. What if he decided to end his relationship with Magdalena and just didn't know how to tell her?

"I'm sure he's okay." Tadzio hoped his voice sounded convincing. "I'll tell him to call as soon as I see him."

Tadzio hung up and sighed. *Poor Magdalena. Soon Lech will break her heart,* he thought.

But Lech didn't return that evening. Or the next. Or the next month.

Tadzio spent as much time as possible with Magdalena and the children at Auntie L's, trying to keep up their spirits. He visited at least twice a week to rehearse piano and violin duets with Magdalena. Once he played card games with Henio, now eight, Lucyna, Yacob, and Magdalena. And he helped Lucyna with her Polish school assignments whenever she asked. Despite his efforts, Magdalena appeared thinner and more sullen each week.

Near the end of March, there was still no sign of Lech. Tadzio's worry increased when Andrzej called all the Scouts together for a late night meeting at the Krasiński apartment. Tadzio rubbed his arms to ward off the chill, both inside and out.

Magdalena sat on the couch next to Anna where she grasped her Scout leader's hand as if she were about to fall off a cliff. Maybe she was. Magdalena's usually large brown eyes all but disappeared behind her tightened, fearful face.

Letting his gaze dart from one Scout to another, the absence of Lech, Zoshka, Alek, and Rudy hit him hard. Did this meeting have something to do with the missing Scouts? Were one or more of them hurt or captured?

The only one in the room he didn't recognize was the young man sitting on the threadbare chair across from Andrzej. He was about two years younger than the Scout leader. The young man's pensive eyes, classic Greek nose, the way he scrubbed his palms back and forth across his legs—there was something familiar about him. *Of course. He is Andrzej's younger brother, Jan.*

With a down-to-business clearing of his throat, Andrzej began. "I'm afraid I've got some bad news."

A squeak escaped Magdalena's lips. She clamped her hand over her mouth.

"We're still out of touch with Zoshka," Andrzej continued, "and we haven't heard anything from Lech for over a month. We know that the Gestapo picked up Rudy and his father yesterday for interrogation."

Tadzio's stomach turned rock-hard. His throat tightened, cutting off his breath. He'd heard about the Gestapo's brutal interrogations. He knew Rudy would never reveal any secrets, but how would he hold up if the Gestapo used his father's torture as leverage?

"We've got to rescue Rudy," Andrzej's brother insisted, half rising from his chair.

The apartment door flung open, giving Tadzio a start.

In walked Zoshka.

Anna jumped to her feet and threw her arms around her brother's neck.

"You're safe!"

"I came as soon as I heard about Rudy's arrest."

A second later, Alek entered the apartment.

Andrzej gave the Scout leaders a half-smile. "I assume you two have a plan to break Rudy out?"

"What about Lech?" Magdalena broke in, her voice thick with emotion. "Have you even bothered to search for him?" Her eyes narrowed as she gazed at Zoshka. "What if he needs rescuing too?" With a fisted hand she rubbed her hand across her cheek.

An arrow of pain pierced Tadzio's chest.

Zoshka raked a hand through his thick brown hair. "No one has seen or heard from him all month. I've even asked our contacts at the Gestapo's office and the prison. It's like he's disappeared off the face of the earth."

Magdalena buried her head in Anna's shoulder and wept.

The next two days blurred together. During the day, Tadzio, Krzysh, and Andrzej shuttled weapons from various safehouses around Warsaw to the Krasiński apartment where they stashed them under the kitchen floorboards. In the evenings, although she appeared as if in a fog, Magdalena helped Tadzio tap out coded messages to Gray Ranks members about what they referred to as "Operation Arsenal." Benyameen and Stefan spent most of their time running errands for Zoshka or Alek.

On the evening of March 25, they all met together in the boys' apartment to review the final plans.

While Zoshka stood to address the Scouts, Tadzio sat on the floor next to Krzysh, and the others sat on chairs or the couch. Zoshka's neatly parted brown hair, his naturally arched eyebrows, and confident exterior stood in stark contrast to his own inner trembling.

"I've learned," Zoshka began, "that late tomorrow afternoon, after their interrogations, the Germans will transport about twenty-five political prisoners from Gestapo headquarters back to Pawiak Prison.

We'll make our move at the intersection of Bielańska and Długa Street. We'll ambush the prison van just before it passes the Arsenal."

"Are you leading the operation?" Tadzio asked.

Zoshka shook his head. "Our Gray Ranks Chief will head it up, using his code name, Orsza. I'll command the Attack Group, which includes all of you, except Magdalena and Anna."

"You can't leave us out." Magdalena pursed her lips as she and Anna huddled next to each other on the couch.

"I hadn't planned to." A faint smile flitted across Zoshka's face. "Orsza has enlisted the help of twelve other Scouts to form what he calls a *Cover Group*. You two will join them."

Magdalena shrugged. "What does that mean?"

"The Cover Group will watch for any German activities along the van's course. You'll be spaced out along the route so you can signal us if it looks like we need to terminate the mission."

Zoshka gazed around the room. "Stefan, Krzysh, and Benyameen, I know you three have experience throwing petrol bottle bombs." Zoshka raised an eyebrow. "You'll be in charge of fire-bombing the transport. Alek, you're in charge of grenades."

Alek let out a whoop.

Folding his arms across his chest, Zoshka continued. "Armed with Sten guns and pistols, the rest of us will position ourselves on the intersection's corners as lookouts until the van comes. When the vehicle reaches the intersection, we'll stop the vehicle and free the prisoners."

Tadzio, sitting cross-legged on the floor, grabbed his knees to keep them from shaking. Scenes from the Wawer Operation flashed across his mind. He envisioned his trembling hands as they gripped the German Luger while the soldier fought with Andrzej in the snow. He recalled how his insides froze when Andrzej told him to shoot. And how Krzysh wrenched the cold metal from his hands in order to do what he couldn't.

What if my cowardice ruins this mission?

Approaching Zoshka after the briefing, Tadzio squeezed his toes inside his shoes, hoping to steel his courage. "I don't think I can be involved in this operation." He let his gaze fall to the floor.

"I know you can." Zoshka lifted Tadzio's chin and held him with a stare. "Otherwise, I wouldn't have included you. I know it's not easy to kill a man, but I've seen what you can do on the rifle range. We need your expertise tomorrow. I need to know I can count on you."

Tadzio stuffed his hands into his pockets and glanced down. "But, when I see a German up close, I freeze."

Gripping Tadzio's shoulders, Zoshka's dark bushy brows knit together.

Tadzio wagged his head and shook his tingling leg, hoping his calf wouldn't cramp.

"I've got it," Zoshka said. He released Tadzio's shoulders and stepped back. "Last week, one of our Gray Ranks Assault Groups captured a German sniper rifle. Tomorrow we can set up a sniper position for you on a rooftop at the intersection where we'll stop the transport van. It might be easier for you to take your shots from a distance. When you shoot, I have no doubt you'll hit your mark. What do you say?"

Tadzio imagined the cruel prison guards who oversaw his mother's concentration camp. He saw the twisted smiles of those who had herded young men off Warsaw's streets to work as slave laborers. He recalled the enemy soldiers who'd gunned down Piotr when he jumped off the tram to avoid capture. And the soldiers who laughed while they kicked him as he bled out.

Yes, he could kill—from a distance.

CHAPTER 27

Stones for the Rampart

March 26–30, 1943
Żoliborz District, Warsaw, Poland

Tadzio willed his trembling hands to steady as he peered through the scope of his Kar 98k bolt-action rifle. His rooftop advantage gave him a clear view of the intersection below.

Off to his left, on the southeast corner, Zoshka's hand rested on the butt of his gun. He had stuffed the pistol into his pants pocket and covered it with his sweater vest. Krzysh stood inside a shop on the southwest side and gazed out the store's window. Jan and Andrzej chatted with each other near the Polish Bank. Orsza, Stefan, Benyameen, and Alek remained somewhere out of sight.

Where were the other Gray Ranks members? He tapped a finger on the side of his rifle as he scanned below. Finally, he picked them out as they worked to blend in with the other Warsaw citizens strolling the streets.

When he shifted his focus back to Andrzej, his heart nearly thumped out of his chest. The Scout leader waved his checkered newsboy hat, signaling the prison van's approach.

A second later, the truck's grinding gears sounded as it downshifted and turned left onto Długa Street.

Orsza, fingers to his lips, let out a sharp whistle.

Krzysh, Stefan, and Benyameen darted out from their positions and lobbed petrol bombs at the vehicle.

Zoshka planted himself in front of the tarpaulin-covered truck.

Would they run him down? Tadzio held his breath until his lungs screamed for air.

Before the truck reached him, the Scout Leader whipped out his pistol and fired.

The windshield exploded, littering the street with shards of glass.

Seconds later, the van's hood and engine burst into flames as it swerved left, then right.

Frightened citizens scattered in all directions.

The truck jumped the curb, bounced, and rolled to a stop near the old Arsenal building.

Other Scouts whipped out their weapons. Several shot at the vehicle's tires. Another brought down a German soldier as he exited the passenger's side.

As he peered through his scope, Tadzio saw the driver scramble out, his gray uniform alight with fire. The soldier dropped to the ground and rolled to extinguish the flames now torching his body.

Tadzio winced, then squeezed his trigger and put the man out of his misery. Sweat trickled down his back. He shuddered.

No time to think. Just act. He turned his attention to the van's rear as two Gestapo agents scuttled out the back. He took aim and fired, flinching with the rifle's recoil. He hit one of the men in the shoulder. They disappeared around the side of the truck. From the safety of their cover, the agents gunned down two Scouts.

Guilt squeezed his heart. He had aimed for the German's head, not his shoulder. *If I hadn't flinched, would one of the Scouts still be alive?*

An SS officer rushed up from Nalewki Street. Alek stood about fifteen feet away, his back to the man. The officer raised his pistol.

Tadzio lined up his sites. Sweat damped his forehead. This was it. He pulled in a breath. *Remember not to flinch.*

Before he squeezed the trigger, Alek swung around and shot the German. The SS officer buckled to his knees and collapsed onto the street, blood oozing from his chest.

Tadzio cursed himself. He should have had Alek's back. He thanked God the Gray Ranks leader was alert and a good shot. Otherwise, there'd be one more dead Scout in the street. His body heated with anger. He had to act faster. No hesitation.

A movement behind the truck grabbed his attention.

An SS officer crept out. With pistol in hand, he crouched low and surveyed the area.

Tadzio aimed, held his breath, and fired.

Blood spattered as the man fell onto the paving stones.

Adrenaline raced through Tadzio's veins. His heart thudded against his chest, and he gasped for air. He was a musician, not a soldier.

Zoshka's words echoed in his head. "I know I can count on you." Tadzio worked to slow his breathing. He had a job to do.

He surveyed the scene again. All seemed quiet.

Andrzej approached the truck. It appeared the mission was a success. Then, a glint of light sparkled near the front of the crashed vehicle. Pulse rushing, Tadzio resumed his sniper position. He viewed the intersection through his scope and made out the tip of a rifle poking out near the truck's front left tire.

The rifle tip inched forward. Who held it? A German? A Scouts? The rifle's barrel appeared, then a head wearing a German helmet.

Should he shoot? What if it was a Scout wearing a German uniform? His pulse pounded in his ears.

The person holding the rifle aimed it at Andrzej.

Tadzio gasped. He squeezed his trigger and landed a bullet in the man's forehead.

Six dead Germans now lay in the street.

Moments later, Alek ran to the rear of the truck, lowered the tailgate, and shouted Rudy's name. Alek, Zoshka, and a few other Scouts helped the prisoners slide out, aided by their more able-bodied companions. After twenty people exited, half of them women, Zoshka and Alek lifted Rudy out of the truck and onto their shoulders. They then rushed him to a waiting car.

Tadzio hooked his arm through his rifle's sling and raced down the stairwell. His rifle beat against his back with every step.

The Scouts carried off their fallen comrades and the battered prisoners, exiting by various streets. The only bodies remaining were dead Germans.

As prearranged, Tadzio ran east down Długa toward Miodowa Street. He stopped when he came upon Alek and a few of his grenade-throwing Scouts. They crouched near the Ministry of Labor and Social Welfare building. Several German officers guarded the entrance, making it impossible to pass.

"Back by the wall!" Alek shouted.

Tadzio and the other Scouts flattened themselves against the concrete structure.

Alek whipped out a grenade and rushed the doorway.

A mind-numbing explosion rocked the ground, followed by a swish of bullets. With blood pulsing in his ears, Tadzio pushed away from the wall and pointed his rifle at a German who had survived the blast. He targeted the man's heart, but when the soldier's eyes went wide, he flinched and hit the German's shoulder.

The soldier fell to the ground, but then rose up and fired at Alek.

Alek doubled over and collapsed on the sidewalk.

More shots came from the building's open doorway. Tadzio drew back his bolt and readied to fire again.

Alek rose on one knee and pulled out two more grenades. He released the safety latches with his mouth and hurled them into the entrance.

Seconds later, with debris still floating to the ground, Tadzio and Alek's grenadiers scooped Alek up and carried him to safety.

The adrenaline pumping through Tadzio's veins compressed the next two hours into a matter of moments. After he and the Scouts took Alek to a safehouse, Tadzio ran fifteen more blocks to his assigned stop. When he reached the designated apartment, he found Zoshka, Andrzej, and Magdalena there with Rudy.

A doctor scurried from his medical bag to Rudy, and gave Magdalena instructions on how to cleanse the Scout's wounds and wrap his bandages.

Tadzio pulled Zoshka and Andrzej aside and told them about Alek.

Every muscle in Tadzio's body quivered. He couldn't slow his pulse. When he sat, his trembling worsened. He paced back and forth, shifting his gaze from the Scout leaders to Magdalena at Rudy's bedside.

Thirty minutes later, Andrzej and Zoshka left to check on Alek.

As if in a stupor, Tadzio stood by while Magdalena bathed and bandaged Rudy's broken fingers. Rudy slipped in and out of consciousness as Magdalena washed the caked blood from his matted hair.

Three days of brutal Gestapo interrogations had literally beaten Rudy within an inch of his life. In his conscious moments, Tadzio heard Rudy recite the Gray Ranks pledge. Tadzio repeated it out loud with him.

"I pledge to serve with the Gray Ranks, safeguard the secrets of the organization, obey orders, and not hesitate to sacrifice my life." Tadzio finished the last phrase alone. Rudy had slipped off again.

Tadzio leaned back in his wooden chair and closed his eyes

"Great work out there, Tadzio." Orsza's voice came from behind him.

Tadzio's eyes flitted open. He'd fallen asleep.

"I heard your quick shooting may have saved Alek's life today."

"Thank you, sir." Tadzio turned and glanced at the short, stocky man, then looked away.

People think I saved Alek's life? If they only knew the truth. He wagged his head. *It was my fault Alek got shot.*

He stayed with Magdalena for the next several days as she nursed Rudy. The doctor checked in with them every day. He always left shaking his head.

On the fourth day, Rudy's lips turned blue. Tadzio guessed from his labored breath and fitful sleep that Rudy was in a lot of pain. Whenever the Scout groaned, Tadzio's stomach twisted. Despite it all, in his wakeful moments, Rudy sometimes joked with them. *A loving God would save this brave, honorable Scout. Wouldn't He?*

Sometimes Rudy mumbled Lech's name. It brought tears to Magdalena's eyes. No one had seen Lech for over a month. Not since he'd fought with Rudy outside their apartment. For Tadzio, not knowing what happened to Lech seemed almost worse than staring at Rudy's beaten and mangled body. It was like staring into a deep, dark, bottomless pit, knowing it would suck you in if you got too close. And Magdalena was closer to the hole than he was.

Tadzio began to doze off again but came to life when Rudy stirred once more. "Alek? Is Alek okay?"

Rising from his chair, Tadzio swabbed Rudy's swollen, cracked lips with water. "Yes, Alek is fine." Tadzio bit the inside of his cheek with the lie. He'd heard from the doctor that Alek's most recent operation had failed to stop his internal bleeding.

Rudy grabbed Tadzio's arm with his bandaged hand. "Don't lose hope, Tadzio," he whispered. "Ever."

"How is he?" Magdalena said as she stepped to Rudy's bedside.

Tadzio shook his head.

Rudy groaned. "Does anyone know that line about hope from Słowacki's poem, *My Testament*?"

"Yes, I know it," Tadzio said. Last year, Professor Lewandowski had them memorize it. "Why do you ask?" Tadzio brushed loose strands of hair from Rudy's red-rimmed eyes.

As if reciting the poem, Rudy's lips moved, but no words came out.

Tadzio leaned closer.

"*I implore the still living not to lose hope,*" the Scout whispered.

"*I implore the still living not to lose hope,*" Tadzio repeated, pushing the words out through his dry, constricted throat.

The two continued in unison: "...*but, when the time comes, to go forth to their death, like stones thrown by God upon a great rampart.*"

The poem's meaning was not lost on Tadzio. Alek and Rudy were living examples of the poem's stones. Their young lives had been thrown against the fortified strength of the German stronghold, and, seemingly, with no result. But, perhaps, if enough stones were thrown against the German fortifications, perhaps if they did not lose hope, others would follow. Perhaps there was still a future hope, somewhere in the distance, for Poland to become its own free nation again.

In a hoarse whisper, Rudy's blue lips repeated the line. "*I implore the still living not to lose hope.*" With that, he blew out his last breath.

Chapter 28

Lech Returns

April 2, 1943
Warsaw, Poland

"I made this for you. Thought it might cheer you up." Henio laid a drawing on Magdalena's lap as he plopped down next to her on Auntie L's parlor couch.

She ruffled his light brown hair and sighed. Tension and fatigue gripped her shoulders like a vise. She'd been on her feet since five that morning, having worked eight hours at the Żoliborz hospital, and another four at the theater. The pounding in her head worsened as she massaged her neck. She needed rest and lots of it.

Henio pointed to his drawing as he leaned over her lap to view it. "When I saw this sign on buildings all over town, Tadzio said the Scouts did it. They wanted to scare the Germans. He showed me how it makes the letters P and W. He says the letters stand for *Polska Walcząca*, Poland Fighting. I think it's clever how it looks like an anchor, don't you?"

"Yes. It's very clever. Thanks for the picture." She kissed the top of his head. "I'll treasure it forever."

A week had passed since she'd watched Rudy die. She'd never felt so helpless. Alek died at almost the same time. She kept reciting Rudy's last words, looking for comfort—*I implore the still living not to lose hope*—but she found none. Maybe Henio's picture would help.

Henio rattled on about a fight he'd had that morning with Lucyna, but Magdalena let her mind drift. Hadn't the aunties told her about another anchor? She searched her memories. *The train. Yes.* When they'd come back from purchasing black-market potatoes and sugar. They had mentioned a verse of Scripture that talked about an "anchor of hope."

The aunties believed it was possible to have faith in God's unchanging character, no matter how bleak the circumstances. They said trusting in God to be true to His character would provide an anchor for her soul. She wasn't sure how to do that. Maybe she'd ask Fr. Wacław. She tousled Henio's hair again and tried to tune in to his story. He'd already seen and heard more than any eight-year-old should.

From down the hallway, the phone rang. Auntie M answered. "Yes, she's here. May I say who's calling?" Auntie M paused and called out. "Magdalena, it's for you. The caller won't give me his name."

Magdalena rushed to answer. "Hello?"

"It's me," someone said in a hushed tone. "Meet me at the end of the block in five minutes. Tell no one." He then hung up.

She felt lightheaded and leaned against the wall. Lech had called! She hadn't dared to believe he was still alive. And now, he wanted to meet her in five minutes.

Four minutes later, she stood on the corner under the stars searching for him.

Hands touched her waist. She startled and spun around. Her knees went slack. Lech wasn't dead. He was here in front of her. She fell into his arms. The warmth of his body relaxed her taut muscles. Pressing her head to his chest, she heard the rapid beat of his heart. She breathed in his scent. A mix of freshly cut grass with a hint of mustard and sweat. She kissed him long and hard.

"Where have you been?" she finally gasped. "I thought you were dead. Why didn't you call? What have you been doing?"

"I've been preparing for our future. And now, I've come for you." His smile radiated a confidence she'd never seen before.

Puzzled, she narrowed her eyes. "What do you mean? We all thought you'd been captured, like Rudy."

"I'm a hard one to catch." A smile spread across his face. "But *you* managed to catch my heart." He bent down on one knee and grasped her hand. "Magdalena, will you marry me?"

She pressed her free hand to her mouth. "Oh, Lech. Do you really mean it?"

Standing, he lifted her at the waist and spun them both around. "I mean it, with all my heart." He gently set her down. "I've saved enough money to rent a small place in the country." He opened the leather satchel that hung from his shoulder. "Look. We have enough to last until the end of the war."

She glanced inside. The shoulder bag was stuffed with Reichsmarks. "Lech." Magdalena hesitated. "If you weren't captured, what have you been doing? Where did you get all this money?"

"I've been hiding out at my country house for the past two months while I established a new identity. I got a job transporting goods from a nearby factory to the railway station."

A buzzing rang in her ears. It almost drowned out his words. *How could he make that much in two months?* She watched his lips move, but barely took in his words.

"And you can start a garden and fix up the place while I'm at work. Then we can make love all night, waiting out this horrid war together until things get sorted out. What do you say?"

She shook her head and stepped back. "Do you even know what's happened since you left? Someone turned Rudy over to the Gestapo. We ambushed the transport and rescued him, along with the other prisoners, but not soon enough. He died." Her voice quavered. "Alek is dead, too."

He pulled her to his chest. "I know," he whispered. "But putting our lives on hold won't bring them back. It's time we think about ourselves. It's foolish to think we can defeat the Germans. We tried, and we failed. We have to move on and make the best of things."

Lech stepped back, raised Magdalena's chin with his finger, and gazed into her eyes. "Come away with me. We can't say anything to anyone. I have a car parked around the corner. Because of my transport business, I have a pass to drive at night."

She pushed him back. "What are you saying? You want me to leave Henio and the other children behind so I can sneak away with you? Without even saying goodbye to Tadzio, Auntie M, or Auntie L? And what about your brother, Stefan? What's happened to you, Lech?"

He grabbed her hands and tugged them. "Wise up, Magdalena. The Allies aren't coming. We're outgunned and outmanned. It's time to stop playing soldier and get on with our lives."

His tone cut her to the quick. She shook him off. "No, Lech. Rudy died begging us not to lose hope." Her throat constricted. "We have to fight on—for Poland—for our future." Tears trickled down her cheeks.

He yanked open his leather pouch, grasped a handful of bills, and shoved them under her nose. "Look. This is all we need. We can get through this war together. After it's over, we'll contact our families and everything will return to normal. You'll see."

Magdalena let her jaw drop. She widened her eyes. "Lech, you didn't have anything to do with Rudy's arrest, did you?" She swatted his money-filled hand away.

Not answering her question, he shoved the bills back into his pouch. Anger brewed behind his eyes.

Her knees weakened. Her stomach dropped. "How could you?" She retreated a step.

The high-low pitches of a German police car cut the air from somewhere nearby. Lech grabbed Magdalena's arm in a vise-like grip. "Get into my car. Now!" He dragged her toward the corner.

She stomped on his foot and wriggled to break free. "Lech, I won't go with you. I won't marry you. We have to fight for Poland. For our future. I'll never give up."

He grasped her shoulders and shook her until her teeth rattled. "We can't win. I want to marry you. Isn't that enough?"

Stiffening her spine, she slapped his face. "No. You're not the man I thought you were."

The police car's siren blared louder. It was past curfew.

"And you're not the woman I thought you were." Lech shoved her back.

She tripped and fell to the ground.

He climbed into his car and drove away.

Scout Sabotage

June–September 1943
Warsaw, Poland

Energy surged through Tadzio as Professor Handelsman stood to address the Scouts assembled in his home on Wilcza Street. Something big was coming. Tadzio sensed it. Why else would the professor come out of hiding and call this meeting?

"We know the Gray Ranks want to do more to fight the Germans," the professor said. "I've returned so I can personally introduce you to Major Pług of the Underground Army. He has a special announcement."

"Thank you, Professor Handelsman."

As the major stood before them, Tadzio noticed the man's bushy brows and penetrating eyes, his receding hairline and no-nonsense expression.

"In my younger days," the major began, "I too was a Scout. I have great respect for the organization, and for you. That's why I asked Professor Handelsman to call this meeting." He paused, gazed around the room, then continued. "The Underground Army wants to form a special group, the *Kedyw* Division, comprised of seasoned Scouts such as yourselves."

A collective buzz filled the room.

The major turned to the professor. "Do the boys know about Stalingrad?"

"I don't think so," the professor said. "We haven't passed that information down the line."

Tadzio sat cross-legged on the floor next to Krzysh. He poked his friend. Tadzio's underground history teacher told them a little about Germany's failed invasion of Russia. Tadzio tried to explain it to Krzysh, but he hadn't seemed interested.

The major raised a brow. "Boys, as you may know, in '41, over three million German troops invaded Russia. Within days, they advanced 483 kilometers into Russian territory." The major paced over the professor's Aubusson rug in front of the group. "By the end of '41, however, a strong Soviet counteroffensive pushed the Germans back about 257 kilometers."

Krzysh nudged Tadzio. "That must be why we saw so many injured German soldiers on the train. Remember? That frigid November morning in '41 when Andrzej took us to Choszczówka for training exercises?"

Tadzio nodded, then turned his attention back to the major.

"We have received reports," Pług continued, "that between the summer of '42 and the winter of '43, Germany and its allies fought to conquer Stalingrad in southern Russia. They failed, even though they mercilessly bombed the Soviets, including civilians. We've learned the Germans killed over two million people. To date, the fight for Stalingrad was one of the bloodiest battles in warfare history."

Tadzio's breath froze in his lungs. He couldn't fathom that many dead bodies. That much blood. That much tragedy. He wondered where this brief history lesson was going.

The major clasped his hands behind his back and continued to pace. "Germany's defeat at Stalingrad severely weakened Hitler's forces."

"I never thought I'd say this," one Scout spoke up, "but thank you, Russia."

Major Pług shot the Scout a wry smile. "When the Germans retreated from Stalingrad," he continued, "they amassed their forces near Kursk, 370 kilometers south of Moscow. Now, here's where you come in."

Tadzio leaned forward, his interest piqued. Maybe they'd get to blow up a train depot or rob a German weapons station. Rudy and Alek's deaths had triggered something inside him. He itched to take a more active role against the Germans.

"To ensure their victory at Kursk," the major said, "the German High Command plans to ship their new heavy Tiger tanks and medium Panther tanks east."

"Those armored vehicles will have to travel by rail through Poland in order to get to Russia, right, Major?" Benyameen said.

"Correct." The major nodded.

Andrzej broke in. "Let me guess. You want us to blow up those shipments before they reach the Eastern Front?"

A faint smile spread across the major's face. "That's right. The Allies' spy rings have informed us Hitler plans to send at least 2,450 tanks to ensure a victory at Kursk."

Zoshka eyes widened. "If we blow up rail-lines running through Poland, we can halt Germany's invasion of Russia."

"Exactly," the major said. "That will give our allies, the Russians, an upper hand against the Nazis."

Once again, the room filled with noisy voices.

Tadzio pulled his brows together and shook his head. *Germany and Russia. What hypocrites. No honor between them.* He recalled when Germany invaded Poland in '39, and how Germany and Russia signed a pact not to fight each other. They split Poland between themselves. Germany agreed they'd invade Poland from the west, while Russia advanced from the east. In 1941, however, the Nazis went back on that pact and took over Polish areas Russia had claimed for themselves. Russia then changed sides and became Poland's ally.

"What's wrong?" Krzysh asked Tadzio. "This is great news."

Tadzio pulled his knees to his chest. "I don't trust the Russians." He fisted a hand and pounded it on his knee.

"Face it, Tadzio," Krzysh shrugged. "We can't defeat the Germans on our own. If we ever hope to become a free nation again, we need Russia's help."

Tadzio faced Krzysh and narrowed his gaze. "Russia's just in it for themselves. They don't care about us."

Krzysh punched his arm. "Haven't you ever heard the saying, 'the enemy of my enemy is my friend'?"

"Russia's never been Poland's friend." Tadzio scowled. "I doubt they'll start now."

After a moment, the major raised the Scout sign and silenced the group. "The Home Army's commander, General Bór, has named this endeavor Operation Belt." Pług glanced at Zoshka and Andrzej. "Some of you already hold ranks in the Home Army and have received sabotage training. Now you will train those willing to join this Gray Ranks' *Kedyw* Division so they can join you in further acts of subversion. We hope this will help us in our fight against the Nazis and free Poland once again."

Every nerve in Tadzio's body tingled. Yes. He'd put aside his hesitation to fight Germans face to face. Whatever the task, even if it meant killing the enemy up close instead of from a sniper position, he'd do it.

June–August 1943

Throughout the summer, Tadzio and his roommates took part in several sabotage missions under Andrzej's command. Raiding a German arsenal. Blowing up police stations. Stealing German uniforms from a storage facility.

In August, however, Andrzej said they'd participate in a larger mission under Zoshka's leadership. Along with fourteen other *Kedyw* Scouts, Tadzio's team of six would travel to the eastern Polish town of Sieczychy to bomb a military transport station.

At midnight on August 21, Tadzio hunkered down in a ravine next to Krzysh and the other Scouts. He peered through the darkness at their target. A military transport station. A pale moon cast eerie shadows of tanks sitting on the tracks, and the wire fence surrounding the depot's barracks. Although thrilled to take part in a mission led by Zoshka, Tadzio's insides twisted. Was he really ready to kill a German face-to-face?

Zoshka whispered his final orders. "Krzysh and Stefan, go with Mackiek's Scouts to set charges on the tracks and supply trains." He pointed to the railway.

"Yes, sir," Krzysh and Stefan said.

He then motioned toward a hill above the ravine. "Tadzio, you'll provide sniper cover from up there."

Blowing out a breath of relief, Tadzio gave Zoshka a thumbs-up.

Their leader nodded toward the structure near the tracks. "I'll go with Długa and his men to take out the barracks."

Andrzej and Benyameen returned from their reconnaissance mission.

"We took out the two sentries." Andrzej huffed to catch his breath. "Ready when you are."

Zoshka waved the Scouts forward.

With sniper weapon in hand, Tadzio pulled in a breath and crept to his spot on the ridge. From there, he watched the others slip into place.

Krzysh, Stefan, and Mackiek's Scouts set the charges without incident.

A chill tickled Tadzio's spine. In a few minutes, the tanks loaded on the stationary railcars would burst into a ball of flame.

He followed Zoshka's movement through his scope. His Scout leader and his crew crept toward the building.

Tadzio wrapped his finger around the rifle's trigger. Beads of sweat trickled down his back.

Zoshka cut the wire fence, then signaled the others forward with his flashlight. A Scout in Długa's group tossed a grenade at the wooden structure. With guns raised, the insurgents stepped closer.

Tadzio tensed. The grenade didn't detonate.

Shots erupted from the barracks.

Several Scouts fell.

With blood pounding in his ears, Tadzio scanned the area through his scope. The tip of a rifle pointed out a window. He held his breath and fired. The soldier fell back on impact.

Ka-shhung!

The grenade finally exploded. Bits of wood shot into the air.

The Scouts charged the building. All except the Zoshka.

Tadzio scoped the scene. He gasped. Zoshka's crumpled body lay on the ground.

Get up Zoshka. Get up!

Tadzio's chest heaved as he pulled in air. He bit his tongue so hard, he tasted blood. His hands shook.

A German rushed out the front door.

Focus. He had to focus. He slowed his breathing. Tadzio lined up his sites and squeezed off a shot. The soldier crashed to the ground.

Ice now filled Tadzio's veins. He scoped out another Nazi. The man had crouched and aimed his rifle toward Krzysh and Stefan's position.

They're sitting ducks! Tadzio fired again. He hit the German in the chest.

A second later, the dynamite near the tracks exploded. The ground shook. A ball of fire engulfed the railroad tracks and tanks, permeating the air with the smell of sulfur and burnt rubber. A taste of metal filled Tadzio's mouth. His heart beat against his chest as he returned his gaze to Zoshka. His leader still lay in the dirt.

Tadzio and the others regrouped a few days later at Auntie L's house. As soon as they crossed the threshold, Zoshka's sister, Anna, grabbed Andrzej's arms.

"Something terrible happened, didn't it!"

With his heart in his throat, Tadzio turned away and moved toward the couch.

Still standing, Andrzej gazed down at Anna and grimaced. He shook his head but said nothing.

Anna beat Andrzej's chest with her fists. "You were supposed to protect my brother! You promised!"

"No. Not Zoshka!" Magdalena wailed. Wide-eyed, she rose from her chair and knelt in front of Tadzio. "What happened?"

He couldn't meet Magdalena's gaze. Instead, he glanced at Anna who continued to beat Andrzej with her fists.

Stone-faced, Andrzej didn't move.

"We accomplished our mission." Tadzio swallowed hard against the rock of grief that clogged his throat. "Zoshka was hit when his group rushed the station's barracks. He took a bullet to the heart." He finally let his gaze meet Magdalena's. "He didn't suffer. He died instantly."

For the next few weeks, Anna barely spoke. Magdalena, still mourning Lech's betrayal, tried to console her friend. At least they had each other. They became inseparable.

Almost hourly, Tadzio recited Rudy's last words. *I implore the still living not to lose hope.* And yet, more and more each day, hope slipped from his fingers.

CHAPTER 30

The Róg

September 1943

After Zoshka's death, Kedyw did not send Tadzio or the others on any more missions. Instead, they were ordered to stay close to home. Near the end of September, however, Tadzio grew restless.

He suggested they help with deliveries of the *Information Bulletin*. Everyone agreed, including Magdalena, Anna, and the children. The Scouts on the other side of the Vistula were short-handed because the Gestapo had arrested several leaders in the Praga District.

On the morning of September 29, Tadzio carried ink to the house in Praga where they printed the *Bulletin*. While still several blocks away, he sighted Henio, Yacov, and Lucyna across the street. The children all carried satchels of the *Bulletin*. Tadzio sighed, knowing the dangers of delivering it. He'd tried to talk the children out of helping, but they refused.

"We want to help fight, too," Henio had said one afternoon when Tadzio was at Auntie L's. "I want Poppa to be proud."

"I'm sure Poppa is proud." Tadzio kissed the top of his head. "But I think he would also want you to be safe."

Auntie M had shaken her head. "Children do what you do, not what you say. Henio knows you take a stand for Poland. You can't expect him to do less."

When the three youths reached Tadzio's side of the street, Henio tugged Tadzio's sleeve.

Tadzio bent down.

"I'm almost done with my deliveries," Henio whispered in his ear. "See you back at the *Róg*. And you'd better hurry. Magda really needs that ink."

The *Róg*. Tadzio was proud of the codename Henio had invented for the corner house where they printed the *Bulletin*. Henio had pointed out that the Polish word *róg* not only meant "corner," but also meant a "bugle" or "a horn."

Henio had said, "It's like our newspaper is a bugle announcing news that's really true."

His little brother was becoming quite the child-soldier. His heart ached as Henio scampered away. Dressed in his knee-high stockings and shorts, Tadzio was reminded that, although Henio had joined the fight, he was still his sweet little nine-year-old brother. Tadzio tapped the hidden cannister of ink beneath his sweater vest. He buttoned his overcoat and hurried on his way.

When Tadzio rounded the next corner, a passing newsboy whispered in his ear.

"*Łapanka*."

Tadzio glanced around. The codeword warned Germans were conducting roundups. Anyone caught with illegal weapons, publications, or black-market items would be arrested. However, no German trucks or police cars were in sight. He shrugged and continued on his way.

The ink grew heavier with each step. He crossed an intersection and scurried down the next street. Still no Germans. When he reached the corner house where they published the *Bulletin*, a taxicab pulled up. His knees went slack.

Andrzej met Tadzio on the walkway. "Get rid of the ink," he warned in a low voice. "I've received word that Germans have already taken away three truckloads of people from around here. More trucks will arrive in about forty-five minutes." He pressed a few Reichsmarks into Tadzio's hand. "Have the taxi driver take you to the florist on Konopacka Street. Buy a dozen roses. Then, pick up a pound of apples at the market. Bring everything back here as quickly as possible."

Tadzio arched a brow. "Why?"

"Just do it," Andrzej hissed. "Hurry."

Tadzio rushed to the taxi and gave him directions.

On his way back, two German trucks trailed them. Tadzio gripped his knees until his fingers numbed.

When he entered the house, he found Magdalena and Andrzej stuffing bundles of the *Bulletin* into large suitcases. Their pinched eyes reflected the same worry that had tied his stomach in knots.

"Give Magdalena the roses," Andrzej said.

Tadzio inclined his head.

Andrzej shot him a tense grin. "They're Magdalena's wedding bouquet. We're off to our honeymoon."

"Okay." Tadzio scratched his head. He handed the roses to Magdalena and helped Andrzej carry the suitcases to the waiting cab.

Neighbors appeared outside the house and cheered as Andrzej and Magdalena approached the taxi. Magdalena held the bouquet in one hand and an apple in the other. Andrzej loaded the suitcases into the cab's trunk, then opened the back door for Magdalena.

Five Wehrmacht soldiers emerged from a neighboring house.

"Stop," they ordered Andrzej. "Open the trunk."

Every muscle in Tadzio's body froze. *Oh, God. What now?*

Andrzej faced the soldiers. "Our suitcases have already been searched. We just got married and are now leaving for our honeymoon. Surely, you don't have the heart to detain a young man from that."

Two of the soldiers grinned. One winked at Andrzej and waved him on.

As the cab sped off, Tadzio exhaled. He had no idea how long he'd been holding his breath.

Tadzio hurried to warn Henio and the others to stay away from the *Róg*. His pulse pounded in his ears. He ran four blocks before spotting Henio across the street. About to call out, he stopped when two German policemen approached his brother from behind.

Tadzio froze in place. Bile rose to his throat.

Groups of citizens in front of their homes stepped back.

"Halt!" one policeman shouted.

Henio's eyes widened.

"Halt!" the officer repeated, drawing his gun.

Henio, still with his back to the policemen, froze and raised his hands.

Tadzio wanted to run across the street and scoop up his brother. But that might put him in more danger. His mind raced. He had to save Henio. His whole body went cold. He dug his fingernails into his palms.

"*Was ist das?*" the policeman with the gun shouted as he yanked Henio's satchel from his shoulder. He handed the bag to the other German.

The second officer opened the satchel and tossed out several copies of the *Information Bulletin*. He showed one to his partner.

Seeing the illegal paper, the policeman's face twisted into a malicious grin. He pointed his pistol at Henio's back. As if in slow motion, the officer pulled the trigger.

Blam!

Only one shot.

Henio's arms flew up. His fine light-brown hair lifted in the breeze as his face contorted in pain. His legs went out from beneath him.

Tadzio's heart stopped.

Several women screamed.

With a laugh, the two policemen turned and walked away.

Adrenaline rushed through Tadzio. He sprinted across the street, knelt beside Henio, and raised his head.

"Tadzio." His brother gasped.

"I'm here." Tadzio choked out a sob. "You'll be okay."

"Poppa would be proud, yes?" He gasped again.

Tears trickled down Tadzio's face. His heart clutched. "Yes. Poppa would be proud."

Slipping his arm beneath Henio's head and the other under his legs, Tadzio stood and shouted, "Someone get a doctor!"

Henio winced. "It hurts."

Tadzio buried his face in his brother's soft neck. "I know." He glanced at the people milling about. "Please! Somebody! Help!"

A woman rushed forward with a blanket and wrapped it around Henio. "Bring him to my house." She pointed toward an open doorway.

Tadzio readjusted Henio's weight and staggered into the home.

Henio gazed up and winced. "I just wish… I could hug… and kiss Momma one more time."

The edges of Henio's faint smile sliced Tadzio's heart. He turned his head and wiped his wet face on his shoulder. "Shh, now. Save your strength."

Henio squeezed his eyes. "Hurt… only lasts… a little while. But happy… is forever."

"Oh, Henio." Tadzio choked out a sob.

Henio blinked and reached up to pinch Tadzio's cheek. "I love you," he whispered.

Henio's eyes closed for the last time.

CHAPTER 31

Zoshka Battalion

November 1943
Warsaw, Poland

For the next two months, Tadzio walked about in a fog of grief. Having lost Henio, he'd lost a piece of his heart. Like a wooden soldier, he took part in sabotage missions, but found it harder to engage as the weeks wore on.

In November, his spirits perked a little when the Home Army created a special battalion for Scouts. Instead of working alongside the Underground Army, they'd now be part of it with their own special battalion. The Scouts named it Zoshka in honor of their fallen scoutmaster. Andrzej, as leader of the battalion's Second Company, made sure Tadzio, Krzysh, Benyameen, and Stefan all served under his command. The boys adopted Alek as their as platoon name.

Thanks to his radiotelegraphy skills, Tadzio attended a secret meeting of Zoshka Battalion officers at a safe-house on Regal Street on November 20. As the apartment swelled to capacity, he breathed through his mouth to avoid the unpleasant odors of cigarette smoke, unwashed clothes, and desperate men. At seventeen, he guessed he was the youngest in the group. His fingers twitched as he set up the transmission equipment. Hunching over his battalion's shortwave, he jotted down the coded message that now clicked through.

The weight of his assignment, to receive and decipher the Commander-in-Chief's communication, pressed in on him. Had all the air been sucked from the room? Breathlessly, he urged his trembling hands to still as he transcribed the transmission.

Order No. 1300/111: I hereby order all Home Army commanders and units currently fighting the retreating Germans to reveal themselves to in-coming Russians. We must assert the existence of the Polish Republic to our Russian neighbors. My order conflicts with those I have received from our exiled government in London. Our Polish Prime Minister and our English allies would prefer that those of us fighting here in Poland not fight out in the open. They would rather we only stage covert missions of sabotage against the Germans. However, in light of the Soviet Union's recent break in diplomatic relations with Poland, if we do not fight alongside the Russians, who will defend our territorial and political integrity once the Germans are defeated? Certainly not the Russians. It is up to us to defend our freedom, despite all, and against all who would seize it from us.

Tadzio handed the decoded message to Zoshka Battalion's commander. Code-named Jerzy, the man appeared about 30, average-sized, and well-built. The commander first read the transmission to himself, then to his surrounding officers.

Murmurs arose from the group. A few heads nodded.

Commander Jerzy raised a hand to quiet his men. "I concur with General Bór. We need to fight in the open against the Germans and alongside the Russians."

Kuba, leader of Felek Platoon, spoke up. "But, sir? Why should we fight alongside the Russians if they've broken off diplomatic relations?"

"To give a show of strength." The commander pointed to a wall map. "Two weeks ago, I received news of activity in Ukraine. The Soviets took back Kiev from the Germans. However, once the Russians arrived, they installed pro-Communists to run the capital. The city's previous leaders were murdered or sent to prison camps. The Soviets have done the same thing in every area they've *liberated* from the Germans."

Andrzej raked a hand through his hair. "And, as the Russians continue to push the Germans west, it won't be long before the Soviets reach our Polish borders."

A strange mix of excitement and fear laced Tadzio's lungs. He couldn't pull in a breath. He was proud to be part of this briefing, but what would Russia do once they reached his country? What would become of him and his friends—of Magdalena and the little ones?

"Morro's right." The commander grimaced. "It won't be long before the Russians reach Warsaw. But if we fight alongside them before they reach the capital, we'll have a better chance of maintaining our sovereignty. Otherwise, once they're here, we can expect the same fate as the Poles buried in Kiev. Or Katyn Forest."

A hush blanketed the room.

Tadzio's head spun. The room seemed to shrink in size. The meager contents in his stomach threatened to spill out. He swallowed the bile that rose in his throat.

Commander Jerzy had briefed the battalion about the Katyn massacre last month. When the Germans retreated from their failed invasion of Russia, they discovered mass graves of Poles buried in Katyn Forest. Searching corpses for documents, they found none dated later than April 1940—a time when Russia controlled the area.

Hoping to discredit the Russians in the eyes of the allies, the Germans called for a European Red Cross Committee to examine the remains. The committee identified over 8,000 Polish officers, who, with hands bound behind their backs, were shot from behind and piled twelve layers high in deep graves. Tadzio shuddered at the image.

The committee eventually recovered 22,000 bodies, including Polish lawyers, teachers, government officials, landowners, and priests.

The commander continued, pulling Tadzio back to the present. "Of course, Russia denies any responsibility for the massacre at Katyn. Despite the evidence, they maintain Germans perpetrated this horrific war crime."

Andrzej scowled. "And that's why, to answer Kuba's question, even though Russia is supposed to be our ally, Stalin broke off diplomatic relations with us. He refuses to admit what we now know is true."

One of the company commanders made a twisting motion with his hands. "I'd like to break off something with Russia. And it has nothing to do with diplomatic relations."

July 1944

Tadzio's frustration grew with each passing month. While other battalions gained key victories with Russians in Ukraine and eastern Poland, his Zoshka Battalion remained in Warsaw. They only conducted local missions such as an attempt to kill their German mayor, Fischer, and the derailment of trains traveling to and from Germany.

After a hot afternoon of working all day at the coffee shop, Tadzio sauntered home in a foul mood. Next month he'd turn eighteen. He should be going to movies and dating girls, not setting bombs and ambushing traitors.

When he entered their Krasiński apartment, he found Krzysh on the couch reading the *Warsaw Courier*. He ripped the paper from his hands.

"Why are you reading that German pack of lies?" Tadzio crunched the newspaper between his hands.

Krzysh wide-eyed, stared at Tadzio. "Who crossed your path on the way home?"

Tadzio tossed the paper ball at his head. "Jesus, Mary, and Joseph! Why is it so hot in here?" He strode to the far side of the room. "Can't you even bother to open a window?" He lifted the sill, and a slight breeze drifted in off the Vistula.

"Ahh." Tadzio inhaled the cooler air.

Before he breathed in again, Andrzej burst through the door.

"It's official!" He raised his arms. "General Bór wants us to prepare for an uprising against the Germans here in Warsaw."

Krzysh leapt to his feet. "When? How?"

Still angry at Krzysh and exhausted from work, Tadzio blinked to take in Andrzej's news.

"Our government in London has approved it. We don't have an exact time or date, but we're calling it *Wybuch*—Outbreak Hour."

"W-Hour." Tadzio rubbed a weary hand across his face. "An uprising. You say we're supposed to start it here in Warsaw before the Russians arrive?"

Andrzej nodded. "That way, if we defeat the Germans on our own, the Soviets can't take the credit. General Bór's asked our allies to provide supplies and military reinforcements. He's also requested our government in London to send the First Parachute Brigade and the Polish fighter squadron."

Finally stirring to life, a surge of hope rose in Tadzio's chest—the first he'd had since Henio's death.

Time for open warfare had come to Poland's capital.

CHAPTER 32

The Rising Begins

August 1, 1944
Żoliborz District

The morning of August 1, Andrzej met the boys at 6 AM for a final breakfast before the W-Hour. After polishing off his platter of fried mashed potatoes and cabbage, Andrzej issued assignments.

"W-Hour begins tonight at five. Zoshka Battalion will launch an attack from Wola District." Andrzej rubbed his hands together. "At the same time, battalions all over Warsaw will strike. Until then, you're assigned to help a Bastza platoon collect weapons from nearby safehouses."

Andrzej checked his watch. "Start in an hour. Deliver caches to the platoon on Tucholska and Krasiński."

Excitement pulsed through Tadzio's veins as Andrzej fixed his gaze on him, then the others.

"Remember, General Bór wants the Rising to start at the same time throughout the city. No skirmishes until then. Finish up by three, then join Zoshka Battalion in Wola by five."

With his heart in his throat, Tadzio stood and saluted. The others followed.

Standing tall, Andrzej returned their gesture of respect.

Everyone's fist shot into the air as they shouted, *"Cuwaj!"*

After Andrzej left, Tadzio finished his breakfast in silence, but his mind raced. A twinge of dread shot through him. *What are our odds of success? None, unless the Allies come to our aid.*

An hour later, his pulse racing, Tadzio grabbed his pistol and headed out with the others. He and Krzysh agreed to collect weapons from safehouses east of Słowacki and Mickiewicz. Benyameen and Stefan combed locations to the west.

Tadzio scurried alongside Krzysh as they carted weapons from various places to the platoon on Tucholska Street. Hiding stockpiled arms and ammunition beneath their clothing made for slow work.

Three hours later, Tadzio paused to check his watch. "Eleven o'clock." Winded, he inhaled quick breaths and wiped sweat from his forehead. "That gives us four hours until we leave to meet the others in Wola District."

Krzysh parked himself on a pile of rubble near the edge of the street and sipped from his canteen. "We'll never finish in four hours," he said between sips. "We need a better way to do this."

"You're right." Tadzio glanced around. A gutted utility store shrouded in burnt beams and charred walls stood behind them. As he entered the ruins, shards of broken glass crunched beneath his boots. The charcoal odor reminded him of nights around the campfire in Kampinos Forest—their summer Scout Camporee of 1939. Back then, he didn't know why or how he would use the radio operator training and riflery expertise he learned there. Now, after four years of German occupation, he would finally use those skills in the Rising. After rummaging through the store's debris, he brought Krzysh a battered wheelbarrow and a load of blankets.

A corner of Krzysh's mouth shot up. "Now you're thinking."

At the next safehouse, Tadzio winced as he wrapped boxes of homemade grenades in blankets. One wrong move with these unstable devices and he'd play piano with one hand. Or maybe not at all. After Krzysh set a blanketed bundle of rifles in the cart, Tadzio lowered his grenade box on top of them.

Thankful he still had all his body parts, Tadzio blew out a relieved sigh. He lifted the rig's handles and pushed their cargo toward Tucholska Street.

"Wait." Krzysh grabbed his arm after a few steps. "How will we sneak this load past German patrols?"

Tadzio ran a hand across his face, then wriggled a brow. "We'll pretend we're using the wheel-barrow to get you around, since you have a broken leg."

Krzysh glanced down. "I don't have a broken leg."

A pile of wood lay in the safehouse's front yard. Tadzio scavenged through it and pulled out a leg-sized post. Moving back to the cart, he cut strips of cloth from a blanket and tied the short pole to Krzysh's leg. "Now you do."

"Okay." Krzysh smirked. "I get it." He hobbled to the wheel-barrow and lowered himself next to the blanketed box of grenades. "If it looks like I have a broken leg, we're less likely to attract attention. But, Tadzio?"

"Yes?"

"After we deliver these weapons, it's your turn to sit in the cart."

Tadzio spotted several youths roaming the area as he wheeled Krzysh down Suzina Street. The boys' jackets bulged with what Tadzio assumed were pistols or Sten guns. Most likely, they patrolled the street in case those collecting weapons encountered trouble. Tadzio's stomach clenched. If he had noticed their hidden weapons, so would the Germans.

As Tadzio and the patrol turned down a side street, a German transport truck rolled into the intersection, then stopped.

Tadzio pulled in a quick breath.

The soldier on the passenger's side rolled down his window and shouted, "Halt!"

The boys in the patrol glanced at each other with panicked faces, then sprinted across the street.

Blam! Blam! Blam!

Blood pounded in Tadzio's ears.

Three insurgents fell.

Tadzio stopped his cart. "Out! Now!" he screamed.

As Krzysh clambered out, Tadzio grabbed a rifle from the carrier. With his heart thudding against his rib cage, Tadzio crouched behind a pile of paving stones. He raised his rifle and picked off two Germans who scrambled out the truck's rear.

Krzysh yanked a machine gun from the barrow. Tearing off his splint, he dove behind a pile of rubble and fired off a round.

The truck's windshield shattered. Blood oozed from the driver's head. He slumped against the steering wheel.

Tadzio's hand shook as he trained his rifle on the rear of the truck. He drew in a lungful of air, hoping to slow his pulse.

Stefan and Benyameen appeared on the other side of the street. One shot a German emerging from the vehicle's passenger side.

Two more Germans piled out the back, then crouched low, out of Tadzio's sight.

A second later, they crawled beneath the truck and turned their pistols toward Stefan and Benyameen's position.

Tadzio drew in a sharp breath and held it. Sweat drizzled down his back. He aimed beneath the truck and fired.

Blam!

Recoil. The sulfur smell stung his nose.

Blam!

Recoil.

Two shots. Two more dead Germans.

Tadzio raced to the cart and handed grenades to the remaining patrol members.

One tossed his at the truck.

Boom!

Even though Tadzio ducked and covered his ears, the blast reverberated in his head. Once the debris settled, he glanced out from behind his cover. The grenade had missed its mark.

He pulled in gasps of air. None seemed to reach his lungs.

Two more Germans piled out of the truck and sprinted toward the safety of rubble near the sidewalk.

With sweat dripping into his eyes, Tadzio aimed at one and fired.

Blam! He missed.

Another grenade exploded.

Again, Tadzio ducked behind his barricade.

"Yes!" one of the patrol boys shouted.

Tadzio looked out. The blast had taken out several Germans who had charged in from a side street.

Out-flanked and out-gunned, the remaining soldiers piled into the truck and sped off.

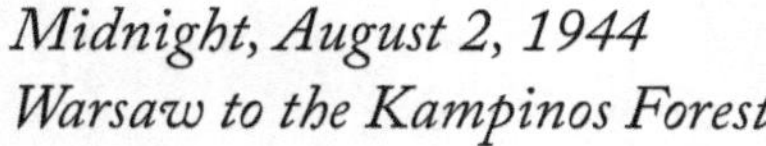

Midnight, August 2, 1944
Warsaw to the Kampinos Forest

"Come on, guys!" Tadzio shouted above the rain's patter. "We're falling behind." He waved his lagging friends forward. Rain clouds took turns sliding past the moon, alternately hiding or allowing thin shafts of lights to reach the earth. It wouldn't take much to lose sight of Baszta Battalion.

Krzysh shook his head, rain dripping from his helmet. He scurried beneath the cover of an oak. "I can't take another step. It must be midnight by now. We've hiked for two hours, and I'm soaked to the bone."

"We can't stop now." Tadzio swiped drops from his face. "We have to follow Baszta to the forest."

"But it's not even *our* battalion," Stefan said. He rushed to join Benyameen and Krzysh beneath the tree.

"Yes," Tadzio said, "but we've got to keep going."

Krzysh pulled out his canteen and sipped. "Just a brief break."

A dry, hacking cough cut the air. Stefan. He'd been sick for two weeks.

As a light rain continued to fall, Tadzio threw up a hand. "All right. Only a minute." With a reluctant grunt, he adjusted his helmet and stood beneath the canopy.

Before the Rising, he had seized his oversized headgear from a fallen soldier's grave. He figured the deceased insurgent wouldn't mind. He shivered beneath the tattered uniform Auntie M had given him. Her husband had worn it during the Great War. To better shield his rifle from the rain, he tugged his jacket more firmly around his ever-thinning waist.

Stefan, Krzysh, and Benyameen wore SS camouflage jackets and helmets stolen by Bastza Battalion earlier that morning. Like others who fought in the Rising, they wore red and white armbands on their upper right arms. Tadzio mused the only thing worse than getting shot by a German would be getting shot by a Pole who mistook him for a German.

He blew out a sigh, massaged his neck, and sat. They had fought all afternoon in Żolibroz District and missed their five o'clock rendezvous with Zoshka Battalion. Now, under Colonel Żywiciel's command, they fled to the safety of Kampinos Forest.

"I'm cold, I'm wet, and I'm hungry." Krzysh sat next to Tadzio and hugged his arms to his chest.

"Me too." Shivering, Benyameen pulled jerky from his rucksack, tore off a piece, and handed it to Krzysh, then devoured the rest.

From a map he'd scanned before leaving Warsaw, Tadzio guessed another ten miles lay between them and the safety of the forest. He clenched his jaw. "We need to go." With a grunt, he shouldered his rucksack and moved out from beneath the tree.

The annoying drizzle once again spit droplets onto his eyelashes and nose. He shivered from the chill.

Seized by another hacking cough, Stefan bent over and struggled to inhale.

Frustration and fear twisted Tadzio's gut. Did Stefan have enough strength to trek the next sixteen kilometers?

Benyameen turned to Stefan. "You all right?"

Stefan waved him off. "I'm fine." He coughed again. "Go on. I'll catch up."

Tadzio stepped closer. "No. We stick together." He spoke with a confidence he didn't feel. He scanned the darkness for a sign of Baszta Battalion. The light rain, combined with the moon's soft light bathed the area in a wispy glow, but no soldiers were in sight.

Once again, Tadzio joined the group. "We'll rest one more minute." As he leaned against the oak, Tadzio fought to keep his eyes open. He lost.

"What's the problem here?"

Tadzio jerked awake.

Their assigned platoon leader, Korwin, emerged from the darkness. Two others trailed behind him.

"Stefan's sick," Tadzio said. "We needed a quick break."

"You can't stop," Korwin barked. "We spotted German anti-aircraft gun positions up ahead. Move out. Now."

The boys groaned.

Stefan hacked again.

"You heard him." Tadzio waved the huddled group forward. "Let's go."

The boys followed.

At least the rain had stopped.

As they trudged on, Tadzio peered into the gray, wet fog ahead, hoping for a sign of the forest. Soon, an open field came into view. Tadzio shuddered. The eerie mist distorted the field's birches, willows, and wild apple trees. They appeared as Warsaw's dead, crying out for justice. But how could he, a Scout of eighteen, avenge their souls against a horde of evil Nazis? Like a rock dropped from a cliff, a ball of fear sunk to his gut.

A veiled ribbon of woods appeared in the distance. Relief washed over him. Soon they'd have a chance to rest.

For thirty more minutes, Tadzio and the others crept across a soft wet field covered with tall grasses. Slumbering, misshapen hamlets appeared off to the right.

Stefan stopped again, racked by another spasm.

Tadzio held up a hand. "Here." He turned to Stefan. "I'll carry your rucksack." Not waiting for an answer, he slid Stefan's backpack from his shoulders.

As his comrade doubled over in another coughing fit, Tadzio's insides chilled. He doubted Stefan could hike the rest of the way.

"I'll help, too." Krzysh reached out. "Let me take your rifle and belt."

Stefan shook his head. "I should keep my weapons handy." He coughed into the crook of his arm.

Benyameen sidled next to Tadzio and spoke in a low tone. "If there's a German anti-aircraft position ahead, Stefan will give us away."

Tadzio scanned the area and observed a large willow several feet ahead. Motioning them to follow, he led them beneath its branches. "Let's rest here. We'll catch up with Korwin in a few minutes."

They all agreed. Placing his rucksack beneath the tree, Tadzio sat.

A plane's engine roared overhead.

Tadzio jumped up. Adrenaline flooded his veins. He scrambled out from beneath the tree and peered into the black sky. Had the Allies come to their aid?

Like flashes of lightning, tracer bullets lit the sky.

Pa-shuu! Pa-shuu!

The boom of German ani-aircraft guns sent Tadzio racing back to the tree. Dread shot up his spine. Had the Nazis hit the plane? He listened for the whine of a descending plane. None came. Relieved, he pulled in a full breath.

He once again moved away from the tree and scanned the skies. Krzysh and Benyameen followed.

"Do you think the Russians have finally come to our aid?" Krzysh said.

Tadzio shook his head. "I doubt it's the Russians. Maybe it's the British or the Americans."

Benyameen nodded. "I heard Korwin say Russian troops recently reached Vistula River's eastern banks but didn't cross over. He thinks they'll camp there until the Rising's over. Then they'll swoop into Warsaw and *liberate* us from the Germans."

Once again, tracer bullets lit the sky and German cannons boomed. Then, an earth-trembling explosion.

Tadzio's insides shook. The whine from a plane's engine pierced the air, followed by a crash. His heart sank as he envisioned an allied plane crashing to the ground.

Boom! Another explosion sounded. This time, from somewhere nearby. The discharge reverberated in Tadzio's ears. Shrieks of pain filled the air.

Tadzio whipped around. What caused the blast?

Eying Stefan, Tadzio let his jaw drop. A homemade grenade from Stefan's belt must have exploded. Part of Stefan's stomach lay in a shredded, bloodied mess.

His mind reeling, Tadzio glanced at Benyameen.

Blood oozed from Benyameen's upper arm. Fragments from the grenade must have hit him as well.

With adrenaline coursing through his veins, Tadzio fought the urge to panic.

"Krzysh!" he shouted. "Take care of Benyameen. I'll see to Stefan."

"Those damned homemade bombs." Stefan groaned through clenched teeth.

Kneeling at Stefan's side, Tadzio whipped off his WWI jacket and cinched it around Stefan's mid-section. "We'll make you a stretcher and catch up with a medic."

For the first time, Tadzio took stock of himself. He wasn't bleeding anywhere. Then why did his entire body shake?

Stefan grabbed Tadzio's arm in a death-like grip. "A stretcher? Who ya fooling, Dombrowski? I'm not … gonna make it. Leave me here. Better yet, put me … outta my misery."

The scent of fear cut through Stefan's brave words. His face twisted into a mirror of pain. He pressed on Tadzio's now blood-soaked jacket.

Benyameen and Krzysh approached. Tadzio locked eyes with them and shook his head.

"Oh my God!" Benyameen shouted as he stepped closer.

Krzysh turned and retched.

"Tell Lech what happened." Stefan clutched Tadzio's knee. His eyes grew wide. "Find … Lech. Tell him … it's worth the fight."

He hadn't seen Lech for months, but Tadzio nodded. His eyes burned. "I'll tell him."

Stefan's breath came in short gasps. With wild eyes, he took in the three Scouts around him. "You've been … the best family … I've ever had." He gasped once more. Then he was gone.

CHAPTER 33

The Dinner

August 2, 1944
Warsaw, Poland

"I hate the *Schutzstaffel*," Captain Hosenfeld muttered to himself as he closed the College of Physical Education for the evening. Having just conducted a tour of the facilities for a group of SS officers from Berlin, he shuddered. During the tour, the men joked about new methods of interrogation they planned to use on Polish insurgents captured yesterday during Warsaw's Rising.

Hosenfeld checked his watch. Seven o'clock. He wanted to go home and shower, but there wasn't time. His old army buddy from the Great War, Kurt Kleinhoffer, would be here in thirty minutes. The captain locked the front door behind the SS officers and then worked his tight neck muscles. Why had he scheduled tonight's dinner with Kurt? The Pole's uprising yesterday had taken the German leaders by surprise. Everyone's nerves were frayed. Especially his.

Last year, when he first heard of Kurt's appointment as aide to the *Wehrmacht* Army's Chief-of-Staff, his heart swelled with pride for his old friend. Recently, however, he learned Kurt had accepted a position as aide to SS-General Erich von dem Bach. That's why Kurt was in town. He had to prepare for the SS general's arrival.

Hosenfeld hated the SS.

He hated von dem Bach even more.

He was glad, however, that he'd chosen to meet Kurt here at the college. It afforded more privacy than his own quarters or a public restaurant. Tightly gripping the polished oak railings, he climbed the marble staircase to the second floor where a local chef was setting out the meal he'd ordered for the occasion.

As his steps echoed off the walls, his mind reviewed the atrocities perpetrated by the SS during his five years in Warsaw. In the beginning, the SS only served as a special protection squadron for Hitler and other Nazi party leaders. Now, however, it had grown into the private army of the Nazi party.

After the Warsaw Poles' uprising yesterday, Hitler appointed von dem Bach as Commander-in-Chief over all German forces in Warsaw. A putrid taste rose in his mouth as he reached the last step. Over the past three years, the SS general had supervised the mass murder of 35,000 civilians in Latvia, and over 200,000 in eastern Poland and Belarus. Now, Hitler had appointed von dem Bach to deal a hammer-blow to the rebellious Poles.

In three more days, he, along with all Wehrmacht soldiers, would serve under that SS butcher's direct authority. During his meeting with Kurt, he would have to keep his opinions about the general to himself. No sense in getting off on the wrong foot with the aide of his new commander.

As he entered the meeting room where he and Kurt would sup together, he scanned the square table in the middle. Everything seemed in order. Atop a pristine white tablecloth, the chef had set out a tureen of white bean soup, pork with gravy, carrots, and pumpernickel bread.

The chef lifted a metal cover from a large platter. "And, the *spargel* in my special sauce, just as you ordered, Captain."

Wilm nodded. Spargel in wine sauce. It had always been one of Kurt's favorite dishes.

"And, as a treat for you," the chef added, "I surprise you with my Black Forest cherry cake. I know you have a weakness for it." The chef straightened his tall white cap and pointed to the three-layered cake on a side table.

Eyeing the treat, he let a corner of his mouth curve up. "You've outdone yourself, Gerhardt." As he studied the chef's masterpiece, however, his stomach soured. Topped with dark chocolate shavings, whipped cream, and red cherries, the dessert reminded him of the black, red, and white Nazi flag that waved everywhere in Warsaw. A flag his heart no longer honored. His gaze flitted to the beverages. A carafe of coffee and a decanter of Cognac. At least he'd made sure he had plenty of Kurt's favorite French after-dinner brandy on hand.

Finished with the preparations, Wilm led the chef back downstairs, unlocked the door, and let him out.

Just then, Kurt arrived. His friend removed his officer's visor cap, tucked it under his arm, and shook Hosenfeld's hand. "Wilm. So good to see you after all these years, old friend."

After exchanging greetings, Wilm led Kurt upstairs.

Kurt removed his officer's jacket and hung on the back of his chair. "So, Wilm, how are Annemarie and the four children?"

"I've got five now." Wilm let a grin spread across his face. "Little Ute was born two years ago." His heart pinched as he withdrew a family photo from his pocket and handed it to Kurt.

Kurt pointed to Wilm's jacket which he still wore. "I see from your shoulder boards that you've risen to the rank of captain since I last saw you."

Pouring Kurt and himself a bowl of soup, Wilm nodded. "When I was tasked with overseeing the construction of a prisoner-of-war camp, I received a promotion. It helped me send home a larger check." Thinking of home made his eyes burns. He needed to quickly change the subject.

Kurt talked about his travels and offered tidbits about his own family, but Wilm wished he could probe his friend deeper. He was careful not to talk about the war, but the pallor of his friend's face and his haunted gaze—they disturbed him. What had happened to the boisterous, life-loving Kurt he once knew?

Moving on to dessert, Kurt took one bite, then dropped his fork to his plate. He leaned back and studied Wilm's face. "Why is it that, throughout the entire meal, you've not said a single word about our current war?"

Wilm swallowed a sip of brandy to moisten his dry throat. "What can I say? It's war. It's hell. What's new?"

"I'm wondering…" Kurt hesitated, then raised a brow. "What are your feelings about the Schutzstaffel's involvement in all of this?"

"The SS?" Wilm sipped more brandy. "It's nothing like the Great War."

Kurt shook his head. "I had hoped that moving from the ranks of the Wehrmacht to the SS would provide me with greater security."

Wilm lowered his glass. "And? Has it?"

Seeming to ignore his question, Kurt leaned closer. "Truthfully, Wilm, what do you think about the SS?"

"I think truth is relative." Wilm shrugged. "Especially when talking with an aide of SS-General von dem Bach." Picking up his fork, Wilm stabbed a piece of cake off his plate.

A grin played across Kurt's face. "I always said you'd make an excellent politician." Grasping the Cognac decanter, his friend refilled his goblet. "However, I guess what you think doesn't really matter. I came here as a friend to tell you what *I* think. And then later tonight, I'm going to shoot myself."

Wilm's bite fell from his fork. Crumbs littered the tablecloth. A chill ran through him.

Suicide?

Leaning forward, Wilm held his friend with a stare. "Are you serious?"

"I've made up my mind." Kurt crossed his arms over his broad chest. "I've seen and heard too many deplorable things. *Mein Gott.* I've even approved and participated in them."

With a faraway gaze, his friend fingered his glass, then continued. "Only Germany's madmen believe we can win this war. There's no way out. There will be no revolution at home from those who disapprove of Hitler. No one has the courage to stand up to the SS. What use is there to try? You saw what happened after the July attempt on Hitler's life. The Nazis have too much power. The Wehrmacht is willingly being driven to its death."

Wilm's head spun. Every muscle in his body quivered. He'd never heard an officer speak so boldly. "What do you suggest?"

"Do you mean for those who choose not to kill themselves?" He offered Wilm a wry smile. "I suppose you just go on to the bitter end. Eventually, our entire nation will pay for the crimes we've committed."

He shook his head. His friend's words rang true. "I've felt the same way for quite some time but never felt safe to admit it."

Kurt let out a sour laugh. "Well, there's no one safer than a dead man."

Silence hung in the space between them.

After another sip of brandy, Kurt set down his glass. "I can't work another day for von dem Bach. The reason Hitler chose him as Commander-in-Chief of Warsaw's forces is because the *Führer* knows that SS-spawn-of-Satan won't show the Poles any mercy. Now, with this damned Rising, Hitler has issued a decree to destroy the entire city. His exact words to Von dem Bach are to not 'leave one stone upon another.' If any Poles survive the city's destruction, von dem Bach will ban them to the countryside, prisoner of war camps, or labor camps."

Wilm widened his eyes. "Destroy all of Warsaw?" The faces of his Polish friends came to mind. The Ciecioras. Father Wacław at St. John's Cathedral. The orphans for whom he'd bought shoes.

Shrugging his shoulders, Kurt pushed back his chair and stood.

Speechless, Wilm stumbled to his feet.

"Thank you for dinner." Kurt shook Wilm's hand then donned his jacket. "Now, if you'll excuse me, I have an execution to attend."

Chapter 34

The Kiss

August 2–4, 1944
Warsaw, Poland

The morning after Stefan's death, Tadzio and the Baszta Battalion abandoned the safety of the forest and marched back to Warsaw. If you could call what they did marching. Fatigue from yesterday's battle coupled with the damp, sleepless night in the woods, left Tadzio bone-tired.

At one point, Tadzio screamed, halted, and gripped his stomach. In his half-awake state, he thought it had twisted into a bloodied mess. Another time, he caught himself fingering the keys of an invisible piano as if performing at a school concert. Several times he fell asleep on his feet. He eyed the rag-tag group around him and saw he was no worse than the rest of them. How would they battle the Germans on the streets of Warsaw?

When they re-entered the capital, Tadzio's physical exhaustion paled in comparison to the gut-retching scene before him. Rubble and dead bodies lay everywhere. The sights and the stench seized his stomach. He choked on bile in an attempt to vomit, but had nothing to spew.

Tank shells had blasted through buildings in Old Town and near the Royal Castle. Chunks of concrete and splintered wood littered the fractured streets. Flattened rows of houses and apartment structures gave silent witness to bombs disgorged by German *Stukas*. Vigilant to escape notice, Tadzio and the others slunk into defensive positions around Żoliborz.

Did Auntie L's house still stand? Tadzio's heart clutched at the question. *Were the two aunties, Magdalena, and the children safe, in a hospital, or....*

No. He refused to let his mind go there. As he plodded on, he viewed more dead bodies. His insides twisted and suffered another dry heave.

Bombs would fall again today, and they had no anti-aircraft guns to protect themselves. He grit his teeth. How would they be able to hold back the onslaught of the German army?

No time to check on Magdalena and the others. He'd have to entrust them to God's care. While the Baszta Battalion took up defensive positions in Żoliborz, Tadzio, Krzysh, and Benyameen were ordered to report to the Wola District to rejoin their Zoshka Battalion.

After reporting to Commander Jerzy, a runner dispatched the boys to a spot near Okopowa Street. There, they found their platoon lying in wait for a German Panther tank that approached from the north. As soon as Andrzej saw them, he waved them over to join him behind what remained of a brick wall.

"Glad you made it back." Andrzej thumped Tadzio on the back.

Tadzio's vision blurred. "Not all of us."

"I'm sorry." Andrzej rubbed his stubbled face. "Fill me in later. Right now, we need your help near Mireckiego Street. Another tank's approaching from that direction." Andrzej pointed to a cache of weapons. "Grab as many petrol bombs and grenades as you can carry. Felek Platoon needs your help. They're west of here. Hanka will show you where."

Tadzio glanced behind him. Standing next to the weapons pile stood a young blonde. He remembered her from somewhere. Her deep-set eyes, tentative smile, and braided hair pinned to the back of her head pricked an old memory. Even dressed in a dusty gray skirt and crumpled white blouse, she appeared as attractive as when he'd first met her. "You're Anna, right?" He wiped his weary face with a hand. "I remember you from the 1939 Scout Camporee."

A slow smile framed her face.

Before she could answer, Andrzej stepped between them and

scowled. "Codenames only. This is Hanka Biała. White Hannah. She's a courier and nurse assigned to our Rudy Company. She'll direct you to Felek's position."

The back of Tadzio's throat stung. That was Andrzej. All business.

As soon as they met up with their assigned platoon, Lieutenant Kuba ordered them to lie in wait behind a cement barrier as the Panther groaned forward.

Two minutes later, Kuba shouted, "Attack!"

Grasping two cylindrical grenades, Tadzio summoned his remaining strength and charged out. Bending low, he pitched them at the tank's tracks.

Ba-chew! Ba-chew!

The blast pressed Tadzio back toward the cement barrier. He struggled to stay on his feet. A strange mix of shoe polish and bitter almond-like odors permeated the air.

Through dust and debris, he spotted Benyameen and Krzysh on his right as they lobbed petrol bombs at the tank's hull. Glass clinked and shattered. Flames whooshed to life against metal. Tadzio raised his arms to ward off the blaze.

More chemical grenades and petrol bombs exploded around the tank. After several disabling hits, the tank slipped on the pavement and crashed into a small house on the opposite side of the street. German crewmen popped open the hatch. They raised their hands and surrendered.

With his heart thudding against his chest, Tadzio joined Krzysh and Benyameen in pumping their fists into the air.

"I'll take the prisoners to our holding barracks," Lieutenant Kuba shouted above the din. "Jan and Ryk, with me. The rest you, secure the tank."

By the end of the day, The Zoshka Battalion had captured two Panther tanks. They dubbed the first *Magda*, and the second *Felek*.

Over the next three days, the battalion worked to retain control of Wola District. Tadzio slept only a few hours each night, but a renewed sense of purpose energized him. After five years of German occupation, he could finally fight back.

On August 4, Captain Jerzy assigned his fighters to storm the

German police barracks on Żelazna Street. Those inside put up a fierce resistance. As Tadzio and the rest of his platoon crouched behind a pile of rubble in front of the barracks, Andrzej relayed new orders.

"Maintain this position," he said. "Kolegium-A Company plans to set the building next door on fire. We'll provide cover. Once the fire spreads to the police station, Tadzio will continue to cover us while we storm the building."

Tadzio nodded.

Several Kolegium-A fighters ran out and tossed fire bombs and grenades into the adjoining structure.

A glint of light from the police barrack's second-story window caught Tadzio's attention. A German standing next to the open window had his rifle trained on those setting the fire. Tadzio pulled in a breath and held it.

Blam!

Blam!

Tadzio's second shot hit its mark. Tadzio released his breath.

Although flames licked a few walls inside the next-door building, the blaze refused to spread to the barracks. Tadzio swallowed, hoping to soothe his scratchy, dry throat. It didn't help.

After several more unsuccessful attempts to catch the police station on fire, Kolegium-A's commander shouted, "Attack!"

Krzysh, Benyameen, and Andrzej shot out from behind the rubble to join the fray. Three soldiers from Kolegium-A brought over a downed metal pole and used it as battering ram against the entrance. Loud thuds reverberated in the street, but the immense door refused to yield.

Sweat beaded Tadzio's forehead. Keeping his rifle trained on the police barrack windows, he blinked away a salty drop that trickled into his eye.

A roar of voices rose behind him. Tadzio glanced toward the sound. A crowd of civilians had gathered to cheer the insurgents. One man played a fast-paced tune on his accordion as others clapped and sang.

Tadzio shook his head at the incongruity of the situation, but the music and the citizen's cheers fueled his flagging spirit.

Turning back to the fight, Tadzio glimpsed a German in a third-story window. The soldier had his rifle trained on those at the door.

Taking aim, Tadzio squeezed his trigger and took him out with one shot.

Another German took his place, but he didn't have a rifle. Instead, as if in slow motion, the soldier pulled back his arm as he readied to launch a grenade on those below.

Tadzio yelled, "Watch out." With sweat trickling down his spine, he took aim and fired.

Ka-blam!

His bullet pierced the Nazi's forehead.

The man fell back, but not before his grenade fell onto the Polish fighters below.

Ka-chaw!

Shockwaves from the explosion threw Tadzio to the round. As if submerged underwater, voices around him sounded muffled and garbled.

He made out the screams of a nearby soldier. "My leg, my leg. Ohhh!"

Struggling to his feet, Tadzio peered through the dust and debris as Hanka and another nurse scurried to the injured man's side.

"Quick," Hanka shouted. "Help me stop Antek's bleeding. He's taken a lot of shrapnel."

Tadzio wiped the dust from his eyes. He stepped forward, but stumbled. The blast still rang in his ears. He barely heard Lt. Kuba's command to rush the seriously injured to the Karolkowa Street hospital.

He checked himself for missing body parts. To his relief, he found everything intact.

Later that night, Andrzej's Rudy Company billeted down in an abandoned shell of a house on Okopowa Street. Every muscle in Tadzio's body quivered with fatigue. "We haven't rested for three days," he complained as he dumped his rucksack on the floor next to Krzysh. He attempted to sit, but bending required too much effort.

Across the room, Andrzej placed his rucksack between himself and the parlor wall and collapsed against it.

Tadzio dragged himself over to his leader. "Have you seen Magdalena since the Rising started?"

Glancing up, Andrzej offered a tired nod. "I saw her earlier today when I helped take our casualties to the Karolkowa Street hospital."

"She's at the hospital?" His heart thrashed against his ribs. "What happened? How bad is she? I should be with her."

Andrzej raised a hand. "No, no. She's okay. She's working there." He ran a hand through his dirt-encrusted blond hair. "So many were injured on the first day of the Rising that we had to open up the Karolkowa hospital. The Żoliborz hospital staff asked her to go and help."

Benyameen leaned over. "What about Yacov and Lucyna? Are they still with Auntie M and Auntie L in the Żoliborz District?

"The Baszta Battalion's defending that area." Andrzej rubbed his stubbled face. "Last I heard, they were safe."

Lieutenant Kuba strode over. "Sorry, men." He shifted his gaze from Tadzio to Andrzej. "I need a word with Morro. Give us a moment."

Nodding, Tadzio hobbled away. He glanced around the cramped quarters and counted twenty-five exhausted soldiers scattered about. Some sprawled on the few remaining pieces of furniture that had survived the last two days of fighting. Others had collapsed on the dusty floor. At some point a tank shell had blasted a hole through the deserted home's front door and entryway.

Tadzio allowed his gaze to follow Hanka as she distributed tin cups to the soldiers. A girl carrying a cooking pot trailed behind her. It cheered him to see Hanka offer each man a smile as she ladled a scoop of brown liquid into the soldier's cup.

Moving back to his rucksack, Tadzio sat.

When Hanka reached him, he let his hand linger on hers for a few seconds before taking the cup. "Thanks."

She offered him a tired grin before moving on the Krzysh.

In two gulps, Tadzio gulped down his tepid broth and its bits of floating cabbage.

After the girls moved out of earshot, Krzysh pressed a hand to Tadzio's forehead. "Aha. Just as I suspected. You've got a fever. I'd diagnose it as a severe case of lovesickness."

Raising a brow, Tadzio set his empty cup on the floor. "I have no idea what you're talking about."

"Right." Krzysh play-punched his friend's arm.

Tadzio let a corner of his mouth turn up. "Back in '39, before the war, I met Anna—I mean Hanka—on our Scout Camporee in the Tatra Mountains. Remember? I sat next to her that night as Professor Handelsman spoke about the possibility of war with Germany. I never dreamed I'd meet her again like this."

"Yeah, I remember." Krzysh rubbed his hands on his bent knees. "And I bet you my wad of toilet paper you can't get her to kiss you tonight."

"Ewww." Tadzio wrinkled his nose. "What would I want with your wad of toilet paper?"

Krzysh flashed him his impish grin. "It's clean. I doubt *you've* got any clean paper to help you *take care of business*, if you know what I mean."

Leaning against the home's battered wall, Tadzio considered Krzysh's offer. Since the Rising began, he had eaten little, and as of yet, hadn't needed any toilet paper. But he figured the time would come. "Okay, I'll take you up on that bet. If I kiss Hanka before the end of the night, you owe me your wad of toilet paper. If I don't, I'll give you—"

"You'll give me half of your next meal." Krzysh extended his hand to close the deal.

Tadzio shook it. "Agreed."

After Andrzej finished speaking with Lt. Kuba, he stood to address the company.

"Men, we've got some good news. Earlier today, the Home Army secured both the power station and the main post office."

Benyameen raised his tin in a toast. "And don't forget our two captured tanks," he added.

The weary soldiers raised their cups and shouted, "Hurrah!" All except one. Starba. He sat in the corner with his left arm in a sling.

"Starba," Tadzio hollered from across the room. "Don't you feel like toasting our victories?"

Scowling, Starba adjusted his sling. "Not much of a victory, if you ask me. Reports say we lost over 2,000 soldiers yesterday. The Germans only lost about 500. Sounds more like a defeat than a win."

Tadzio ticked a muscle in his jawline, then turned his attention back to Hanka.

Their soup task completed, the girls checked and re-bandaged soldiers' wounds. When Hanka finished with her last patient, Tadzio approached her.

"Would you like to join me outside for some fresh air?"

She rubbed her nose and nodded. "It is rather ripe in here, isn't it?"

For the first time, Tadzio noticed the smothering scent of the sweat-infused room and gagged. He hadn't considered the odor until she mentioned it. It smelled like ammonia and cat poop.

As he guided her to the backyard, he tried to recall the last time he'd taken a bath. He drew a blank.

Eyeing a cement bench near a birch tree, he led her to it. They sat in silence and gazed at the August sunset. As the sun slipped past the horizon, ripples of rose-colored clouds adorned its descent.

"I love watching the sun set." Hanka breathed out a sigh. After another few seconds of silence, she turned to Tadzio. "I've thought a lot about what you asked me that night at the Camporee."

He drank in the warmth of her brown eyes. "You have? That was five years ago. I can't even remember what I asked you."

Hanka grinned. "We were only thirteen, but you asked if I knew what I wanted to do with my life." She flattened her hands atop her gray cotton skirt, then slid them toward her knees as if to smooth out the wrinkles. Appearing to give up, she tucked each side of the mid-length skirt beneath her knees. "It impressed me you would ask such a serious question."

Right now, serious questions were the last thing on his mind. He thought about Krzysh's bet. It made his stomach growl. Even though Krzysh was his best friend, he didn't want to share half of his next meal with him. He also thought more about toilet paper. It might come in handy sooner than he thought.

Tadzio leaned closer to Hanka. "And *have* you decided what you want to do with your life?"

She smiled—that cute, gentle one that only revealed a glimpse of her two beautifully even front teeth. Teeth hidden from full view by those lusciously full lips. His insides tingled.

"Yes." Hanka nodded. "After this dreadful war is over, I want to be a writer." Her voice picked up speed. "I want to travel, visit new places, meet new people, and write about what goes on in other parts of the world."

He loved the way her eyebrows arched above the curve of her eyes. When she smiled and her cheeks lifted, it was like part of her soul spilled out. He raised a hand as if to touch the glow. "You have the most beautiful brown eyes."

He pinched himself. *I can't believe I said that. She probably thinks I'm a cad.* "I'm sorry. I'm so exhausted, I don't know what I'm saying."

Hanka's cheeks flushed. "Are you saying you don't think I have the most beautiful brown eyes?"

"Ah, ah. You have, well, I mean—"

"It's all right." She laid a hand on his knee. "I'm just teasing." Grinning, she shifted her position on the bench. "And what do *you* want to do when all of this is over?"

Tadzio sat taller and pulled in a deep breath. He glanced around the garden, then back at Hanka. "I just want to survive this war. I don't want to be a hero. I just want to return to my piano music and my books."

"That's it?" Hanka tilted her head.

"Well," Tadzio leaned closer, "I might want to do a little traveling, too."

Hanka blushed again.

He placed his hand on her knee and pecked her cheek.

She smiled and kissed his forehead.

Dare I dare kiss those lips?

Before he could make good on his thought, Krzysh stumbled out the back door. "Tadzio, come quick. Magdalena's here. She's been shot."

CHAPTER 35

The Inferno

August 4, 1944
Wola District, Warsaw

"**N**urse. Water please," another feeble patient called out. Eager to take part in the Rising, Magdalena had volunteered to help at the Karolkowa Street hospital. Five days later, the facility filled to overflowing.

She urged her muscles to move faster, but they pulled, groaned, and flat-out refused. *I guess that's what comes of working eighteen hours a day.* At twenty-one, she'd seen enough brutality, suffering, and death to last a lifetime.

As she poured the wounded soldier a cup of water, she wistfully recalled how, at sixteen, she had only longed for the fragrance of fresh-cut roses, the heart-thrill of staring at a cute boy, and the excitement of imagining her first kiss. Now, only the smell of urine, blood, and antiseptic assaulted her nose. Only painful, contorted faces awaited her nurse's touch. Only bloodied and dismembered bodies lay beneath her as they anticipated the kiss of death.

After slaking the patient's thirst, she squeezed through a row of beds to check on a young man who'd come in yesterday. Grenade fragments had shredded one of his legs. "What's your name, soldier?"

"They call me Antek." The soldier managed a weak smile.

"Watch out for him," warned the soldier in the next bed. "He's a heartbreaker."

Magdalena glanced over. The man who warned her about Antek wore a white bandage over his right eye.

"Oh, come on, Stasinek." Antek groaned. "You're already married. Let the single guys have a chance."

She moved to Stasinek's bed and checked his chart. Yesterday, he'd broken his right occipital plate after an explosion threw him to the ground. As a child, he'd lost vision in his left eye. Now, according to his chart, he'd probably lose sight in his right eye as well. Magdalena swallowed hard and glanced at him again. She couldn't imagine going through life blind.

"Stasinek," a nurse addressed the man with the bandaged eye. "Are you giving Antek a hard time?"

"No more than usual, my dear Krystia." Stasinek reached out a hand.

Krystia moved to his side. Bending down, she kissed his cheek.

"You certainly look beautiful today, my bride." Stasinek smiled.

"That's a safe bet." She laughed. "Right now, you're blind."

The crackling of machine gun fire cut through their banter and reverberated off the basement walls.

A scream froze in Magdalena's throat. Her clipboard clattered to the ground.

Two nurses near the bottom of the staircase crashed to the floor. Blood oozed from their chests.

Shrieks rang out around the room.

Several soldiers pounded down the steps. Magdalena didn't recognize their uniforms. As they waved their guns, they shouted something in a language she didn't understand.

"What do they want?" she screamed to no one in particular. The men weren't speaking either German or Polish.

"They're ordering us to vacate the building!" Krystia shouted above the chaos.

Magdalena and Krystia helped Stasinek out of bed and up the steps.

"*Schnell*," a soldier on the basement floor yelled.

There *were* Germans in the group. Magdalena glanced back to see who had ordered them to move faster, but the man wasn't looking at her and Krystia. He was shouting at two nurses who were lifting Antek onto a stretcher. With his mangled leg, there was no way Antek could walk or even hobble out.

"*Nein!*" the soldier screamed. He shoved the nurses aside. He whipped out his Luger and pressed the barrel against Antek's skull.

Blam! Blam!

Magdalena turned away and vomited.

When she and Krystia reached the first floor, soldiers thrust them out the hospital door and into the street. They followed along behind other patients and staff as they guided Stasinek down several blocks.

"What's going on?" Stasinek's voice wavered as much as his faltering steps.

Before Krystia could answer, a soldier nudged Stasinek's back with his rifle's bayonet. "*Shvydshe!*" he shouted. "*Shvydshe!*"

Crunching her eyebrows, Magdalena glanced at Krystia.

Krystia draped her husband's arm over her shoulder. "He says to move faster."

"You understand them?" Magdalena shouldered Stasinek's other arm.

Krystia nodded as they plodded along. "They're speaking Ukrainian."

Other unintelligible words poured out of the soldiers' mouths as they pressed their captives forward.

When a few of the soldiers near them stopped to light cigarettes, Krystia glanced over at Magdalena. "I overheard them say they are leading us to a place where they plan to kill us."

Magdalena gasped. "Jesus, Mary, and Joseph!" She crossed herself with her free hand.

Stasinek gripped Magdalena's shoulder. "You two must escape. I'll fall to the ground, and, in the commotion, you two sneak away."

"I'm not going anywhere without you, soldier boy," Krystia said.

"And I'm with her," Magdalena shot back.

Raising his head to the sky, Stasinek sighed. "Women. There's no reasoning with them." A smile shadowed his face.

Magdalena pulled in a shaky breath. "Who are these soldiers, Krystia? I don't recognize their uniforms, except for the few that are German."

"Most are Ukrainian or Belarusians." Krystia kept her voice low. "My parents were from Ukraine, so I'm familiar with the language. They say the Germans got them out of prison in order to join this brigade."

"But why would Ukrainians and Belarusians agree to help the Germans? After taking over Poland, Germany invaded their countries too."

Krystia readjusted her husband's arm across her shoulder. "From the bits of conversation I've picked up, a German commander, Dirlewanger, is in charge here. He's promised these criminals freedom and money if they fight for the Germans. They don't seem to mind being drafted by the Nazis since they're getting paid to kill Poles. Most of them hate Poles more than Germans. As a bonus, before they murder us, they'll get to keep any valuables they poach off our bodies."

Magdalena shuddered and her vision swam. She didn't want her life to end this way. How could these monsters justify the slaughter of innocent people? Their victims were only wounded men and women, doctors and nurses.

Up ahead, soldiers herded patients and staff into an open shed next to a burning house. It appeared the soldiers were collecting their documents and valuables.

Pulling Stasinek and Krystia to a halt, Magdalena stopped in her tracks. As if weighted down by bricks, her legs refused to move. No nearby soldiers prodded them forward. With her mouth agape, she continued to stare ahead.

As the helpless victims exited the shed, the mercenaries ordered them into rows. Line by line, the ghoulish soldiers shoved them into the front yard of the burning home. At the opened doorway, one by one, the soldiers flung their captives into the inferno.

Magdalena snapped out of her trance when two Polish doctors standing near her bolted across the lot and disappeared around the side of the house.

Slavic voices shouted. Several shots rang out as soldiers chased after them.

She turned to Stasinek and Krystia. "Now's our chance. Let's make a run for it."

"Magdalena's right." Stasinek said. "Go now. Both of you. Leave me here."

"You can't get rid of me that easily," Krystia said. "I'm not leaving you behind." She pointed to the right. "There's an overpass about ten feet ahead. Maybe we can hide there. The soldiers might not even notice we're gone."

Magdalena nodded. "Let's go."

The trio scurried toward the span.

More shots rang out.

Since neither she nor her companions dropped from bullet wounds, Magdalena figured the soldiers weren't shooting at them. She kept moving.

Once they reached the overpass, Krystia stopped to catch her breath.

Stasinek urged her on. "You won't get far with me tagging along. Go. Meet up with the Zoshka Battalion on Okopowa Street."

Krystia squeezed her husband's arm. "You're not making a widow out of me today, mister."

Glancing at Magdalena, Krystia tilted her head. "But you should go. You'll have a better chance on your own."

"Forget it." Magdalena said. "The Karolkowa nurses are famous for taking excellent care of their patients. We all leave together."

Stasinek squeezed the girls' hands. "God bless you brave women."

The three scuttled out from beneath the bridge and turned onto Okopowa Street. As they crossed Żytnia, something zipped overhead, then pinged off a pile of bricks.

"Ahhh!" Searing pain bit through Magdalena's leg. She fell to the ground.

"My God, Magdalena!" Krystia shouted. "You're bleeding!"

More bullets zinged through the air.

"Find cover!" Stasinek shouted. "Krystia, if Magdalena can't walk, help me lift her legs while you drag her by the shoulders."

"My leg is on fire!" Magdalena tried to stand, but fell again.

Working in ragged tandem with Magdalena between them, Krystia dragged Magdalena by the armpits as she steered her blind husband forward.

With her head tilted back, Magdalena glimpsed a bombed-out building ahead. If only they could reach it in time.

More shots peppered back and forth. Bits of shattered brick flew through the air. Several bounced off Magdalena's arm. A few landed in her hair.

Once they reached the battered building, a soldier wearing a red and white armband rushed over.

"Kuba," Magdalena gasped. She clenched her teeth to hold back the pain. "Am I glad to see you." Recognizing him as one of the Zoshka Battalion's lieutenants, she reached for his hand and squeezed it.

"What are you doing here?" He wiped his grimy face with his shirtsleeve. "You just walked through the middle of a battle zone between my platoon and the Krauts."

Krystia ripped off the hem of her skirt and tied it around Magdalena's leg. "We need to get her medical attention right away."

Kuba gave a hand signal, and a soldier behind the crumbling wall came out. He helped Krystia with Stasinek while Kuba hefted Magdalena over his shoulder. "My men will lay down cover while we take you to the battalion's headquarters," Kuba said.

The last thing Magdalena remembered was seeing a cloud pass overhead before everything went black.

CHAPTER 36

Goose Farm

August 5, 1944
Wola District, Warsaw

"Don't worry," Magdalena whispered as Tadzio tiptoed into the bedroom where she lay. Hanka hovered over her, redressing her wound.

Tadzio's heart tore at the sight of his sister's soiled bandage. Too much blood.

Last night, he'd stood by as Kuba rushed her into their house barracks. He'd stayed at her side as a doctor removed the bullet. The doctor warned she'd lost a lot of blood. He'd have a better assessment in the morning. How could Magdalena tell him not to worry?

"The doctor just left." Hanka glanced up at Tadzio, her warm brown eyes meeting his gaze for only a moment. "She's stable now and can be transferred to the Długa Street Hospital in Old Town."

Old Town. How long would she be safe there? He'd already lost Henio. He couldn't lose her, too. And what about Yacov and Lucyna? The Aunties now cared for them at their home in the Żoliborz District. How long would it take the Germans to overrun that area?

Before he could ask, Magdalena raised a shaky hand. "The children are safe at Auntie L and Auntie M's, and I'll rejoin them after I recover." Her thin smile twisted into a wince of pain as Hanka secured the new bandage.

Tadzio stepped closer and gripped his sister's hand. "The Underground Army tasked Baszta Battalion with protecting Żoliborz

District, but what if they can't hold it? Who'll protect you then?" He clenched his jaw to stop its trembling.

"Then we'll find a safe place to hide until the Rising is over. I'll be fine. We'll all be fine."

Perhaps she thought she could fool him as she feigned to brush away a strand of sweaty hair from her eyes, but she didn't. His heart wrenched as she swiped at a tear that slid down her cheek. He studied Magdalena's unfocused eyes, then quirked a brow at Hanka.

"Her wound is clean," Hanka said. "The doctor removed all the bullet fragments. The hospital will monitor her for several days. After she returns home she'll need at least a week of bedrest. But she will recover."

"Like I said, I'm fine." Magdalena wrapped her fingers around Tadzio's. "Just make sure *you* stay safe. Enough about me. I heard you had a few victories in the Wola District."

The iron-framed bed let out a small creak as Tadzio sat next to her. He widened his eyes and nodded, hoping to appear optimistic. "We did. We captured two German tanks on the second day of the Rising. Later, we took control of the German police barracks on Żelazna Street." Gazing out the shattered bedroom window, Tadzio squinted to push out mental images of the bloodied, mangled bodies he saw that day.

Magdalena circled the top of his hand with her thumb and drew in a ragged breath. "I know. Whenever I close my eyes, I see them too. We cared for many of the men wounded in that battle before that butcher, Dirlewanger…" She paused and tugged her blanket more snugly around her body. She didn't finish her sentence.

What could he say to bolster their sagging spirits? If he lied, she'd see right through it.

She moistened her cracked lips. "So, what's your next mission?"

He swallowed hard to choke back his despair. "Now that we control the police barracks, Andrzej—I mean Morro—says our next goal is to capture Goose Farm on Gęsia Street. That will strengthen our position in Wola District. After we take Goose Farm, we'll link up with companies in Old Town. With both districts in our control, we can cut a path to the Vistula River." He withdrew a wrinkled sketch of Warsaw from his pocket and pressed it atop her blanket.

"The Vistula." She dragged a trembling finger over the river. "I see. We'll take Warsaw back from the Germans without the Soviets' help so that when the Russians do come, they can't claim our victory as their own."

Tadzio nodded and stuffed the map back into his pocket. "Right. The Russians are on the other side of the river, but have yet to help."

Once again, Magdalena's tired gaze met his. "Tell me more about Goose Farm. The Germans turned it into a concentration camp?"

"It's in the former Jewish Ghetto." He nodded. "Near Pawiak Prison." His voice picked up speed. "Andrzej says the camp has eight guard towers overlooking the surrounding streets and buildings. We plan to take out those towers with one of the captured German tanks. Then we'll storm the facility."

A knock sounded on the open door's framing. Not waiting for an invitation, Andrzej entered. A smile teased his lips. "You know, Magdalena, we've nicknamed one of our captured tanks *Magda*."

Tilting her head, Magdalena blinked several times. "After anyone I know?"

"After an old, wrinkled, heavy-set woman." Andrzej scrunched his face into a scowl.

Magdalena pouted. "Now you're just being mean."

"Actually, since Lieutenant Wacek's driving the thing, we let him name it. He said the beast reminds him of his grandmother. Big, mean, and powerful."

Andrzej stepped to Magdalena's bedside and rested a hand on Tadzio's shoulder. His grin faded. "I'll do my best to make sure your brother's safe."

An hour later, Tadzio, Krzysh, and Benyameen trailed the Felek Platoon down Gęsia Street. Andrzej had assigned them to Kuba's platoon for the Goose Farm mission, since Kuba's platoon had lost several men in their police barracks raid.

The captured Panther rumbled on in front of them. Kuba, his hand on the back of the tank, gave further instructions. "Lieutenant Kołczan and the Alek Platoon will engage the Goose Farm towers from Okopowa Street. They'll draw the Germans' attention to the eastern side while we attack from the front."

Kuba affectionately patted the rear of the tank. "We'll follow along behind Magda until Wacek blasts out the first tower on Gęsia Street. We'll have the element of surprise. The Krauts'll think they're being rescued by their own troops."

"And then we'll storm the camp?" Benyameen asked.

"Not until Wacek fires his second round. That'll be everyone's signal to enter."

Tadzio took stock of those around him. Like Krzysh and Benyameen, most were outfitted with stolen German uniforms and helmets. Others had civilian clothes. He still wore the WWI uniform Auntie M had given him. Several sizes too large, it encased him like an oversized shroud. The only thing binding the rag-tag crew together was their red and white armbands—that, and their shared sense of desperation.

As soon as the tank neared Goose Farm's gate, shots rang out at the eastern end of the camp.

Kuba turned and mouthed, "Alek Platoon," then waved the patrol forward.

They crouched behind the tank as it creaked toward the prison's entrance. Tadzio leaned out from the back and stole a peek at what lay ahead. He cringed at the sight of the large iron gates. The Germans had blocked the gate using concrete blocks, railway tracks, and other large objects, stacking them at least one story.

Impenetrable.

To his surprise, Wacek revved the tank forward. Little by little, he edged the beast over the top of the mound. No shots or shouts came from inside the camp. Why would they? After all, this was a German tank. Magda crawled over the pile, thundered down the other side, and crashed through the gates.

The tank's gears churned as it approached the tower. Wacek swiveled the turret —*Wrrrr… Click… Krrrr…*—until it aligned with the entryway's guard station.

Now, loud shouts and German swear words rang out. The enemy had broken through their gate using their own tank.

A cluster of grenades exploded near the tank's tracks. The ground trembled, and Tadzio lost his footing, eating a mouthful of dirt as he fell.

The grenades' blasts lifted the vehicle off the ground, but its tracks held firm.

With a shudder, the tank's turret discharged a shell. Its deafening *ka-shaw* reverberated throughout the camp. As the first tower fell, splinters of wood shot into the air.

A few eager men ignored Kuba's orders and streamed out from behind the tank before Wacek launched his second blast. With a rat-a-tat of their machine guns, the insurgents opened fire on soldiers in the second tower.

Still spitting dirt out of his mouth, Tadzio waited for Wacek's second shelling before leaving the safety of the tank.

With Krzysh to his left and Benyameen on his right, Tadzio ducked low. He trained his rifle on SS soldiers who now fired at them from the middle of the compound.

Boom!

The ground shook again. With another blast from the tank, the second tower exploded in a rain of debris. Tadzio choked on the dust as more rounds sounded and brought down the third and fourth towers.

Through the haze, Tadzio made out the ghostly shapes of Nazis fleeing the remaining four towers. Moving to a more protected spot behind several barrels, Tadzio observed several black-clad SS officers streak toward a building near the east end of the compound. Then, from his right, a lone German ran toward the southwest corner of the camp. With a machine gun slung over his shoulder, the soldier made a beeline for one of the now abandoned, but still standing watch towers.

Tadzio's pulse pounded in his ears as he sized up the situation. The tank, busy blasting the northern towers, wouldn't be able to fire at the southern end for at least another ten minutes. That gave the lone gunner, now climbing the watchtower stairs, freedom to rain down deadly fire on his friends at the far end of the compound. To make matters worse, prisoners dressed in what looked like striped pajamas now poured out of several prison buildings. Oblivious to the danger, they raised their arms and sang.

Lieutenant Kuba frantically waved them back inside. "For God's sake, take cover!" he shouted.

Instead of returning to their prison wards, they huddled together and gestured toward Kuba. Perhaps they wondered why Polish words streamed from the mouth of a man wearing a German uniform.

Kuba slapped his red and white armband. "Friends! We're friends!"

With all the confusion, no one took notice of the lone gunman.

"Watch out!" Tadzio warned. His voice rose in pitch. "The tower! Over there!" The raging battle swallowed his screams. It was up to him. He had to stop the gunman.

All else—his sweat, the screams, the swell of gunfire—faded into the background.

He scanned his surroundings. A rusty bicycle lay nearby. Rifle in hand, he raced toward it. Propping it up, he pedaled like a mad man. Bullets zinged overhead. The wind whipped his face. His chest refused to suck in air. He skidded to a stop at the south end of the camp. No time to slow his racing heart.

The gunman in the tower.

His friends.

A life for a life.

His vision sharpened. He pegged the man's face and fired. A scream rang out. A machine gun clattered down. A deathly silence followed.

No more b*ratatatatat* machine-gun fire.

Tadzio pulled in a breath.

The sounds of the battle brought him to the present moment. He raced back to the compound's center and brought down several Germans who raced toward the exit.

As he neared, Kuba shouted to him, Krzysh, Benyameen, and two others, then pointed to what looked like an administration building. "Check out the north wing. Flush out any Germans hiding there. Kołczan's platoon will secure the rest of the building."

Kuba then approached the prisoners who still stood in front of their prison barracks. The frail men assembled themselves into two long lines.

"Attention! Eyes left," their leader shouted in Polish as Kuba neared. "Sergeant Henryk Lederman, sir." The man saluted, and did not lower his arm until Kuba returned the gesture. "The Jewish Battalion is ready for action."

Overcome by the men's resolve and fortitude, Tadzio clenched his jaw to hold back a wave of emotion. Even in their weakened condition, these brave men stood ready to fight.

As directed, Tadzio, Krzysh, and Benyameen secured the administrative building's north wing. Kuba then assigned Tadzio and a few others to keep watch over the German prisoners that had been rounded up and assembled in the dining area.

When Tadzio entered the detention area, his stomach twisted. Well-fed, well-groomed SS men sporting clean black uniforms sat tall against the dining-room walls, hands fastened behind their backs. They stood in stark contrast to the starved, bedraggled Jewish prisoners he'd seen outside.

A table draped with a white tablecloth stretched across the center of the room. In the middle of the dining table sat a large, uncovered tureen of soup. It smelled like chicken. Bottles of liquor sat next to platters of untouched bratwurst, sauerkraut, spaetzle with sauce, carrots, and rolls. The overturned chairs gave silent witness to the enemies' hasty attempt at a retreat only moments earlier. In a corner of the room, an antique grandfather clock chimed eleven times. Their successful assault had only taken thirty minutes.

"You should have seen him, Morro," Kuba told Andrzej when they returned to their quarters later that night. "Your boy was brilliant. If your Scout hadn't ridden that bike like the devil himself, we would've lost more than just one soldier today. I'm recommending him for the *Virtuti Militari* award."

Tadzio drank in the gaze that Andrzej shot his way. His leader's raised brows, the nod of his head, and the curve at the corner of his mouth made Tadzio's chest fill out his gangly uniform a bit more. *If only Poppa could see me now.*

That night, Tadzio sat alone on the cement bench in the garden of the Okopowa house. He searched the skies for a glimpse of the North Star, but it kept slipping behind clusters of clouds.

Thoughts of his father invaded his mind. Where was he tonight? When Tadzio was young, his father had always been his North Star—his reference point. For the past several years, however, like tonight's star, Poppa's had become distant, his memory slipping in and out of view.

His stomach cramped. The walls of his chest chilled. The image of the old well at their manor house flashed across his mind.

Why the well? Why now?

The same twist in his gut.

The same frozen lungs.

He had experienced the same sensations and emotions after falling into the well.

Why did Poppa take so long to find me?

As if providing a cinematic background for his thoughts, a familiar strain from Paderewski's Violin Sonata in A Minor took center stage. He and Magdalena had played the piece at their last recital before Germany's invasion. While people applauded, Tadzio had scanned the audience for a glimpse of his father.

He had promised to come.

He never did.

He searched his memory. What were Father's last words that day at their summerhouse? *I need to leave now on an important business trip, and I'm not sure when I'll be back.*

Father had charged him to take over as man of the house.

A space pinched between his ribs.

Like viewing a grainy film, his mind replayed a reel of Father dragging two heavy suitcases out of the manor house barn, then shoving them into the back of Andrzej's Fiat. He hadn't seen his father since.

Why were those bags important, Poppa? Were they more important than our family? Perhaps Father had withdrawn the rest of their family fortune and was smuggling it out of the country before the Germans took over. Perhaps it was Father's way of ensuring their family's future. But would it?

What kind of future do we have without you to protect us?

A burning rose from his chest to his throat. No. Father was no longer his North Star. He needed a new star. A star he could keep in view.

CHAPTER 37

Hanka

August 7–11, 1944
Wola District, Warsaw

Two days after their Goose Camp victory, Tadzio barely recognized Hanka when she dragged herself through the doorway of Zoshka's Okapowa headquarters. "What happened to you?" He took a step back. "You look like you walked through a swamp."

Krzysh pinched his nose. "I hate to say it, but you smell like it, too."

Hanka sniffed the air. "As if you're all a bed of roses." She handed Krzysh the two satchels slung over her shoulders and wiped her muddy hands on her disheveled skirt. It didn't do any good. There were no clean, dry spots left on her wrinkled, torn clothes to receive the slimy residue.

Grabbing an abandoned shirt hanging on the back of a nearby chair, Tadzio used it to wipe smudges from her face.

"Thank you." The trace of a smile touched her lips as she took the shirt from him and wiped her hands and arms with it. "I just got back from Old Town. German patrols and Home Army barricades block all the intersections. I mucked through the sewers to get to the army's headquarters and back."

Krzysh suspended Hanka's bags by their straps as far from his body as possible. "Whatever's in here must be pretty important to tromp through sewers to get them." He shook his head. "I've been told the sewage can reach as high as your knees."

Still wiping her arms, Hanka nodded. "Worse. In some places, it comes up to your chest. Sometimes, a swift current rushes in and almost knocks you over. Even then, you're bent over, almost in half, trying to feel your way in the dark."

Tadzio shivered. Talk of dank sewers reminded him of the time he'd spent in the well at their manor house. "I'm sorry you had to go through that."

Swiping at the caked mud on her blouse, Hanka glanced at Tadzio. "Even worse is what's beneath the sludge. To keep from falling, you have to be careful to step over things you can't see. Branches, pieces of broken furniture, rocks, or…" She bit her lower lip. "Corpses."

Bile stung his throat as Tadzio fought to erase the gruesome scene from his mind. The stench that human waste had left on Hanka's clothes, however, wouldn't let him.

Apparently giving up her battle with mud, Hanka stopped wiping the grime. "Well, right now, sewers provide the only way to get from one district to another." She handed the now-soiled shirt to Tadzio.

Gripping it between his fingers, he tossed it into a corner.

Andrzej's whistle entered the hallway before he did. "Whew, Hanka. I smelled you from the back of the house. Bet you can't wait to get changed."

Twisting her mouth into a wry smile, Hanka pulled at the sides of her skirt as if to curtsey. "You boys really know how to flatter a girl."

"I know it was a tough assignment." Andrzej lowered his head. "But, the General Staff in Old Town wanted us to get our new armbands as soon as possible."

"Armbands?" Tadzio raised a brow.

Andrzej took a satchel from Krzysh and opened it. He pulled out a red and white cloth, turned it over in his hand, and pointed at a number stamped there. "Since the Home Army can't outfit us with proper uniforms, they've issued us new armbands. They've stamped each with a company's number. It'll make it easier to identify one another."

Tadzio winced. *And help identify our bodies if we're shot or blown up.*

A few hours later, after washing her hair and donning a clean blouse and skirt, Hanka distributed the numbered armbands to the battalion members. Another nurse followed to check names off a list.

After they received their new red and white ID bands, Andrzej stood and read an update Hanka had brought from the General Staff.

"Old Town is holding strong, but the Germans have rolled more tanks and heavy artillery into the Żoliborz District. Most of the civilians in Żoliborz have moved into the cellars as the enemy tries to blast our fighters out into the open.

Krzysh clutched Tadzio's shirt sleeve. "That means Lucyna and Yacov—"

"Are still being taken care of by Auntie L and Auntie M," Tadzio said to reassure his friend. He swallowed hard. If he could only reassure himself. He turned his attention back to Andrzej.

"Soldiers join the citizens in the cellars at night to get some rest. At first, the civilians cheered them on. But now, with food and water shortages, some citizens are questioning the wisdom of our fight."

Glancing across the room at Benyameen, Tadzio's heart sank. His friend had lowered his head onto his bent knees. Tadzio knew all too well the gut-wrenching spasms that stop your breath when you know your little brother or sister is in danger, and there's nothing you can do about it. Continuing to scan the room, he let his gaze rest on Starba. The young man, his arm still in a sling, slumped in the far corner of the room and stared out at those gathered there.

Starba glanced up and met Tadzio's gaze. A fire burned beneath the soldier's eyes as the wounded man now shifted his attention toward Andrzej. "Yeah." Starba huffed. "Things in the Żoliborz District might be bad, but what about what's happening right here in our district?"

"Starba." Benyameen lifted his head from his knees. "If you can't say something positive, then just shut up."

Starba shrugged and continued. "Sure, we had a momentary victory with Goose Camp. But today, while my group manned a barricade, the dirty Germans and Ukrainians herded hundreds of civilians in front of their tanks as they closed in on our position. We didn't want to risk killing innocent civilians, so we abandoned the barricades and pulled back. Those barbarians. If you ask me, it's hopeless."

Krzysh picked up a fragment of cement from the dusty floor and flung it at Starba. "No one's asking you."

Ignoring Krzysh, Starba droned on. "And what about the massacres? I hear the Germans have slaughtered about 30,000 citizens in our district over the past few days. And when that stupid SS general von dem Bach realized his mass murders only enraged us to fight harder, he ordered the brigades to stop their slaughters. Now, the Nazis just send captured citizens to concentration camps. Or put them into work groups."

Andrzej opened his mouth as if to say something, but a loud voice spoke up first.

"I saw it myself. Yesterday, while on patrol."

Tadzio searched the room to see who had spoken. The man sat with a group of middle-aged men near Andrzej. He was Pan Plonski, the butcher his mother had used when they ordered meat.

"The Germans ordered groups of citizens to pile up dead bodies and then dump them into nearby homes." Pan Plonski ran a large hand over his stubbled face. "Then, the Krauts set the houses on fire. Once they torched all the evidence of a mass slaughter, they shot those in work groups and burned their bodies, too."

Andrzej raked a hand through his unwashed mop of hair. "You're right, men." His voice rang out louder than usual. "Things are bad here in Wola District. But we've also had our successes. The Germans' aim is to break through from Wola to the Saski Gardens. That will give them access to the Kierbedzia Bridge. From there, they can cross the Vistula River. If they secure an east-west corridor through Warsaw, they'll be able to attack Russians gathering on the other side." Standing taller, he boomed louder. "But all along the way, the Germans run into fierce opposition from our forces at every barricade. Every house. Every kilometer."

"Yeah," Starba added, "until we're all dead."

The man was right. How could they hope to stand against the invincible German horde? How much unnecessary pain and death would their fool-hearted bravery cause? As if falling into their manorhouse well all over again, the edges of Tadzio's vision narrowed. He let his head drop to his knees. His head spun. His insides twisted.

A hand touched his knee. He jumped.

"Here's your new armband, Tadzio."

As Hanka handed him his new red and white striped cloth, he squeezed her fingers. His tired eyes fought to focus on hers. "What if Starba's right?" He pushed the words past his dry lips. "What if things really are hopeless?"

She gripped his hand. "You can't lose hope." Her jaw stiffened. "Once you lose that, there's nothing left."

"But what's the use?" He shook his head. "We're out-manned, outgunned, and before long, they'll overrun our positions here in Wola District." He glanced at her moist brown eyes, her full lips, her supple white skin. For her sake, he wanted to believe they had a chance to survive the Rising. But how could he have any hope in the face of such naked hopelessness?

The next day, Jerzy, the battalion commander, laid out plans to shore up Zoshka's control of Wola District. After assigning various companies to strategic points, Jerzy directed Andrzej's Rudy Company to engage German forces hunkered down in a school building that lay along the path to the Vistula River.

As instructed, when they reached the site, Tadzio rushed up the staircase of the building next to the school. From here, he picked off German officers leading the enemy's defense of the building. By the end of the day, the Zoshka Battalion flushed out the Germans and took control of the school.

For the next three days, Tadzio's Rudy Company rebuffed German counterattacks. They ate and slept inside the building with rifles in hand. While Tadzio and his friends struggled to keep the enemy at bay, Hanka and other nurses distributed instructions, ammunition, and meals, and cared for the wounded.

On the third day, Tadzio peered out a broken window facing the front of the school. No Germans in sight. Then, his ears perked at the sound of a whine. An incoming shell.

"Run!"

Too late.

Ka-blam!

The wall of the room next to him crumbled.

His ears rang. He coughed, choking on a cloud of dust. He braved another glance out the window. A German inched toward his position.

The soldier raised an arm to toss a grenade.

Tadzio landed a bullet in the man's skull.

The grenade burst before it left the man's arm.

"Retreat!" someone shouted from another room. Other voices down the hallway repeated the order.

We can't give up now! Clenching his teeth, Tadzio peered out the window again. Three Germans charged his position.

Blam!

Blam!

Blam!

He brought down all three.

"Tadzio!" Hanka ran into the room and seized his shoulder. "We've got to get out. Now!"

He gripped her hand, and they ran out together. Gunpowder and dust stung his eyes. He tripped over pieces of brick and broken glass as they darted toward the rear of the building. Through the haze, Tadzio recognized Benyameen up ahead.

"This way." Benyameen pointed down a hallway.

Tadzio tracked Benyameen's lead.

When they reached a back door, Benyameen ran across an open area in a crisscross pattern. Others in the company laid down fire to ensure his escape.

Tadzio turned to Hanka. "Keep your head down. Zig-zag to the other side. I'll go first. You follow."

He kissed her on the lips and ran out. Bullets zipped around his head. One grazed his arm, but he dashed to safety. He turned and glimpsed Hanka more than halfway across. "Come on. Just a little more."

Only three meters. So close. He imagined her in the safety of his arms.

Rat-a-tat-tat-tat! Machine gun fire ripped through the air.

Hanka jerked and fell as bullets riddled her body.

"No!" Tadzio screamed.

Chapter 38

Sewers

August 12—15, 1944
Długa Street Hospital, Warsaw

Tadzio hunkered down behind a pile of paving stones. He winced as one of the battalion nurses bandaged his right arm. He then scowled at Andrzej. "What do you mean, there's no time to bury Hanka?"

"Our position's overrun. We've got to leave. Now." Andrzej peered over the top of their barricade. "We've been ordered to abandon Wola District. We'll evacuate through sewers to Old Town."

Sewers. Tadzio's breathing came hard and fast. Those dark, putrid-smelling cesspits. Hanka had braved them. Could he? *Hanka.* He couldn't erase the image of her bullet-ridden body from his mind. Losing her stripped away his last shred of hope. Starba was right. They had pitched a battle against an impenetrable force.

Andrzej glanced at the nurse bandaging Tadzio's arm. "Lidka, as soon as you can, meet us on Chlondra Street." Motioning for others to follow, Andrzej dashed out.

Krzysh crouched next to his friend. "Ready?"

Tadzio shook his head.

"He's ready to go." Lidka cinched the bandage and packed her supplies in her rucksack.

Benyameen placed his hand beneath Tadzio's left armpit. "Come on. I'll help you up."

His right arm burned, and his head pounded. When Benyameen raised him, the world spun. He opened his mouth to pull in more air and panted faster. He forced himself to stand, then collapsed to the ground. "I can't feel my right leg. It's numb."

"You're hyperventilating." Lidka cupped her hands around Tadzio's mouth. "Purse your lips and breathe slowly. That should help."

Tadzio obeyed.

"We've got to leave now." Krzysh glanced over the barricade. "The others are almost out of sight."

With Krzysh on one side and Benyameen on the other, Tadzio half-walked and let his friends half-drag him to their rendezvous point on Chlondra Street.

Starba, rifle in hand, stood at the manhole's entrance. "About time you got here. I'm bringing up the rear. Climb in."

After Lidka descended, Benyameen clambered down. He guided Tadzio's numb foot to each rung. "One more," Benyameen said.

Reaching the sewer floor, Benyameen and Krzysh sandwiched Tadzio between them. As Tadzio followed Benyameen, the pins-and-needles sensation in his leg eventually subsided. But his panic remained. Why couldn't he slow his breathing? Every muscle vibrated. He bent at the waist to avoid hitting his head on the oval pipe. It didn't matter whether his eyes were open or shut. Darkness swallowed him.

Scenes flashed in his mind. Tumbling down their summerhouse well. Searing pain in his right arm. Suffocating blackness. Screams from a little five-year-old boy trapped inside him screamed. *Poppa! I'm down in the well. Come find me. Where are you?*

"Grab the leather strap across my back." Benyameen's voice sounded far away.

Tadzio reached out until he found Benyameen's weapon strap. He clutched his fingers around it as they plodded forward.

"And I'm right behind you," Krzysh added.

Krzysh's tap on his right shoulder didn't lessen his dread. The putrid stench of sewage flooded his nostrils and wrenched his insides.

Air. He needed fresh air.

He stumbled over something beneath the sewage, but his hold on Benyameen's strap kept him from falling. They plodded on through knee-high wastewater.

At last, a blast of fresh air rushed in. Light shone ahead. Hands reached down and pulled him out.

"Welcome to Old Town," a fellow-soldier greeted.

Two days later, Tadzio glanced up at the nurse tending his arm. "When can I get out of here?" He'd spent the last two days at Długa Street Hospital in Old Town.

"Not until we've gotten your infections under control." The nurse handed him his meds and a cup of water.

When he reached for the cup, fiery pain shot down his arm. He sipped the water and downed the pills. After swallowing them, his stomach cramped. "Bedpan. Please," he said between clenched teeth.

The next day, he willed his infection to clear. He reasoned he could still fight with a bandaged arm. His dysentery, however, was a different story. It left him nauseous and weak. The last time he tried to make it to the latrine on his own, he passed out.

Alone and depressed, he wished Magdalena had been assigned to work at the hospital. Her skills were needed elsewhere, however. She now worked in Old Town as a radio operator for the General Staff.

Resting his head on his pillow, he closed his eyes and fell into a fitful sleep. Feverish dreams haunted him. Ghostly apparitions of wide-eyed friends shot down in battle. Hanka's blood-soaked body, face down in the dirt, only two feet away. Nazi foreheads pierced by his sniper bullets. He'd told Hanka he didn't want to be a hero. He still didn't. He wanted revenge.

On August 15, the vicar of St. John's Cathedral visited Długa Street Hospital. The black-clad priest scraped a wooden chair across the cement floor and pulled it to Tadzio's bedside. "How are you doing, soldier?"

"I just want out of here, Father," he said between parched lips.

"In good time, son." Father Wacław handed him a cup of water.

Propping himself up on one elbow, Tadzio took the cup and sipped. "How's the battle going?"

The priest raised a brow and offered a faint smile. "Our forces laid a telephone line through the sewers. It now connects General Monter's headquarters in City Center with General Bór's hub here in Old Town." The vicar pulled in a heavy breath. "But the enemy is closing in. Ukrainian butchers captured Royal Castle, and Germans attacked Old Town's southern end." A muscle in his jaw ticked. "If help doesn't come soon, it won't take long before they reach us here."

Tadzio handed Father Wacław his cup and narrowed his gaze. "I've given up looking for help. British forces aren't coming. American G.I.s aren't coming." His voice rose. "Russian Communists camped across the Vistula aren't coming. Everyone's left us to die. We're pawns in their game of chess. Expendable. Abandoned."

Leaning closer, Father Wacław's gaze bored into Tadzio's. "We must not lose hope. Even if it seems all have abandoned us, we know God hasn't."

Tadzio swallowed, broke off the priest's stare, and raised his chin. "Do you really believe that, Father?" His words sounded sharper than intended, but he pressed on. "I know what it's like to be abandoned. My father abandoned me. My mother's in a prison camp. My little brother…" The image of Henio's bullet-pierced body flashed across his mind. Hot tears raced down his cheeks. He swiped them with a fist. "The least I can do is get out of this stupid hospital. Kill those damned Nazis. As many as I can. You've seen their evil acts. There's no justice. Only death. Slow, sickening death. How can you say God hasn't abandoned us?"

Father Wacław pinched his eyes shut, then slowly opened them. "Tadzio, I wish I could say more. But, know this. Your earthly father did not abandon you. Your heavenly Father hasn't abandoned you, either. I know these two very well, and I trust them to act according to their true natures."

My father didn't abandon me? What does Father Wacław know that I don't? Tadzio stared into the priest's sad but gentle brown eyes. "Do you know where my father is?"

Fingering the crucifix around his neck, Father Wacław gazed around the room. He then focused again on Tadzio. "About four months before Germany invaded Poland, your father met with me one Sunday after church. I remember because he seemed very distressed. I had never seen him so upset."

Tadzio readjusted his position on the bed. "I think I recall that day. We were already at church. He arrived about ten minutes late, but he kept checking his watch all through Mass. Then, after your sermon, he grew calm. When Mass was over, he sent us home. He said he needed to stay and talk with you."

The priest nodded and continued. "He asked about a passage we read that morning. It was about three Jewish men who vowed not to serve an evil king. When confronted with either bowing down to the monarch or being thrown into a fiery furnace, the young men told the king, *God is able to save us from the fiery furnace. But even if he doesn't, know O king that we will never bow down to you. We serve the one and only most high God.*"

Tadzio glanced at the wounded soldiers around him. Like the young men in the story, they'd given their all to fight against the pagan dictator, Hitler. His gaze returned to the priest.

"Your father asked how he could latch onto the kind of hope those young Jewish men had," the priest continued. "A hope, a confidence in God to provide him with an anchor for his soul."

Tadzio shook his head. It felt as heavy as a mortar shell. "And what did you say?"

"I said to focus on what is true, just, and good. People may fail you, but God never will. Even when evil seems to prevail, God remains sovereign. Until the Lord brings about His justice, we must continue to choose acts of love and sacrifice over cowardice and greed. To choose what is right over what is convenient."

Tadzio's mouth went dry. His tongue felt thick. "I don't know if I can do that."

The priest inhaled, as if to say something, but then pressed his lips together. "It's time for me to say Mass for the patients." He stood. "Don't lose hope. Your father didn't."

Father Wacław moved to the brick wall in front of the patients' beds where he had mounted a cross. A table with candles stood in front of the wall. He put on his vestments and said Mass.

From his bed, Tadzio moved his lips as Father Wacław recited the liturgy, but his heart and mind drifted to thoughts about the war. Would Russians come to their aid before Germans slaughtered all of Warsaw's fighters? Was their uprising doomed to fail?

For the next seven days, Tadzio's mood continued to decline. Magdalena visited and tried to cheer him, but Warsaw's mounting losses drowned out any hope of victory.

CHAPTER 39

Don't Lose Hope

August 30–August 31, 1944
Old Town to City Center, Warsaw

Two weeks later, the doctors cleared Tadzio for duty. He rejoined his battalion in Old Town as they fought to maintain a position in the ruins of the Sapieżyńska Street Fiat Factory. Hour by hour, the Germans closed ranks around them. Each time Tadzio brought down a soldier, another took his place.

On the night of August 30, Andrzej and Captain Jerzy returned to the factory after their briefing with Colonel Radosław.

"Men," Jerzy began after calling the battalion together, "I'm proud to announce that Colonel Radosław has appointed Morro as Zoshka's new commander. He will assume his position once we vacate Old Town and reach City Center."

Tadzio had always admired Andrzej's leadership skills. His chest now swelled with pride. The promotion made Andrzej, at twenty-one, the youngest battalion leader in the Home Army.

Benyameen rose to his feet. "You mean we're giving up our position here in the Fiat Factory?"

The room buzzed. "What?"

"We're retreating from Old Town?"

"Give up 600 years of Polish history?"

"No. We can hold out. They can't take Old Town."

"Forget it. Staying here is suicide."

Tadzio raised his voice above the rest. "Where do we go next, Commander Morro?"

As if responding to his new title, a corner of Andrzej's mouth turned up. "I'm not Commander yet. Captain Jerzy's still in charge. Until we reach City Center, I'm only Rudy Company's leader."

Captain Jerzy laid a hand on Andrej's shoulder. "Go ahead, Lieutenant Morro. Explain our evacuation plan."

Andrzej nodded and unfolded a large hand-drawn map. Captain Jerzy held up one side as Andrzej held up the other.

The soldiers crowded around.

"Tonight, the remaining forces of Radosław Group will evacuate Old Town through sewers here on Bielanska." Andrzej pointed to the street on the map. "We leave in an hour to join them. The plan is to meet up with Czata and Broda Battalions near the Bank of Poland by midnight."

"Then what?" Starba shrugged. His face pinched into a dismal frown.

"Then we'll surprise Dirlewanger's forces from behind." Andrzej's words picked up speed as he tapped the map. "Our combined battalions will cut a path through German lines laying siege to Old Town. That'll give the sick and wounded trapped in Old Town a chance to escape to City Center before all our forces retreat."

Krzysh's eyes widened. He held up his hands. "We can't give up our position here. Once the Germans take over Old Town, who will stop them from advancing to Żoliborz District?"

"Not much to give up," Starba grumbled. "Most of Old Town's a pile of rubble."

Tadzio winced. Although he agreed with Starba, his insides twisted as he gazed at Krzysh. His friend's face whitened with Starba's remark. Krzysh's sister Lucyna, along with Magdalena, Yacob, and the two aunties, were still in Żoliborz. Tadzio's throat and chest burned. Would everyone he loved end up like Hanka and Henio?

Captain Jerzy pointed to the district north of Old Town. "Colonel Żywiciel's division is holding strong here in Żoliborz. For now, the northern end of Warsaw remains protected." He let his gaze rest on members of his battalion. "Our Radosław Division began the fight for Old Town with five thousand. Now, our numbers are down to fifteen hundred."

A cold darkness flooded Tadzio's insides. He shivered, even though sweat plastered his shirt to his back. How many more would die before this was over?

Andrzej's jaw ticked as he folded up the map. "And our own Zoshka Battalion began with 300. Now, we're down to 80. We can't possibly protect Old Town's 200,000 citizens with such meager forces." He handed the map to Jerzy.

"And our ammunition stocks are depleted. We can't go on," the captain added as he stuffed the map into his shirt pocket. "General Bór and his staff have already evacuated Old Town through the sewers."

General Bór already retreated? Tadzio's insides flamed. *Through the sewers?* The weight of retreat. The abandonment of Old Town. The unknown fate of those left in Żoliborz. Something inside Tadzio snapped. He dropped to the floor, bent his knees, and held his head between his hands. Darkness flooded not only his body, but also his soul.

"As you can see," Andrzej added, "it's vital we link up with Czata and Broda Battalions to take Dirlewanger by surprise. Cutting a safe corridor from Old Town to City Center is the only way to provide the sick and wounded a way of escape."

Tadzio squeezed his eyes shut and covered his head with his hands. He'd heard Magdalena's stories of what happened at her Karolkowa Street Hospital. Andrzej was right. Unlike the soldiers, Old Town's sick and wounded wouldn't be able to travel through the sewers. If they reached City Center before the Germans seized the district, if they created a passage for them to escape to City Center, the sick and wounded would have a chance. If not, the German Army would butcher them for sure.

Tadzio hadn't slept for more than four hours at a time since he rejoined his battalion. Now, at 1 AM on August 31, he and the others crept out of the factory and scurried to the manhole on Balienska street. They were already an hour late for their rendezvous with Czata and Broda Battalions at the Bank of Poland. Tadzio hoped they wouldn't be too late for those still trapped in Old Town. He guessed their tromp through the sewers would take another hour or two, putting them almost three hours behind schedule.

After climbing down the manhole's ladder, Tadzio raised his rifle over his head and waded into the foul sewage water. He tripped on something beneath the sludge, but steadied himself on the slippery sides of the sewer's wall. Despite a splitting headache and the stench that engulfed him, he willed himself forward—until Benyameen, a few steps in front of him, cried out.

"My leg!"

Tadzio blinked in the darkness. Sewage sloshed around him. "What's wrong?" he yelled. His limbs tingled and his mind whirred. Had something or someone grabbed Benyameen's leg?

Krzysh, traipsing in front of Benyameen, turned and clicked on his flashlight.

The beam blinded Tadzio, and he shuttered his eyes.

When Krzysh lowered the light, Tadzio opened his eyes. Krzysh's beam focused on a roll of barbed wire. Wire that now encased Benyameen's leg.

"Shut off the damned light," a voice cried out in the darkness. "The Krauts'll see it through the manhole covers and drop a grenade on us."

"And if they can't see the light," another man whispered, "they'll definitely hear our voices. Keep quiet!"

Before Krzysh clicked off his light, Tadzio moved to Benyameen's side. With the butt of his gun, he dislodged most of the wire from Benyameen's leg. A final strand, however, still hung on. Handing Krzysh his rifle, Tadzio wrapped his jacket around his own arm and hand. As he pulled off the remaining wire, barbs cut through his jacket, piercing his arms and hands. He bit his tongue against the pain. At least he had freed Benyameen's leg.

His friend grimaced. "Thanks."

Before Krzysh clicked off his flashlight, splotches of blood appeared on Benyameen's pants leg.

As Tadzio plodded on behind Benyameen, he raised his punctured arms and hands to keep them out of the bacteria-infested sewage. His limping friend would certainly need antibiotics once they reached the City Center. So would he.

They arrived at their rendezvous point at 3 AM—three hours late. After scrambling out of the sewer, Tadzio bent and retched. His head pounded. A moment later, after catching his breath, he glanced around his moonlit surroundings. Had Czata and Broda Battalions waited for them?

Once everyone had emerged from the sewer, Andrzej waved his straggling company to follow him across a rubble-strewn street. As soon as they stepped out, German tracer bullets zipped through the air.

Andrzej swerved left and pointed toward a low wall. "Quick. Find cover over there."

Everyone obeyed.

Tadzio glanced behind him. Starba lumbered forward, bringing up the rear.

Bullets pinged off the wall as they neared it. Bits of plaster pecked Tadzio's face. He raced behind the barrier, his heart thudding against his chest.

German shouts pierced the darkness. "*Halt! Hände hoch*! Stop! Hands high!"

Andrzej ignored the warning and pushed them on to the next broken-down wall.

Rat-a-tat. Blam. Blam. Blam.

Gunfire rained down.

Blood pounded in Tadzio's ears. As he dove behind the next barricade, a scream rang out. Starba? He peered around the crumbling wall.

Starba's bloodied, unmoving form lay crumpled in the street.

From somewhere in the dark, Andrzej called for them to move again, but Tadzio couldn't budge. Another man down. What was the point?

Krzysh grabbed his arm and tugged. "Come on. There's nothing we can do for Starba now."

Shaking his head and sucking in a breath, Tadzio trailed Krzysh and the others. He snaked between low brick walls and mounds of rubble. Several blocks later, a nine-foot stone wall blocked their way. Andrej jumped and grabbed at protruding stones, then scaled the hurdle in one more jump.

Tadzio lunged at the wall and grasped for a hold. Finding none, he tumbled to the ground. The stones scraped his barbed wire wounds, making them they bleed again. He gritted his teeth against the sting. On his second try, he gained a foothold, but when he reached the top, his strength gave out. He couldn't pull himself over. He slipped and fell to the ground.

Benyameen, despite his gouged leg, scrambled over the wall in two attempts. "Try again," he urged Tadzio. "I'll help." He leaned down and extended his arm.

Panting, Tadzio lunged at the wall. With Krzysh pushing from behind, he scrabbled over the stones and grasped Benyameen's hand.

"Thanks," he said when he reached the top.

With machine-gun fire riddling their way, Tadzio mustered his remaining strength. He raced with the others to a burnt-out flat across the street from St. Anthony's Church.

Once everyone reached the flat, Tadzio dropped to the floor and counted their number. *Nine.*

German soldiers closed in.

Tadzio's breath came in short spurts.

He moved to peek through cracks in the wall. The Germans only shot from behind barrels and piles of debris, their bullets falling short of the flat. Thankfully, none had rushed their building. Yet.

He caught glimpses of the morning sun as it broke through the spaces between the buildings in front of them. Their pre-dawn sprint to the flat had disoriented him. Staring through the cracks again, he made out the familiar shape of Saski Gardens not far away. That meant the Bank of Poland was behind them. Tadzio guessed they had missed their rendezvous with Czata and Broda. Where was the rest of his Zoshka Battalion?

With their limited numbers, the nine of them had no way of escape. Overcome by exhaustion, Tazio sat against a wall to wait for the inevitable.

A wounded soldier in the street cried out. "Medic!"

Blam!

No more groans. A German bullet finished him off.

"I'm scared." Krzysh's voice trembled as he sat next to Tadzio.

"Me too," Tadzio admitted. He glanced around the gutted remains of the flat and rubbed his nose against the scent of its charred walls and beams. For some strange reason, it reminded him of the popcorn his father had burned the evening before he left the manorhouse.

I'll never ever see Poppa again. Or Magdalena. Tadzio's throat burned. Tears threatened to fall. He fought them back and gripped his rifle, willing his trembling hands to still.

He glanced across the room at Benyameen. His friend lay on his left leg as he crouched beneath a broken window. His right leg was covered in blood.

Benyameen met Tadzio's gaze. "Do you think the Allies will come to our aid?"

He wanted to give Benyameen hope. Hope that he'd see his little brother again. Tadzio swallowed hard, then shook his head. "I doubt it. Not in time for us. But I believe the Allies will eventually defeat the Germans. When they do, we can only hope that Churchill and Roosevelt will convince Stalin to allow Poland to hold free elections again."

"Even if our Rising fails," Andrzej low voice came from across the room, "at least we'll have shown the Allies our resolve to maintain a free Poland. Like Rudy said, 'stones thrown against the rampart.'"

As if sizing up the group, Andrzej glanced around the room. His chin steeled. He barked out, "We're not done yet, boys! Throw out your impact grenades. Now!"

Tadzio didn't have any, but two other fighters bounced theirs into the street.

Cha-blang! Cha-blang!

Blinding flashes and deafening explosions ripped the air. A cloud of dust hung like a shroud between the Germans and the insurgents' burnt-out flat. The enemy's gunfire stopped.

"Move to the church!" Andrzej shouted.

In one swift motion, they sprinted for the cover of St. Anthony's. A soldier loping next to Tadzio took several bullets to the chest and dropped to the ground. Ahead of him, Andrzej jerked his head, but kept moving.

"You made it out!" Captain Jerzy greeted when they arrived.

Tadzio blew out a grateful sigh as he glanced at the remaining members of their Zoshka Battalion. Neither had known the others were near. Maybe they *could* make it out of this alive.

Lidka rushed over to Andrzej. "Looks like a bullet pierced the fleshy part of your nose."

"Cover the entrances," Andrzej's muffled voice shouted as Lidka worked to stop his bleeding.

Tadzio took up watch in a small outdoor area near a side door. Peering over a low wall, the surrounding area looked clear. Krzysh joined him in the courtyard.

Distant German and Slavic voices rang out, followed by a barrage of bullets. A few pinged off Krzysh's helmet.

Tadzio pushed his friend to the ground.

Crouching behind the stone wall, Tadzio spotted two Germans near a window on the upper floor of the adjacent building. He took aim and fired, but his gun jammed. *Damned dust.*

A groan came from somewhere nearby.

Tadzio glanced down. Blood oozed from Krzysh's neck. "Medic!" Tadzio screamed.

Bullets zinged the air.

Tadzio's heart pushed against the walls of his chest. He crouched low. As he attempted to pull Krzysh to safety, pain ripped through his right shoulder. He dropped to the ground next to his friend.

Two nurses rushed out and dragged both of them into the church.

Tadzio sat and cradled Krzysh's head in his lap while Lidka attempted to stop Krzysh's bleeding. Another nurse examined Tadzio's shoulder.

Krzysh, with an out-of-focus gaze, stared up at Tadzio. "Do you think Auntie M and Auntie L will take care of Lucyna if I don't make it?" Krzysh's words came out in a garbled whisper.

"Of course. Until you recover." Tadzio clenched his teeth. "Then you'll take care of her, like the doting brother you are."

Tadzio glanced at Lidka as she pressed more bandages to Krzysh's neck. She shook her head, as if to say there wasn't much she could do.

Someone outside screamed in Polish, "Help me! I can't move my legs!"

The man's pitiful voice was then drowned out by a Slavic one. *"Tey swinya Polska!"*

Between sounds of a stomping boot and repeated shouts of *Tey swinya Polska*, more pitiful groans arose from the wounded soldier. "Someone help me. God, save me!" he called out.

Tadzio envisioned the scene. A wounded Polish fighter pummeled to death beneath a Ukrainian's boot. And there was nothing he could do to stop it.

As Tadzio gazed at his bleeding, gasping friend, a dark despair filled his soul. Every muscle in his body twitched. Like the wounded soldier in the street, he doubted any of them would make it out alive.

A Polish saying came to mind. *Jak trwoga to do Boga.* In mortal peril, one turns to God. Like the patriot in the street, he should pray.

No. He balled his hands into fists. War's ugliness had hardened his heart. *I'd be a hypocrite to pray now, just because death's literally staring me in the face.*

"Tadzio," Krzysh whispered. "Tell me again what Rudy said before he died."

Tadzio brought Słowacki's poem to mind. "Rudy said, *I implore the still living not to lose hope.*" Tadzio tried to swallow, but his dry mouth and thick throat made it impossible.

Krzysh grabbed Tadzio's arm. "Whatever happens, don't lose hope." Krzysh's voice came stronger. "Tell me the next line."

Even though blinding pain seared his shoulder, Tadzio pushed out the words. "*When the time comes, go forth to death, like stones thrown by God upon a great rampart.*"

Tadzio's eyes and nose stung. Raw emotions flayed his soul. In the face of naked hopelessness, he'd lost heart. Even in Krzysh's last moments, he couldn't offer his friend the consolation of the living.

"Tadzio." Krzysh clutched Tadzio's hand. "Even if Poland survives this war, we may never get the justice we deserve." Krzysh pulled himself closer to Tadzio's face. "But God's bigger than we are." His voice gathered energy. "All we can hope for is to be stones in His hands."

A tear trickled down Tadzio's cheek. He nodded. "You mean, let God throw us where He wills?"

"That's right." Krzysh attempted a smile as Lidka pressed harder against his neck. "I believe that one day freedom *will* win out." He clenched his teeth. "Freedom and truth will always win out against oppression and lies. Against hatred and injustice." He gasped for air. "Don't lose that hope."

As Krzysh's hand released its grip on Tadzio's, his friend's last breath lingered in the air like a ghost.

Hope Lost

September 1–14, 1944
City Center, Warsaw, Poland

Tadzio received an unwelcome nudge. When he opened his eyes, Benyameen's face hovered over him. Tadzio checked his watch. It read 5 AM. He'd fallen asleep with Krzysh's head still in his lap.

"We need to leave soon," Benyameen said.

Tadzio shook his head. "We need to bury him first." His voice came thick and heavy. He gently laid Krzysh's body to the side and stood. A shot of pain seared his shoulder. He winced. He crept to the courtyard's wall and glanced through a crack. No Germans were in sight. It was as quiet as a crypt.

"Here. Drink this." Lidka offered Tadzio a cup of water. "The bullet in your shoulder must have pinged off a wall. It wasn't very deep. I dug it out and closed the wound, but be careful you don't pull out the stitches. We need to keep changing the dressing until it heals."

Using only his left arm, Tadzio grabbed a shovel and plunged it into the courtyard's rocky soil. He stomped on its blade's head, forcing metal to split soil. Benyameen found another shovel and joined him. Together, with the sound of steel swishing through stone and earth, they dug Krzysh's grave.

Andrzej stepped over and pulled the spade from Tadzio's hand. "We leave in an hour. We'll escape to what's left of the Zamoyski Palace."

A bulky bandage covered Andrzej's nose. Tadzio grimaced. When

Andrzej spoke, he struggled to form his words, allowing his lips to move as little as possible.

With a quick glance at Krzysh's corpse, Andrzej looked away. "Captain Jerzy's ordered us to remove our Polish armband," he said. "And those not wearing a German uniform need to find one and put it on."

Like Andrzej and Benyameen, Krzysh was dressed in a German uniform. He still wore the WWI outfit given to him by Auntie M. His insides twisted.

Benyameen leaned on his shovel. "What's the plan?"

Drawing a hand across his days-old stubble, Andrzej sighed. "Captain Jerzy says we'll disguise ourselves as Germans and march right through enemy lines." His weary gaze met Tadzio's. "There's no other way to reach what's left of the Home Army in City Center. Either we die here or we all disguise ourselves so we can reach the far side of Saski Gardens." Andrzej returned the shovel to Tadzio. "I'm sorry about Krzysh, but you'll need to exchange uniforms with him before you bury him."

Strip off Krzysh's clothes and wear them? Bile stung Tadzio's throat. He turned and spewed out green acid. More digestive fluid threatened to erupt. He swallowed to keep it down. Trembling, he obeyed Andrzej's order and donned Krzysh's SS uniform. After burying his friend, he and the others crept out of the church into the still dawn of morning.

Tadzio trailed Benyameen as their dwindling battalion straggled through Saski Gardens. Germans passed by without notice.

Emerging from the area, they plodded on for several blocks until they reached the bombed-out remains of Zamoyski Palace. With no roof and four floors of naked windows, the palace looked like a bald blind man.

Dust and soot swirled through the air as they stepped through the burnt-out structure. Broken beams and debris from blackened walls crackled beneath Tadzio's boots. He choked on the sweet, gas-like odors.

"Over here." Captain Jerzy motioned toward an opening in the floor. The cellar.

After climbing down the stone steps, Tadzio collapsed with his friends on the ground.

A soldier near him moaned.

Andrzej shushed the man.

Tadzio glanced over. The man's arm lay limp at his side. Tadzio guessed a grenade had shredded it.

"Remain absolutely quiet," Captain Jerzy whispered.

Through dirty cellar windows, Tadzio spied German boots patrolling Warsaw's streets. By 11 AM, rivulets of sweat drizzled into his eyes. He supposed the temperature had risen to at least 37 degrees Celsius. Between the heat generated by the burnt-out building, and the warm September day, he didn't even have spit to swallow. But he knew better than to ask for water. It was reserved for soldiers with more serious wounds.

Cha-klung!

An explosion rocked the cellar.

The blast reverberated off the basement walls. Debris clattered to the floor. A high-pitched buzz rang in Tadzio's ears. Smoke and dust permeated the air, making it hard to breathe. Tadzio tucked his head in his armpit to muffle his coughs.

The Germans had probably heard the wounded groaning. A Kraut too fearful of descending the cellar steps had tossed down a grenade.

Once the dust swirls dissipated, a grim silence filled their wake. Everyone slid behind mounds of rubble and into narrow wall niches to await the cover of darkness.

Around noon, another grenade bounced down the staircase. Tadzio's ears rang again. Machine gun fire rat-a-tatted through windows. As bullets pinged off walls, pea-sized pebbles of cement sprayed the room. Pieces landed in Tadzio's hair. To his amazement, the attack only wounded a few men.

Once more, all went quiet.

"When it's dark," Captain Jerzy whispered, "we'll cross enemy lines and join our forces on the other side of Saski Gardens."

The captain's escape plan did little to relax Tadzio's taut muscles. For the moment, he couldn't decide which was worse—his pounding head or throbbing shoulder. The minutes painfully ticked by. Then, at nine that evening, Captain Jerzy signaled to move out. Tadzio helped Benyameen and the soldier with the shredded arm crawl out a window and into the garden outside.

Once he exited, a whispered command cried out. "Down!"

Tadzio hugged the ground. Three German vehicles packed with military police rolled by.

His stiff muscles quivered from fatigue and stress.

Once the trucks rumbled past, Captain Jerzy ordered them to march in a tight formation across Saski Gardens toward the Polish line.

As he stood, Tadzio's leg cramped. He bent his foot back to release the spasm. It worked. He tapped the red-and-white armband hidden in his pocket. Could they get to City Center without detection?

"Dobrosław," Andrzej whispered to one of his soldiers. "If we encounter an enemy patrol, use your best German accent to make them think we're a special detachment sent from German headquarters."

When they reached the intersection of Królewska and Marszałkowska, a German roadblock barred their way.

"Who goes there?" a voice rang out.

In perfect German, Dobrosław confronted the soldier. "Direct us to the Polish insurgents' position."

"Password!" the soldier demanded.

Dobrosław stepped forward and shouted in the man's face. "Idiot! We're a special detachment sent from headquarters." He pointed his weapon toward Saski Gardens. "Obviously we're coming from our own side. What do you want a password for, *dummkopf?* Stand at attention when you address us."

Studying their SS smocks more carefully, the guard snapped to attention. "*Jawohl!*" he shouted. He clicked his heels, stepped aside, and let them through.

Tadzio inhaled, then blew out a sigh. He tapped his hidden armband once more. Only a few more blocks, and he could display it again.

When they reached City Center, Colonel Monter emerged from behind a cement barrier, grasped Captain Jerzy's hand, and gave him a weary smile. "Glad you made it."

Jerzy pulled his brows together. "Have you heard anything yet?

Since we couldn't provide a safe corridor, did Old Town's wounded citizens and soldiers make it through the sewers?"

Colonel Monter shook his head. "I'm sorry. A radio operator informed us that, as soon as you escaped, Germans swooped in, shot our old, sick, and wounded, then trucked healthy prisoners to concentration camps."

Guilt flooded Tadzio's soul. He couldn't pull in a breath. Why did he escape when so many others hadn't? He turned Krzysh's words over in his mind. *Our hope is that freedom will one day win out despite the odds against us. Don't lose that hope.*

Tadzio and the rest of Zoshka Battalion spent the night in an abandoned warehouse in City Center near New World Street. He hoped for a bit of uninterrupted sleep. Five hours later, he stirred to the sounds of rocket blasts, the crackle of flames, and frantic shouts.

When he forced himself awake, the scent of sulfur and smoke filled his nostrils.

"Out, now! The warehouse is on fire!" Andrzej shouted. "We're being bombed with rockets from Saski Gardens."

Tadzio and the others grabbed their gear and exited behind their new captain. Another rocket exploded. Tadzio crouched and covered his head. Once the danger passed, he glanced at Andrzej. "Where to now, Captain?"

"North to Saski Gardens," Andrzej shouted above the din. "We'll push back the enemy's position from there."

Tadzio and his battalion smashed through the shared apartment walls of buildings near the intersection of Królewska and New World.

"Why aren't we just running through the streets?" a recent recruit asked.

With a wry smile, Andrej glanced back. "This way we stay inside the building, undetected, as we advance. We'll keep moving forward like this until we meet up with Colonel Monter's forces on Saski Garden's west side."

Adrenaline pumped through Tadzio's veins as he raced to keep up with his fellow soldiers. Despite a throbbing shoulder and piercing headache, he crawled through hammered wall openings created by those in front of him. He focused on the hope that once they linked up with Monter's other battalions they could launch a counterattack. Weakening German control of Saski Gardens would keep those in City Center safe.

After sprinting through several apartment buildings, Tadzio and the others ran another block without cover to reach the next tenement complex. Bullets zipped overhead as Tadzio wove his way through Home Army barricades of paving stones, rubble, and tram carriages.

"Only two more complexes," Andrzej encouraged the men. "Keep it up!"

Midway through the next building, a sharp pain shot through Tadzio's side. He leaned over and placed his hands on his knees to catch his breath. His pulse thumped in his ears, and his vision blurred. Afraid he might pass out, he forced himself to slow his breathing.

"Can't stop now," Benyameen shouted as ran by.

Still panting, Tadzio raised an index finger to signal, *Give me one more minute.*

Benyameen paused. "You have thirty seconds."

Offering a weak smile, Tadzio nodded.

After thirty seconds, Tadzio trailed Benyameen through two more apartment buildings. Finally, they reached Marszałkowska Street.

"We'll make our stand here," Andrzej said when they came to the corner apartment structure. "If we can keep the Germans from advancing, it'll cripple their ability to bombard City Center."

Their plan seemed to work. Facing a wall of insurgents, the Germans pulled back.

Tadzio's hopes swelled. Over the next three days, he either stood guard from their apartment's upper-story window or caught a few hours of sleep in a room's back corner.

On the third day, he awoke to the banshee sounds of Stukas followed by the ear-piercing explosions of bombs.

Andrzej addressed his battalion's dwindling forces. "Men, we just received information that Dirlewanger attacked our eastern positions along New World Street and is moving toward us." He blew out a heavy sigh. "Our battalion lost twenty men in our fight to push the Germans back from Saski Gardens. Other divisions suffered even greater casualties." He drew a hand across his weary face. "Colonel Monter has ordered us to fall back."

Groans arose around the room, but Tadzio couldn't muster the energy to respond. As he slung his rucksack and rifle over his shoulder, a radio operator handed Andrzej another transmission.

"Stukas and heavy artillery have pulverized Napoleon Square in City Center," Andrzej read aloud. He paused, then finished the message. "Bombers also targeted St. Alexander Church and Holy Cross Church where citizens had gathered for sanctuary."

As if he'd received a punch to the gut, the air whooshed from Tadzio's lungs. His heart rose to his throat.

Churches.

Bombed!

Churches where citizens sought sanctuary after German rockets burned their homes.

Churches that now only provided a sanctuary for smoldering rubble.

The room spun. Tadzio blinked and pictured Three Crosses Square where, five years ago, he carried out his first clandestine mission.

"We'll fall back south to Wilanowska Street," Andrzej said. "Move out!"

As if his legs had filled with cement, Tadzio couldn't move.

Once again, Benyameen came to his rescue. "Snap out of it, Tadzio. Do it for Magdalena. For Lucyna." Benyameen's voice tightened. "For Yacov."

Yes. Family. He couldn't give up now. He huffed, then hefted his rucksack and rifle. He forced himself to trail behind Benyameen as their battalion marched six kilometers southeast. Each step threatened to undo his remaining thread of hope. *What's the point? No one's coming to our aid. We should just surrender. Let them take us to POW camps. That way, at least some of us might survive.*

Tadzio's shoulder had begun to heal, thanks to the stitches, antibiotics, and bandaging he'd received. He doubted, however, that healing existed for his shredded soul.

CHAPTER 41

Hope Regained

Once they reached Wilanowska Street and settled into a burnt-out house near the corner, Andrzej assigned guard duty positions and rotations. After completing his shift behind a nearby street barricade, Tadzio returned to their billet, stretched out on the dusty, ashen floor, and closed his eyes. Before he entered a deep sleep, Benyameen's cry jolted him upright.

"Yacov! What—how did you get here? Tadzio!" Benyameen shouted. "Yacov's here!"

Tadzio popped his eyelids open and stared up at Yacov. Dressed in a Scout's garrison side hat, baggy trousers, and an oversized button-downed coat, Yacov carried a leather satchel.

Tadzio barely recognized him. He looked as though he'd grown eight inches since he'd seen him last.

Benyameen enveloped his brother in a hug. "What are you doing here?"

A grin split Yacov's boyish face. He pointed to his pouch. "I'm delivering letters. Since I turned eleven last month, I began working as a Boy Scout mail courier."

Tadzio knew the Underground government had established mail delivery throughout Warsaw, and despite constant fighting throughout the city, their system seemed to work well. Gray Ranks Scouts from ages 10–15 delivered many letters via sewers. However, neither Tadzio nor Benyameen were aware that Yacov served as one of those carriers.

"It's all very official." Yacov beamed as he withdrew a letter from his pouch. "Every piece of mail has a postmark and an official stamp." He handed Tadzio an envelope and pointed to its stamped imprint. "See. Inside this circle it says, *Scout's Post*, and it has a picture of our Scout's lily symbol."

Tadzio's heart raced as he read the sender's name—*Magdalena*. His hands trembled as he tore his sister's envelope open.

Yacov turned to Benyameen and bounced on his toes. "And we have a letter from Grandpapa." The brothers huddled in a dusty corner of the room to pore over their treasure.

Tadzio sat alone and read his note from Magdalena.

> *Dear Tadzio,*
>
> *Yesterday I married a young man named Pawel. We met working at Długa Street Hospital. In this war, we must grab happiness wherever we can.*
>
> *Magdalena*

Tadzio turned the letter over. Nothing on the back. *That's it?* Smacking his sister's note against his hand, he strode over to Yacov. "Are you sure this is all you have from Magdalena?" His face grew hot. "She says she's married. Did you know? She doesn't share any details. Is she safe? Where is she?"

Peering up at Tadzio, Yacov frowned and shook his head. "I haven't seen Magdalena since the Rising started."

"I want more information." Once again, Tadzio slapped the thin paper against his hand. "What kind of character is this Pawel? Is he a soldier or a civilian? Why didn't she share more news?"

Yacov winced. "All mail sent through the Underground postal system is censored and limited to twenty-five words. She couldn't write more than that."

Tadzio sighed. "So, someone reads everything that's sent?"

Yacov nodded, then glanced sideways at Grandpapa's letter.

Tadzio stole a glance over Benyameen's shoulder. "Your letter is much longer than twenty-five words. Why's that?"

"It didn't come through our Underground mail system." Yacov stared at the floor. "Someone named Father Wacław gave it to me."

"It's a letter from Grandpapa," Benyameen whispered. "He's in the Auschwitz concentration camp."

Tadzio swallowed hard. His sting of jealousy over the boys' long letter faded as he digested Yacov's news. *Grandpapa was in a concentration camp and Yacov's letter came through Father Wacław.* "Father Wacław's my priest at St. John's Cathedral." Tadzio pulled his brows together. "How do you two know him?"

"We don't." Yacov shrugged. "Somehow, he knew I lived with Auntie M and Auntie L. He personally delivered Grandpapa's letter. Said someone who escaped from Auschwitz asked him to give it to me and Benyameen."

Tadzio crouched next to the boys and glimpsed Grandpapa's flowing handwriting. He struggled to keep his voice steady. "What does he say?"

Benyameen read most of the letter out loud. Grandpapa shared that, two years after he fled Warsaw, Gestapo agents caught him and sent him to Auschwitz. Due to his lapidary skills, his captives kept him busy reworking jewelry that they stole from prisoners. German officers forced him to reset stones in new settings and to engrave special pieces of jewelry dedicated to their wives or mistresses.

Benyameen paused. "We haven't read the next section yet, but it looks like Grandpapa shares a song and some scripture he wants us to know. Yacov and I can read those parts together later."

Turning over the last page, Benyameen cocked his head to the side. "Look at this, Yacov. The last two paragraphs are in a different handwriting."

"Read it out loud," Yacov said.

Benyameen cleared his throat.

Your Grandpapa asked me to smuggle out this letter when I escaped from Auschwitz. He knew he was too old and frail to attempt his own escape, but he wanted you boys to know he was still alive and that he loves you very much.

He thinks about you every day. I passed this letter along to a priest who knows many insurgents in Warsaw, and I trust it will eventually make its way to you.

Roman

Returning to the first page, Benyameen ran his fingers over Grandpapa's neat script. "We love you too, Grandpapa," he whispered.

Tadzio's heart clenched. He wished he had a letter from his father.

Or, at least, a longer letter from Magdalena. Would he see either of them again?

Tears drizzled down Yacov's cheeks. "I wish I could hear Grandpapa sing once more."

Tadzio's nose burned. He bit the inside of his cheek to hold back a flood of emotion. "Would you mind reading the part you skipped?"

"Sure." Benyameen nodded, then grinned. "If you don't mind hearing a sermon. Like I said, it looks like he wrote parts of scripture and a song. I think Grandpapa would have made a good rabbi if he hadn't bought a jewelry business." He held the letter closer.

Boys, you have seen much evil in this world. However, we cannot let anger and hatred consume us. Many in Auschwitz once believed in God, but now their hatred of Germans has pushed out recognition of anything good.

Benyameen paused. "Next, Grandpapa quotes words he says were written by a Jewish prophet named Habakkuk."

"That figures." Yacov gave a half smile. "He always wanted us to study what he called the *Holy Writings*, but he never had time to teach us before he left."

"He says these sections are like a riddle." Benyameen held the paper higher. "They're a little hard to understand, but if we work at it, we can unravel the meaning. He said they will help us find hope in the midst of evil."

"I could certainly use some hope right now." Tadzio grimaced. Rudy, Henio, Father Wacław, Hanka, Krzysh, and now, a Jewish man in a concentration camp. They had all urged him to not lose hope. The least he could do was listen. He pulled in a breath. "Go ahead, Benyameen."

Grasping the letter with both hands, Benyameen read aloud in a clear voice.

The wicked doth beset the righteous;
    Therefore right goeth forth perverted.
Look ye among the nations, and behold,
    And wonder marvelously;
For, behold, a work shall be wrought in your days,
    Which ye will not believe though it be told you.

They gather captives as the sand.
   And they scoff at kings,
And princes are a derision unto them;
   They deride every stronghold,
For they heap up earth, and take it.
   Then they sweep by like the wind,
Guilty men, whose own might is their god.

Tadzio scratched his head. "That's a bit hard to understand." He leaned closer to review the letter. "Some of that sounds like what the Germans have done here in Warsaw. They surrounded good people with wickedness and perverted justice."

"What does perverted mean?" Yacov asked.

"It means corrupt, or evil," Tadzio said. "Like arresting Lucyna and Józefina for handing out newspapers that tell people the truth."

"And look here." Benyameen pointed to the third section. "It sounds like what the Germans did to Auntie M's husband and sons. It says they 'gather captives as the sand.'"

"Right." Yacov nodded. "That was per... per..."

Benyameen grinned. "Perverted."

"Perverted." Yacov nodded. "It was perverted that they shipped Polish people to work like slaves in their German factories and consatration camps."

"*Concentration* camps." Tadzio ruffled Yacov's blond head of hair.

Benyameen glanced at the letter again and raised a brow. "And yet, read the last line again. It says they will sweep on like the wind, guilty men, whose own might is their god."

Tadzio rubbed his jaw. "I think that means the Germans won't get away with all they've done. Father Wacław reminded me that God is holy and just. I may not see it in my lifetime, but I believe He will hold them accountable." A small flame of hope ignited in Tadzio's chest. His pulse quickened.

"There's one more quote from the prophet Habakkuk," Benyameen said. He pulled in a breath and continued.

Write the vision, and make it plain upon tablets, that a man may read it swiftly. For the vision is yet for the appointed time, and it declareth of the end, and doth not lie; though it tarry, wait for it;

*because it will surely come, it will not delay. Behold, the righteous
shall live by his faith.*

Tadzio's mind swirled. He was taught that Christians had a more
complete understanding of God than Jews because they believed
Jesus was the long-awaited Messiah and God in the flesh. And yet,
here was Grandpapa, a Jew, who seemed to have a stronger faith in
God than he did. He pushed out his lips. "What do you think the
prophet meant when he said, 'the righteous will live by his faith'?"

Benyameen turned to Yacov. "Remember Warsaw's bombing back
in '39? How Grandpapa calmed us with a song?"

Yacov nodded. "I remember he said his father composed it, but I
don't remember how it went."

As if studying the ceiling, Benyameen raised his gaze. He then
began to hum a soothing tune.

Yacov grabbed Benyameen's arm. "That's it! I remember it now."

Glancing at the page before him, Benyameen added Grandpapa's
final words to his melody.

> *For though the flock shall be cut off from the fold,*
> *and there shall be no herd in the stalls;*
> *yet I will rejoice in the Lord, Adonai,*
> *I will exult in the Elohim, the God of my salvation.*
> *Elohim, Adonai is my strength.*
> *He maketh my feet like hinds' feet,*
> *and He maketh me to walk upon my high places.*

Benyameen's gaze locked onto Tadzio's. "I think Grandpapa means
that even when God doesn't seem to provide things we want or need,
we can still have faith in who God has revealed Himself to be. Faith
like that will give us the strength to wait for, as the Scripture put it,
God's appointed time. God is just and holy. Even when wickedness
and injustice seem to reign, God's still in control."

Tadzio's flame of hope burned brighter. Once more, he recalled
Krzysh's last words. *Freedom and truth will always win out against
lies, hatred and injustice. Don't lose that hope.* For the first time since
the battles had begun, an assurance stirred his soul. An assurance
that, despite the outcome, his efforts weren't in vain.

CHAPTER 42

Reunion

September 14—28, 1944
Czerniaków to Mokotów, to City Center

Tadzio had no time to settle in on Wilanowska Street. The day after Yacov delivered their mail, Zoshka Battalion received orders to secure Czerniaków's waterfront.

An abandoned paint factory west of the Vistula River now provided cover for resistance efforts. Tadzio hoped they didn't spend much time inside. The chemical, ammonia-like stench of the factory turned his stomach. The odor reminded him of when their cat spent too much time indoors.

After they arrived, Andrzej pinned a hand-drawn map to a wall near the front entrance. "Right now," he said, pointing to the map, "Dirlewanger's closing in from the west. Schmidt's descending from the north, and Rohr's forces are moving up from the south."

Tadzio glanced around the factory. His heart contracted. As if trapped in a press, the walls seemed close in on him. Had their sacrifices been for nothing? He raised a hand. "So what's the plan, Commander?"

"I'm getting to that." Andrzej adjusted the bandage on his nose. He then pulled a pencil from his pocket, pointed to the map, and drew a boat on the riverbank. "There's a half-sunken pleasure ship, the *Bajka,* not far from here. Tonight, under the cover of darkness, we'll establish a beachhead near there."

Benyameen stepped closer. "You mean—"

"Yes." Andrzej nodded. "The Russians are finally coming to our aid. They'll send small boats across the river filled with *LWP* soldiers."

"About time," a young man next to Tadzio said. "Haven't the Soviets been camped east of the Vistula River for weeks?"

"Yeah," another insurgent spoke up. "But the Russians have been waiting for the Germans to kill off all of us with the will to fight. That way, it 'll make it easier for the Communists to take over once they *rescue* us."

"Wait," Tadzio said. "Did you say, *LWP* soldiers?"

Before Andrzej could respond, another soldier broke in. "*LWP*. What a joke. The Polish People's Army." He snorted. "*Ludowe Wojsko Polski*. I'm sure the Soviets dubbed them The Polish People's Army hoping we'd think those Polish soldiers were *willingly* joining the Communists. We all know half the *LWP's* officers are from the Red Army, and most of the Polish fighters were previously imprisoned in Russia. The Polish soldiers are only fighting alongside the Russians because they have to."

"Right," Benyameen added, "but at least many *are* Polish. They'll be more sympathetic toward our cause than Russian soldiers."

That evening, under a moonlit sky, Zoshka Battalion crept from the paint factory to Vistula's shores.

Once they reached the waterfront, Andrej waved over one of his leaders. "Lieutenant Skalski. As soon as you spot *LWP* boats, move your platoon to the sunken ship and signal your position. When the boats get close, furnish cover in case they take on enemy fire. We'll establish a beachhead here to provide a safe place to land."

While Skalski and his men waded toward the sunken ship, Tadzio and the rest of the battalion dug trenches in the sand.

Soon, with moonlight glinting off the waters, small crafts bobbed into view.

Tadzio's heart thumped against his chest. Finally, help had arrived.

As the *LWP* boats neared, enemy fire exploded around them.

"Alek Platoon!" Andrzej shouted. "Find a higher position. Take out those German gunners!"

Tadzio sprang from his trench and sprinted to an outcropping of rocks. Andrzej and the others laid down cover for several boatloads of *LWP* soldiers who approached the shore.

Bullets zinged everywhere. Polish insurgents shot Germans. *LWP* fighters targeted anyone they thought was shooting at them. Germans targeted both Home Army and *LWP* soldiers.

Tadzio brought down two machine-gunners. Then his blood froze. An *LWP* soldier scrambled from his boat and aimed his weapon toward Andrzej's position.

"No!" Tadzio shouted at the Polish fighter.

The battle's confusion tore Tadzio's warning from his lips and whisked it into the smoke-filled air. As if in slow motion, a bullet pierced Andrzej's chest. He collapsed to the ground.

Tadzio's heart stopped.

The next day, Tadzio moved as if in a dream. When someone spoke to him, he made no reply.

While others in Radosław's division continued the fight for Czerniaków's bridgehead, Zoshka Battalion members held a Mass for Andrzej. Tadzio attended, but his prayers, singing, and readings took on muffled tones, as if he were a disembodied soul watching from afar.

When they returned to the paint factory, Benyameen attempted to lift Tadzio's spirits. "So far, twelve hundred *LWP* soldiers have crossed the river," Benyameen said.

Tadzio made no remark. He simply sipped his watered-down soup in silence. The new influx of soldiers, weapons, and ammunition had brightened everyone's mood. Everyone's except his. Nothing could make up for the loss of his friend and leader, Andrzej Romocki.

Tadzio's depression deepened as German Stukas bombed *LWP* landing sites. Soviet artillery east of the river did little to stop them. Russian aircraft dropped weapons and food, but, since they chose not to use parachutes, much was destroyed or damaged on impact before reaching the Czerniaków area.

In the aftermath of Andrzej's death, Captain Jerzy re-assumed the command of Zoshka Battalion. After four more days of intense fighting, Colonel Radosław and Captain Jerzy called a meeting in the paint factory.

Tadzio stood next to Benyameen to hear the briefing. To help him focus, Tadzio studied Radosław's angular face. His jutting chin. But his mind still wandered. *Andrzej is dead. And where is Magdalena? How was married life with what's-his-name? Was Poppa still alive? How many more friends and family members would die before the war ended?*

He shifted his gaze to Colonel Radosław's bandaged left shoulder and finally corralled his thoughts.

"I've already shared this news with Czata and Broda Battalions," Radosław said as he paced in front of the men. "Of the forty-nine hundred LWP soldiers sent across the river, fewer than fifteen hundred survived. The Red Army never provided enough air or battery support. Then, tonight, when the Germans installed their own heavy artillery, the Soviets refused to shell our enemy's exposed positions. We're out-numbered and out-gunned. I'm ordering our troops to evacuate south through sewers until they reach Mokotów District."

Groans went up around the room. "Sir." Lt. Skalski raised a hand. "If it's all the same to you, I know many of us want to stand and fight until the last man."

"That's right," another spoke up. "For Captain Morro."

"Hear, hear," a few others shouted.

Tadzio shrugged. *Go? Stay? What does it matter?*

Radosław eased into a nearby chair and sighed. Splotches of blood soaked through his bandage. "I admire your courage and loyalty." He wiped sweat from his tall forehead with the back of his hand. "But Zoshka Battalion now has less than eighty men. The battalions holding out in the canning factory have a combined total of only two hundred. And half of them are wounded." Radosław paused and met Lt. Skalski's gaze. "We'll evacuate those in the canning factory first."

Captain Jerzy nodded and faced his battalion. "All right, men. We'll defend our position here at the paint factory while the others escape through the sewers. I'll take half of you with me to the canning factory to keep up the fight there. Maintain your usual positions here and sleep rotations. Halszka and the other girls will bring you soup and dress your wounds."

Tadzio stood watch next to Benyameen near the factory's front entrance.

"Thanks, Halszka," Benyameen said after slurping his first cup of soup. Can I have a little more?"

"Yes. I think we have enough." Halszka poured a second cup.

The nurse gave Tadzio a cup, but he pushed it away. "I can't stomach any food. The chemical smell in here makes me sick."

"You've got to keep up your strength." Halszka offered the broth again. "Besides. It's not food. It's more like colored water. But at least it's something."

Tadzio shrugged and took the cup. "Where's Lidka? I haven't seen her for days."

Without a word, Halszka lowered her eyes and moved to the next soldier.

Puzzled, Tadzio stole a glance at Benyameen.

"Lidka died two days ago. Halszka joined our battalion last week."

His scarred heart flayed open once again. *Too much death. When will it all end?*

For the next three days, he fought and slept next to Benyameen but said little. The wounded from Zoshka's battalion evacuated with Radosław's group, leaving behind a total force of sixty.

After several days of heavy fighting, Captain Jerzy addressed his men once more. "Our ammunition is almost exhausted. We've been ordered to leave. The LWP will keep one hundred and forty men here while we evacuate through the sewers or attempt to cross enemy lines to reach Mokotów District."

"Maybe we could swim across the river," one fighter suggested.

"There's the wreckage of the *Bajka* just off the shores of the bridgehead." A wounded insurgent fastened the bloodied wrap around his arm more securely. "If we can make it that far, maybe the Russians can rescue us from there."

"Good luck with that," a soldier with a bandaged head said. "I'll take my chances in the sewers."

"The route you choose is up to you." A muscle in Jerzy's jaw ticked. "I'll accompany those who try to cross enemy lines. Whatever happens, if we don't see each other on the other side, I want you to know it's been a privilege serving with you."

Tadzio flexed his stiff shoulder and winced. It still ached. No.

He wouldn't attempt to swim the river, even if it was only to the wrecked ship.

Benyameen nudged him. "We still have our German uniforms. Let's go with Captain Jerzy. It worked once before."

Most of the wounded opted to swim to the *Bajka*. Others braved the sewers. Tadzio hoped he'd made the right decision in joining the remaining four who crept into the night with Captain Jerzy.

Tadzio gritted his teeth as artillery and gunfire ripped through the air.

Benyameen glanced back. "Sounds like it's coming from the waterfront."

Tadzio feared for those attempting to swim to the sunken ship. He looked down at his SS smock. Would it fool any Germans who stopped him? Would he have the will to fight if he was stopped?

After several blocks, Captain Jerzy held up a fist. Everyone halted, then crept into the shadows.

Ahead, four Germans patrolled the streets.

Sweat drizzled down Tadzio's back.

A few breathless moments later, Jerzy gave an all-clear signal. Once again, they moved out.

They reached Mokotów District without further incident. Two from their battalion stepped out from a street barricade and greeted them.

"Glad to see you're safe." A soldier named Karol thumped Benyameen's back.

Stench emanated from Karol's soiled uniform. Obviously, he'd chosen to escape through the sewers.

The group moved behind the barricade. "Have you heard how many from our battalion made it out?" Captain Jerzy asked.

Karol rubbed his grimy hands on his damp trousers. "An LWP fighter radioed a report thirty minutes ago. He said machine gun fire and mortar rounds wiped out most of those who swam to the *Bajka*. A few crossed the Vistula at other points."

Another soldier arrived and escorted them to their Mokotów safehouse where they downed cans of sardines. All except Tadzio. Even in his half-starved condition, the smell made him gag. He wrinkled his nose at the fishy aroma. He hated sardines. Besides, he was too exhausted to eat. He stretched out on a cot and fell asleep.

Several hours later, the sound of a crackling radio woke him. Sitting up, he studied the operator's scrunched face. *More bad news*, he guessed.

Captain Jerzy strode over. "What's the report?"

"Von dem Bach's troops gained control of the Czerniaków bridgehead, sir," he said. "A civilian witnessed Germans rounding up LWP fighters. Said they took them away as POWs." The radio operator grimaced. His voice lowered. "He also said the Germans executed our remaining Home Army insurgents."

Tadzio's throat threatened to close. Even Halszka? She had stayed behind to care for those too wounded to escape. Had she survived? A tingling crept from his legs to his chest. He threw himself on his cot and curled into a ball.

The next morning, Tadzio woke to the whistle of bombs. Seconds later, explosions rattled their building. He scrambled off his bed, shoved on his boots, then grabbed his rifle.

"Men," Captain Jerzy shouted above the din, "General Bór's headquarters in City Center has been hit. Soviet troops have stopped crossing the Vistula. Von dem Bach has now received reinforcements. We're to hold our positions here as long as possible, but once again, we're on our own."

That afternoon, as Tadzio and Benyameen manned a barricade on Pulawska Street, Tadzio grumbled. "It's impossible. I hear von dem Bach's sending thick-plated Sturmpanzer tanks our way. Our homemade bombs won't be able to take them out."

Benyameen stared down at his machine gun. His face twisted. "And our weapons are no match against a Sturmpanzer's howitzers."

A runner joined them behind the barricade. "Two Panzer-Division battalions are approaching from the south." He panted for several breaths, then continued. "They're hemming us in. You're to join Baszta Battalion near Królikarmia Palace."

By the time Tadzio and Benyameen arrived, the Germans had already overrun the area.

As night set in, Captain Jerzy endeavored to rally his men at a new safehouse. "We're not beaten yet, boys. The Home Army still has two thousand troops here in Mokotów District. Together, we can do this."

Benyameen raised his voice with the others as they howled and raised their fists.

Visualizing the scene of Andrzej's death, Tadzio squeezed his eyes shut. They had also cheered before that battle.

Tadzio fought alongside Benyameen all night as the Germans attacked from the south. By morning, they were ordered to retreat a block north to a school on Woronicza Street.

Tadzio's fingers numbed as he crouched down in a classroom and reloaded his rifle. He guessed it was noon, but he had no way of knowing. His watch had died long ago. He paused and gazed around. Bloodied bodies littered the floor between desks where children once sat. Were they to fight to the last man?

A lieutenant entered the room. "Move out!" he shouted. "We're to reinforce Olza Battalion on the west."

Two hours later, Olza's protective barrier around Mokotów's western side crumbled. The district commander ordered all battalions to fall back towards Mokotów's fortified northern end.

The next day, Tadzio guarded a barricade on Szustra Street. He overheard a one-way conversation as Captain Jerzy consulted with another commander over the radio.

"They're sending an armored assault group toward Pulawska Street?" Jerzy paused.

"What?" Another pause. "They've overrun the barricades near St. Elizabeth's Hospital?" Jerzy frowned.

"Assault guns?" The captain ran a hand over his face.

"We'll do what we can."

The next night, Captain Jerzy roused those on rest rotation. "The Home Army has negotiated a temporary cease-fire for our district. In the morning, the nine thousand citizens here in Mokótow will surrender to the Germans."

Tadzio rubbed sleep from his eyes. *A cease-fire?* He swallowed hard. *If the Germans had executed insurgents who stayed behind at Czerniaków, what would happen to them?* He couldn't pull in a breath.

"I suppose it's better than having people slaughtered in their homes," mumbled a soldier to his left.

"Captain?" Benyameen asked. "Will we stay to fight?"

Jerzy shook his head. "Tomorrow, we'll evacuate through sewers and meet up with our remaining forces in City Center."

Tadzio fell back onto his cot. He stared into nothingness, trying to erase the image of Andrzej's ashen face from his mind.

Early the next morning, while the Mokótow citizens surrendered to the Germans, Tadzio climbed into a manhole on Szustra Street. He followed Benyameen and several others into the dark, foul-smelling passages.

"Watch out for debris on the floor," Benyameen called out over his shoulder. "Let's not run into any more barbed wire."

Before Tadzio could remark, he tripped and twisted his ankle. Catching his balance on the slimy curved walls of the sewer pipe, he groaned. Now, both his shoulder and his ankle throbbed.

A soldier behind him clicked on a flashlight.

In its faint glow, Tadzio gasped at two dead bodies lying in the shallow water that swirled around his feet.

Benyameen glanced back. "Tadzio. Pick up the pace." His friend seemed to ignore the bodies. "The guys in front of us just turned a corner. We need to keep up. Otherwise…" Benyameen didn't finish his sentence.

Or else we'll get lost. Tadzio completed Benyameen's thought and shuddered. He'd heard of people losing their way in sewers. Some had spent over twenty hours in a putrid labyrinth before they got out. Others, like the corpses he just passed, never escaped. Trailing Benyameen, Tadzio steadied himself on the sewer wall. As they turned a corner, the pipe sloped down.

"Any sign of those in front of us?" Tadzio whispered.

"No. It's too dark to see anything," Benyameen said.

He sensed a slight quiver in his friend's voice.

"I don't think I should turn on my flashlight, though," Benyameen called back. "Remember, if the Germans notice light shining above manholes, they might toss down a grenade."

"Right." Tadzio quivered

"And be careful." Benyameen gave a whispered warning. "The water's faster and deeper here."

After several more steps, a stronger current churned around Tadzio's ankles. As he slithered forward, the sewage water slowly rose higher and higher. Eventually, it reached his knees. His gut roiled. The foul-smelling flow now carried not only excrement but also thick gravel and hard stones. It pounded his legs as it rushed past.

"Hope we get out of here soon." Tadzio swallowed back an eruption of bile. Scenes of being trapped in their summerhouse's well flooded his mind once again. His throat constricted, making it difficult to breathe. When he pulled in a breath, the fetid air made him gag.

The tunnel took another turn, then shrunk in size. He hunched over to avoid hitting his head. The current slowed, but the latrine sludge made every step more strenuous.

"I see them up ahead," Benyameen cried out.

"Quiet." An urgent whisper hissed. "The Germans are right above us."

Tadzio tilted his head. The rumble of vehicles and the boom of artillery pierced the darkness. He moved forward in silence, careful not to splash any water. After what seemed like ages, a manhole opened above them.

Soldiers in front of Benyameen climbed out, aided by someone above them.

After Benyameen exited, Tadzio mounted the ladder.

"Here, let me help you up," a strangely familiar voice called down.

Tadzio grabbed an outstretched hand. "Thanks."

When he reached the surface, Tadzio pulled in a deep breath, grateful to inhale the fresh air. When he finally looked up, he gazed into his father's face.

CHAPTER 43

Surrender

September 28–October 5, 1944
Warsaw, Poland

Filth and stench permeated Tadzio's uniform, but he wrapped his arms around his father's neck anyway. A million questions flooded his mind. After a few moments, he pulled back. "Where—? Why—? Did you—?"

His father raised a hand. "Answers will have to wait until we're safe."

Anticipation surged through Tadzio. He urged his fatigued limbs forward toward their City Center billet. In the dusk's faint light, he made out shells of bombed-out buildings and heaps of broken bricks. Eventually, they reached Marszalkowska Street and entered a burnt-out row of flats.

When he flopped onto a cot, his body shook as his adrenaline crashed.

A nurse came by. "You need to eat something. And clean clothes." She offered him a weak smile and a dented can of SPAM.

Another nurse entered and handed the new arrivals used but laundered uniforms. "Have you heard?" she asked them. "General Bór has begun talks to discuss surrender."

Grief and gloom churned Tadzio's insides. He sat on the edge of his cot and wagged his head. "I'm not surprised. It'd be suicide if we continued to fight without more aid from the Allies."

"It's not like they didn't try." A soldier Tadzio knew as Kotwa sat on a crate and pried open a can of SPAM. "We heard that both British and American pilots asked to refuel in Soviet-occupied territories, but the Russians turned them away. Aviators had to fly to Italy for refueling before dropping supplies."

Two other nurses, a brunette and a blonde, entered. They carried in towels, soap, and a water basin.

Kotwa's gaze followed them as he pivoted on his crate.

The soldier next to Kotwa stole several spoonfuls of SPAM from his tin. "That's right," the second soldier said around a mouthful of meat. "Because of that, the Allies were forced to transport less and make more runs."

"Hey, Jan!" Kotwa shouted when he peered into his partially-eaten can. "Get your own!"

The brunette nurse smiled. She grabbed another tin from a stack near the wall and handed it to Jan. She glanced at Kotwa. "Even then, half of those supplies fell into German hands."

The blonde nurse set her water basin on a nearby table and joined in. "But at least we've gotten goods from Russia since mid-September."

"Too little, too late," Kotwa groused, holding up his dented can. "Most of that came damaged or destroyed. The Soviets shoved them out of planes without parachutes."

Tadzio had witnessed the smashed airdrops. Shattered cases of medicine. Battered crates of broken sub-machine guns and rifles. What a waste. The memories deepened a brooding well of anger in his gut. He finished his SPAM and crushed the tin. He had no love for the Communists, especially since the failed fight for Czerniaków's bridgehead.

While Tadzio washed and changed, his father spoke with a group of men on the other side of the room. Tadzio's mind whirred with questions. He pulled in a ragged breath. *Where has Poppa been all this time? Why is he here now? Who is he talking to?*

Moments later, Tadzio's father came over with two other men. "Roman, Bear Cub, this is my son Tadzio and his friend Benyameen."

Tadzio shook the strangers' hands and sized them up. Bear Cub, short and stocky. Roman, lean and muscled. *Must be codenames.*

Benyameen grasped the thin man's hand between his own. "Roman?" His pitch rose. "The one who delivered Grandpapa's letter to Father Wacław?"

Roman nodded. "That's me. Glad you got it."

Tadzio's father motioned toward the shorter man. "And, boys, this is Bear Cub. I've worked with him since the Rising began. He's General Bór's Operations Chief."

Tadzio pinched his eyes into slits. *All this time, Poppa's been working with General Bór's right-hand man?* A flame of anger pricked his heart. Why didn't his father contact him sooner?

"Good to meet you, boys." Bear Cub nodded. He then checked his watch. "Mateusz, I must attend a meeting. I'll send for you later." With that, Bear Cub left.

"Mateusz?" His father's first name was Henryk. Tadzio tilted his head.

"Codename," his father said.

The flame in Tadzio's chest ignited. He fought to keep his voice even. "Why do you have a codename?"

Before his father could answer, gunfire exploded.

Adrenaline shot through Tadzio's veins. He grabbed his rifle. Answers would have to wait. Again.

A Baszta officer ran in. "Our position's overrun. Everyone out. Now!"

As Tadzio rushed out, the Baszta lieutenant stopped him, along with Benyameen and five others. "All of you. Take positions outside the building. Give us ten minutes. Then retreat two blocks south. We'll regroup there."

After ducking behind a pile of broken concrete and bricks, Tadzio brought down two Germans.

Benyameen shot another that appeared from around the corner.

Kotwa and Jan tossed grenades.

Ten minutes passed. Could they make a run for it? With sweat trickling down his back, Tadzio nodded to the others.

Through a cloud of debris, he and his comrades rushed south.

October 2, 1944
City Center, Home Army Headquarters

After four days of intense fighting, General Bór ordered the Home Army to cease fire.

Regret and fear depleted Tadzio's reserves as he awaited further orders in a bombed-out flat near General Bór's headquarters. Had he done enough? What would happen now?

After several grueling hours, Captain Jerzy entered their cramped, ashen apartment. Tadzio's breath hitched as he studied Jerzy's face. Five years of war had taken its toll. The events his leader had witnessed and the demons he'd wrestled had etched themselves into the man's forehead and jawbone like stories carved in deep lines. "We've entered negotiations with von dem Bach." Jerzy's voice came heavy, as if a stone was attached to every word. "After our surrender, the Germans have agreed to treat us as POWs."

Air whooshed from Tadzio's lungs. So many had suffered and died. And for what?

A quiet pall enveloped the room.

"Look at it this way," Benyameen broke the silence. "Labelling us as prisoners of war obligates the Krauts to give us humane treatment."

"As opposed to massacring us as rebel insurgents? Not much of a bright spot." Tadzio tried to swallow another forkful of SPAM, but the news left a bitter taste in his mouth. He spit it back into the can. Would the Germans send Magdalena to a POW camp? Where was Father? He hadn't seen Poppa since he pulled him from the sewer.

"What will happen to Warsaw's civilians once we surrender?" a nurse asked the captain as she changed a soldier's arm bandage.

Before the captain could answer, the soldier with the bandaged arm spoke up. "Once we surrender, there'll be no more Warsaw. I heard Hitler has ordered the city's complete destruction. *Leave no stone upon a stone*, he's been quoted to say. Germans will force civilians to evacuate and shoot those who refuse."

The captain lowered his head. "I'm afraid that's true."

The well of anger in Tadzio's gut leaked into his soul. His vision clouded with rage. He envisioned Hitler's smug, mustached face as he blasted a hole through the man's skull.

The day before the soldiers surrendered their weapons, Tadzio and

Benyameen were assigned duties at General Bór's headquarters. A lieutenant briefed them on how to sort papers into piles of items to be burned or saved.

At first, work was slow. After a while, Tadzio could better distinguish between the two.

"Boys." Captain Jerzy entered the small room, his face less grooved than last week. "In thirty minutes, there's a Scout meeting at Professor Handelman's old place on Wilcza Street. Anyone who wants to take part has permission to attend. However, you must return as soon as possible to complete this work."

Although still weak from battle fatigue, meager rations, and a lack sleep, a renewed vigor flowed through Tadzio. He turned to Benyameen. "Want to go?"

Benyameen nodded.

They scurried out and hurried toward Wilcza Street.

Arriving at the professor's gutted home, Tadzio studied the faces of those around him. He recognized some as Underground mail couriers. Others he'd met while printing or delivering Underground newspapers. Many he'd known as Girl Guides who served as nurses during the Rising.

Forming a large semicircle around Professor Handelsman's shell of a house, the group joined hands. Tadzio counted almost 100 Scouts as he scanned the crowd for Magdalena, Lucyna, or Yacov.

Fear clenched his stomach. No sign of them.

Orsza, the Gray Ranks' Chief Commissioner, honored forty Scouts with either a Cross of Merit or Cross of Gallantry. Tadzio pulled in a deep breath. He knew every recipient.

"And for his bravery and quick thinking while rescuing prisoners at Goose Farm Concentration Camp," Orsza continued, "I award the Cross of Merit to Tadeusz Dombrowski."

Adrenaline shot through Tadzio as he stepped forward. Scenes from the battle flashed before him. Wacek revving their captured tank into the compound. Explosions reverberating in his ears. His mad bicycle ride toward Goose Camp's southern tower. The soldier's machine gun clattering to the ground as he took him out. No time to think. He'd acted on impulse to protect his friends.

After shaking Orsza's hand, Tadzio returned to his spot next to Benyameen.

A movement across the group caught his attention. Scouts on the far side dropped hands to create an opening. Four new people slipped in. Spotting Magdalena, Yacov, and Lucyna, he swallowed hard. His Adam's apple struggled to bob inside his constricted throat. They were alive! Then he noticed a young man standing beside Magdalena. He guessed the man was Magdalena's husband, Pawel.

Not wanting to disturb the solemn ceremony, Tadzio resisted the urge to run and embrace his sister.

"And now," Orsza said as he raised his head, "let's recite our Gray Ranks' Pledge."

Tadzio forced his breath to come in even draws as a mix of joy, pride, and sadness threatened to undo him. How long had it been since they pledged those oaths at their manorhouse? After surrendering, would any of them live long enough to utter them again?

... to serve God and Poland with the whole of my life ...

Reciting the words, Tadzio glanced again around the circle. His stomach spasmed. Sadness twisted his soul. So many missing. Henio, Józefina, Stefan, Krzysh.

... and to obey the Guide and Scout Law.

Images of Rudy's bruised and beaten body filled his mind. Alek, Zoshka, and Andrzej felled by enemy bullets. Tadzio shuddered. His Scout leaders had faithfully fulfilled their pledge.

"And now, join me in singing our Scout Hymn and National Anthem," Orsza said.

Pride swelled Tadzio's chest as he raised his voice with the others.

... Poland is our life, so we go to live. The dawn is rising, let's open the gates ...

At the end, Orsza, choked with tears, proclaimed, "Scouts, Poland still lives. Poland will always live. *Czuwaj!*"

The Scouts around Tadzio raised their fisted hands and shouted, "*Czuwaj!*"

Tadzio clenched his jaw in determination and also punched a fist into the air. *Czuwaj.* No matter what happened, he'd be vigilant. He'd be prepared.

Although ordered to return to Bór's headquarters after the meeting, Tadzio ran to Magdalena and embraced her. He then held her at arm's length. "Did you know? Father's alive! He's working alongside Bear Cub." He lowered his voice. "We haven't had time to talk yet, but I hope to learn more soon."

"Father?" Tears rushed down Magdalena's cheeks. "I feared he was dead. Oh, Tadzio." She swiped her face with the back of her hand. "I wish we could visit longer, but we have to take the children to Auntie L and Auntie M. Then we must report to Pawel's billet and prepare for surrender."

With promises to meet again soon, vows beyond their ability to keep, they exchanged sweet but sorrowful hugs and kisses. Biting back tears, Tadzio ripped himself away and returned to headquarters.

The next day, as he completed his job at the general's billet, he scanned the final issue of the *Information Bulletin*—the paper Henio had given his life to deliver.

> *The battle is over… From the spilled blood, from the common hardship and difficulties, from the suffering of our bodies and of souls, there will rise a new Poland—free, strong and great.*

He placed the *Bulletin* onto the stack of papers labeled, To Be Saved, and contemplated his friends and family's fate. *Would* a new Poland arise from the blood they'd shed? And what about those who lived? Tomorrow, he, Benyameen, Magdalena, and Pawel would march out of City Center along with the rest of the Home Army. Lucyna and Yacov would move to the country with the Aunties until Germany surrendered to the Allies. He, Benyameen, Magdalena, and Pawel would be sent to POW camps.

And what about his father? Tadzio's throat constricted. Apprehension and fear threatened to choke off his air. Poppa was nowhere to be found.

The morning of October 5 came as cold and gray as Tadzio's heart. For the last time, he fastened his red and white armband around his right upper arm. Joining the others in forming long columns, four abreast, he stood tall, his rifle shouldered. As one, the group proceeded in formation to the weapons drop-off point behind German lines. Ranks of women, including Magdalena, marched in front of them carrying their first-aid kits, postal bags, or radio equipment.

When they crossed the enemy line, Tadzio scanned a group of German officers standing to the side. He gritted his teeth. Although wounded, exhausted, and hungry, he passed by with his head held high.

"*Stolze Polen,*" a German captain said.

Tadzio glanced sideways at Benyameen.

A faint smile lit Benyameen's face. "It means, Proud Poles."

Tadzio kept his face as hard as flint, but his soul smiled at his enemy's compliment.

When they reached the outskirts of Warsaw, Tadzio added his rifle to the growing mound of discarded weapons. As he let his gun slip from his hands, all the adrenaline drained from his body. He joined Benyameen on the side of the road.

Breathe in. Breathe out. After Tadzio forced in several draws of air, he turned to face Benyameen. "Do you remember your Grandpapa's final words where he talked about faith?"

"From his letter? I have it right here." Benyameen pulled the folded paper from his pocket. Opening it, he read aloud.

The vision is for the appointed time. It hastens toward the goal, and it will not fail. Though it tarries, wait for it. The righteous will live by his faith.

Tadzio leaned back and mulled over the words. "You know," he said as he tossed a pebble into the road, "the Germans can take away our weapons, our country, and our freedom, but they can't break our spirit."

"You're right." Benyameen returned the letter to his pocket. "I believe Warsaw will rise again. Like Grandpapa said, the time might tarry, but I need to have faith in God."

The vision is for the appointed time.

Tadzio pictured a restored Warsaw. Yes, the day would come. Until then, he too would trust in God. Neither the Germans nor the Russians could distinguish that hope. Eventually, the flag of freedom would once again rise over Poland.

CHAPTER 44

NIE—No Subordination

October 5, 1944
Warsaw, Poland

When the final group of soldiers neared the weapons-drop-off site, thousands of Polish citizens roared and cheered. Some fell to their knees.

Had their sacrifices been worth it? The lump in Tadzio's throat said, *Yes!* The cost had been high. But how could one put a price on hope?

Once the last soldiers surrendered their arms, the Germans directed them toward trucks waiting to transport them to POW camps. Before the men in Tadzio's battalion boarded, a Wehrmacht officer dressed in black battledress stepped forward. He spoke in German while a translator interpreted.

"Men of Zoshka Battalion," the facilitator translated, "I congratulate you on your bravery and strong resistance. I am proud that my division had the chance to fight against such courageous soldiers."

Stunned by the officer's praise, Tadzio stared at the man.

Benyameen tugged his sleeve. "Time to leave. We're boarding."

As Tadzio climbed into the back of the truck, a din of voices arose behind him.

Benyameen, already in the vehicle, pointed across the street.

With his foot on the truck's last step, Tadzio paused and turned toward the sound. A surge of civilians came into view. Emerging from side streets, two vast streams of humanity, each appearing to number a thousand strong, began their own trek out of Tadzio's beloved city. The rattle of carts, the wails of children, and the stomp of feet filled the air with a somber discordance.

In the confusion, someone grabbed Tadzio's arm.

"Come with me," a voice demanded.

Tadzio glanced down. Below him stood his father, dressed in a black SS uniform.

"I'm with Bear Cub," his father whispered. "He wants you to join us."

Stunned, Tadzio descended the steps and trailed his father. He followed him into the back seat of a German staff car. Roman sat behind the steering wheel wearing a black Wehrmacht uniform. Bear Cub sat next to him in the front passenger seat. He, like Tadzio's father, wore an SS officer's uniform.

As Roman maneuvered the black 260D sedan past crowds of civilians, Tadzio's father twisted in his seat to face him. "I'm sorry I couldn't contact you before this." Lines of sadness creased his father's face. His tone sounded weighted. "I'm sure you have many questions."

Tadzio's throat burned. He couldn't speak. Emotions leaked from his eyes. Finally, he choked out his most pressing question. "Why did you leave us?"

As if recoiling from a blow, his father's face pinched. "It wasn't an easy decision."

Tadzio faced forward and stared out the car's front window.

"As you know," his father's voice assumed its normally firm, clear tone, "before the war, I was a trustee of the Bank of Poland. As such, I attended several meetings with the bank and our government's leaders. That's why I was away so often. In the weeks leading up to the invasion, we discussed how to manage our nation's capital in the event the Nazis overran us. We resolved that, if Poland fell, volunteers would transport our gold reserves to Britain or Canada so our government could continue to function outside of Poland." His father paused. "I was one of those volunteers."

Tadzio's insides churned as he faced his father. "Why couldn't you tell us?"

"We were sworn to secrecy. Only your mother knew."

Tadzio clawed his fingernails against the seat's leather upholstery.

He pushed words out around his heavy tongue. "So that's why the Germans ransacked our manorhouse after you left? And carted Mother off to prison?"

His father winced. "Yes. They were looking for evidence of where to find the gold. Failing that, they imprisoned your mother, hoping she would provide information. Our sources reported she repeatedly denied any knowledge of my activities."

Tadzio gritted his teeth. *Was she tortured?* His stomach spasmed at the thought. He studied his father's moist eyes. "And after you transported the gold, why didn't you return?"

His father pulled in a breath. "Before I left, I sought Father Wacław's counsel. He helped me realize I had only volunteered to transport Poland's gold because it provided an opportunity to ensure our own family's wealth. The Sunday before we escaped to our summerhouse, Father Wacław delivered a sermon about three Jewish men who willingly entered a fiery furnace rather than bow down to the wicked king and deny God. After hearing that sermon, something inside me changed." His father's features relaxed.

"I remember that sermon." Tadzio slowly nodded. "You did seem different after that. When I was in the hospital during the Rising, Father Wacław visited me. I had begun to lose hope in our cause, in God, and…" He let his gaze bore into his father's. "And in you."

Sweat gathered on Tadzio's forehead. He swiped at it. "Father Wacław told me you asked how you could have confidence in God like those men in the fiery furnace. A confidence that would provide an anchor for your soul. At the time, I had no idea what he was talking about."

Grasping Tadzio's hand, his father's eyes widened. "That sermon made me realize I needed to trust God to take care of my family. And I needed to do what was right, not just convenient."

Eyes burning, Tadzio blinked hard. He was a soldier. He had survived the Rising. He couldn't show weakness now. Not in front of Bear Cub, or Roman, or his father. And yet, how could he deny his shattered heart? After all the pain, all the loss, his father's explanation sounded hollow. He clenched his jaw. "How was allowing Mother and Henio to die doing what was right?"

Releasing Tadzio's hand, his father leaned closer. "Even if I had stayed, there was no guarantee they would have survived." The leather seat crackled as his father leaned back and sighed. "Your mother and I discussed our options before I left. She agreed I needed to leave. My financing skills helped secure our country's capital. It also helped fund Poland's covert operations during the occupation. As it turned out, when emergencies arose, I spent most of our family's savings to help the resistance."

Until now, the men in the front had remained silent. Bear Cub now turned in his seat. "Your father secured financing for our intelligence efforts and helped keep our government-in-exile going. Winston Churchill himself told me forty-three percent of all British Secret Service reports regarding Europe came from Polish sources. Your father played a huge role in that. Your father's a hero."

Tadzio's head whirled. His father, a hero?

Their vehicle jostled and shook. "Damn ruts," Roman swore as he grasped the wheel. "I'll be surprised if they don't take out an axle."

Tadzio rolled down his side window, fearing he might lose the partially digested SPAM he had for breakfast.

Bear Cub faced front. When the road smoothed out once again, the general turned to face Tadzio. "Your father begged our government-in-exile to send him back home. They agreed, but asked if he'd consider returning as an SOE operative."

Tadzio opened his mouth, then closed it. *His father, part of Britain's Special Operations Executive group?* Wide-eyed, Tadzio stared at his father. "I heard SOE agents parachuted into Warsaw to help with our Rising, but I thought they were all British. How…?" Tadzio dropped his jaw again and let his voice trail off.

His father pressed his lips together, then explained. "As a British SOE operative, I became one of Poland's *Cichociemni*—one of the Dark and Silent Ones. Four months ago, the SOE dropped the general and me into Warsaw to help prepare for Warsaw's Rising. Now, with General Bór's surrender and his arrest by the Germans, our government-in-exile has asked Bear Cub—ah, now General Bear—to lead a new resistance group. We're calling it *NIE*. It stands for *Niepodległość*—No Subordination."

Turning to grasp the back of his seat General Bear nodded. "Once Germany is defeated, we believe our allies will give us over to the Russians. To counter this, *NIE* will form a network of spies. We will share information with the West and, one day, regain our freedom."

Adrenaline wound its way through Tadzio's fatigued body. His head began to clear. His chest swelled as he studied his father with new respect.

"All this time I thought you had abandoned us. Or were dead."

His father pulled in a shaky breath and grimaced. "I'm sorry, son. We were ordered to maintain strict secrecy. I know it's been difficult for you."

Bear cleared his throat. "Much was at stake, Tadzio. Our question for you is—do you want to be part of it?"

"Me? Part of *NIE*?" Tadzio widened his eyes. Blood pulsed in his ears.

Bear and Tadzio's father glanced at each other, then Tadzio.

His father nodded. "That's right, son."

"*Tak*! Yes! I want to see Poland rise again."

Tadzio's father gripped his shoulder. "Glad to hear it. I believe that, out of its ashes, Poland will rise once again. And now, together, we can play a part in it."

About the Author

Marie Sontag enjoys transporting middle grade and young adult readers to various time periods and locations by creating stories that bring the past to life. Her fifteen years of teaching middle school and high school have given her insight into what students find entertaining, and her B.A. in social science and M.A. and Ph.D. in education provide her with a solid background for writing historical fiction.

Born in Wisconsin, she spent most of her life in California, but now lives with her husband in Texas. When not writing, she enjoys romping with her grandkids, playing clarinet and saxophone in a community band, and nibbling red licorice or Tootsie Pops while devouring a good book.

Visit Marie online at:

http://www.mariesontag.com/

Author's Note

Dear Reader,
Thanks for joining me in this WWII adventure. For a downloadable link to a list of the characters, pictures, and Polish pronunciations, view my webpage at https://www.mariesontag.com/books/underground-scouts. Here you can also find links to a book trailer, colored maps, and an interview I had with one of the historical Scouts in the story, the nurse code-named Halszka (Chapter 42).

Please consider leaving a review of *Underground Scouts* on your favorite social media platform or bookseller's website. If you enjoyed the story, tell a friend. Word-of-mouth is the best way to introduce stories to new readers.

I'd love to hear from you. You can message me at mesontag@gmail.com or post on my Facebook page, facebook.com/AuthorMarieSontag.

Until our next adventure!
Marie Sontag

Acknowledgements

I'm grateful for my faithful critique partners, especially Jennifer Ashcraft, Heather Chock, Julie A. Marx, Marcia McIntosh, Lori Z. Scott, Paul Thrower, and Gayle Veitenheimer. I've learned so much from each of you. Most of all, I'm grateful to my forever friend and spouse, Mark. I look forward to our next trip to Poland!

Sequential Cast of Characters in Undercover Scouts

Tadzio Dombrowski—(Tahd'-jeo Dahm-brahf'-skee) with a rolled "r"): A fictional main character in *Undercover Scouts*, Tadzio is portrayed as a member of the Polish Boy Scouts. When the war starts in 1939, Tadzio is thirteen. At the end of the book he is eighteen. Tadzio is the name of a young Polish boy whose given name is Tadeusz (Tah-deh-oosh'). It is the Polish equivalent of the English name, Thaddeus. In Polish, Tadzio's last name is really Dąbrowski, but for ease of reading in English, it is spelled Dombrowski or Dombrowska throughout *Underground Scouts*. This is the closest sound in English to imitate this name.

Professor Handelsman—A historical person born in Warsaw, Poland (1882–1945), Marceli Handelsman taught modern history at Warsaw University. Although a Catholic, Handelsman's Jewish roots forced him to go into hiding during WWII, while continuing to serve as a professor in the underground Warsaw University. After 1942, Handelsman worked with the Bureau of Information and Propaganda of the Home Army. According to author Norman Davies, (*Rising '44)*, in June 1943 a discussion was held in Professor Handelsman's home to discuss the formation of a special unit of armed youths to fight the German police with their own methods. *Undercover Scouts* fictionalizes the professor's role as scoutmaster over all the Scouts in Warsaw.

Magdalena Dombrowska—(Mahg-dah-lane'-a Dahm-brahf'-skee) One of the fictional main characters in, Magdalena is Tadzio's older sister and a Girl Scout (Girl Guide). In *Undercover Scouts*, the historical person of Anna Zawadzka serves as Magdalena's Scout leader. The name Magdalena was the name supposedly chosen for her by her Polish parents because they wanted to name her after her material German grandmother, Magdalena. When the war starts in 1939, Magdalena is sixteen. At the end of *Undercover Scouts* she is twenty-one.

Henio Dombrowski—(Hen'-yo Dahm-brahf´-skee) Henio is a young Polish boy's name when his given name is Henryk. It is the equivalent of the English name Henry. Henio is a fictional character in Undercover Scouts. He is Tadzio's younger brother and is four years old when the war begins.

Andrzej Romocki—(Un´- jzay Rau-maw´-tskee) A historical person in Warsaw during WWII (1923–1944), Andrzej's code-name was Morro. Andrzej was a Polish scoutmaster and later the commander of Rudy Company during the Rising. After August 31, 1944 he became the commander of the Zoshka Battalion. Andrzej is the equivalent of the English name, Andrew.

Lech Lutowski—(Leh´ Lu-tof'-skee) A fictional character in *Undercover Scouts*, he is a Boy Scout and the older brother of Stefan. When the war starts in 1939, Lech is eighteen. For a time, he is Magdalena's boyfriend.

Stefan Lutowski—(Ste'-fahn) A fictional character in *Undercover Scouts*, he is Boy Scout and the younger brother of Lech. When the war starts in 1939, Stefan is thirteen. A classmate of Tadzio's since third grade, Stefan bullies Tadzio for years. Stefan is the Polish equivalent of the English name, Steven.

Krzysh Piechowicz—(Kzhish Pee-yeh-hah´-veetch) A fictional character in *Undercover Scouts*, he is a Boy Scout and Tadzio's best friend. When the war starts in 1939, Krzysh is thirteen. Krzysh is a young boy's Polish name when his given name is Krzystof, the equivalent of the English name, Christopher. In Polish, Krzysh is spelled Kryzś, but for ease of reading in English, it is spelled Krzysh throughout *Underground Scouts*.

Lucyna Piechowicz—((Loo-tsih´-nah Pee-yeh-hah´-veetch) A fictional character in *Undercover Scouts*, she is the younger sister of Krzysh. Her parents die from injuries received during the bombing of Warsaw at the beginning of the war in 1939. Lucyna is nine when the war starts, and at the end she is fourteen, having joined the Girl Guides with Magdalena as her leader.

Józefina—(You-ze-fee´-nah) A fictional character in *Undercover Scouts*, she is a Girl Scout and Tadzio's cousin. Her parents die in the bombing of Warsaw in 1939, so she comes to live with Tadzio's family at the age of eleven. Józefina is the equivalent of the English name, Josephine. Her story of being captured by the Germans while working as a Girl Guide when delivering copies of the Underground newspaper is based on a true story. She and her friends were sent to Pawiak prison. The young Scout sacrificed herself for her friends and was sent to a concentration camp while the others were later set free.

Władysław Szpilman—(Vwah-diss´-wahv Shpeel´-mahn) A historical person (1911–2000), Szpilman was a Polish pianist of Jewish descent. His performances were often heard live on Warsaw Radio. Szpilman managed to survive the Warsaw Ghetto and German occupation by hiding in bombed and burnt-out buildings, scavenging for food and water wherever he could find them. His true story has been told in his 1946 Polish book, *Death of a City*, and in the movie, *The Pianist*. A 1999 English version of his book, retitled, *The Pianist*, includes extracts from the Diary of Captain Wilm Hosenfeld, the German officer who gave Szpilman food and a warm blanket near the end of the war.

Benyameen—(Ben´-yah-meen) A fictional Jewish character in *Undercover Scouts*, he is a Boy Scout after he leaves Thalau Germany and comes to Warsaw with his younger brother, Yacov. Benyameen is thirteen in 1939. By the time of the Rising, Benyameen is eighteen.

Yacov—(Yah´-cof) A fictional Jewish character in *Undercover Scouts*, he is the six-year-old brother of Benyameen in 1939. He becomes a Boy Scout and helps deliver mail through the sewers by 1944 when he is eleven.

Grandpapa Lebowski—(Leb-off´-skey) A fictional Jewish character in *Undercover Scouts*, Grandpapa Lebowski serves as the adopted grandfather of the orphaned boys, Yacov and Benyameen.

Anna Zawadzka—(An´-na Zah-vahd´-zka) A historical person in Warsaw (1919–2004). Anna was a leader of the Girl Guides in Warsaw during the German Occupation.

In *Undercover Scouts*, Anna plays the role of Magdalena's Girl Scout leader. Anna Zawadzka was the sister of Tadeusz Zawadzki (codename Zoshka).

Zoshka—(Zoe'-shka) Codename for a historical Scout leader in Warsaw during the German occupation, Tadeusz Zawadzki was born 1921. He served as a scoutmaster in Warsaw and later as a second lieutenant in the Polish Underground Home Army. Zoshka (Zośka) is the Polish equivalent of the name Sophia, which means "wisdom" in Greek.

Tadeusz Zawadzki—(Tah-deh-oosh' Zah-vahd'-zkee) Born in 1921, Zawadzki was a historical Scout leader in Warsaw during the German occupation. He went by the codename of Zoshka. Zawadzki was eighteen in 1939 when the war began. He was a close friend of Jan Bytnar (codename Rudy) since the boys had been part of the Beeches Patrol in Poland before the German occupation in 1939. Zawadzki later became a leader in the Gray Ranks during the German occupation of Warsaw, commanded sabotage activities, and eventually rose to the rank of second lieutenant in the Polish Home Army. Tadeusz is the Polish equivalent of the English name, Thaddeus. Tadeusz Zawadzki's sister was Anna Zawadzka.

Wilm Hosenfeld—(Vil'-m Hoe´-zen-felt) A historical person (1895-1952), Hosenfeld was born into a devout Catholic German family. Hosenfeld's diary shows his struggle to reconcile his Christian beliefs with the German war crimes he witnessed while serving as a Wehrmacht officer in Poland. Despite the official Nazi decree making it illegal for Hosenfeld to attend Mass, Hosenfeld attended several churches in Warsaw. He befriended numerous Poles, and provided Władysław Szpilman (*The Pianist*) with food and a warm blanket near the end of the war. This enabled Szpilman to survive in hiding until the Germans were defeated. After the Red Army "liberated" Warsaw in 1945, Hosenfeld was taken to Russia as a prisoner of war. He died in 1952 in the Stalingrad prisoner of war camp.

Uncle Ludwik Woźniak—(Lood'-veek Vahjg-nee-ak) A fictional Polish character in *Undercover Scouts* who serves as an "Uncle" for the fictionalized Jewish German orphans, Benyameen and Yacov.

Rudy—Rudy was the codename for the historical person, Jan Bytnar who was born in 1921. Rudy was a close friend of Tadeusz Zawadzki (Zoshka).

Jan Bytnar (Rudy)—(Yon Bit'-nar) A historical Scout leader in Warsaw during the German occupation. Born May 6, 1921 he was eighteen when the Germans invaded Poland in September 1939. Bytnar was a close friend of Tadeusz Zawadzki (codename Zoshka). They were part of the Beeches Patrol before the 1939 German occupation. Bytnar later became a scoutmaster in Warsaw, a participant in sabotage activities, and a second lieutenant in the Polish Home Army during the German occupation. Jan is the Polish equivalent of the English name, John.

Alek—A historical Scout leader in Warsaw during the German occupation, Alek was the codename of Maciej Aleksy Dawidowski.

Maciej Aleksy Dawidowski—(Ah'-lek Dah-vee-dahf'-skee) A historical figure, born November 3, 1920, Dawidowski was a Scout leader in Warsaw during the German occupation. He went by the codename of Alek. He participated in sabotage activities, such as removing the German plaque from the Copernicus statute in 1942. He also participated in the rescue of his friend, Rudy (Jan Bytnar), from the hands of the Gestapo in 1943 during Operation Arsenal.

Father Wacław Karłowicz—(Vats'-wahf Kar-woah'-veech) A historical person, Father Wacław (1907–2007) entered the priesthood at the age of twenty-five. His great-grandfather participated in the Cadet Rebellion (1830–1831) against the Russians (also known as the November Uprising). To protest the conscription of Poles into the Imperial Russian Army in 1863, his grandfather took part in the January Uprising of 1863–1864. During the 1944 Warsaw Rising, Father Wacław served as chaplain for the Gustav Battalion and co-organized the largest insurgent hospital at 7 Długa (Long) Street in the Old Town area. His apartment served as a contact point for Underground couriers traveling between Warsaw and London. In Poland, he is well-known for his rescue of the 16th century crucifix of Jesus from the burning ruins of St. John's Cathedral during the Rising. Father Wacław also prayed for and supplied Home Army soldiers with crucifixes during battles and supplied chaplains with field missals and vestments. He died in 2007 at the age of 100.

Kościuszko, Tadeusz—(Kahsh-chewsh'-kah) A historical figure (1746-1817), Kościuszko was born in a village of the Polish Lithuanian Commonwealth that is now in Belarus. Kościuszko graduated from the Corps of Cadets in Warsaw and later joined the Continental Army during the American Revolution. As an admirer of the enlightenment ideals of human rights, he became a personal friend of Thomas Jefferson. When Kościuszko returned to Poland from America in 1784, he became a major general in the Polish-Lithuanian Commonwealth Army and later organized an uprising against Russia in 1794. This uprising became known as the Kościuszko Uprising.

Kiliński, Jan—(Keh-leen'-skee) A historical figure (1760–1819), Kiliński was one of the commanders in the Kościuszko Uprising. A shoemaker by trade, Kiliński served as an elected member of Warsaw's city council from 1791–1793. During the Kościuszko Uprising he formed a unit of National Militia to fight against the Russian occupation forces in Warsaw.

Krasiński, Zygmunt—(Kreh-sheen´-skee) Krasiński was a historical figure (1812–1859) who, along with Słowacki and Mickiewicz, ranks as one of Poland's Three National Bards. These Romantic poets greatly influenced Poland's national consciousness. Krasiński lived during the time of the Cadet Rebellion against Czar Nicholas of Russia. He is best known for his philosophical Messianic ideas and tragic dramas as seen in the passage where the fictionalized Professor Lewandowski reads a portion of a Krasiński poem to Tadzio and his classmates. This Krasiński poem was set to music by his contemporary, Chopin, in a piece known as the *Melodia*.

Słowacki, Juliusz—(Swah-vah-tski) A historical figure (1809–1849), Słowacki, along with Krasiński and Mickiewicz, ranks as one of Poland's Three National Bards. During the Cadet Rebellion in 1830, Słowacki served as a courier for the Polish revolutionary government. When the rebellion failed, Słowacki settled in Paris, and later Geneva. He wrote his poem, *My Testament*, around 1939–1840 in Paris. *My Testament*, is quoted by the historical character Rudy on his deathbed, and later by the fictionalized character, Krzysh.

This poem is characteristic of the Polish romanticism that idealized self-sacrifice. The poem also served as the inspiration for the title of the 1943 book, *Kamienie na szaniec*, or, *Stones for the Rampart*, by Aleksander Kamiński.

Major Pług—(Pwoog) His codename means "plow" in Polish (1909–1986). A historical person, his real name was Adam Borys. As a youth, he was a Scout of the 3rd Gniezno Team of Scouts. After 1942 he joined the *cichociemny*. The Home Army ordered him to create a special unit of *Kedyw* in 1943 to fight against the SS and the Gestapo.

General Bór—(Boor) A historical person (1895–1966), Bór was the codename of Tadeusz Bór-Komorowski. General Bór helped organize the Polish underground in 1939. In July 1941 he became deputy commander of the Home Army. In March 1943 the government-in-exile appointed him as the commander of the Home Army.

Commander Jerzy—(Yeh´-rjzhe) A historical person during WWII (1914–1992), Jerzy was the codename of Ryszard Białous. He was a Polish scoutmaster who became captain of the Gray Ranks. He was also Commander of the Zoshka Battalion before and during the Warsaw Rising.

Kurt Kleinhoffer—(Kline'-hof-fer) A fictional German officer and supposed WWI war buddy of Wilm Hosenfeld. In *Undercover Scouts*, this fictional character serves as an aide to the historical figure of General von dem Bach.

SS-General Erich von dem Bach—A historical figure (1899–1972) Von dem Bach took command of all German troops fighting in Warsaw as of August 2, 1944. As an SS officer, he also commanded all *Wehrmacht* troops in Warsaw after this date. Born Erich Julius Eberhard von Zelewski, he legally added "von dem Bach" to the family name late in 1933. He went on to have the Polish sounding "Zelewski" name officially removed in November 1941.

Hanka Biała—(Bee-yah'-wah) A historical figure (1925–1944), Hanka Biała was the codename of Anna Zakrzewska. Assigned to the Felek Platoon in Company Rudy of the Zoshka Battalion, Hanka Biała (White Hannah) is fictionalized in *Undercover Scouts* as Tadzio's girlfriend.

Antek—(Un′-tek) A historical figure (1921–1944), Antoni Wojciechowski was a Polish soldier in Company Kolgium A during the Warsaw Rising.

Kuba—(Koo′-ba) A historical figure (1923–1944), was the commander of Felek Platoon during the Warsaw Rising, and part of the Zoshka Battalion.

Stasinek—(Sta′-she-nek) A historical figure, Janusz Stanisław Sosabowski was the wounded soldier Magdalena helped escape from the hospital during the Rising. He was a soldier in Company Kolgium A during the Warsaw Rising.

Kołczan—(Co´-chun) A historical figure (1920–1944), Eugeniusz Koecher was commander of Alek Platoon in the Rudy Company of Zoshka Battalion during the Warsaw Rising.

Dirlewanger—(Dir′-leh-vang-er) A historical figure (1895–1945), Oskar Paul Dirlewanger was an SS commander of one of the brigades responsible for the massacres in the Wola District. The World War II historian Chris Bishop called him the "most evil man in the SS." Timothy Snyder, Professor of History at Yale University, claims, "in all the theaters of the Second World War, few could compete in cruelty with Oskar Dirlewanger."

Halszka—(Hahl´-shkah) Codename for the historical person, Halka/Halina Śliwińska-Butler, a historical character.

Bear Cub—Leopold Okulicki (Ah-koo-lee′-tskee) A historical figure (1898–1946), Bear Cub was one of the codenames of Leopold Okulicki. He served as a General of the Polish Army, and was the last commander of the Underground Home Army in Warsaw. He managed to escape capture by the Germans after the Rising failed, but, after the Soviet Union took over Poland, he was arrested and imprisoned in Moscow where he was murdered in 1946 in Butyrka Prison.

Leopold Okulicki—(Ahw-koo-leats′-ki) A historical figure (1898–1946), Okulicki went by the codenames of Bear Cub and Cobra, *Niedzwiadek* and *Kobra* in Polish.

Roman—He was a historical figure (1901–1948), Roman was the codename for Witold Pilecki (Vee′-told Pea-letz′-kee). In 1940, Pilecki allowed himself to be picked up by the Germans in a Warsaw street roundup. He was sent to Auschwitz and later escaped in 1943. In *Underground Scouts*, he supposedly smuggled out Grandpapa's letters to Benyameen and Yacov, and had it delivered to them by Father Wacław.

Pilecki provided invaluable information about Auschwitz to the Polish resistance, and through them, to the British government in London. After his escape from Aushwitz, Pilecki joined the Home Army's intelligence department. Then in 1944, he joined Poland's secret anti-communist organization, *NIE*. He fought in the Rising, but was then sent to a German prisoner-of-war camp when the Rising failed. Liberated from the German POW camp at the end of the war, Pilecki, under a false identity, returned to Soviet-controlled Poland in 1945 to gather intelligence for the Polish government-in-exile. In July 1946, with his cover blown, Pilecki was ordered by the government-in-exile to leave Poland. He refused, choosing to remain in Poland to collect evidence on Soviet atrocities committed against the Poles, especially against former members of the Home Army. Arrested by the Polish communist secret police (MPB) in 1947 and repeatedly tortured, Pilecki was tried and then executed on May 25, 1948 at the Warsaw Mokotów Prison.

Witold Pilecki—(Pea-letz'-kee) A historical person who used the codename Roman (1901–1948).

Radosław—(Ra-do'-swahf) Codename for the historical person of Jan Mazurkiewicz (Ma-zur-kee-ay'-veech), Commander of the Radosław Group, one of the best trained and equipped Polish units in the uprising because it was mostly comprised of former Scouts. Zoshka Battalion was part of this group.

Alphabetical List of Characters in Undercover Scouts

Alek (codename for Maciej Aleksy Dawidowski)
Andrzej Romocki (codename Morro)
Anna Zawadzka
Antek (codename for Antoni Wojciechowski)
Bear Cub (codename for Leopold Okulicki)
Benyameen
Commander Jerzy (codename for Ryszard Białous)
Dirlewanger (Oskar Paul Dirlewanger)
Father Wacław
General Bór (codename for Tadeusz Bór-Komorowski)
Grandpapa Lebowski
Halszka (codename for Halka/Halina Śliwińska-Butler)
Hanka Biała (codename for Anna Zakrzewska)
Henio Dombrowski
Hosenfeld, Wilm
Jan Bytnar (codename Rudy)
Jerzy (codename for Ryszard Białous)
Józefina
Kiliński, Jan
Kleinhoffer, Kurt
Kołczan (codename for Eugeniusz Koecher)
Kościuszko, Tadeusz
Krasiński, Zygmunt
Krzysh Piechowicz
Kuba (codename for Konrad Okolski)
Kurt Kleinhoffer

Lech Lutowski
Lucyna Piechowicz
Maciej Aleksy Dawidowski (codename Alek)
Magdalena Dombrowska
Major Pług (codename for Adam Borys)
Morro (codename for Andrej Romocki)
Okulicki, Leopold (codename Bear Cub)
Uncle Ludwik Woźniak
Pilecki, Witold (codename Roman)
Professor Handelsman
Radosław (codename for Jan Mazurkiewicz)
Roman (codename for Witold Pilecki)
Rudy (codename for Jan Bytnar)
Słowacki, Juliusz
SS-General Erich von dem Bach
Stasinek (codename for Janusz Stanisław Sosabowski)
Szpilman Władysław
Stefan Lutowski
Tadeusz Zawadzki (codename Zoshka)
Tadzio Dombrowski
Wilm Hosenfeld
Władysław Szpilman
Yacov
Zoshka (codename for Tadeusz Zawadzki)

Bibliography

Cosby, Rita. *Quiet Hero: Secrets from My Father's Past.* New York: Threshold Editions, 2010.

Davis, Norman. *Heart of Europe: The Past in Poland's Present.* Oxford: Oxford University Press, 2001.

Davies, Norman. *Rising '44: The Battle for Warsaw.* New York: Penguin Books, 2005.

Forczyk, Robert. *Warsaw 1944: Poland's Bid for Freedom.* Oxford: Osprey Publishing, 2009.

Halberstadt, Hans (Ed.). *Guide to the Military Vehicle Technology Foundation Collection – Building One.* Portola Valley, CA: Military Vehicle Technology Foundation, 2021.

Korbonski, Stefan. *Fighting Warsaw: The Story of the Polish Underground State 1939-1945.* New York: Hippocrene Books, Inc., 2004.

Królewski, Zamek. *New Constitution of the Government of Poland, the Third of May, 1791: Second Edition.* London: J. Debrett, 1991.

Kulski, Julian. *Dying We Live.* New York: Holt, Rinehart and Winston, 1979.

Kulski, Julian. *Legacy of the White Eagle.* Middleburg, VA: HMP. Inc., 2006.

Likiernik, Stanislaw. *By Devil's Luck: A Tale of Resistance in Wartime Warsaw.* Edinburgh: Mainstream Publishing Company, 2001.

Szpilman, Władysław. *The Pianist: The Extraordinary True Story of One Man's Survival in Warsaw, 1939-1945.* New York: Picador, 1999.

Zamoyski, Adam. *Poland: A History.* London: William Collins, 2009.

Ziolkowska-Boehm, Aleksandra. *Kaia, Heroine of the 1944 Warsaw Rising.* Lanham, MD: Lexington Books, 2012.

Ziolkowska-Boehm, Aleksandra. *The Polish Experience through World War II*. Lanham, MD: Lexington Books, 2013.